*To everyone who
needs novels and
kdramas to stay
somewhat afloat.*

Same.

HEAT LEVEL AND CONTENT WARNINGS

The romance level of this book is closed door, which means that there is innuendo, kisses are descriptive, and characters don't shy away from their attraction.

There is mild to moderate use of language but no f-bombs, religious blasphemies, or known ableist terms.

There are moderate depictions of bullying from the female lead's roommate, and from the male lead's stepmother. There is also moderate violence and mild blood/gore. Adults may consume alcohol on the page.

The story is set in Miami and features some Latino characters. See Glossary of Spanish Terms at the end for translations of occasional Spanish vocabs.

CHAPTER 1
SERENA

My superpower is continuously getting the short end of the stick and then getting beat with it. It's why I should've been suspicious of getting the job offer right after the first interview.

This is the work of hindsight, which is always 20/20, and not my thought process while sitting in front of Cedric Oh, Fortune 500 CEO and the tenth richest guy in the US. He is somewhere in his sixties, with slightly pastier skin than I expect from someone who claims his favorite pastime to be sailing.

In fact, the way he starts my interview is by asking, "Do you like boats, Miss Lossada?"

"I don't know how to swim," I respond.

Rather than getting put off by my curt response, it makes him smile. Wrinkles appear in the corners of his eyes, which are so sharp I fear they can see through to my deepest secrets.

It's not just the enormous, lavish office that has an effect on me. The black marble floors, leather couches, gold appliqués and art pieces that cost several zeroes to the right are only half as intimidating as the man who commands the space.

Meanwhile, I have exactly fifteen dollars and eighty-three

cents to my name in my savings account. My credit cards are almost maxed out, though, and looking at the balance of my student loans makes me as dizzy as getting on a boat would. I need this job like I need air, and not just because working for Comed Solutions will look amazing on my resume. Or because most of my classmates have received mouth-watering job offers after graduation.

"I like your frankness," he says, lacing his fingers in front of his face as if he were meditating a billion dollar deal. "Thus, I would like to meet it with my own. While we don't have a lot of applicants for this position, I find your resume to be lacking."

I pinch my lips to hold back the words that want to jump out. One thing is frankness and another one altogether is the level of alienating rudeness I'm capable of. It hasn't helped me land any job offers so far.

"I speak two languages fluently," I say, sitting straighter. "Spanish and English, which are both the lingua franca of Miami. Comed has several branches in hispanic speaking countries, and I have no doubt I will be an asset in that regard."

He waved a hand. "I've had polyglot applicants in the past. What else?"

Were they as desperate as I am? Probably not. Otherwise, he wouldn't be hiring again.

"I am also a very organized person, which results in a great ability to multitask."

For example, at this second I'm cursing him in my mind, smiling outwardly, wondering where the nearest McDonald's is and if my credit card will work if I order something, and also suffering from the blisters these high heels are giving me.

"And?" he asks, and although he sounds bored, it's almost as though he's willing to give me another opportunity.

That's when I realize he's as desperate as I am.

Someone as important as him, interviewing a college graduate for the position of his son's assistant, has to mean the situation is so dire that it has escalated all the way to him. That he hasn't dismissed me in the first thirty seconds of this interview also means he's looking for any excuse I can give him to hire me.

And then there's the fact that I didn't see any other applicants in the waiting area. At first, my guess was that interviews are by appointment, but maybe there just aren't other candidates—period. It lines up with what I researched in preparation for the interview.

While I stay still as a statue, a rush of excitement washes over me like a splash of cold water. Maybe my luck is finally turning. I best ride the wave while I can.

"I'm also really good at research," I say, which makes one of his eyebrows quirk. "And while there weren't many details I could find online, presumably because of NDAs, I did notice an interesting pattern."

I make a strategic pause and push my glasses up my nose.

Before the silence prolongs further, I continue. "Caleb Oh has had five different assistants in the past year alone. Such high turnover is concerning, and it explains why I currently seem to have no competition."

He leans back on his chair. A bad sign according to body language experts, but I have nothing to lose and I push on.

"So I'll be fully transparent with you, Mr. Oh. I'm not someone who is well connected in the business world, nor am I an heiress who can bring the heft of money to the table. I'm just a poor college graduate whose only asset is determination. If you hire me, I can at least promise you that I won't give up as quickly as the previous assistants."

Mr. Oh hums from deep in his throat, picking up an iPad that he scrolls through as he speaks. "I'm inclined to believe your words. It's not often I meet orphans who have put them-selves through the education system on their own."

Heat travels up my chest and settles on my face. I hate using the orphan card, but job interviews are as gutting as college applications. You have to do whatever you can to stand out, and it's an undeniable fact that I'm pretty much alone in the world. It's up to me to make my place in it.

"My son, Caleb, is a difficult person. But he isn't a villain," he says, setting the device down and giving me his full attention again. "I hope you don't believe the rumors about him online."

How could I, when rumors around him range from deranged, to incorrigible womanizer, to immature baby?

One thing is certain: he must be a terrible boss. But at this point, a terrible boss who pays a steady check is better than no boss at all.

"I would rather make my own judgement," I say, scoring a nod from Mr. Oh.

"Let's get to the real interview, then." His voice comes out light, unlike the expression on his face. This is the make or break moment. "How do you handle stressful situations?"

By screaming on the inside.

Instead, I say, "I break down problems to their smallest components, so it's easier to tackle them."

"Give me an example."

"This interview." I motion at the air around me. "It's a daunting exercise, but after drilling down to the core of the matter it's going a lot smoother, I believe."

This startles a short laugh out of him and I resist the urge to pump my fist.

"You went to business school but here you are, applying for the assistant position of someone notoriously hard to handle. Why?"

Mierda, this is a very good question and I don't answer it right away.

Finally, I explain, "A personal assistant is someone who has to keep on top of the company's pulse. It's not just about booking appointments or ordering meals for the manager, it's about making sure they have all the information—and know all the people—their boss needs to make the right decisions for the company. I think this will give me a closer glimpse at the kind of position I aspire to in the future, than if I start my career at a job where I have to do the same thing every single day."

Mr. Oh whistles low. "I admit I'm impressed by your vision."

So am I. I didn't know my capacity to bullshit my way through tough questions extends beyond college essays.

"Thank you."

"And you're right, a personal assistant is all of those things, but in my son's case, he or she also has to be a bit of a babysitter. It's not something that explicitly appears in the employment contract, but facts are facts." Mr. Oh expels a deep breath, not even bothering to hide his disappointment.

Facts are facts, indeed.

"So," he continues. "Would that bother you?"

Sure, but what bothers me more is my piling debt.

"I'm confident I can be a good influence to your son," I say, smiling like I mean it.

"In that case, let's conclude here." He stands up and offers me his hand. I shake it, hoping he doesn't notice how clammy mine is. "Please wait outside and I will give you my answer in a few minutes."

I almost ask if he's for real because that's not normal. Out of the many red flags, this is the one I would later come to regret missing.

But I do as I'm told and sit in the vast lobby outside his office for what feels like an eternity, though the clock of my beat up cellphone shows it's only half an hour. Then, Mr. Oh's assistant shows up and wordlessly hands me an envelop. As I take out the documents inside, two words jump out at me.

Employment Contract.

I grit my teeth not to let out a squeal.

This is the moment when my life changes, just days before meeting the person who will make every one of my plans careen off course.

CHAPTER 2
CALEB

I wish I had been born a merman.

Calm reigns underwater. Every living creature moves at the rhythm of the current, and if there are no threats you can just drift. There's no noise, which in theory should make it easier to think but instead drains my mind of anything. No worries. No hunger. No obligations.

While I can hold my breath three times longer than a swimming gold medalist, I can't just live here. Too bad.

I take a breath of oxygen from the tank strapped to my shoulders, following a lone angelfish as it swims through the reef. Keeping a good distance in between and not making any sudden movements, makes it realize that I don't want to eat it, and I'm able to snap a few good pictures of it.

A shadow shifts above me and I almost hope it's a shark. That would be a freaking cool closeup. Instead, I make out the vague figure of a boat pulling up beside my yacht, which can only mean one thing.

A pirate is trying to take over my vessel.

I push upwards with my legs, swimming as though I'm one with the water. Regret weighs me down when my head breaks into the surface and I get the first gulps of air. I hoped to stay underwater for an hour longer. The sun feels hot on my head as I wade over to the yacht and latch onto the ladder. I cast one last look at the vast blue of the Caribbean and promise I'll return to it soon. After seeing what the intruder wants.

As soon as I haul myself up on deck, a very familiar voice asks, "What the hell are you wearing?"

I tear my visor away and shake my head, hoping to splash him. He stays put even as salt water hits him in the face and dampens his clothes.

As I take off the oxygen tank, I say in an offhand way, "A swimsuit?"

"You call that a swimsuit?" the old man says, lifting an eyebrow as he looks down at me.

"I believe the more accurate term is a Speedo," I add, snapping the waistband for emphasis. "Be thankful you didn't catch me wearing a thong today."

His eyes grow as wide as saucers. "Does that mean some days you do wear one?"

Trying not to laugh at his patent horror, I ask, "Why are you here, Dad?"

He follows me as I make my way to the cabin. "Just checking in on my son."

I give him a look. There is never a *just* when it comes to interactions with Cedric Oh. Something important is always on his mind when he graces me with his presence. If not, it's to give me a scolding like I'm a little child.

In that spirit, I ask, "What did I do wrong this time?"

As I pick up a towel to dry myself off, Dad sits on a chair and regards me with a funny look. Even though I'm almost naked, I'm glad vampires don't have X-ray vision, because I feel as though he's seeing right through my skull and into the deep recesses of my mind.

"Are you hiding someone?"

"Huh?" I wrinkle my nose.

"Are there any women here?" He motions at me again. "Is that why you're wearing almost nothing?"

I blow a raspberry. "No, it's just easier to swim like this than with something bulkier."

"Or do you and Joe have a thing going on?"

That makes me choke on air. "What the hell?"

"Why else would you be alone in the middle of the Keys with just the yacht's captain?"

"First of all," I say, raising a hand. "Joe is really hot, but I don't bat for his team. Second, my favorite thing about him isn't that, but that he's quiet as a tomb. And that's why I'm here —I want to be alone. So again, why are *you* here?"

"I'm here to drag you back to land," he says, in a few words ignoring my desires.

Typical.

I almost want to remind him of what I just said, but I don't want to deal with the sequitur. Explaining why I want to be by myself would be a reminder of the latest sting caused by my stepmother's tongue. And Dad always takes her side, so that's a losing battle.

There isn't a single battle I've ever won against the mighty Cedric Oh, but there also isn't a single one I've backed away from. Right now, the only strategy I can use is silence.

I towel my hair dry and turn my back on him to flip the TV on. The wet swimsuit is sucked into the crack of my butt and I hope it offends him. It would've been funnier if I wore a thong, damn it.

"Until when do you plan to continue acting like a spoiled brat?" he asks, and I change the channels for a few seconds before shrugging.

"I don't have an expiration date for that behavior."

"A man ought to be responsible," he starts.

And that's how I know I'm in for another lecture. I stop

flipping channels on some cartoons and carry on toweling myself dry. They don't truly interest me but they certainly fit the current brand.

"As the second son, you may not be next in line to inherit the responsibilities of the vampire king, but you are a board member and executive of Comed Solutions. There are roughly fifty employees in your organization, all of whom barely know what you look like."

"And they're doing a fantastic job without me," I say, hanging the towel around my neck. "It's almost as though they're working even harder to prove that they don't need me. Three viral campaigns last year, a twofold increase in the order intake, eleven new portfolios. Why change a successful formula?"

"Because it can be even better if you really put your mind to it."

Dad stands up and squares up against me. Even though I'm almost a head taller, I want to cower under the intensity of eyes that have seen ages pass before him. Although I stay ramrod straight, I know he can snap me like a twig if he wanted to—and I've given him plenty of reasons to. I just don't understand why he doesn't.

"Caleb," he says with a voice so low that I barely hear him. "You're the smartest person in our entire family. I just wish you used that brain of yours for something useful."

I take a deep breath and expel it slowly. "And I am. Keeping away is the best I can do for everybody."

On that I agree with my stepmother. I don't belong, so why bother trying?

Cedric Oh puts the palm of his hand against my cheek and I flinch, not because I expect to be hit but because contact between us is so rare that I'm not used to it.

"I disagree, Son. I think you're capable of greatness."

I groan. "Shit, is this a new strategy?"

Dad offers the first smile I've seen in ages. "Is it working?"

I wish it wasn't, but I can pretend it isn't.

So, I shake my head. "Again, why would I want to go to work when I can just… not?"

"I figured you might say something like that," he says, taking his hand back down. "So I came prepared."

I take a step back, just in case.

"If you don't return to work by Monday," he says, checking out his watch as if to confirm there are, indeed, three more days until then. "I will cut off your credit cards, bank account access, take away your apartment, cars and even the Speedo off your back."

I cross my arms over my chest, gasping. "You would really leave your spare out into the world, naked?"

Dad shrugs. "You might have a promising career in the modeling world, but of course I will not sponsor you. If you don't show up on Monday, you'll have to find your own way in the world from the bottom. Just like you want."

That isn't quite what I want, either. To truly find my path, I need money to explore. Money I don't have on my own because Dad is right, I financially belong to him.

"But it's not like I'm leaving you off to the sharks," he says in a light tone. "If you fess up and return to work, you'll find a promising new assistant waiting to help get your head in the game. What do you say?"

I scrunch up my face. "Is there an option C?"

He stares at me until I finally start to feel self conscious.

"Fine," I say, figuring I'll make my own option C. I'll show up to the office and not work, which will probably drive his new minion—my so called assistant—right up the wall. Win-win.

Dad pats my cheek a couple of times. "That's a good boy."

We'll see about that.

CHAPTER 3
SERENA

People say the first job after graduating from college sets the tone for the rest of your career, and I think the same can be said about the first day of said job.

Anyone who says first impressions don't matter is a liar, which is why I put on my best suit—a two piece jacket and skirt combo in a soft rouge that isn't offensive to the eye and flatters my shape—and paired it with the only pair of shoes and purse I own that fool people into thinking they're expensive.

I'm not too savvy on makeup application, so I keep it light on that front, but I straighten my hair so that not a single strand is out of place from the high ponytail I put it in.

I look good. Professional. In control.

Not at all how I truly feel like.

My roommate's boyfriend ate my yogurt while I was getting ready, but I refuse to let that ruin my mood. Today is the first day of my life as a fully emancipated adult. Today is when I put the lanyard with my full time employee badge around my neck for the first time. The first day that counts toward a good paycheck.

And also the day I meet my new boss.

I walk into the main building of Comed Solutions with the confidence of someone who belongs. The company has a significant footprint all around the city of Miami and beyond, but this building is where Cedric Oh, the executives, and top line of managers sit with their teams. It's also where I'll work now.

"Serena Lossada?"

I halt on my way to the elevators and find a young Black woman waving at me. She might be slightly older than me and is so pretty that it hurts, like someone straight out of a commercial. The smile on her face seems genuine as she heads my way.

"Hi, I'm Marissa Gonzalez, Jon's assistant. It's so nice to meet you."

She offers her hand out to me and while I shake it, I ask, "Likewise, but who is Jon?"

She jumps as though I've zapped her. "Right, you might not know who's who yet. Jonathan Wolkers, or Jon for short, is Mr. Oh's assistant. You met him during your interview with Mr. O."

Ah, I remember. That was the guy who handed me the employment contract. Which must mean that Marissa is the assistant to Cedric Oh's assistant.

"Jon asked me to escort you to Mr. Oh's office before I show you to your work station. Is that okay?"

I don't have the option of saying no, so I follow along. People must know who she works for because they part ways for her, allowing us to get in the elevator even before the throngs of people gathered in the lobby waiting for it.

As if acknowledging this, she explains, "There are some perks to the job but it does come with basically endless hours. If at any point you need someone to vent with, I'm here for you."

"Thank you." I want to add that it won't be necessary

because I'm not a complainer, but I've learned to keep my mouth shut when I'm about to say something people will dislike me for. This is one of those moments.

The top floor, where Mr. Oh's office is located, is much calmer than the busy lobby. We don't have to wait at all, because Mr. Wolkers opens the door as soon as he sees us.

"Miss Lossada is here," he announces.

"There you are," Mr. Oh says, standing up from the sofa and coming to shake my hand. "So glad to finally have you on board. Take a seat."

His office is large enough to have its own living room area, which is where I join him. There's a box on the coffee table that almost looks like a gift, but I do my best to not make my curiosity obvious.

"Jon, if you'll do the honors." Mr. Oh motions at the box and his assistant opens it.

I peek inside and find a puzzling assortment of things. The smaller boxes with a laptop, iPad, and cellphone I can understand. But there is also something that looks like a wallet, a car key, another badge, and what looks like fancy stationary.

I wish I had something smarter to say than, "Uhh…"

Mr. Oh chuckles. "I take it you like it."

"Rather, I'm confused."

Mr. Wolkers says, "These are the basic supplies you will need to work here. If you have need of anything else, feel free to request it through me. I'm the lead for all the personal assistants."

As I squint, I note that the car key has the emblem of a brand I could never afford in a million years. I keep my mouth pressed into a firm line but I'm sure my eyes are bulging.

Mr. Wolkers catches on and asks, "You do have a driver's license, right?"

"Yes, but—"

"Don't worry about the rest," he says. I leave it at that for now, but will inquire later—something along the lines of *what the heck?* Was I really going to get to drive a Lamborghini?

"Remember," Mr. Oh says, and it takes me a moment to tear my eyes away from the box. "Your primary objective is to get Caleb motivated with work, and though he may think he's your manager, it's actually me."

"Yes, sir."

"Good, now off you go." He waves a hand at me.

"Thank you," I say, before picking up the box and joining Marissa outside.

"Ohh, the goodies." She rubs her hands. "What did you get?"

I shake my head. "Too much."

And at the same time too little. I wish they'd told me what I should accomplish with all of this.

I'm disoriented by the time Marissa delivers me to what is going to be my work station, two floors below Mr. Oh's. My desk is built into a massive counter outside a big set of doors, where I presume my new sort-of-boss-slash-work-project is. I set the box down along with my purse and spiffy myself up to go meet him.

Knocking on the door produces only silence. I open the door just a sliver to glance inside, but the office is completely empty.

My clock reads eight thirty in the morning, and I decide to cut him some slack. Executives can keep to their own hours, especially if they're billionaires and with reputations for being rogues. He'll probably show up late.

Instead, I start setting up the company gadgets and that takes me most of the morning. But when noon arrives and my new boss doesn't, I know something's up.

I use the brand-spanking-new iPhone and find the phone

number for Caleb Oh. My index finger hovers over the call button for a second. What if he's busy with something important? Or if he's sick? What if by calling him I make a bad first impression?

Not at all what I want. But I also can't imagine his dad would like to find out that I had nothing to do today because his son didn't show up.

Dale y ya, I tell myself and press the call button.

The call goes all the way to voice mail with no answer. So I try one more time. And another.

By this point I'm pacing up and down. People come and go, tossing glances my way, no doubt wondering who I am and why I'm so stressed out.

That's when I realize this might be why they gave me a car key. Before I make a fool out of myself, I send a quick text to Mr. Wolkers to confirm.

Mr. Caleb Oh hasn't arrived to work yet. Should I go pick him up?

Mr. Wolker's answer comes back right away as, *Yes, drag him to the office if you must. Otherwise we'll cut his cards off.*

All right, I guess that's today's goal.

I pick up the car key along with my purse and head to the parking lot. I probably should've asked Mr. Wolkers where the car was parked, but I find it the second I step into the garage. I had expected a sleek sports car, barely hovering over the floor, but it turns out to be a SUV.

"I can do this," I whisper to myself.

I've only ever driven a beat up Toyota. It belonged to the owner of the pizza place I used to work at through college, and I only drove it when I had to make deliveries. That was stressful enough in Miami's intense traffic, but if I put a dent in a car this expensive I can probably kiss my life goodbye.

Even so, I have to make a delivery now. Of a whole man.

It feels like forever when I finally park in the residential building of one Caleb Oh. Someone set up his address in the car's GPS already, but that was the only easy thing about the whole trip. I cross myself and thank goodness I, and the car, made it safe to our destination before psyching myself up for the next leg of the trip.

The building, located in a prime spot of Brickell facing out directly to the ocean, has a security guy who waves me right in as if he knows me.

"Mr. Oh is on the top floor," he says for all greeting.

"Thanks…"

I figure it must either be the badge around my neck, or he already has my face in file. Probably the latter.

The elevator opens directly into an apartment straight out of a movie. The first thing I see is the infinity pool right across from me, striking even if it wasn't for the fact that the property has no outer walls. It's all floor to ceiling windows spanning across the ocean view and the city center. I can't even catch sight of the decor when my eyes are lost in such a stunning view that it should be captured in a postcard.

But that's not even the most shocking part. That's when a man emerges from the pool like he's the main actor in a movie.

Rivulets of water trickle down muscles so ripped, he might as well have been chiseled from marble. He shakes his head, hair tossing droplets of water all around him, only to catch on his skin and continue their descent down the hard plains of his body, past hard rock abs leading to a Speedo that doesn't leave much to the imagination.

His dark eyes finally catch sight of me and I need no introduction to recognize Caleb Oh. That perfect face is well known in the city, even if I hadn't looked him up extensively before the job interview with his dad.

Dripping, he steps into the living room until he's in front of me. As he brushes the hair off his forehead, his biceps bulge with the motion.

All through the spectacle, I remain quiet and still as a

statue, my expression schooled into the perfect mask of nothingness I have honed over the years.

"And who are you?" he asks, with a deep voice that threatens to crack my composure.

I hold fast to it out of pure spite, and say, "Serena Lossada, your new assistant. And I'm here to bring you into work."

CHAPTER 4
CALEB

"Hmm," I say, looking her up and down.

She's a good head and a half shorter than me but with the way her eyes blaze, I have no doubt that height and size are a construct and she can take me down if she wanted to.

It doesn't mean I have to make it easy for her, though.

"No, thanks." I turn around, running my fingers through my hair to get the moisture out.

Unbeknownst to her, I already went to the office. Checked my badge in at the front door and marched right back outside.

System wise, I'm still in the main building of Comed Solutions. The security guys have seen me pull this trick off enough times that they already know not to bother reporting me.

Unless Dad found out somehow and that's why he sent this new minion.

Sure enough, she follows me on the way to the kitchen. "I apologize for my language, but I'm prepared to drag you to the office if I have to."

I chuckle. "I'm sure."

She stays silent only long enough to let me open the fridge

and get a fresh bottle of organic orange juice with ginger, turmeric, and cayenne pepper. I manage to take one sip before she speaks again. "I heard your credit cards will be cut off if I report you as no-show today."

I inhale all the air in the room.

Damn it, I forgot about that.

"Fine." I gulp down the rest of the juice and lick my lips to catch the last few drops. My eyes are trained on hers all throughout, but all I can see is annoyance.

Dad chose a good one this time. It doesn't look like I'm having any effect on her.

Weird. All of the assistants I had in the past who were into men, showed at least some sign of attraction without me even having to compel them.

"I need to shower first." I wave a hand in her general direction. "Make yourself at home."

With that, I head to my en-suite bathroom and decide to take my sweet time.

Just because I said *fine* doesn't mean I agree. There has to be a reason why Dad is pushing so hard for me to go back to work, especially since the previous arrangements worked so well for everyone. The team is doing great without me and I'm thriving on my own, waking up everyday and choosing to swim in the ocean or in the pool, working out, eating at the hidden gems in the city, fielding off a marriage proposal here and there.

What changed?

As I stand under the hot spray of water and let it rinse the soap suds off my skin, the only thing I can think of is last week's family dinner. I can still see the expression in my step-mother's face as she called me a good-for-nothing baseborn. Maybe Dad's determined to prove her wrong on the good-for-nothing front.

Problem is, I'm tired of trying to prove myself. Winning

swimming competitions did nothing for her. In fact, she told me off for putting our identities in danger and forced me to drop out before I could try for the Olympics. Graduating from the top business school in the world at fifteen years old also disappointed her.

"If you have such a high IQ," she said back then, ignoring the diploma I showed her in my hands. "You should've gone into med school like your brother."

I wrinkle my nose at the memory, especially because right after that I spewed one of the most foolish things I've ever said to her.

"But… I hate the sight of blood."

"You're a vampire!" she shouted in my face. "Or are you not even good at that?"

That was probably what caused the outburst last week. For the family dinner, she had Maria, our housekeeper, prepare filet de mignon—knowing damn well that I'm vegan.

There's absolutely no winning with her, so why keep trying?

Well, I guess if I want to keep tapping into Dad's vast funds is why.

Besides, it might be fun to find out what the new assistant is made of. The rest didn't last very long under the guidance of a lazy, good-for-nothing of a boss.

After toweling off, I choose a three-piece suit in a light grey with a crisp white shirt, and a pair of matching loafers. I tie the towel around my waist and hum a tune I can't hear over the sound of the hair dryer. I style my hair with some pomade, brushing it back in a wave over my temple and finally get dressed.

The new minion is probably losing her mind out there, but if she's any smart she should raid the kitchen or pocket something. A single one of my forks could probably pay off her rent for a month.

But when I finally emerge, she's standing by the farthest window, hands clasped behind her back as she looks over the city. So absorbed is she by the view, she doesn't even hear me as I walk up to her.

"Best view in town, huh?"

This makes her jump. The very first human reaction out of her.

She's puzzling. Most humans I know wear their hearts on their sleeves. It's not like vampires are much different in that regard, but with keener senses we try harder to keep our emotions close to the vest. This girl is a wall, though.

"Yes, it is," she says, pushing her glasses up her nose. "Ready to go?"

I shrug. "Sure."

She hasn't even put her purse down in the hour or so I took getting ready, and she just turns to the elevator without further ado. I have a feeling she'll be a piece of work.

When we're in the parking lot, she points to a Lamborghini Urus and says, "That's us."

I stand by the door behind the passenger, but she gets in the car without catching my hint. It takes all my willpower to not grin as she gets back out in a huff.

"What?"

I give her my best angelic look. "Aren't you going to open the door for me?"

She does a double take. "Don't you have hands?"

"Don't you have chivalry?" I put a hand on my chest. "Or is chivalry only for men to offer?"

She has to know I'm doing this to rile her up, and I can see it's working with the way her nose flares. Ultimately, she must really want to bring me in to work because she walks around the car and opens the door for me.

"Don't hit your head on your way in." The way she says it

makes it very obvious she wants exactly the opposite, so I don't give her that satisfaction and hop in smoothly.

Once we're strapped in and she's driving us out of the parking lot, she says, "I've been tasked with driving you to and from the office every day. Tomorrow, I'll be here at seven thirty sharp."

"It can't be seven thirty *and* sharp," I say, glancing outside the window and watching the downtown streets roll by. "It can only be sharp if it's seven o'clock."

"Seven thirty *sharp*, not seven twenty nine or seven thirty one."

I narrow my eyes at the back of her head. She pushes back in a way the previous assistants didn't dare to, which makes me wonder if she's some hotshot.

I put my elbow against the window and lean my face against my chin. "So, aside from human, what are you? A polyglot? Top IQ in the world? Some kind of record-breaker? A graduate from a super prestigious college?"

I must have touched a nerve because the more questions I ask, the more her shoulders tighten. Before I start theorizing about which one is true, she finally answers.

"The only applicable option is human, just like you and everyone else."

Oh.

So she doesn't know what I am. Interesting.

But then I catch on. "What, so you landed this gig with no qualifications?"

My brow creases. If my stepmother hears about that she may start suspecting Dad of having an affair again.

The girl squeezes the steering wheel hard enough to make the leather crunch. "If you really must know, I'm only bilingual. I speak English and Spanish. My IQ is average, as is pretty much the rest of me. The only record I'm breaking is of patience right now and no, I just graduated from Miami Herbert Business School."

"Really? Just that?" There's a piece missing from the puzzle that would show the full picture of why Dad hired her. Could she really be his new paramour?

"Also," she says, turning back to face me since we're stopped at a red light. Her voice is low but loaded with emotion, which means she's not a robot at least. "I might not be of the caliber of person you're used to dealing with, but I still deserve respect. I promise to extend the courtesy, but if you don't, you will also get the same from me."

Slowly, I tilt my head.

Nope, the different angle still reveals the face of someone determined enough to make me eat my words should they displease her.

This isn't the profile of the girls Dad usually dallied with in the past. He liked women who always said yessir, in contrast to his own wife. Serena Lossada isn't a yessir type of person. She demands respect.

And this must be why Dad hired her. She will break me in two if I let her.

I smile in full. "My apologies, it's true I've been rude. I'll strive to be a gentleman from now on."

My ass.

Game on, Serena.

CHAPTER 5
SERENA

I climb the steps of my apartment complex one by one, not as if I was carrying my weight alone but that of the whole word. I can't help but feel like I made money for doing nothing this week, which sounds like a dream come true—except that it was exhausting.

Every morning, I woke up at a terribly early hour to head to the office, where I picked up the company vehicle. I didn't dare park it around my apartment because the car alone probably costs as much as my entire building, and I don't quite live in the nicest area of town.

Then, I drove to my boss's place and picked him up.

The only silver lining was that he was always up and about, exercising in the gym or swimming pool. But after driving to work, he still spent every day napping in his office.

Like, straight up sleeping on the job.

The first time, I was so stunned that I just stood like a statue in front of him. He sat on the sofa in the middle of his office, legs splayed open and arms wide like a starfish. His head was tilted back, exposing a long neck corded with muscles. His eyelashes were so long they almost looked fake. I hoped he was at least drooling so I could make fun of him, but his lips were firmly closed as he snoozed without a care in the world.

It was almost funny how he got up every morning and dressed to the nines, only to come into the office to hibernate in his couch. He might as well come in his pajamas.

I'm sure if I fell asleep at my desk I'd be fired on the spot. And yet, it was very tempting when all I could do everyday was stare at the blinking screen of my computer, willing it to produce some action.

Essentially, I'm a high paid chauffeur—nothing wrong with that, except it wasn't the kind of experience I needed in my resume.

On the third day of that nonsense, I got up from my desk and spent the whole day introducing myself to the entire Marketing department. Without fail, when I mentioned I was Caleb Oh's assistant, it earned me pitying looks across the room.

A middle-aged woman was the only one kind enough to give me advice. She led me to the kitchenette and put a hand on my shoulder. "Try not to get on his bad side."

"Who?" I asked, frowning. "Mr. Oh?"

She must have guessed I meant Cedric Oh, because she said, "Caleb. A lot of people think he's just dead weight, but when he gets serious, he's the sharpest person in the building."

I kept my expression schooled into polite indifference, but I wish I could've snorted with the vehemence I desired. If he truly was so smart, why did he spent everyday snoozing his brain?

When I finally make it to my apartment complex on Friday, I send a fervent wish to the heavens that Karyn, my roommate, and her boyfriend Richard, leave me alone tonight. All I want to do is crash on my bed, face down, and stay like that until tomorrow.

I take two deep breaths before opening the apartment door

and stand at the threshold, wondering if my prayer is being answered or not.

They're in the kitchen, dressed up in outfits that scream night club. The tell with Richard is that his shirt is unbuttoned almost all the way down to his stomach, showing off a conventionally attractive physique marred by the fact that he's a gross jerk.

Meanwhile, Karyn wears a snake print dress as tight as a second skin, which I find poetic. The hem is so short she will no doubt flash people, but maybe that's the point. She and her boyfriend can't be considered demure by any means.

My roommate retrieves her tongue from inside her boyfriend's mouth long enough to tell me, "The bathroom's dirty."

I grip the handle of my purse tighter. Sadly, if I fling it at her face I'll land in jail and lose my job. And I need my job to save money and move out of this shithole.

Two years ago when we made our arrangement, it seemed like the perfect idea. Paying only forty percent of the rent in exchange for doing the house chores was a bargain, right?

Wrong.

Karyn is one of the messiest people alive and her boyfriend's worse. He pays zero percent of the rent despite hanging out here every day and night, and I still have to clean up after their combined disasters—which sometimes make me wish I could afford biohazard suits.

If that isn't enough, she also drops pearls like this all the time. "Oh, sorry. Does now being a hotshot's secretary mean you're not our live-in maid anymore? Will you finally start paying full rent?"

Affording full rent is my dream. But away from her.

So I respond with, "No, I'll clean it up. Are you guys going somewhere?"

Richard's face is tucked in the crook of her neck as he says, "We're going clubbing so don't wait up for us."

And in case he thinks I don't catch the meaning, he slaps his girlfriend's butt. I feel so bad for the people in the club who will witness their antics. I hope for my sake that they really don't return home tonight and leave me the hell alone.

After going into my room, I bolt the door.

I don't understand how they can be so inconsiderate. I don't care if they're so into each other that they can't keep their hands to themselves, but why do they have to make me see it every time?

It's like they want to rub in my face the fact that I'm single, or that they know I find their displays disgusting and it gives them their jollies. Or both.

I get it. Hormones can be a powerful thing and I've felt their effects too. When Caleb Oh stepped out of that pool, dripping wet and wearing very little, I felt like the world was pitching and gravity pulled me sideways. Every nerve of my body buzzed with electricity.

I drop on my bed, bouncing a little before settling my face against the pillow. Then I scream.

This is probably why I'm so tired. It's very taxing to spend every single day annoyed.

Annoyed that I can't do the job I signed up for. That my boss is an arrogant, lazy-ass. That he's so damn beautiful it physically hurts to look at him directly for extended periods of time, even when he's asleep. That he can still make me want to sock him in the nose when he opens his mouth. And even worse, that I have to suck it all up and have no one to share this with.

The only person in my life who cares about me is Sister Emilia. But I feel weird about venting about all these things with the nun who practically raised me in the orphanage.

Especially when it comes to the inappropriate feelings that arose from seeing my boss emerge from the pool.

No, I have to deal with all this mess on my own. One day I'll be able to look back on this and laugh.

I flip onto my back and stare at the dark ceiling. Noises come from the kitchen and I lie still until the annoying couple leaves. Finally, it's home sweet home.

I tear my work clothes off and chuck them at the floor with violence, kicking my kitten heels for further satisfaction. Come Monday, I'll have to do something about Caleb Oh's laziness, but for now I need to do a little bit more work before I can follow in his example of lounging about.

After changing into sweatpants and a threadbare T-shirt, I set out to clean the bathroom, the kitchen, and pick up the trash in the living room. I turn on a radio station that mostly plays merengue and sweat my frustrations out by cleaning and dance breaks.

A shower and pizza delivery later, I tuck myself in bed with my geriatric laptop and turn on the latest soap opera I'm obsessed with. This one is Korean, but I watch soaps from all across the map. All they need to have is a strong romance plot and characters with a lot of friends and family. It's the only way I can get a fix of all the things lacking in my life.

I fall asleep and dream about being the lead character of a soap, not realizing that is the path my life's headed for.

CHAPTER 6
CALEB

wake up from my nap with an insatiable hunger I can no longer postpone. My stomach doesn't rumble, because this isn't that kind of hunger. If anything, it starts to grow queasy.

Rubbing the sleep from my eyes, I confirm that the office is empty except from me and the sunlight bathing it from the windows. With the sun as my witness, I stand up and stretch my shoulders and back. My whole body feels like lead, as if every system is getting ready to shut down. I grab my hands to stretch my arms and can no longer feel sensation in my own skin. Not the touch, not the heat, not the beating pulse in my veins.

Basically, I'm dying.

It's only by this point that I'm able to bring myself to feed. I hate the thick, metallic taste of blood. I hate the feeling of it on my tongue, coating my teeth and going down my throat.

But it feels great when it hits my stomach.

Unlike with food, my body absorbs it and processes it almost instantaneously. Just a spoonful is enough to make every cell in my body vibrate with energy.

But I know if I drink only a little at a time, I'll have to feed more often. And that I can't stand.

I drag myself across my office, feet shuffling and body swaying. I'm careful not to bump into the furniture because if I collapse on the floor, it'll be much harder to reach the fridge tucked in the built-in cabinets behind my desk. My vision grows blurrier with every step. It takes monumental effort to open the cabinet and put the password into the keypad that opens the fridge.

Inside, bags upon bags of blood taunt me. Picking one out, I wonder if Dad keeps this stocked for moments like this, or if he's hoping it'll tempt me to drink more than usual.

"Vampires need blood to survive," he likes to tell me. "But survival isn't enough. You have to get stronger every day, and you can only do that by consuming quality blood—often."

But I don't need to get stronger every day. And I hate all blood equally. Quality or not. Human, vampire, or animal. I can't stand it.

I gag as I open the bag, but my slowing heartbeat forces me to bring it to my mouth. Instinct takes over and I latch onto the bag as if someone is going to pry it from me. Taking big gulps, I will my brain to shut off and pretend I'm drinking an açaí smoothie.

But it tastes like human blood.

That's the most common source of nutrients for vampires. Comed Solutions has a world-renown hematology research branch, of which a hidden venture is distributing some of the blood people sell for the use of vampires.

Animal blood is good in a pinch. It's less nutritional and the quality ranges from okay to abysmal, depending on how the animal is farmed. But that's also why I can't stand it. While humans sell blood for money or donate it for good causes, animals can't give you that kind of consent. Taking blood from them because I'm stronger doesn't sit right with me, and I don't understand why it does with everyone else.

Especially vampires.

The best blood for us is actually from our brethren. Our bodies produce all the enzymes and proteins we need not just to survive, but to get strong—inhumanly so. The more vampires you sample, the more blood mutations are absorbed into your own bloodstream, and the more your own body can evolve.

But you can only drink the blood of another vampire if they agree to it. Or if you defeat them.

Essentially, we're mosquitoes with a code of conduct. Why can't we extend the same curtesy to animals?

I finish the first bag and toss it aside, leaning against the cabinet to catch my breath for a second. My heart is pounding like I'm swimming in the ocean with a hungry shark on my tail. I draw in gasps of air with the same frenetic pace as I fed a few seconds ago.

More. I need more.

Squeezing my eyes tight, I shake my head to clear it. The world undulates and my head throbs, and this time I realize I *really* need more. One bag wasn't enough to bring me back to normal.

My hands tremble as I open a second bag.

That's when the door bursts open and I freeze. Is it Serena?

I check myself. My back is turned to it and hopefully I'm blocking the blood bag and the fridge from sight.

"What are you doing?" a different voice asks.

I let out a breath that makes my entire body sag in relief, before turning around. "Oh, it's just you."

Dad closes the door behind him and strides over. "Give me one, I need a snack."

I wrinkle my nose but toss him a new bag and sit on my

chair to finish my meal. "To what do I owe the pleasure of your visit?"

I guess it'll be a short one considering he doesn't take a seat, and he sucks in the bag's content in the blink of an eye. Dad licks his lips and says, "I need you to earn your keep."

I was almost thankful for the distraction up until this point.

"I have a meeting with Purchasing that I want you to join." He checks his watch and adds, "In five minutes."

"Why?" I ask.

"Because something doesn't feel right," he says.

That strikes me so hard, the plastic bag falls from my lips and I barely catch it before blood splashes on my clothes.

"Wait a second," I say, waving a finger between us. "Is this you asking me for my opinion on something?"

Dad shrugs. "Consider it more a test for me to see if your opinion is worth anything."

"I see." I suck the remaining blood in the bag. "Is not wanting to have an opinion an option?"

"Nope. And bring your assistant, I'll need minutes after the meeting."

I mumble. "You could've sent Jon for this."

"I wanted to see if it's true that you've been sleeping in your office."

My lips pinch into a tight line. My so-called assistant must have tattled, but at least I didn't give Dad the satisfaction of catching me redhanded—no pun intended.

Once he leaves, I clean up every vestige of my lunch, which definitely takes more than five minutes. I'm brushing my teeth in my office bathroom when a strong knock on the door echoes across the empty space. Dad doesn't knock and he must be in the meeting, which can only mean one thing.

Still brushing my teeth, I stroll outside the bathroom to find my assistant walking into the office. She carries her iPad in her hands and a stern expression on her face.

"We're running late," she says.

I shrug and return to rinse my mouth. Since I know she's waiting, I take more time in putting every strand of my hair in perfect place. Since I know Dad is waiting, I take every step twice as slow as usual, even though my body is so full of energy that I could run across the entire world and back.

As we walk over to the elevator, my assistant says, "You should make it less obvious even if you're dragging your feet on purpose."

The corners of my lips threaten to go up. "Where's the fun in that?"

Her eyes look lethal behind her spectacles, and the smile defeats me and makes itself known. She casts her attention down to her iPad and as I peek, I find that she's studying a map of the buildings, probably trying to find the route to the meeting room. I debate leading her the complete opposite way, but I have a feeling that would end in my untimely demise.

So when the elevator pings with our arrival to the ninth floor, I just tell her, "Follow me."

Even as she does, she walks beside me matching my stride. I like that. Her angry presence behind me would've been upsetting for my stomach, especially after a big meal.

I open the meeting room door without knocking and as if on cue, a big yawn takes over me. Joining this meeting already makes me want to take a nap. But my assistant digs her elbow into my side, jolting me awake.

The attendees break into murmurs at my entrance. The Purchasing Director stands beside the screen, openly annoyed to see me. At the table sit all the managers in his division, whispering amongst themselves.

One of them is loud enough that I can clearly hear him ask, "Who invited him?"

"I did," Dad says, sitting at the farthest end of the table.

Jon sits just behind him against the wall, and he motions at my assistant to join him.

While she rushes over to him, I tuck my hands in my pockets and stroll slowly, making eye contact with each person. I know I'm not well liked in the company, especially by the managers who feel like everything they had to fight for was handed to me because I was born the son of the company's owner. But the way they avoid my eye is kinda strange. Usually they glare.

Is this what Dad meant?

Speaking of, he points at the chair on his right and I take a seat there.

"You may resume," I say to Nick Walters, the Purchasing Director.

Through gritted teeth, Nick says, "Should I brief you on what you missed?"

The jab only makes me smile. "No need. There's such a thing as context cues. Proceed."

So he does. His people turn away from him to focus on his presentation about a potential new supplier of paper products for medical supplies.

Except the numbers he tosses about in the presentation make no sense.

Something is fishy here, and it isn't just Nick's breath.

CHAPTER 7
SERENA

"Fire him," Caleb says to his father.

All I see is the back of Cedric Oh's head nodding before he says, "Bring me the ammo first."

I cast wide eyes at Jon, but all he does is scroll through his phone without any sign of even paying attention.

It's all I can do, because unfortunately I do know my place. As much of a mammoth as Comed Solutions is, it's still a family owned business and here are the main stakeholder and one of his successors. There's nothing I can do to make them change their minds, although I really wish to tell them to value individual employees better.

Caleb lets out a long exhale. "I have no jurisdiction over Purchasing."

"Not as Marketing Director," the older man says. "But as a board member you have jurisdiction over everything. That's how I want you to act like in this instance."

Caleb swivels on his chair, giving me a view of his profile. So far I've only seen two expressions on his face. The first was amusement, when I showed up in his apartment for the first time. The second was the blissful slumber he submerged himself in all last week.

Right now he looks like an entirely different person. His mouth is set in a hard line and his eyes blaze with something I'm glad not to encounter face to face.

Without a word, he stands up and motions at me to follow. I notice he's clenching his fists tight and as we climb into an empty elevator, I pray that Caleb Oh doesn't turn out to be an aggressive boss who takes out his frustrations on his employees.

"It's not the first time he cooks numbers," he says, voice low as if anyone else might hear.

"What?"

"Nick claimed switching to this supplier I've never heard of will save us twenty million dollars."

I recall that comment specifically because the sum is so large. But how was that a red flag? "I'm not following."

As the elevator pings with our ascent back to the Marketing floor, he says, "Compared to which of our existing suppliers? And during what period of time? Twenty million in a month is not the same as twenty million in ten years."

"Couldn't you have asked for clarification in the meeting?"

"I could have," he nods in the most condescending way a person can muster. "But I would have, if I didn't already know we're using the cheapest suppliers in the market. And also if he hadn't already lost us twice as much money on previous reckless choices."

"Whoa."

He reaches forward and presses the button for a different floor. "Let's provoke him into giving us some info."

"Do you have a plan?" I ask, because I certainly don't.

One of his shoulders goes up. "I'm gonna wing it."

I jog beside him to keep up with his long strides, glad I chose ballerina shoes today rather than more elegant heels.

The Purchasing employees glance as we pass across their

floor. Most of them weren't in the meeting earlier, and it must be shocking to see the elusive younger Oh in the flesh.

We find Mr. Walters just outside of his large corner office, chatting with some of the employees who tagged along for his presentation. They clam up like shells upon noticing us, and that alone is suspicious even if we don't find any evidence to back my boss's claims.

"Caleb, my friend," he says in a way that doesn't make me feel like they are friendly at all. "So glad to see you finally join hard-working society."

Caleb's lips smile but his eyes paint a different picture altogether. "Is that where you think you belong? The last time you promised millionaire savings, you ended up causing a lot of hard work for other people to clean up your mess."

That causes a flurry of complaints from the guys flanking Mr. Walters, but not from the man himself. He says, "To err is human, is it not?"

"Sure." Caleb drags the word until its meaning morphs into mockery. "But to continue erring in the same way is probably criminal."

Mr. Walters breaks formation and gets right up against Caleb's face. "What are you implying?"

"I imply nothing. I'll find proof instead." As if he wasn't talking to anyone important, Caleb dismisses him by turning away. "Let's go, Serena."

Hearing my name from his mouth for the first time almost renders me into a marble statue, but I unfreeze myself to follow along. I have to focus on the matter at hand.

"What now?"

We retrace our steps back toward the elevators and as we wait, he says, "I can use his presentation to recalculate everything, which will show only that he was wrong but not any ill intention. We need to find hard proof that he presented misinformation on purpose. Those two things, plus his past history, should be enough for Dad to make the right call this time."

I sigh. "If they hadn't seen me already I could've tried spying on them."

He grins. "If you change your hairstyle you can still probably try. You're plain enough that they probably forgot what you look like already."

"Will I get fired if I hit you?" I ask with perfect calm.

All my question accomplishes is to make him chuckle.

When we finally reach our floor, he sequesters himself in his office to finally do something productive.

Meanwhile, I pace up and down my work area. I know I'm plain but there's no way taking my hair down from its ponytail will make me look much different. And it's not like I can run home to change and pretend I'm someone else.

No, I need to really *become* someone else.

And I know just how.

I grab my cellphone and call the first person to help me in this company. Marissa picks up at the second ring. "Hey, Serena. What's up?"

"I need your help." I walk her through the situation without going into any incriminating details.

"This sounds exciting. I get to play James Bond," she says, chuckling.

"If that gets you to help me, sure. You can be the next James Bond."

"I'm in. Jon doesn't have a lot for me to do today, anyway."

We agree that she'll go to the Purchasing floor on the pretense of collecting some office supplies. I plop down on my seat to wait for her updates. And for almost an hour there's…

Absolutely nothing.

The door to Caleb's office remains closed and I'm glad for it. He can't see the panic that must be written all over my face. If I don't find any proof of malicious intent from the

Purchasing Director, what's going to happen to me? Am I going to become an ex-employee or will I never be given another chance at proving myself?

I have to show that I'm competent, no matter how difficult or bizarre the task.

The first update comes from Marissa via text, and it says, *The employees don't know anything out of the ordinary, which means the presentation must have been prepared by their higher ups.*

I lock my laptop in my desk drawer and make my way back down to Purchasing. My mind races trying to come up with a plan, but the elevator conveys me five floors down a lot faster than I can come up with one.

But then I notice that without Caleb Oh, I'm completely invisible. Not a single head turns my way as I walk across the floor and I curse. Maybe, in his assholery, he was onto something. If I can blend among the people and overhear something, that should be enough. I park myself around Mr. Walters' office, my phone ready to record anything suspicious.

He strolls out of the office with two of the managers who flanked him earlier, and I tuck myself into a nook just in case.

"Are you sure?" Mr. Walters says to one of them.

The man nods. "Yeah, I shredded the report last night and deleted it from the drive. All that is available anywhere is your presentation."

"Good," his boss says, clapping his shoulder.

My heart is racing so fast, it's as if I was running a marathon.

Someone walks by and I slide myself farther back. The motion turns the light on in the nook, and I realize I'm in the supply area. Wall to wall cabinets full of assorted office stuff surround the space, and the only additions are the printing machine standing beside the shredding one.

I suck in air. That's probably where the jackpot is.

On the one hand, I can't believe how thoughtless these

guys are to have printed proof of their shenanigans. On the other hand, I curse them for being smart enough to shred it.

But I'm equal parts desperate and determined, so I march to the machine and lift the top off. Later, I'll give my bosses feedback to protect intellectual property by locking the shredding bins. For now, I'm just going to be thankful for a lead. It's like I'm the James Bond here.

CHAPTER 8
CALEB

The door to my office opens with such abruptness, it swings all the way and slams against the wall. I freeze in the middle of typing up a storm on my keyboard as my assistant barges in with a massive bin. It threatens to tip her over, possibly right into it, and the mental image makes me want to laugh.

She sets it on the floor long enough to shut and lock the door behind her, but rather than picking the bin back up, she pushes it to the center of my office.

Her chest goes up and down and she wipes her forehead before turning to me. "I think the proof is here."

I tip my head toward the thing. "And what is that?"

"The shredding bin." When that produces no response from me, she adds, "I overheard them say they shred a report last night and Walters seemed glad for it."

My eyebrows shoot all the way up. "Well, have fun taping it back up."

Serena puts her hands on her hips. "You're not going to help?"

"Nope, I'm busy." I pick up the sentence where I left off and finish typing it.

The beauty of marketing is that we're the main data hub of the company. We have to know what our position is with regards to suppliers and customers with the same detail so we can put out campaigns that increase the value of our brand, or repair any possible damage to them. It's why I don't need to beg Purchasing for information to help me debunk their business case, and I was in the middle of working on that when she barged in.

"Fine, don't help me, but at least let me use your office."

I glance up and catch her in the middle of pulling out armfuls of shredded paper.

Her thesis sounds good. Unless the Purchasing guys were talking about a different report altogether, it's likely that something useful hides in the endless ribbons of paper. But putting that puzzle together is impossible.

And I guess she's out of her mind, because she clearly is going to try.

"Be my guest," I say.

For a while, the only sounds are paper rubbing together and my typing. I crunch numbers directly on Excel, pulling data from our main suppliers and their sourcing allocation. Already, this tells me that the twenty million savings claim was bogus. The cheapest supplier we use has sixty percent of the global sourcing already, and the new player Walters is proposing costs more.

My nose wrinkles. Why is he interested in working with a more expensive supplier, but pitching it as if it was more cost effective? Does he have stocks in it?

And if so, does he really think we'll never catch on?

A yelp breaks my concentration and the scent of blood hits my nose like a jab. My stomach jolts, torn between the queasiness that blood always causes for me, and the instinct to put it in my mouth.

She murmurs something that must be Spanish, because I can't quite catch the words until she says, "Do you have a first aid kit?"

"In the bathroom," I answer, lifting one hand to pinch my nose.

The second she locks herself in the bathroom of my office, I spring for the windows and open them wide. A gust of hot wind swirls into the room and cleanses it of the smell of blood, and my lungs stop feeling like shriveled up raisins. My stomach settles and my veins stop tingling.

That's when my assistant comes out. I only have a second to spot the bandaid around her finger before she screeches, "What have you done?"

I don't even know how to explain that her blood smells both delicious and nauseating—or should I let her think I farted? But she derails that train of thought by pointing at the middle of the room. All I see are piles of shredded paper.

"I was making good progress and you blew it all away!"

"Really?" I close the window. "It looks the same to me."

"Ugh." She shucks her shoes off and kneels down on the floor, rummaging through the strips of paper. "I had already found a few from the same page. It has some logic, you know? The top layer probably corresponds to the last pages of the report, and so on."

"Well, just don't get any more paper cuts," I say.

She lifts her head to give me one of those blank looks perfectly designed to make people feel like fools. It works, because while my comment has nothing to do with hers, it has everything to do with why I had to open the window. But explaining it would get me in hot waters I'd like to avoid.

So I whistle as though nothing was amiss and sit back at my

desk. She can waste her time all she wants, but I do have real work to do putting together a puzzle of numbers.

I immerse in data until my surroundings start turning dark. Before that is able to pull away my concentration, the office is bathed in light and I continue working.

I only stop when the picture is complete on the screen in front of me.

Twenty million to the penny, all right. In losses.

"Shit," I say, going over my numbers again.

I can imagine him claiming to have made a mistake, that he got excited about diversifying the supplier portfolio further and misread his own number. But even if he didn't do it out of ill intent, this level of incompetence is unacceptable for someone who is supposed to be leading the Purchasing organization at a global scale. I stand by my assessment that he should be fired.

Finally, I pull my eyes away from the screen, only to get a massive eyeful of butt.

I do a double take—but sure enough, my assistant is on all fours, her butt raised high in the air and facing my way as she pores over shredded paper. I tilt my head, about to enjoy the view from a different angle when I realize this could probably count as sexual harassment.

If I make her aware of the view she's giving me, she'll feel awkward. So I stand up and walk around the office until I'm in front of her. That's how I notice that she's actually managed to tape together five pages. A glance at my watch tells me that's the progress she's made in six hours, and I can't help being impressed.

"Anything interesting?"

Breaking the silence out of the blue makes her jump. She composes herself sitting back and folding her arms. "It turns out it's actually twenty million in losses but that's not the most interesting part."

My eyes are wide as saucers. "Oh yeah?"

Serena pushes a stray strand of hair behind her ear and points at the corner of a page. "The report is made by one Luis Fernandez. Somehow I expected it to have that clown's name written all over him."

I hum from my throat. I don't know the names of every employee by heart, but I do know there isn't a Luis in the Purchasing management team. Which means this was actually written up by an employee.

And that's all the proof I need. If I can find that employee and have him testify that he knows the facts are different from what his management team presented, it will be all the grounds Dad needs to make heads roll. Figuratively.

"Great job," I tell her, which makes her jaw drop. "But stop what you're doing and find me Luis Fernandez."

"Uh, I think it's after hours already."

I shake my head. "It doesn't matter. Track him down and drag him back here if necessary."

"I—okay." She tries to stand but her legs must have fallen asleep, because she falls back on her rear. "Ouch."

I snort but offer my hand to help her up. She glares at it and I say, "It's not dirty."

"That's not—whatever."

Finally, she takes my hand and I haul her up easily. The sudden change of position doesn't work well with the noodles for legs she has developed, and they falter. Before she can topple over, I wrap an arm around her waist and hold her upright.

I can see my smile reflected on her glasses as she looks up at me. "Don't get me wrong, I just didn't want you to keep getting injured on the job."

"I can take it from here, thanks," she says, with a voice so pinched she could either be on the verge of tears or of a screaming fest. When she pulls away, her legs hold steady and I'm happy for my good deed of the day.

I turn back to the work she did and start snapping pictures. "While you find Luis, I'll send these to Dad. Walters is toast after this."

Along with my report, I send the pictures to Dad and update him on our next step. He texts me back with, *Aren't you glad I found you a diligent assistant?*

Yeah. If only she was nicer.

But then again, if she was nice *and* also had the curves she does, I'd be in serious trouble.

CHAPTER 9
SERENA

I f anyone ever comes to find me during off hours to drag me back to the office, they'll have to kill me first. I also don't want to be the one dragging in the corpse to work.

Which is why I'd much rather use my brain. I bring my laptop back to life and search for the employee database. A phone number should be listed there that I can try, and a call will hopefully be less intrusive than me showing up at the guy's house while he's asleep already. It's what I presume most people are doing at eleven in the night.

Finally, the system is up and running and I search for a Luis Fernandez in the employee database.

It comes up blank.

I let out a string of curse words in all sorts of languages. That's mostly what I've picked up from watching international soaps.

How can there be no employees with that name?

I pick up the laptop and go back into Caleb's office with it. He's in the middle of texting someone and looks almost guilty when I walk in.

Whatever, I don't care if he's texting his lover in the middle of making me work extra hours. I just want to get this done so I can go to sleep.

"Do you think it's a fake name?" I ask after explaining what I've found.

"I doubt it." His pretty face is scrunched up in thought. Then he stuffs his phone in his pocket and in a few strides is back to his desk. He doesn't sit on his chair, and instead leans down to type on his computer. "Hah! He was an employee until literally yesterday."

"Did he quit?"

"No, he was fired." Caleb slams his laptop shut with such force the device is probably broken now. "I bet he tried to blow the whistle with this report."

I blink rapidly. "Wow, I didn't know something like that could happen in this company."

"Neither did I," he says, voice low as he fishes for his phone again to make a call. He speaks to whoever is on the other end, "I just sent you the last of it. The whole Purchasing management team has to go."

I cringe, because even if their corruption has no room in a serious company like this—and it's already a major embarrassment that it festered until now—it still feels like nails scratching the chalkboard of my soul to know I contributed to someone losing their job.

But then again, these assholes also cost Luis his job.

Caleb nods from whatever the other person says. His eyes stray to me for a second. "Yeah, yeah. Don't get your hopes up."

Judging by the whiny tone of his voice, he must be talking with his dad.

"It's done," he says, shutting the call off. "Dad will take care of the rest. We're free to go."

"Aleluya!" I say, throwing my arms in the air.

That makes him give me a smile I don't like. It's the first

real one I've seen on his face, not filtered by the lens of a camera on a screen, and it has the same effect as looking into the sun. My eyes are blinded but I feel warm, and suddenly the colors seem brighter.

I turn around. "I'll clean this mess tomorrow. Get your stuff so I can drive you home."

I don't wait for confirmation before leaving his office. It takes me a minute to breathe evenly again but at least the sudden jolt woke me up. That smile was stronger than coffee.

After tossing everything I need into my purse and finding the car key, I'm about to call out for him when I find him standing right across my desk. I jump in my skin, not only because he was silent as a ghost, but also because it's a shock to find the object of your thoughts right in front of you.

He extends a hand out to me, palm facing up. "Key."

I assume he means the one in my hand, for the Lamborghini. "I'm the driver here."

"Not tonight, you look about ready to pass out." He closes his fingers around air and opens them again. "C'mon, I'm getting older here."

I bite my lip. The car was given to me to drive *him*, not the other way around. But then he makes a noise from his throat and I give in.

My feet drag as we take the few steps from our office, to the elevators, and then out onto the parking lot. The basement parking is muggy with air so humid that I break into a sweat the second we leave the air conditioned premises. That's the only thing spurring me to the car faster, even though he was right when he said I'm on the verge of losing consciousness.

We approach the car from the driver's side, so I walk around and open the passenger's door. I pause as I catch Caleb staring at me across the car. "What?"

"You can ride in the back," he says. "It'll probably be more comfortable."

"No, that's just weird." After all, he's not my driver but I am his. Tonight is abnormal and I'm not going to make it worse by climbing in the back, pretending like I'm some billionaire heiress.

I climb to the passenger's seat and strap on, about to give him a clever quip when my stomach makes the most ferocious sound.

"Is there a lion in your gut?" he asks with no mercy.

I groan. "Oh my word, couldn't you at least pretend you didn't hear that?"

"Nope." He climbs in and after fastening his seatbelt, turns to me. "What do you want to eat? I'll treat you to whatever you want as thanks for today's work."

My eyebrows go up, and the gesture makes my glasses slide down my nose. I push them up and on cue, my stomach does its party trick again.

Right now, my dream is being served a full course meal from a Michelin starred restaurant while in bed. But I don't think he can accommodate that wish. Honestly, I'd just settle for something warm and comforting.

"Arepas," I say right away, knowing that a taste of the home I've never known is exactly what I need.

There's silence for a second, before Caleb asks, "What's that?"

I shouldn't be shocked that the son of a billionaire has no idea what arepas are, but I do feel bad he's missed out on them his entire life. My mouth waters as I picture myself slicing a freshly made arepa, steam rising as I open it up and fill it with all the food in the world.

"How to describe them," I start, putting a hand on my stomach so it won't betray me again. "They're sort of like a bread made of corn flour, and you can fill them with pretty much anything. My favorite is carne mechada con pico de gallo y queso de mano. Qué delicia."

I don't even realize I switched to Spanish until I catch the confusion on his face. After translating, he asks, "Can they be vegan too?"

In my current state, it takes me a second to process and my filtering capabilities have reduced drastically, which is why I blurt out, "You're vegan?"

He reels back as though I hit him. "Geez, you don't have to say it like it's a disease."

"No, that's not what I mean." I wave a hand in his general direction, keeping it close to me not to smack him in the dark. "I mean, I just didn't know vegans could be so…"

"Uh, what?"

"Huge." For a second I wonder if that's inappropriate. But just in case, I add, "Like, you're super tall and buff. That's all."

He lets me stew in my embarrassment as he turns the car on and adjusts the seat to the length of his legs. "Well, vegans come in all forms and shapes. You shouldn't judge a book by its cover."

"Er, you're right. And yes, we can get yours stuffed with only veggies."

I should also never open my mouth again in front of him. Ever.

"So, where to?" he asks, and I give him instructions to my favorite arepera. It's open all day and all night, to cater to people with day jobs and also for the night owls who party hard in a city that prefers clubbing to sleeping.

Of course, every single person sitting in the terrace of the restaurant glues their eyes to the fancy car and even more so, to the driver, as he climbs out of it. I don't even care to observe the phenomenon and instead rush across the parking lot to join the line of people waiting to place their orders.

Eventually, Caleb catches up to me and I'm reminded again that the vision of him in this joint is as striking as finding a single flower in a field of green grass.

He eyes a plate of arepas as a waitress walks by and tells me, "I think four of them will suffice."

"What?" I'm loud enough to catch the attention of the people around us, and I lower my voice again. "They're super filling, you know. I'm going to be stuffed with just one."

He turns to me, slowly. Very slowly.

And cocks an eyebrow.

I take a deep breath.

"We're officially not at work, right?" I ask.

"Yes," he says, the corner of his lips going up.

Caleb doesn't stop me as I smack his arm with all my strength. "Freaking perv."

And he doesn't even defend himself. Instead, he just chuckles all the way until the front of the line.

CHAPTER 10
CALEB

"I read on your Wikipedia page that you're twenty seven years old, but are you?" Serena wonders out of the blue, which makes me drop the arepa in my hand on my plate. Even though there are bags under her eyes, the way they narrow is slightly menacing.

"What do you mean?" I ask, loosening the collar of my shirt because in the past thirty seconds or so it cinched tighter around my neck. Which is an absolutely baseless reaction because first, she can't hurt me. Second, I really am twenty-seven. If she was asking this about my brother I'd have real grounds to get nervous.

And yet, it's the judgement in her eyes what's causing this visceral effect.

Serena sighs. "It's just that sometimes you act like a fifteen-year-old."

"Ah." My shoulders relax and I pick the food back up. "I can show you my ID, if you want to double check."

"No, I guess this just means your birth age isn't the same as your brain's."

I grin and say, "You were the one who said something with a double entendre."

The power of her glare is diminished by the fact that her cheeks are so full of food that she looks like a squirrel with glasses. I use all my willpower not to laugh.

"Listen," I say, after polishing my plate clean. Four arepas stuffed with pico de gallo, avocado, and vegan cheese were exactly what I needed. "If I say or do something that makes you uncomfortable, you can let me know. I promise not to act like a brat in those instances. But in all other instances I will probably keep being insufferable."

Especially because riling her up is the most fun I've had in ages.

She nods and finishes her one arepa. "I guess I can work with that."

"Anyway, this really hit the spot but we should probably get going."

My assistant looks down at the table, first at her plate and then at the four empty ones I stacked in front of me. "You're right, but let me hit the restroom real quick first."

She shoulders her purse and collects all the plates, used napkins and empty soda cups. I glance around and catch someone else doing the same thing, which means that's the custom. In this place, it must be the customer and not the wait staff who cleans the table after the meal. I make a mental note to clear the table next time, and also to never bring my stepmother here.

Since there's a line of people waiting for the bathroom, I vacate our table and follow Serena to wait close by the entrance to the restrooms. That's when I notice a shadow slink away from the restaurant and disappear into a corner.

Is it a cat? A burglar? It probably has nothing to do with my assistant and I, and yet I must be the cat because I'm curious.

I follow along, rounding the same corner. This side is pitch black and so hot it makes me regret the existence of clothes, since it has the exhaust system of the restaurant's HVAC. There's a rustling sound and I make out the movement of the bushes. with something big—about human sized.

I splutter as I walk through a cloud of heat and when I emerge on the other side, I find a guy talking on the phone.

"Yeah, it's him. He's alone with a woman."

Serena and I weren't the only ones to fit that description, but if this guy is looking to cause some trouble for anyone, I won't be able to sleep well if I don't stop him.

"Tell me you're not up to something nefarious," I say. It makes the guy clamp his mouth shut and when he sees me walking over in the dark, he bolts.

Too bad for him, I fed today. In all forms.

Even though there isn't a streetlamp in sight, I can see almost as clear as day which direction he takes. I bend my knees and jump. It lands me directly in front of him and he brakes before crashing into me. This close, I catch a whiff of his blood, enough to realize that he's also a vampire. He won't be freaked out by a random dude who can jump higher than a gymnast in the dark.

"Caleb Oh," the man says, not bothering to run anymore.

I put my hand over my heart. "What a relief, I'm glad it's me you were tailing and not some innocent bystander."

"Shit." He puts his phone back in his pocket and I don't know if he kept the call engaged, which reminds me that whatever this is about, this guy isn't doing it on his own.

"What do you want?" I ask, advancing slowly.

We're now in the back of the restaurant. There's dim light coming from the back door, open just a sliver. The night is noisy with the sound of the air conditioning, the kitchen employees talking and working, and the faint murmur of customers at the front. Behind the guy, there are bushes as high as a wall but beyond that I don't know. There could be an actual wall, or a parking lot, or an empty road. I stretch my neck, trying to anticipate any direction he could try to escape through.

"I just wanted to see what the king's son looks like," he says, taking tentative steps back in an attempt to put distance between us.

I snort. "My picture's all over the internet, bro."

Clearly *seeing* me wasn't the true intent, because he pounces.

I bob my head in time to dodge his swipe. Before he can react, I grab his arm and twist. He flies over me and slams onto the ground with a hard thud.

"You're not going to be able to get a good look at me from the floor," I say, which makes him snarl.

He bounces back up, showing no signs of his bell truly being rang. I may have to work harder.

"I guess you're not the weakling of the Oh family, like people say you are," the stranger says.

"Trust me, I absolutely am." I shrug. "But I guess that makes you even weaker."

Just that is enough to provoke him into coming at me again. This time I can't avoid the punch to my stomach. But my guard is up and he can't land the jab to my face. It also must have distracted him and I land a knee in his gut. He doubles over and I grab a fistful of his face.

"In any case, if you really wanted to check if I'm the weakest Oh, you'd have to square against my mother and brother too." I lean down. "Is that your intention?"

If so, I need to warn them. Small fry like this won't hurt them, but several small fries together could be annoying.

He spits at my hand. "Damn you."

"Dude, gross." I cringe.

I land my elbow on the top of his head, hard enough that I

know his bell is really rung this time. He drops on his knees and I catch the gleam of saliva dripping from his mouth. Lifting his head by his hair shows he's out of it.

"Oh shit, did I hit you too hard?"

I'm glad this guy caught me today, after having fed on two bags of blood. Otherwise, he probably would've taken me down and if my assistant was a target too, it would've put her in danger.

Because he was right, I'm the weakest Oh.

Dad is the king of vampires, he's drank the blood of every vampire family on earth and has gained all the mutations in our species for the three hundred plus years he's alive. No vampire can defeat him. My stepmother is close in age to Dad and I once saw her punch through a cinderblock wall because she was angry. Meanwhile, my brother Daniel has trained all his life to succeed Dad and every time we spar, I'm the one who ends up on his knees.

I crouch down in front of the guy and shake him until consciousness comes back to his eyes. "I'll let you live under two conditions."

His voice is slurry as he asks, "What are they?"

"First, tell me why you're after me and who sent you. And second, give me your blood."

He blinks slowly through the sweat dripping from his forehead. "Isn't that three?"

"I guess the good news is that you may not have a concussion if you can still count."

"Screw—"

I nod. "Yes, screw me. Now talk."

"I don't know," he says with a grunt. "My buddy from the motorcycle club told me to test you, that's all. I don't want any real trouble."

"Okay, fourth condition. Give me your buddy's phone."

"Take it," he says, giving me his cellphone. "Can I just go now?"

"Blood," I say, extending my hand out. He tries to stand, probably to leave, but he's in no condition.

Without waiting further, I grab his arm and bite. The food from earlier revolves in my stomach as though it turned into a blender, threatening to spill out as I drink. His blood tastes more metallic than a regular human, like drinking mercury instead. Just two big gulps are enough and I let him go, tightening my jaws to stave off the gag reflex.

I stand there for a few minutes even after he leaves, breathing in the damp night air and willing my stomach to settle down. I can't afford to throw up the blood. Not only is it even more disgusting when it comes back up, but I also can't absorb his strength unless I digest his mutations.

My phone buzzes in my pocket and I take it out, finding ten missed calls from my assistant. I take out the handkerchief from my breast pocket and wipe my face just in case. No doubt she's angry that I made her wait for no reason, but I'm glad she didn't witness any of this. Even if I'm not happy that she's making me work, I don't want to put her in danger.

So, apologies at the ready, I walk back out to meet her.

CHAPTER 11
SERENA

Two strong cups of coffee later and I'm still not fully awake.

I sway in front of the mirror in my room as though hungover. There are dark circles under my eyes and I can see them even without wearing my glasses.

And it's all my annoying boss's fault. Why did he have to go missing for like half an hour last night? That was half an hour more I could've slept.

Or I could've taken up on his offer of arriving to work later today. I feel like that would've benefitted him more than me, though, which is why I didn't.

I tuck the tails of my white blouse into a secondhand maroon pencil skirt. Pairing it with kitten heels in the same color makes me feel well put together, and I complete the look with some concealer under my eyes.

Today, I plan to survive on caffeine and willpower. This exhaustion won't defeat me.

A few minutes later, it absolutely defeats me as I sit on the bus headed downtown. I almost miss my stop close to the Comed offices, if it wasn't for an old lady talking loudly on the phone in front of me. When I finally get in the company car, I turn the radio all the way up and smack my cheeks.

"Vamos, sí se puede," I tell myself before starting the drive to my boss's place.

I don't guarantee his safety if he's asleep when I get there. He's probably as tired or more, having worked hard for once, but I'm still miffed about him making me fight sleep waiting for him for what felt like forever.

"Good morning, Mark," I say to the security guy in the lobby of Caleb's building. We've become somewhat friendly, what with him being the first person I see every morning.

"Is it?" he asks, his wrinkled forehead growing more so with the worry etched on his face. "Are you being overworked, kid?"

"Aren't we all?" I say back, pushing the elevator button. He grunts as response, because it's a truth universally acknowledged that this is life for us, poors. Most of us don't make millions in our sleep.

I lean against the cool wall of the elevator and sigh. While I definitely wish I was in bed instead, I also can't fathom it when there's a shitstorm waiting as soon as we arrive to the office today. All the information was sent to Cedric Oh last night, but this morning is when the heads are going to roll. The coffee in my stomach churns at the thought.

There isn't a single sound when I step into Caleb's apartment. The windows are still obscured from the early morning sunlight, and the kitchen shows no signs of life. I leave my purse there and tiptoe toward the back of the apartment, passing the stairs leading to the level below. His bedroom door is closed.

He's probably asleep and I may be acting as a chauffeur, but I'm not an alarm clock to gently wake him up from his slumber.

So I knock on the door and shout, "Good morning, Mr. Oh! I'm here to pick you up."

I expect some sign of life but nothing happens for a solid minute, and also not when I try again. Casting my pride aside once more, I push open the heavy door and peek inside his room.

It's just as dark as the living room, and almost as big. I push my glasses up and squint at the bed. The sheets are rumpled but show no human-shaped lumps.

"Hello?" I call out, and get absolute silence in return. "Well, at least he's up."

If he's not in his room, or bathroom, he must be in the gym. That he has that kind of energy after the day we had yesterday annoys me. I stomp all the way down the stairs to the lower floor of his apartment.

Occasionally, this is where I find him in mornings when I come pick him up. They're the worst mornings, too, because I have to wait until he finishes his workouts, showers, and gets ready before we're able to go to the office. It makes us arrive at midmorning at best, which makes every person we come across on the way to his office give us funny looks. And of course he had to choose today of all days to be difficult.

The weights and equipment area are empty, which can only mean one thing. He's taking a swim in the full size pool— which is not to be confused with the infinity pool in the main apartment. I sigh heavily.

Not only he's going to make us late today, but he's also going to make me see him in a swimsuit again.

"Caleb Oh," I shout as soon as I make it to the pool. Sure enough, he's swimming a lap in the middle of the water and I have to wait until he reaches the end and surfaces for long enough to hear me. "Caleb Oh, we're going to be late."

Even though he's at the farthest end, my voice echoes

across the otherwise empty chamber and I have no doubt he hears me well.

Caleb pulls his goggles up and wipes his face. "Good morning, Miss Lossada."

"Good morning my ass," I murmur only to myself. To him, I say, "Swim time's over. Today's an important day and you're going to make us late."

I hear him groan as I turn, but the sassy quip in my lips is replaced by a shriek. Everything tilts and I realize too late that I'm flying. My arms flail, trying to find something to grab onto but all I catch is air.

And then I slam into the water. The shock steals the air I had in my lungs and I sink like a boulder. I try to fight the water off but there's no use, it sucks me in. I can't feel the bottom of the pool under me. I also can't see the surface of the water. Or is it because I lost my glasses?

My mouth opens as if to scream and water rushes in. I pray in my mind and try to fight the pull of gravity. I'm pretty sure I'm crying but the water doesn't care about that.

Shit, is this how I'm going to die? Why did I get so close to the edge when I can't even swim? Why did I have to slip?

Then, something cinches around my waist. It pulls hard at me, defying gravity, and I cling to it. I know it's my boss and a cocktail of emotions blend in my gut. While I'm thankful that Caleb Oh is here, I'm also angry that I got in this mess because of him.

I want to curse at him when we finally break into the surface, but all I can do is splutter water and cough for air.

"You don't know how to swim?" is the first thing that comes out of his mouth.

I try to hit him, but while the water was quick to suck me in, I'm too slow in it and I don't land the blow anywhere near him.

With my arm around his neck, he swims us to the edge as though he was born underwater. A shock goes through my skin where it touches his bare one, and I have to look away to not focus on the fact that he's half naked and we're both wet. But I can still feel his muscles against me as they work, and no amount of closing my eyes will make this new knowledge go away.

When we reach the edge, I push him away and grab onto the bare concrete. I breathe in and out harshly, which stings my lungs.

"Are you okay?" he asks, ripping the cap from his head and shaking the water off his hair. It splashes me and makes me want to hit him again.

"I think so." I fight to regulate my breathing. It should help me get rid of the cold and hot sensation flashing through my body. "Thanks for helping me but let's be clear, this was your fault."

He chuckles and pushes himself up over the edge, which gives me an eyeful. I didn't know there was such thing as visual poetry until seeing the sinew of his shoulder muscles working to pull himself out of the water, rivulets of water trickling down his smooth skin. Even worse, he's wearing those swimming briefs that stick like a second skin, and I didn't know someone could have muscles that defined on top of their bubble butt.

My grasp of the pool edge slips and for a second I'm submerged again. Probably not a bad idea, considering how high my temperature is running. Two hands reach under water and pull me out. I hear laughter.

"Wow, I'm gonna have to teach you how to swim."

Please, no, I think to myself.

I slide myself over the edge, scrapping my knees against it. The pain is nothing compared to finally being on the surface with plenty of air.

I wipe my face and notice two things. First, I lost my

glasses. Second, my boss's bare feet are right in front of me and I better not look up. Not that I'll be able to make out details without my glasses.

"Here you go," he says above me, holding said devices in front of me. "Also," he says, sounding on the verge of laughter again. "We're going to be really late today."

I point at him. "Your fault!"

"Actually, this time it'll be yours." He crouches down in front of me and I thank the droplets of water on my glasses distorting the view. I still make out his pointed glance down at me. "You're going to have to wash and dry your clothes, unless you want to give everyone at the office a shock."

"What?"

Then I glance down at myself. My blouse has gone so fully transparent, I might as well not be wearing one.

CHAPTER 12
CALEB

can't stop laughing. It's either that, or marching right back to my bathroom for a very cold shower.

Taking a quick peek at my assistant's chest wasn't quite what I had on my list of things to do today, but now for the life of me I can't remember what the list contained. In the seconds after pulling her out of the water and noting her wardrobe malfunction, I debated whether to tell her on the spot or let her discover it on her own.

Either way, it's a fact that I'm toast. I'll have inappropriate dreams about that vision for weeks.

But I don't make it a habit to be an asshole, so I told her. She covered herself right away and I gave her the towel I'd brought down for myself. We headed back upstairs in silence. Her shoulders went up as high as her ears—which were red like streetlights—as she tried to make herself smaller.

My shoulders still shake with mirth as I knock on the door of the spare guest room. It's where she's sequestering herself while her clothes get dry.

"Hey, what shoe size are you?" I ask. For a while, there's no response until I hear some rustling.

"Why?" she asks through the locked up door.

As if I'll pounce on her because of a little boob. Whatever.

"I guess the more accurate question is, do you want to wear your sopping wet shoes all day?"

That leads to a pause before she finally says, "Eight."

"Cool. Also, your clothes should be ready in like twenty minutes."

I leave before I can think too hard about the fact that my assistant is hanging out in just a bathrobe in my guest room. We don't more fodder for my imagination.

My cellphone buzzes and I take it out from the pocket of my slacks.

Oh shit.

"Hey, Dad," I greet.

"Where the hell are you?" he says, which is his version of good morning.

A glance at my Omega reveals it's already past ten in the morning, which for Dad's intents and purposes is way too late.

"I'm still home." There's no good way to put this, so I just say, "My assistant had a small accident this morning when she came over to pick me up, and we're still sorting it out."

"What?" I pull the phone away from my ear after the question nearly pierces my eardrum. "What happened? Is she okay?"

Why is he so worried about my assistant?

You know what, that's not a question I really want an answer to.

"Yeah, she's fine. Just slipped into the pool."

Dad grunts. "Glad no one was hurt. When are you coming into the office then?"

"As soon as her clothes dry and traffic allows us to get there." Which could be anywhere between half an hour and three. No one knows how or if downtown Miami traffic will flow.

Besides, I need to find shoes for Serena.

"Fine, try to hurry. I'm waiting for you to make the announcement."

I scrunch up my face. "Why? Just get it over with."

"Because I want you there, you fool."

"Aww, Dad. You're so sweet."

He lets out a long breath. "You're going to be the death of me, child."

With that he hangs up before I can say that his most likely cause of death will be his wife, especially if she finds out that he cares about my assistant a lot.

Shaking my head, I relocate to the kitchen and pour myself a glass of orange juice while I call the only person who can help me out of this situation. After a few seconds of ringing, she picks up.

"Caleb, baby! How I've missed you."

Her use of the word *baby* in association with my name is in the literal sense, seeing as I'm the baby brother of her husband.

"You should only call Daniel baby," I say.

"But babies are tiny and cute, none of which fits my husband." She lets out a rush of air. "Danny is a big, manly man and—"

"Okay stop." I want to laugh just as much as I want to barf. "I'm also not tiny or cute—But that's not what I'm calling you about, anyway."

"What's wrong, baby?"

I lower my face onto the palm of my hand but I have to let it go if I want this conversation to head in the right direction.

"What's your shoe size?"

"Are you going to give me a gift?" she asks.

"No, don't ask for details but my assistant's in a pickle and she basically doesn't have any shoes."

"You can't tell me something like this and expect no questions from me," she says, her voice light and ready to pry out the gossip.

"Tell you what, bring me a sensible pair of shoes in size eight and I'll tell you everything."

Lara squeals. "Deal. Be there in five."

It takes her way more than five.

By the time she bursts in from the elevator, Serena is already dressed in her clothes and sits in the living room with me. While I browse the internet looking for my next diving spot, Serena checks her work email on her iPad as if she couldn't abide wasting one more second of work hours.

Or it could be in an effort to not meet my eye. It works until Lara shows up.

"And who is this pretty lady?" my sister-in-law asks.

Serena's expression is what I imagine someone to look like if they have to perform life-saving surgery on themselves with no anesthesia. I have to bite my lips not to laugh.

"Lara, this is Serena Lossada, my new assistant." Then I motion the other way around. "Miss Lossada, this is Lara Khouri, my sister-in-law."

The latter dumps herself on the couch and wraps my assistant in a hug. That's when I notice that she can't possibly have brought one pair of shoes—but several. Five shopping bags scatter to the floor where she drops them.

"Ugh, aren't you just the cutest little thing?"

For the first time since The Accident, my assistant deigns me with a look. It reads *what the hell?*

I wave a hand. "Don't mind her, she thinks everything is cute."

"No, you both are cute." Lara points at us, before putting her hand on her chest. "My husband and I are hot."

"I detect some bias," I say. "Anyway, did you bring *one* sensible pair?"

Lara gives me a blinding smile. "Define sensible."

I have to think about it for a second, but the answer is simple. "Exactly the opposite of your style."

Lara is a fashion designer and even though it's a Wednesday, she's decked with clothes and accessories most fitting for a pictorial than the office where she came from. Meanwhile, the most exciting clothes I've seen on Serena were a suit in a burnt pink color and a white blouse. The highest heels she's worn are actually the ones in my laundry room.

"Hmm." Lara sets her attention on the products she brought. She arranges seven shoe boxes on the coffee table. "There are many ways to define sensible, but I hope one of these options fits your particular definition."

"Miss Lossada?" I tip my head toward the selection.

Still without saying a word, my assistant treads on bare feet across the plush carpet and opens the nearest box as if expecting a snake to come out. She drops the lid back on it just as fast.

"So, not the snake print ballerina flats," Lara says, her eyes shining in amusement.

I snort, but a look from my assistant warns me that I will probably taste the snake print shoes if I laugh. Shifting my attention to my sister-in-law, I say, "Anyway, thanks for the assist."

"You'll owe me."

"Geez, why does that feel ominous?"

"These are fine," my assistant cuts in, picking up a pair of white shoes with no heel. "Thank you so much for the help."

Lara claps. "Oh, she speaks!"

Serena cringes. "Sorry, it's been a weird morning."

Weird isn't quite how I'd describe it.

It gave me two unexpected gifts: an excuse to be late for work, and boobs.

Finally, the three of us make our descent in the elevator.

While Serena is focused on her iPad, my sister-in-law leans closer to me and pulls me down to whisper in my ear.

"I like her."

I lift an eyebrow. "So what?"

Lara's lips curve in a dangerous way. "I want to play with her."

Serena's either not listening, or is really good at pretending that she isn't. Either way, she looks like a serious type of person, not someone who would enjoy partying hard with Lara until morning breaks. Besides, she's being paid for me to nag her, adding Lara to that scope won't get her a bonus.

So, I whisper back, "My assistant's off limits."

We finally make it to the office at eleven in the morning. As soon as Serena and I walk in through the lobby, Jon picks us up and carts us over to the auditorium.

And in case I can't already guess, he says, "Your father's probably going to kill you after this."

I smile.

"I hope the employees haven't been waiting long," my assistant says, hopping in quick steps beside Jon and I. "I tried to reschedule the conference to our precise arrival, but we ran into all the red lights possible."

"You were in on this, too?" I ask her.

She pushes her glasses up her nose. "Yes, it's called working."

Jon lets out a muffled laugh, before clearing his throat. We follow him into the auditorium where Dad is in the middle of saying a thorough audit of the Purchasing organization will be conducted, and as if this was timed perfectly, he points at me.

"And it will be conducted by the interim Head of Purchasing, Caleb Oh."

Barely moving my lips and keeping my voice low, I say, "What. The. Hell."

My assistant's glasses gleam as she whispers to me, "Time to work, boss."

CHAPTER 13
SERENA

"I hate this," Caleb says while he rifles through papers strewn across his desk.

I know exactly what he's looking for, and I pluck the inventory report from the main warehouse and hand it to him. "I don't know why. I love it."

His pretty face twists like he's chewing on a lime. "Not all of us are workaholics."

"It's only been two days." It's very hard to refrain from rolling my eyes, but I succeed by sheer power of will. Only two days of actually having to work and he complains as though it's been twenty years. "Besides, the audit hasn't even started."

Caleb Oh groans. Anyone would think he's under severe torture.

"Reminding me is like pouring salt on the wound." He scans through the report and extends his hand out, finally accepting the cup of coffee he asked me for. "Did you send me all this by email?"

"Yes, I even organized your inbox for you so it's easy to find all the information."

I broke it down into the different topics, labelled them in

intuitive ways and even color coded it. All he has to do is think about what he wants to find, which I'm not entirely sure he's determined yet. There are piles of papers on his desk in a haphazard mess.

"Are you sure you know what you're doing?" I ask, which certainly crosses the lines of my duties as his assistant and reaches more into critic territory, but I wasn't the most deferential assistant from the start.

Besides, ever since the pool incident he gets this look on his face when I'm around—no doubt caused by that incident—like he wants to laugh. It makes me want to take even more swipes at him.

Absentmindedly, he says, "Let's just say I'm winging it."

Ay, caramba.

"Well, let me know what I can assist with."

Since he doesn't respond, I trace my steps back and leave the office. It's disconcerting to see him awake for so many hours in a row. Hopefully this will keep him from naps for a good while, and that way stave off the boredom that plagued my first week.

When I turn to my desk, I find a guy standing by it with his hands in his pockets. He turns around and I almost drop the tray in my hand.

"Hi," he says, smiling in a way that lights up the entire place.

This can only be the one and only Daniel Oh. His face appears in almost every article associated to Comed Solutions. Where Caleb is the subject of tabloid gossip, Daniel's accomplishments in hematology research for the scientific branch of Comed is what gains him notoriety—aside from the fact that he's the heir to Cedric Oh's entire business empire.

"You must be Daniel Oh." I set the tray on the counter at my desk and offer my hand. "I'm Serena Lossada, your brother's new assistant."

"Very nice to meet you at last. I've already heard about you from Lara." He shakes my hand and leans forward just a notch. "Also—sorry? My wife can be tough to deal with, especially if she and Caleb get the same idea. You'll have to be patient with them."

Daniel doesn't look a day older than Caleb. The shape of their eyes is pretty similar, but Daniel's irises and hair are darker, and he doesn't have the freckles that pepper Caleb's nose. The biggest difference is that looking at the older brother doesn't make me want to strangle anyone.

"I appreciate it." I offer a polite smile. "I presume you're here to see him?"

"He must be busy but may I?"

Probably not busier than you, I think to myself.

In any case, Caleb has actually been productive this morning, and it's not like I can turn the Oh heir away because I want to. I knock on my boss's door and enter.

"Excuse me, Mr. Oh—"

Before I can finish the sentence, Caleb says, "Just call me Caleb. We should have enough trust by now for that."

His definition of trust is very loose, if he's basing it on the pool incident alone.

He keeps his head in the papers and misses the way I press my lips in a tight line, so for the sake of keeping his attention away from me I say, "Fine. Caleb, your brother's here to see you."

"Dan's here?" He finally looks up, eyes shining just the same as when I drive him home after work.

On cue, his brother peeks in and whistles. "Never thought I'd see the day when Caleb is finally working his ass off."

"Save me." His younger brother whines.

I let out a sigh. "Mr. Oh, is there anything I can bring you?"

"Some water would be great," he says. "And please call me Daniel. Mr. Oh makes me feel like I'm my dad."

Caleb makes a sound like it's the grossest thing he's ever heard and I swear he's like a teenage boy sometimes.

"Very well, Daniel." And because my boss gives me a pointed glance, I add, "And Caleb."

The smile in his face has the effect of chafing my pride. It's as if he won a battle I didn't know I was fighting.

As I head back for the door, I catch Daniel saying, "You sounded weird on the phone, so I decided to talk in person."

I close the door behind me.

And panic

Oh. My. Word. What if this is about the pool incident? It certainly turned what already was a dysfunctional work relationship into a weirder one. I'm self-conscious all day, wondering if every time Caleb glances my way he can see through my clothes like his memories work like X-ray. What if he called his brother to talk about this, and how awkward it's made the past two days?

What if he wants to fire me?

I force myself to take deep breaths and discard that option. It's not like I flashed him on purpose. If anything, he's the one who flashed me with his tiny swimsuit. Maybe I should fire *him* for indecent exposure.

"I'm going wild," I murmur to myself as I grab a cool bottle of Evian to bring over.

When I open the door, Daniel is saying, "Nothing weird around Lara and I, but thanks for the heads up."

I clear my throat. "Excuse me, here's your drink."

As I approach, a cold tingle travels down my spine. I haven't seen that expression in Caleb's face. Like he could snap a brick with his bare hands.

"Thank you," Daniel says, taking the bottle from my tray and facing his brother again. "You should tell Dad."

Caleb shakes his head. "No, he'll overreact."

That's the last I catch before I return to my desk. From that little context, it doesn't sound like the Oh brothers were talking about my boobs.

Not a sentence I ever thought I'd form in my mind.

Relief comes out with a sigh, and with that I set out to focus back on my tasks.

After meeting with the audit team this morning, Caleb decided there are three fronts he has to tackle to clean up this mess. First, it's putting out a statement with the PR team to control the damage to the company's image. Second, and linked to the PR statement, is reengaging with our current suppliers to assure them about our relationship with them. And third, it's to conduct the actual internal audit of our practices.

The audit team, formed mostly by accountants and legal experts, already has their plate full basically deconstructing every deal made by the Purchasing organization in the past couple of years.

Meanwhile, Caleb booked himself solid for weeks to meet with suppliers, starting today. I'll tag along with him for every in-country expedition. I ping Caleb with a reminder that we need to leave the office soon.

A few minutes later, the siblings step out of the office and I grab my bag and car key.

"By the way, when are you going to join us for family dinner again?" Daniel asks his brother, who is busy putting his blazer back on.

"Hopefully never," Caleb responds.

Daniel sighs. "You can't avoid Mom forever."

My boss ignores that and addresses me. "Ready?"

"Er, yes."

The three of us get on the elevator together. I stand behind the brothers, both of whom tower over me.

From the back, you'd think Caleb is the oldest one. His

shoulders are wider than Daniel's, a strange irony seeing as Daniel will carry the burden of the inheritance. It's probably why Daniel sounds like a reasonable person and why Caleb is a brat.

Still, clearly there's love between the brothers. They part ways with one of those hugs guys give each other, including hard thumps of each other's back. My chest pangs with longing for that kind connection with someone, and it's another reminder of how vastly different I am from Caleb Oh. Not only he has ridiculous amounts of money, but he also has a family.

Sighing, I get on the driver's seat of the Lamborghini and set the GPS up to guide me toward the supplier. It'll take at least one hour to get there, and I pray that Caleb doesn't provoke me into murder during the drive.

CHAPTER 14
CALEB

get a text from my brother that feels ominous. *Be careful*, it reads. Almost as if he, too, expects danger to find me at any moment now.

After getting in the back of the Urus, I loosen the tie around my neck and pop a couple of buttons open. Maybe I should just focus on what I have in front of me, instead of imaginary shadows. Dad finally maneuvered me into working for my buck, and my assistant looks almost gleeful about it. That already is enough to keep me busy.

"Do you need me to take notes for this meeting?" Serena asks a few minutes after we're on the road.

"Nah, it'll consist mostly of me kissing ass. That doesn't need to go on record."

Her eyes shift from the road to me via the rearview mirror. "Are you sure? Your ego can stand getting knocked down a peg or two."

"Wow, is that really the way to talk to your boss?"

She snorts. "If we want to get really technical, my real boss is your dad."

"True." I lean my head back and close my eyes. "I'll take a nap and spare you having to put up with me for a while."

"Sleep tight," she says, and I don't detect the usual bite in her voice. It must mean she truly is glad for me to leave her alone for a bit.

My chest shakes with silent laughter. She was a porcupine from the beginning but after a little wardrobe malfunction she's been outright cutting.

"You know, if this is so uncomfortable for you I can show you my boobs too and we'll be even."

She draws a sharp breath. "What I wish above all else is that you forget about that, but at this point I'll settle for you getting some sleep."

"Aye, aye."

Of course, all I can see with my eyes closed is the water dripping down from her transparent blouse, and the fabric clinging to her shape like something straight out of a fantasy.

That's when I catch a buzzing sound, too strong to come from a cellphone. I look out the window and find a burly guy on a motorcycle, driving down the road right beside us. That's not abnormal, but the fact that he's looking through the window straight at me is.

I glance at the other side and what do you know, he has a twin.

"Serena," I say, tempering my voice so she doesn't detect anything weird. "Can you speed up a bit?"

"We're making good time," she says, checking the GPS.

"Just do it."

She turns to look at me for a second. "If I get a traffic ticket you're paying for it."

"Deal."

While she speeds up just a bit, not only do the two guys do the same, I also spot a third one trailing behind us.

Under my breath, I whisper, "Shit."

"What was that?" my assistant asks.

Rather than answering, I undo my seatbelt and scoot to the middle of the backseat. "Coming through."

I give her just that warning before contorting myself over the middle console, one leg first and following with the rest of my body.

"What the—what are you doing?" Serena keeps the car in its lane even despite her confusion.

I let out a breath once I sit on the passenger's seat and fasten my seatbelt. "We're being followed."

"The what?"

"Stay calm," I tell her and fire off a couple of text messages. One is for Dad and the other one for Daniel. "How far are we from the office?"

"Uh—about half an hour. Why do you sound so calm?"

"It's not the first time," I say, without dwelling. It probably won't be the last either. "Okay, stick to main roads. I sent our location and I'm sure help is on the way."

Of all the reactions I expected from her, the last one is praying. But that's exactly what she starts doing and in Spanish. Her knuckles turn white as she grips the steering wheel hard, eyes darting around to the mirrors and to me. Her chest goes up and down faster than normal.

"Deep breaths will help us stay safe," I murmur gently.

"This must be why all your previous assistants quit." Her lower lips trembles. "Too much wild shit."

The guy on our right speeds up until he's beside my window, trying to peek in again. The glass is tinted as dark as it can go and is bulletproof. It can buy us time in case there's a shooting.

To divert Serena's attention from the danger, I say, "Actually, you've just been lucky."

"Just so you know, if we make it out of this alive I'll consider quitting."

"Aw, but I don't want you to. You're actually a lot more fun than I thought you'd be."

She glares at me.

Then, the guy on her side rams against our car.

Serena screams and lets go of the steering wheel. I grab onto it and keep the car on course. I'd return the favor if I was the one driving. But for now, I need to take control of this situation before we get into an accident.

I glance around again and confirm it's only three guys. I can do this.

"Serena, I need you to do exactly as I say."

Her voice trembles. "Okay."

"Take the next exit."

Serena bites her lip. "But you said to stick to the main roads."

Yeah, that would've worked if these guys were just trying to intimidate us. We could've hopped onto I-95 and just drive until the cavalry arrived. But it looks like they want to engage, and rather than putting Serena and I in danger, I have to find the way to only endanger myself.

"Change of plans, we need to find somewhere deserted."

Her voice comes out as a shrill as she asks, "Why?"

"Just trust me, okay?"

Her dark eyes hold fast onto mine, long enough that it's almost dangerous. "Do you have a plan or are you just being reckless?"

Both.

Instead, I respond, "I have a plan."

Somehow, that works. She takes a sharp turn that makes one of the cyclists pull a feat of physics to get out of the way. We're going so fast that I can't even see what the exit sign said, but Serena drives at breakneck speed past relatively busy streets until traffic begins to thin out. The three guys are right on our tail and start to overtake us.

"Good," I say, unstrapping. "I want you to brake and after I get out, lock the car up and drive away."

"What?" she screams. "No!"

"Yes, that's an order."

"I don't care. Why the hell should I do that?"

I shrug. "I dunno, so you can stay alive?"

"And leave *you* to die?" she asks, her voice several octaves higher than the norm.

Against common sense, I find it in me to smile. "Aww, I didn't know you cared."

She surprises me by whipping her arm out and smacking me right in the middle of my chest with all her strength. "Shut up, I don't want your death on my conscience."

Two of the drivers swerve in front of us, forcing Serena to brake. We lurch forward. The seatbelt digs across my chest, which was already stinging from her hit. More than that, my hand hurts. I caught her head in time before it smacked into the steering wheel, getting the brunt of the blow instead.

Slowly, Serena looks up, first at the men climbing down from their bikes, then at me. And I smile again, all placid.

"Don't worry, I'll die one day but not today."

"Are you out of your mind?" she asks, her voice low as if afraid the assailants might hear.

I consider the question seriously. If I was a human, the answer would be yes. If this was happening three days ago before feeding, it'd also be yes. But like I said, not today.

"Lock up and leave, okay?"

Before she can react, I jump out of the car and slam the door shut. Sure enough, I hear the click of the safety engaging.

The location's not bad. We're in the middle of a dirt road by an abandoned building, in what looks like a derelict industrial complex. The sun is high in the sky and the air is stifling hot, especially from the fumes of the parked bikes.

"Well, well," one of the guys says, twirling a metal pipe. "Looks like we'll catch a hefty reward for this one."

As if. Even if I get killed, Dad will bite their heads off.

I take a good sniff at the air. Past the smog, the humidity, the smell of dirt under my feet and the yellowing grass, past the lingering scent of the sea salt in the air and beyond the sweat in their skin, the leather of their jackets and the cheap cologne… I smell vampires.

Excellent. I really don't enjoy hurting humans.

I glance back. Serena sits still, her hands on the wheel and her wide eyes on me. With a hand, I motion at her to leave but she doesn't react. Panic has rendered her still as a statue and while I guess it's safer if she doesn't drive that way, there's no way I can prevent her from seeing what's coming next.

The first guy comes at me swinging the pipe.

CHAPTER 15
SERENA

"¿Qué carajo está pasando?" I shout to the silence inside the car. It blocks all outside noise, and it's almost like I'm watching an action film with the television on mute.

One of the strangers swings a pipe at my boss and I yelp. But Caleb dodges out of the way. I try to warn him that a second guy is creeping from behind. He swings a metal rod as if my boss was a baseball. Caleb must sense it because because he ducks low and disappears from my view.

The third guy goes flying backwards. I brace myself with the steering wheel, trying to see whatever's happening on the ground. But then Caleb is back on his feet, parring the other two guys as they alternate trying to land blows.

My jaw unhinges. Is my boss some martial arts master?

With a high kick, he catches one of the guys by his jaw and sends him flying back. The guy who had fallen is now recovered and circling Caleb. I do a double take when the flying guy finally lands about two yards away.

How is that even possible?

Out of the blue, one of the guys shoots back and lands on

the windshield of the Urus. I cover myself, screaming through the sound of glass shattering. I can't open my eyes. Who knows what sight could be waiting for me. The way that guy crashed against the car was almost as hard as if he'd dropped from a building. He can't possibly have survived that.

As I resume praying under my breath, a swatch of light washes over me again and a familiar voice says, "Serena, are you okay?"

From between my arms, I peek and find Caleb looking down at me, crouched over the hood of the car. His voice filters in through the broken glass, and that's also how I see the shadow looming behind him.

"Look out!"

Caleb turns but can't react fast enough to avoid the metal pipe. It hits him square in the back.

Somehow, I thought he had it all under control. But that's when I realize it really was three guys against one and I'm doing nothing about it. I fumble with my purse. Where's my phone? Why's everything slipping from my hands?

A snarling sound tears my attention away and I look ahead, almost expecting the worst. But Caleb has one guy by his throat, lifted in the air as though he weighs no more than a child. The guy swipes his hands at Caleb, catching him in the face. But my boss doesn't let go.

A second guy struggles to get his balance just a few paces behind Caleb. But his legs keep faltering and there's a steady stream of blood leaking out from his mouth. No matter how hard I try, I can't catch sight of the third guy. I wonder if he's the one who crashed into the windshield and if he's even alive.

Caleb is saying something, but I can't tell the words from the roaring sound in my ears. It takes me a moment to understand it's because I'm breathing so hard.

And then—

Caleb bites the guy.

Straight up sinks his teeth on the guy's throat.

I put my hands on my mouth, trying not to scream—not to puke.

Caleb's throat works with big pulls, as if he's drinking. My mind goes blank for a second and my body grows slack.

When I blink back, I find Caleb strolling to the second guy. He's on his knees, offering his forearm out—and Caleb bites it.

Everything goes dark.

*

When I come back to the land of living, Caleb sits in the passenger's seat beside me, wiping his mouth with the back of his arm. Crimson red smudges taint his blazer. And I start screaming.

He flinches and puts his arms up as if I was the threat.

"Your lungs are fine, but are *you* fine?" he mumbles.

"I'm not fine!" I yell back at the top of my lungs. "How can I be fine after all of this?"

I glance around. We're still parked in the middle of the empty dirt road. The three motorbikes are parked around the car. But where are the three guys?

"Did you kill them?"

"No." Caleb gives me a look, like I'm off my rockers. "I tied them up there."

Following his line of vision, I find the three guys tied up with chains to an old utility pole. They look like they got into a car accident instead of getting a thorough beat up.

Meanwhile, Caleb has bruises and scrapes. His clothes are marred with dirt and blood, and torn in places. But he doesn't look like he'll need the same urgent care as those guys.

He sighs and leans back on his seat, making himself comfortable as though he wants to take a nap. "Backup's almost here. I scouted the area and didn't find any other suspicious activity. We should be safe in here for a while."

My voice comes out in a thin thread as I ask, "Really? Am *I* safe?"

A moment later, Caleb turns to face me and I retreat until my back is glued to the door. There's a red glow in his eyes I didn't notice until he turned them all the way to me.

"What are you?" my voice shakes.

His chest expands as he takes a deep breath and runs a bloody hand through his hair. "What do you think?"

A beast.

A monster.

Not like me.

Not human.

Vampire.

"No way," I whisper.

Caleb looks away and I notice the scratches on his neck where one of the attackers tried to choke him. His hand closest to me is on his lap, the knuckles bruised and split. He was decked in his back too, and who knows where else. But he's much calmer than I am.

I remember his earlier words, that this isn't his first time in a situation like this.

"I was hoping you never found out," he says, propping his elbow against the passenger's window.

I press my hands against my chest, feeling my heart beat as fast as a rabbit's—which is also the level of bravery I feel right now. "Tell me this is a nightmare. A hallucination."

Caleb turns back but the irises of his eyes still glow red. When he talks, I notice his canines protruding more than usual. "Unfortunately, it's very real. I'm a—"

"Don't say—"

But he says it. "Vampire."

Everything in my vision blurs but him—him, and the traces

of what I wish I didn't see. The smudge of blood across his lips. The sharp teeth. The unnatural eyes. The strength in his body, which made grown men fly.

All signs point at the fact that it's true. He must be a vampire. He certainly isn't human.

"But vampires aren't real," I try to reason.

"Mermaids aren't real," Caleb says, as if that makes any sense. "And before you ask, werewolves aren't real either."

My bottom lip starts trembling.

A buzzing sounds makes me jump, but Caleb fishes in his pocket until he takes out his phone. The screen is cracked but flares to life with a call. He swipes his finger across to accept it, though it leaves a trail of red in the broken glass.

"Yeah," he says, leaning his head back against the seat. "Situation's under control, we're just a bit shaken."

A bit is putting it mildly.

Something catches my attention from the corner of my eye. One of the guys tied to the pole stirs and shakes his head. I'm glad he's not dead, and that's something I never thought I'd think in my life.

"Got it, see you in a bit," Caleb says and shuts the call off. "Serena?"

I release the lower lip I was chewing on. "What?"

"Can you do me a huge favor?" he tosses the phone on the dashboard and brushes his hands off. A couple of small glass shards fall off, along with a couple of blood droplets. "Can you please keep what I am a secret?"

His voice sounds light. Anyone would think he's asking about the weather—not about me staying silent about the fact he's a damn vampire.

I can't even fathom myself sharing this information. Who would I tell? My asshole roommate? Reporters? Or even Sister Emilia? No one would ever believe me. I hardly could, even though I saw everything with my own four eyes.

Not to mention, Caleb will probably off me if I spill.

In the cloying silence, he says, "It's for your own sake. You'll be in danger if anyone knows you know. Even from my family."

I suck in air. "Your family are vampires too?"

The sound of an approaching engine pulls his attention away from me. Caleb glances back for a second. "Serena, please. Promise me."

"I—I promise." I bite my lip again. "But how are we going to explain all of this?"

Caleb gives me a sad little smile. "Leave it to me. I'm an expert at excuses."

CHAPTER 16
CALEB

"Dad's going to kill me."

Daniel puts something on my knuckles that makes me flinch. As he bandages my hands, he says, "No, he's going to kill *me*, for knowing someone had already threatened you and not doing anything about it."

"Yeah, and he's gonna kill me for not telling him anything." Since he's done patching me up, my brother passes a white T-shirt over to me and I put it on. "Any chance we can keep this a secret from him, too?"

Dan gives me a look that could cut. I check to see if giving him a smile softens it, in which case I might have an opening to convince him. But no dice.

Instead, he says, "I'm assigning Phelan to you, no ifs or buts."

I push my wet hair off my forehead. "Dude, it's not that bad. You need Phelan more than I do."

Daniel's the heir, the one Dad and my stepmother need to protect no matter what. And Phelan is the king's enforcer, the top fighter dog in Dad's arsenal. Even if I get ambushed by fifty vampires, I can't possibly take Phelan away from Dan's side.

"No ifs. No buts." My brother packs up his first aid kit and stands up.

"Daniel." I get up from the bed and square up to him. "What happens to me doesn't matter, but if you get hurt because Phelan's by my side, your mother will kill me and Dad will bring me back just to kill me again."

"I can't leave you unprotected," he says, his eyebrows scrunching together in the middle. For a second, he looks so much like our dad. Full of so much worry that it's carving his face up from the inside.

"If it makes you feel better, I'll work to get stronger," I say.

We both know what this means. I have to drink more vampire blood if I hope to hold a candle on my own.

Ugh.

"Good. I'll get you a bodyguard, anyway."

Together, we head over to the kitchen. The apartment is so eerily quiet, it's almost as if we're all alone. Daniel casts a look toward the hall leading to the guest room, where my assistant is fast asleep after the ordeal she went through.

"She's physically fine but very stressed out. I gave her some sedatives that'll probably knock her out the whole night." Dan glances up and down at me. "Are you sure she didn't see anything?"

It was what I told him as soon as he and Phelan showed up —that Serena passed out from the shock and came to her senses well after I was done dispatching the assailants. It's one of the least sophisticated excuses I've come up with, but if we both stick with it, it will work.

"Yeah, she clonked out the second those guys surrounded us."

I can tell Daniel doesn't believe me just the same way I can tell the sky is blue and the grass is green. But I'm not going to prove him right.

He sighs. "Be careful, Caleb."

I salute him and stay frozen like that until he finally takes his leave. Then I collapse on the couch, my head on my hands.

Shit, what now?

In my twenty seven years of life, I've mostly been surrounded by vampires or humans who, by virtue of working closely with us, know what we are.

This is actually my first time dealing with someone who was previously in the dark. What if she like, calls animal control on me?

Because that's probably how I look in her eyes now. Like a beast that doesn't belong in this world. When actually, we do. We're part of it. We just have to hide the fact that we're a different species because the homo sapiens tends to be judgy as shit. Anyone unlike them is seen as a threat.

"What if she thinks *I'm* a threat?" I ask myself, glancing back at the dark hallway. "I mean, it's not like I'm going to eat her up."

I have to try to put her at ease, show her that I'm… Well, I'm not normal even for the vampire definition of the word, what with being one of the king's sons and all. But I can at least try to prove that I'm not going to hurt her. I have to act like I'm average.

But how do I do that, when, for example, my injuries are already fading away?

"Nah," I say to myself. "It's impossible."

I just have to keep being myself. Soon, she'll realize I'm harmless.

So, I make myself some popcorn and pop open a soda. I could go to the private cinema I have on the second floor, but I stay in the living room in case Serena wakes up. I don't want to make her feel alone, especially if she's still scared.

I keep the volume of the TV low not to bother her, and in any case I can hear better than ever anyway. I think one of those guys had enhanced hearing.

That's also how I detect the second she wakes up. Captain America and the Winter Soldier are fighting each other on the TV, and beyond that, and the crunch of my fifth serving of popcorn in my ears, I hear Serena's feet shuffle on the floor in the guest room. I think she's tiptoeing, probably trying to sneak out without me noticing.

Sure enough, when she leaves the room she's carrying her shoes and purse in her hands and freezes when she catches me looking straight at her. I put another mouthful of popcorn in my mouth and chew, waiting for her to make a move. She doesn't.

"Are you okay?" I ask with my mouth full.

She gulps so loud, I don't even need super hearing to make out the sound.

I turn back to the TV. "You're free to leave but I recommend you get some rest here. Just in case."

Oh, this is my favorite part in the movie. When the characters communicate their brotherly bond through their fists. It reminds me of when Daniel and I spar together. We love each other, but not enough to let the other win.

To my surprise, Serena shuffles forward and instead of making her way to the elevator, she sits on the couch. Granted, my couch is about twenty feet long on one side and as long as on the other, so she's very far away from me, but her choosing to remain in the same room as me is promising.

I offer the bowl of popcorn to her. "Hungry?"

Serena shakes her head and drops her shoes and bag on the carpet. "No, I kinda wanna puke."

"Please, not on the couch. I'm fond of it."

She gives me this look like she wants to throttle me. "Is this why all your assistants quit?"

"Because I'm a little shit?" I think about it, running the mental tally on all my previous assistants. "It's true most of them couldn't stand me. But one left because she found a better job, another one literally won the lottery and retired right then and there, and the other one became a small business owner."

"No." She waves a hand. "Because you're a vampire."

The word hangs heavy in the air, until I crunch on some popcorn. "If you quit because of that, you'll be the first."

As she looks down, I notice she's been wringing her hands all the while. Since she's not outright saying that she's not going to quit, it must mean that she's considering it. And shit, I can't blame her.

"Listen." I set aside the snacks. "I understand this whole thing has been traumatic, and I want to do what I can to help you feel better. If you want to quit, I'll help you find a similar or better job somewhere else. You don't have to figure all this out by yourself."

"Thanks." She mumbles, and for a while says nothing else until she lifts her head. "For now, I think I need some answers."

Oh, boy.

I turn the movie off. "Okay."

Serena takes a deep breath and asks, "Can silver bullets hurt you? Stake to the heart? Fire?"

I shrug. "Just as much as they'd hurt you."

"What about crosses and holy water?"

"I'm a Christian," I respond, smiling at her obvious shock.

"I take it that you don't sleep in a coffin," she adds with a touch of sarcasm.

"No, I prefer comfortable beds, thank you very much."

She clears her throat. "And sunlight? Does it do anything in particular?"

I motion around us. "Given that I live in Miami, the

answer is no." I also add, "And no, I don't glitter like a diamond, either."

"What about…" She makes a pause to clear her throat. "Do you need blood to survive?"

My head bobs. "Yep, let's say it's the top of the nutritional pyramid for us. Especially other vampire's blood."

Her mouth opens and closes. She pushes her glasses up her nose. Runs a hand through her loose hair. "This is kind of gross, but I need to ask anyway."

I brace myself, expecting her to ask about the mechanics of drinking blood or if any more of the cliches are true.

Instead, what comes out of her mouth is, "So, like, can you smell someone's period?"

Silence reigns.

My jaw unhinges.

Serena jolts to her feet. "You know what? Forget it. I'm just going to go drown in the pool now."

I start laughing.

"Stop," she demands, her face growing redder by the second.

But I don't stop. I laugh harder, until I'm curled up on my couch and everything hurts. She hasn't left to go drown herself, rather she glares down at me with such intensity that I'm afraid for my life.

I wheeze for air and have to wipe the tears off my face. "Wait, you still want an answer?"

She grumbles, "Yes."

Chuckling, I deliver the killing blow. "Yes, I can smell when people have their periods and no, it doesn't make me hungrier."

Serena collapses in a heap on the couch and stays there for the longest time. So long, in fact, I go back to watching the movie.

Of all the things she could ask, I never imagined that one. I have to stuff my face with snacks to keep from cackling again.

CHAPTER 17
SERENA

will the earth to open up and swallow me whole, but it doesn't. And out of all the day's events, having asked that is what I regret the most. Especially because now I know he'll know when I'm on my period, and the thought of that makes me more uncomfortable than knowing he feeds on blood.

An age later, when Caleb's already immersed back in his movie, I ask, "What if I wear a ton of perfume on those days?"

He gives me a side glance. "You should've just done it without telling me. Now I'll know."

"Damn it."

Caleb pauses the movie. "Seriously? That's what you wanted to know about the most?"

"No." I hate that I sound like him when he doesn't want to get ready for work. "That was just one of the least scary questions."

He bends one leg over the couch and turns my way, putting an arm over the headrest. It's patched up with bandages here and there, especially around his hand. There are patches on his face, neck and I'm sure under his clothes. But by the way he moves, it's as if he's not hurt at all.

"Hit me," he says, even though that's the last thing I'd think of doing. Especially since I now know if he were to hit back, I'd fly clear across the living room and out a window. "I'll try to answer most of your questions and I promise to *try* not to laugh."

I scrunch my face up. "What the hell kind of promise is that?"

Caleb's lips lift up at the corners. "I'm afraid that's the best I can do."

I sit up straight, taking a moment just to breathe in and out. That's all I can control in a world that suddenly feels even larger and more terrifying than it already was.

Seeing my struggle to even form sentences anymore, Caleb says, "Let me help you out. Most popular lore stuff is wrong. We're not undead or whatever that's supposed to be—I'm very much alive, just like you are. Basically, we're just a different human species. We don't combust under the sunlight or glitter like diamonds... What else? Oh, yeah. There's absolutely nothing erotic about drinking blood. It's as if someone got off from having breakfast cereal."

My head is positively spinning.

"Wait, wait." I put my hands up and he clams up. "Different human species? And like, no one's talking about this in the news?"

"We have to stay under radar." He shrugs. "It's true that humans have hunted us in the past."

I shake my head, but that doesn't magically align my thoughts in a way that makes sense.

"Then, were those guys vampires too?"

"Yup."

"How could you tell?" I scratch my head. "Or is it that you asked them before beating them to a pulp?"

"They knew about me," he says. After a pause he adds, "Also, vampires smell different from humans. Let's say we have some stuff in our blood that you guys don't have."

"Why did you bite them? Isn't that like cannibalism?"

Caleb gags. "Heck no. You're making me want to barf."

"Sorry," I say, my voice low. "This is all so weird."

Especially this conversation.

"It's sorta like if you have to change your eating habits because your blood sugar and fat levels are out of control," Caleb explains, shutting the television off again. "With every healthy meal you have, your body starts gradually feeling better. Until a year later, you can now climb stairs without getting tired and your skin looks healthier. That's sort of what vampire blood does, but in the course of like half an hour."

This is harder to understand than any math class I've taken.

"How?" I ask.

"I guess it boils down to what we are. Evolved humans." He shrugs, as if we're talking about Captain America post-serum and not of people like us. "We carry that evolution in our blood. So, by drinking another vampire's blood I basically take what made them strong for myself, and essentially I evolve one level higher than them."

My mouth forms a perfect O shape. "Oh."

And because he's truly a little shit, he says, "Just Caleb, please."

I reach out for one of the couch pillows and throw it at him. My aim is so far off that he doesn't even have to dodge.

"What about human blood?" I ask, as if I didn't just stoop to his maturity level.

"As nutritional as french fries and just as filling. It'll do in a pinch."

"So you're not out hunting for blood every night?" I ask, picturing just that. I have the urge to hide my neck from view.

Caleb snorts. "Puh-lease. We have blood delivery nowadays."

"I—My head hurts."

"Let me get you some ibuprofen."

More than the fact that my boss is bringing me medicine, I'm confused that he even has it. But I don't ask about that—I saw how roughed up he was earlier. Clearly vampires can feel pain too.

Caleb puts a tray on the coffee table with a bottle of ibuprofen and a glass of water. I stare at it for the longest time, my mind finally quieting down. Only one important topic remains that I'd like some clarity on right now.

As I reach for the pills and water, I ask, "Why did those guys target us?"

For the first time since this little chat started, Caleb shows signs of discomfort. He bites his lower lip and I note his canines have gone back to normal. I decide it's the least weird thing of the night.

"Not us. Me." He scratches at the bandage around his left elbow. "It happens every so often."

"Why?"

His brown eyes lock on mine. His expression, normally so expressive, is as blank as a statue. Caleb shakes his head slightly. "That I can't answer."

I swallow thickly. "Does that mean I'm in danger just by being next to you?"

Caleb's head reels back as if I threw another pillow and socked him directly. "I—shit. I hadn't thought about that."

I should quit.

He'll probably do right on his word to help me find another job. Cedric Oh will be pissed I broke my promise to last long in this job, but he'll get over it. Soon, he'll find unwitting applicants who are desperate to put one foot in Comed Solutions, and maybe some of them will be vampires who don't care for danger. This job is not worth my safety.

But then what?

There's now life before vampires and after. And I don't know how to navigate this after, especially if I have to do it on my own.

Caleb looks down at his lap. The top of his hair is long enough that it falls forward obscuring his eyes. "As you know, I have to make peace with our suppliers after the debacle at work, so I'll be out of the country for three weeks. Why don't you take that time to think about what you want to do?"

Three weeks.

Three weeks to decide if I want to plunge face first into a world I didn't know existed along with mine. Or if I want to close my eyes and pretend I can't see this new reality.

It's tempting.

"For now," he says, changing the tone of his voice to the lighter one I'm more used to. "You should eat something and go to bed."

"I should go home," I say, but my body refuses to move.

"I'll drive you tomorrow, I promise." Then he puts a hand on his chest in an exaggerated manner. "Or are you afraid I'm going to sneak into your bed tonight and bite your neck?"

I glare at him. "Not funny."

"You're right, it's not. You'd probably elbow me in the face if I even breathe too close to you."

"I'm very tempted to do that right now," I admit, which only amuses him.

"Is vegan pizza okay? Or I can make you a tofu scramble."

I shake my head and murmur, "A vegan vampire... I've seen it all."

"Almost all." He corrects me, wagging one finger. "You haven't seen me naked yet."

"*Yet?*" I gasp. "I should quit for that alone."

He leaps back over the couch in one smooth motion, chuckling on his way to the kitchen. "Just kidding."

But of course, that's what appears in my dreams later that night, as I sleep in his guest room.

Instead of nightmares about vampires attacking me, sinking their sharp fangs on my flesh until I lose consciousness, what I dream about is my boss. Caleb appears like a vision in the dark, crawling under my bedsheets and showing me everything else I haven't seen of him yet.

I wake up in the middle of the morning, but it's not the sunlight pouring in from the window what has me sweating. Right there, I decide if I want to stay sane, I have to quit.

CHAPTER 18
CALEB

t's been about half an hour since I arrived, and I still can't bring myself to get out of the car. The row of windows on the ground floor give the illusion of the mansion grinning at me. Its gothic structure and appliqués have never been comforting, never the first thing I picture when someone says the word *home*. And yet, it's where I was born and raised.

But it's also where I have some of my worst memories.

The breeze lifts up a plume of humid fog from the sea, lending an extra eerie quality to a sprawling house that already looks out of place. Surrounded by palm trees and placed on an artificial island off the coast of Miami Beach, it's like someone plucked it from an eastern European country and relocated it to the last place it should belong to.

That was Dad's vision some fifty years ago when he decided to settle down here, while my stepmother was expecting Daniel. And while the old man has lost most of his sense of humor, he's where I got mine from. Certainly not from Diana Mancini-Oh, his wife.

I lean my head down until it rests against the steering wheel of the Bugatti Chiron. What if I just stay here all night long? Or if I just drive right back to the city?

Dad will hunt me down, that's what.

"Shit, shit."

Normally, I dread coming to these family dinners because of my stepmother, but today I also dread it because of Dad.

My epitaph will be *survived an attack by three vampires, only to be killed by his progenitor for getting attacked in the first place.* But hey, maybe if I die tonight I won't have to go on a world tour of supplier visits for the next three weeks.

It's that thought what finally gets me out of the car. I fix up the polo shirt I wore for tonight, a pristine white that Stepmother can use as a canvas with her glass of wine, like last time. Should be an action-packed family dinner.

The front door opens before I even reach it, revealing Lara in a golden gown that would fit a red carpet better than this occasion. Her smile is the most genuine I'll see directed my way tonight.

"I won," she says, and when I cock an eyebrow she adds, "Daniel bet you wouldn't get out of your car and would instead head back home, and I bet you would face us."

"Ah, so that's why you were smiling. Not because you were happy to see me."

"Of course I'm glad to see you, silly. Otherwise, I would've lost the bet." My sister-in-law gives me a hug. "But mostly I'm just glad nothing bad happened to you."

Yesterday's scrapes and bruises are already gone, but I flinch as her hand pats my cheek like it still hurts. "That's because the truly bad thing is waiting for me tonight."

"Don't be so fatalistic," my brother says, appearing behind his wife with a glass of Old Rip Van Winkle in hand, his favorite. "Your big bro and sis have your back."

I sigh. I know they do. That's what usually makes Diana more pissed, and also what could detonate Dad's temper.

Daniel and Lara spoil me too much, and though tonight I need it the most, it's also when I least want it. I should be the only one to catch the shrapnel of Dad's explosion.

That's why I ask, "Where is he?"

"Last I checked, Cedric's in the backyard," Lara says. "And before you ask, Diana is in her boudoir."

"Lucky me," I grumble as I walk past them.

My limbs grow heavier with every step I take. Clearly my body is on board with my mind's desire to run. I force my lungs to work through breathing exercises. They stop the second I reach the open door leading to the backyard.

Dad's playing golf by himself, in the middle of the night, and the club in his hand looks like a really good weapon.

"Are you going to stand there all night?" he asks, without turning.

But of course he knows it's me. He could probably smell me as I drove down the bridge.

I gulp. "If it gets me to stay in one piece, yeah."

With a smooth swing, Dad hits the ball and sends it into a high arch that disappears in the night. A few seconds later I hear the distinctive clunk of a hole in one. He uses the club like a cane while he walks over to me. "If you're so scared to face me, it's because you know you did something wrong, right?"

Well, where to begin. I've done many wrong things in the past week alone.

"If you'd told me of the first attack, I could have prevented this second one," he says, standing in front of me. "Why did you stay quiet?"

"Wait, how did you find out about the first one?" I'm doing mental gymnastics, trying to figure out the answer but I can't.

Dad snorts. "I interrogated the guys we captured, of course. You didn't even think of doing that?"

No. I was too busy trying to keep my assistant calm after what she saw. But of course I don't tell him *that*.

I run a hand through my hair and scratch my nape. "It's no big deal. I didn't want you to worry."

"Well, I'm more worried now." He tosses the golf club on the porch, where one of the staff will pick it up later. I breathe out a sigh of relief that I'm not the next one who'll fly in an arch because of it. "Caleb."

"Yes?" I look back at him and it shocks me that he looks almost sad.

Not at all what I expected.

"Why do you assume it won't be a big deal if something happens to you?"

Because I don't matter.

The crickets in the backyard answer for me. Leaves rustle with the breeze, as if emphasizing the message. I avoid Dad's eyes because the answer has to be written in mine, with the way they're welling up on their own accord.

"Anyway," I say, stuffing my hands in the pockets of my khakis. "What's for dinner?"

"Son," he says, grabbing my arm.

I twist it out of his grasp and head over to the kitchen. If Dad wanted to, he could stop me a million ways... but he doesn't. And even though I'm glad I don't have to continue that conversation, and that I walked away alive from it, my chest also hurts.

Seeing Maria, the family cook for the past thirty years, brings a smile to my face. She's a human in her sixties who hailed from the Dominican Republic and didn't mind working for a bunch of vampires, as long the work was decent and helped her raise her son.

"Maria!" I spread my arms wide and she meets me halfway, chuckling as I lift her off the ground and pepper her face with kisses. "How I've missed you."

"It's only been two weeks," she says, smacking me until I

set her back down. "This time I'll be the one serving the meal so there won't be any issues."

What she's referring to is the previous dinner, when Stepmother decided to play hostess and serve our meals. I can still recall the smile on her face as she set an enormous plate of barely cooked meat in front of me.

I'm about to tell Maria that she's the best when a different voice fills the air.

"Where are my greetings?"

It's as if an ice cube trickles down my back when I hear Diana's voice behind me. She waltzes into the kitchen, wearing a dress that matches the style of Lara's, with a champagne flute on her hand.

"Hi," is all I say. Maria gives me an admonishing look, but it's not like a more formal greeting will put me on my stepmother's good graces.

Her blue eyes are glacial as she looks me up and down, sipping on the last of her champagne. "You look as if nothing happened."

"Sorry to disappoint," I say under my breath.

Diana extends her glass out to Maria, who hurries to top it off with more Armand de Brignac.

"I was frankly surprised you came out of that unscathed," Stepmother says as she enjoys the drink's scent. "But I guess there must be weaker vampires out there."

From behind her, Maria gives her a glare and I almost smile. Almost. It's hard to remember what mirth feels like in the presence of the woman who hates me the most in the world.

She takes one step forward until she's at arm's length from me, tucking hair the same color as her drink behind her ear. "I guess Cedric's blood in your veins must have saved you this time, but who's to say about the next, if it's more than a handful of lesser vampires?"

I tilt my head. "Don't tell me it was you who sent those thugs after me?"

"Please." The woman snorts. "As if I spend any of my precious time thinking about you. All I'm saying is that you should try not to embarrass your father any further."

That stings even more than the blows I got from the small-time thugs that ambushed Serena and I. My hands squeeze into tight fists, but Diana must be done with me for now because she breezes by.

The kitchen feels much warmer when she's gone.

Maria huffs. "That woman. Why does she have to be like this to you?"

Because I'm the reason her life isn't a perfect fairy tale. She's the queen of the vampires, a former model, one of the richest women in the planet. If I wasn't in the picture, she would have it all.

And that's why it doesn't matter if I'm attacked. Or if I die. Because in the Oh family, I'm worse than a secondary character. I'm just an extra.

CHAPTER 19
SERENA

When Monday comes, I wake up an hour later because I only have to head straight to the office. Caleb is already out of the country, which will make this a lot easier. In my purse, there's a piece of paper with some ideas scrawled on it about how I'm going to structure my resignation letter in a way that doesn't make me sound like a wuss. But that's exactly how I feel.

After I make it to my desk and fire up my laptop, I sit in front of a blank document, watching the cursor blink as much as my eyes do.

Why should I feel bad about wanting to quit? Especially since I'm planning on giving the two weeks notice officially when Caleb returns. Partially, this way I extend my paycheck but it'll also buy him time to find me a replacement. It works out for everyone.

Right?

My phone buzzes and I jump in my skin. Marissa's name appears on the screen and a pang goes through my chest. Something like disappointment, though I can't figure out why.

"Good morning," I say once I pick up.

She returns the greeting and then adds, "Jon just told me his boss wants you in his office in five minutes."

"Oh, shit," I say aloud without meaning to. "Um, do I need to bring anything?"

Like a box with my belongings, for example?

"He didn't say. Maybe bring something to make notes with just in case."

We end the call off after that and I scramble to grab the essentials. It's not like Mr. Oh knows what I'm about to do—unless Caleb told him. He did say he'd make some excuses after the whole mess, but I should've asked for more details to have a solid alibi.

I'm short of breath by the time I walk up to the office of the Comed Solutions founder, just as nervous as the first time but for an entirely different reason.

"Wait here," Marissa says, stepping away from her desk and knocking on the massive oak door. She opens it just a smidge, enough to pop her head in and talk. "Excuse me, Miss Lossada is here."

After a second, she nods at me to come in. Jon stands beside Mr. Oh, showing him something on his iPad. The older man nods upon whatever data is before him, and that's when it hits me like a ton of bricks.

Mr. Oh is a vampire.

I would never have guessed it if it wasn't for Caleb's own confirmation.

Sitting at his desk, Cedric Oh looks like a regular magnate with grey tinging his perfectly combed hair, and the few signs of age on his face would've led me to believe he had cosmetic procedures done. He's probably a hundred years for all I know, though he doesn't look a day over sixty.

What about Jon? Is he a vampire too? And Marissa? Who else have I met in my life who is actually not human?

I have to shake my head when my vision gets too foggy.

The motion sends my glasses careening to the floor, and I have to get on my knees to palm the floor until I feel the frames. When I put them back on, both men are looking at me.

"I'm sorry, please proceed."

"My apologies," Mr. Oh says. "I was so engrossed in work I didn't realize you were already waiting. Jon, leave us for a few minutes."

"Yes, sir." Jon takes his iPad and leaves a whole lot of silence in his wake.

Mr. Oh stands up, buttoning his blazer. "Please, take a seat."

I'm like a newborn foal as I get back on my feet, and morph into a robot as I retrace my steps to the seating area.

As he sits across from me, Mr. Oh says, "Frankly, I wished to talk with you earlier but I hope you understand that I had to take care of my family first."

"Absolutely."I say even though, frankly, I have no idea what he's talking about.

"We were distraught about Friday's events, and I have to apologize that you went through such a harrowing experience."

"Oh, thank you." I wring my hands and when he notices the motion, I still every muscle in my body.

"Are you sure you're okay?" he asks.

I nod. "I'm fine, all things considered."

His expression almost makes me think he cares—until he asks, "Did you by any chance see anything out of the ordinary?"

The question reminds me of when Caleb asked me to keep his secret, including from his family.

My first guess is that it'll get him in trouble. It's not the kind of thing he should go around telling people. But what if it also gets *me* in trouble? If humans who find out about vampires were allowed to keep on with their lives as usual, everyone would know vampires exist already.

What if those humans are rounded up and kept captive? Or worse, killed?

Resisting the urge to squirm, I finally respond, "It's not everyday I see a kidnapping attempt, but to be honest I lost consciousness the second I thought we were as good as gone. It's kind of embarrassing."

Mr. Oh's shoulders relax. Meanwhile, I'm breaking into a sweat because lying isn't my forte.

"And I understand Caleb agrees to the possibility of you resigning as a consequence, correct?"

That snitch.

But maybe that's the excuse he came up with, to keep me safe from this hullabaloo. Just paint me as an innocent damsel in distress who needs someone to help her navigate the dark, dangerous world.

The thought makes me grind my teeth.

"Yes, he did."

"Are you planning to resign?" he asks, point blank.

I'm transported back to the job interview, when I basically swore to not be a quitter.

It was so easy to say it back then, when my life had never been in danger and when I thought the only creatures with two legs and opposable thumbs were humans. And some primates, too.

The point is, I don't want to quit just as much as I do, and after having made up my mind over the weekend that today I would send my resignation letter in three weeks, I hate that it's right in this moment when I realize that part of me doesn't want to give up just yet.

"I'm considering it," I say, if only because I don't want to lie again.

He sighs, disappointment clear in the gesture. After a

pause, he says, "Considering it, but not outright resigning. Why is that?"

"I'm asking myself the very same question," I say under my breath. When he smiles, he reminds me a lot of his younger son and I feel even worse.

"What if I tell you that I'm going to assign a security detail to you and Caleb?" Mr. Oh leans forward and places his elbows on his knees.

Er, the fact we need one at all is already pretty out there.

Even though I don't say this with my voice, I must have said it with my face because Mr. Oh continues, "The motive of the attack seems to have been petty crime, so I don't expect a repeat of it. Still, I would like to help you and my son feel at ease and I'm willing to put you in the care of my best."

That would've been solid reasoning if Caleb was a normal billionaire heir, looking like a hot ATM for petty criminals looking for a quick buck. But he's a freaking vampire who was attacked by strangers of his kind.

Then again, he was able to fend them off by himself. I assume the security detail would be just as strong, if not more, and made of only vampires too.

Carajo, if anything I'm safer in that circle than by quitting and having to fend for myself. In my mind, the scale of reasons not to quit starts tipping heavier.

"Personally, I'm really hoping you'll consider staying on board," Mr. Oh adds along with a deep breath. "You've already had such a positive impact on Caleb in just a couple of weeks."

"You think so?" I'm unable to hide a grimace.

Mr. Oh chuckles. "The fact that he's traveling for work right now and not for pleasure is a good indicator."

"Honestly, I don't feel like I've done much." Other than drive him back and forth from his residence to the office. And give him the occasional verbal jab here or there.

"You have. Imagine how much more you both could accomplish if you stay by his side, pushing him in the right direction." He takes an envelop out of the inner pocket of his blazer and sets it on the coffee table. "I would like you to join him abroad. Caleb needs an ally right now, more than ever."

Since I'm at a loss for words, I pick up the envelop and find first class tickets inside. For departure tonight.

"Um…"

"If you still wish to resign after three weeks working intensively with him, I will accept that outcome." Mr. Oh's eyes hold mine steady, and I feel sweat trickle down my temple. "But I would much prefer if you give us an opportunity, Miss Lossada."

Before I can comprehend, I open my mouth and say, "Very well. I'll try."

CHAPTER 20
CALEB

I sit at a table, staring down at my plate stuffed with buffet goodies, certain that I'm not hungry for them. I eat a slice of pineapple, but a deeper hunger rears its head. It's in the way my skin tingles, in how my nostrils flare to catch the scent of blood all around me. Mostly humans but a few vampires too.

Instead, I eat more fruit.

Shit, why am I so hungry again? I fed less than a week ago. Twice.

"Look, isn't that…"

Two giggles follow the whispered words from a couple of women at a nearby table. They make no effort to hide who they're gossiping about. One of them lifts up her phone while the other one points at me. I turn my head just enough to catch their scent and confirm they're vampires. Which means they know exactly who I am.

"It definitely is him. Look," one of them says to her friend and points at her phone, probably showing her a picture of me from some tabloid.

"Should we talk to him?" the second girl asks.

"We totally should." The first girl laughs low. "He's sitting all by himself and could probably use with some company, right?"

I eat a slice of mango, knowing they're saying all of this so I can hear them.

On the one hand, if they approach me it's because they want something from me. It can go anywhere from a handshake, to a picture, to attempting to seduce me for money or for blood. I almost wish for the latter so I could ask them for blood in return. Or I could just get in touch with my cousin here and ask him for an emergency supply. That might be safer.

The two women stand up, but before they make it too far, someone plops on the other chair at my table.

My eyes bulge. "Serena?"

"Good morning, boss," she says, tucking into her omelet without further ado.

Her appearance makes the two vampires retreat back to their table. It also makes me drop my fork.

"The hell are you doing here?"

She takes her time chewing and downing half of her orange juice. "Your dad sent me to back you up."

"Wow, somehow you answered my question but I'm even more confused than before." I tuck into a tofu scramble with veggies and for a moment there's only peace. I don't let it last too long. "Weren't you going to quit?"

My assistant sighs. "I'm still considering it, but your dad asked me to support you during your trip and see if that changes my mind."

Which means in theory I'm the one in charge of making her change her mind. Messaged received, Dad.

But do I want to? It'd be a lot easier for everyone if she just goes her merry way and continues to live in the world of humans. I wouldn't have to worry about keeping her safe that way.

Actually, I'd worry even more if I can't make sure she's okay.

My face scrunches up, and it's not just because of the sour piece of fruit I put in my mouth. If last week's mess hadn't happened in front of Serena, I wouldn't feel responsible for her.

Serena pauses from her breakfast. "So, I was thinking if we want this to work, we need some ground rules. First, no more lying or sneaking around. I don't want to continue being in the dark."

I cock an eyebrow. "I never sneaked around. I just omitted a truth you shouldn't have learned about in the first place."

"Can't put that cat back in the bag, though." She shrugs. "Second, I want you to tell me every time there's a you-know-what around us. Information is power, and I can't protect myself if I don't know who might want to take a bite out of me."

"That's not very likely to happen," I say, but she waves a hand and the argument vanishes in the air. "Fine, so you want me to start pointing at people and saying that one?"

"Let's use a safe word." She looks around, as if trying to find inspiration and says, "Onion. Let's use that. You did say you-know-what's smell different, right?"

I chuckle. "Really? When garlic was right there?"

"That's a more obvious keyword, isn't it?" Serena squints at my food. "By the way, *can* you eat garlic?"

"Yup, in fact I love it."

She shakes her head. "My whole life was a lie."

Grinning, I ask, "Any other rules?"

"Yes." She leans forward. "You'll let me know immediately if I'm in danger."

I'll one up her and protect her from any danger, even if it's from myself. Especially in that case.

"Deal." I focus back on my meal, filling up my stomach with food that'll make it busy for a bit, but not nourish me in the way I need. "Anyway, you said you're going to join me for the whole trip?"

"Yes, luckily I don't need a visa for any of the stops."

That's true. The only stops are Mexico, Malaysia and Spain, where we have our main suppliers of paper products and with whom we need to heal the rift caused by the recent scandal. It's also why I was able to arrange the trip so quickly.

"It's going to be a bit intense. Are you ready?"

She nods, and although she schools her expression into polite indifference, there's no hiding the way her eyes spark. "I was born ready."

*

Serena proves a trooper. We spend the rest of the day, visiting the factory our supplier has in Juarez before flying down to Mexico City. The next couple of days go by from one meeting to the next, and from one meal to the next. She translates where suppliers struggle to find the right words in English, and I whisper about onions in her ears every time we stumble upon any you-know-what's.

For the last night of our stay in Mexico, our supplier has arranged a cocktail dinner on the rooftop of the most exclusive restaurant in Polanco. Strings of lights hang above us imitating the stars that can't be seen in the sky of such a densely populated city. They dance in front of my eyes even though there's no wind.

"Are you okay?" Serena asks beside me. It takes me a moment to focus on her face.

"Yeah, fine."

The CEO of our supplier approaches with three women in tow. "Señor Oh! Are you enjoying the party in your honor?"

He sways a bit but since his face is red and hiccups interrupt his speech every so often, it tells me that it's not my vision playing tricks. He's just tipsy.

And as if I also was in my cups, I discreetly grab onto the high top table. "Yes, thank you very much for your hospitality."

"I hope we continue doing business in the future."

The man shakes my hand and I have to plant my feet firmly not to fall over. I might've considered compelling him just a bit if I wasn't under the weather, enough that every time he thinks of Comed Solutions he gets a warm feeling in his chest. But thankfully, I don't need the help of my weak vampire abilities. The visit has been successful.

"But enough about boring stuff." He grins at the women around him. "Let me introduce you to my friends."

Humans. All three of them. They've all drank too much to make their blood any good.

A server walks by with a tray loaded with food, including a steak so rare it probably still moos. My stomach lurches with the visceral war between disgust and hunger.

My assistant grabs my arm in a vise. "I'm so sorry to interrupt, but something urgent has come up and I need to speak with Mr. Oh in private."

The supplier says something in Spanish that he finishes off with a wink. It causes Serena to give him a tight smile, before she hauls me away from the group. The floor looks farther than I remember it being, and I stumble upon my feet.

"What is wrong with you?" my assistant hisses.

It's only when we stop at a lobby by the restrooms, that I slide down on an ottoman and say, "I'm hungry."

"Okay, what can I get you?" She tucks the skirt of her black dress behind her knees and crouches before me. "A salad? Crackers?"

I undo my tie and yank it out. "Not that kind of hunger."

Her eyes go as wide as saucers.

"You told me to be honest, right?"

"Yes, but…" Her brow furrows. "Where do I get blood from? Should I ask for a rare steak?"

I gag.

She gives me a side eye. "I'm *not* going to give you my neck."

"It's not like I'm asking for that. I'll call my cousin, he's the one who supplies me with blood when I'm in Mexico." I pull out my cellphone and scroll through my contacts list until I find my cousin, Fernando. He picks up on the second tone.

"Whoa, to what do I owe this call?"

"Hey, Nando. I'm in town and I'm in a pinch."

"Oh, shit." I don't even need to explain what kind of pinch because he's an onion. He knows. "It's my girlfriend's birthday and the whole family and I are celebrating in Cancun, güey. How long can you hold out?"

"Don't worry about me, I'll figure it out." I pinch my nose. "Say happy birthday to Vanessa."

"Dude, seriously. I can be there in four hours tops."

"No, it's okay. I got it." After a minute more, I'm able to convince him to stay put. Once I disconnect from the call, I say, "Shit."

I arranged a blood supply in Malaysia, the next leg of the trip, because I honestly never imagined I'd get so hungry so soon. What do I do now? Prowl for a willing victim like old school vampires? The thought makes bile rise up my throat.

"Don't worry," my assistant declares, and I'm surprised she's still there. She stands up, hands on her hips. "I have an idea."

CHAPTER 21
SERENA

After delivering lies to the supplier that Caleb has food poisoning, I haul him and myself into the back of a taxi and give the driver an address I found off the internet.

Looking at Caleb, it's easy to pretend he's sick. He's so pale, it's almost like he was drained of blood. His eyes can't seem to focus on one thing and his skin is clammy with cold sweat. When I look at his hands, I find they're shakier than leaves. If this plan doesn't work, I don't know what else I can do.

Because I'm *not* going to give him my blood. That's too messed up.

"Where are we going?" His voice comes out like a tendril. He might be about to pass out.

"You'll see when we get there." I chew on my lower lip but can't stop the question from tumbling out. "How did you get like this?"

Caleb squeezes his eyes shut tight. "I'm asking myself the same."

He leans his head back and his whole body sags the second he's out like a light.

To distract myself from the panic I'm feeling, I ask the driver, "¿Está seguro de que va a estar abierto?"

"Sí, señorita," he says. "Es el mercado al que voy siempre. Abre hasta las ocho."

My knees bounce as he weaves in through the dense traffic of the city. "¿Y cree que llegamos a tiempo?"

Because that's the key. It's already seven and we haven't advanced much.

"Sí, está cerquitica."

It turns out to be true and we arrive to the market just before eight. The next hurdle becomes waking Caleb up, but a couple of slaps do the trick. The driver is kind enough to help me pull my boss out of the car, but it's clear he's wondering why I'm taking this drunk-looking gringo into a meat market at almost eight in the night, instead of to a hotel.

"Can you sit here and wait for me?" I ask my boss as I push him until he sits at a bench.

"I—yeah. Okay." Clearly, he has no fight left in his body.

I rush into the market, almost pouncing on the butcher. He's a portly man with an easy smile, who greets me as though we were friends even though it's the first time he sees me.

"Necesito sangre," I say, which does make his smile falter. I take a couple of deep breaths and spill more lies. "Es para una sopa. Así la hace mi mamá."

"Ahhh." The man laughs. "Por un momento pensé que era para un vampiro."

I give out a weak laugh. "Claro que no, ni que existieran. ¿Sí tiene?"

"Sí, ¿cuánta quiere?"

I end up buying one liter because I have no stinking clue what I'm doing. Just looking at the thick, dark liquid in the container makes me want to hurl.

I find my boss slumped on the bench, so still that for a second I fear he's dead. Sprinting the rest of the way, I send a prayer that I'm not too late. It's striking how he can be so weak just a week after he kicked so much ass.

"Caleb." I set the purchase down on the ground and shake him. "Wake up. I got you what you need."

His eyelids flutter open and my lungs start working again. But all he can manage is to roll his head forward.

"Oh, no. Don't you dare make me feed you."

Caleb sighs. "Where is it?"

I shove the tub of cow's blood in his hands and step back. "Bon appétit."

As he fumbles with getting the container open, he says, "Look away."

I'm very glad to do so.

A second later, the sounds of gulping come from behind me. I position myself so none of the passerby can see what's happening, but most of my focus goes in keeping the contents of my stomach down.

I want to cry, too.

Instead, I hum a tune to try to drown the sounds and help me forget what's happening.

"Do you have a napkin?" he asks.

"One second." I swallow with difficulty while I rummage through my purse and find a pack of clean tissues. Without looking back, I reach my hand out to give it to him.

"Thanks."

A couple of minutes later I hear a sigh that makes me think he's done with his meal. Nearby, I locate a trashcan.

"You done?"

"Yeah," he says.

Still without fully turning, I reach my hands out to him. "I'll throw it away."

"I can do it." Caleb still stumbles past me and throws away the container. The way it clunks at the bottom sounds hollow.

He drank it all.

As he turns, my boss's irises are red like rubies glinting under the streetlights. He plops back on the bench and I collapse beside him, as tired as if I'd killed the cow to give him the blood.

"This isn't what I had in mind when I signed up to be your assistant."

Caleb flinches and rubs his nape. "If you weren't sure about quitting before, I guess now you're convinced."

We sit facing a small street, with cars driving by every minute or so. It's a residential neighborhood and people walk about, probably returning home after a long day of work.

We catch a fair number of glances. Two strange people sprawled on a bench by the entrance of a meat market, especially one of them so notoriously foreign, are bound to make a few eyebrows rise.

And that's because they don't know what just happened.

"This is definitely bizarre beyond my imagination." My head bobs, and that's all I have energy for aside from speaking. "But that's also probably why I don't think I can pretend none of this happened."

Caleb turns those eerie eyes to me, but somehow he doesn't scare me. "What does that mean?"

I look up at the dark navy canopy of the sky. Even though I'm grossed out enough to maybe need antacid, I'm also glad I was able to help him. Already, he sounds stronger and his body isn't trembling anymore.

Instead of answering his question, I volley another one back. "What would you have done if I wasn't around to help you?"

He makes that typical Caleb expression like he's sucking on a lime. "I probably would've had to go hunting. Although, I don't think I'd have been very successful in the state I was already in."

"Right." I face forward again. "I helped you."

His body jolts. "You're right. I don't think I've thanked you."

"You already did."

Caleb waves a hand. "That was just for the napkins."

"The point is," I say, turning my body to face him. "I helped you. That's what I'm supposed to do as your assistant. It's also why your father sent me along for this trip. Without me just now, you might have been in serious trouble. Who's to say something like that won't happen again if I leave?"

He mumbles. "In all fairness, I should've fed days ago. I won't wait so long the next time."

"The point is," I say, drowning his voice with mine. "We can be a good team. A weird team, but a good one nonetheless, don't you think?"

My boss blinks those disconcerting eyes at me. I hope anyone who sees them thinks they're cosplay contacts. "Does that mean what I think it means?"

"Yeah… Against my better judgement, I'll stay on this job."

The corner of his lips lifts and I don't like how it makes my heart skip a beat. With his hair tousled by the wind, and the unnatural eyes that stand out in a face already unrealistically beautiful, anyone would feel affected.

Clearing my throat, I say, "I think it'd be a good idea if I manage your feeding schedule."

"The what?" Caleb's jaw drops.

"I mean, clearly you need some help," I say, motioning around us as I infer that the mess tonight became is his fault.

"I have a schedule," he says, grunting. "I feed every couple of weeks or so. I don't know what happened this time."

"Maybe you were still weak from last week's smackdown?" I ask, giving him an up and down scan.

The first time I saw him at the hotel in Juarez, I was stunned to find no blemishes on his skin, you'd think the scars and bruises had never happened. But who knows, maybe the damage in his skin faded before the damage on the inside.

Caleb rubs his chin. "Could be. I can't think of any other reason why I'd get hungry so quick."

"So onions don't need to feed every day?" I ask, using the keyword even though no one is close enough to make out our words. It makes him smile, and under the streetlights I can see color has returned to his face.

"Most onions do, but I hate blood."

I do a double take. "How can you possibly hate what you need to survive?"

Caleb leans his head back. "Life as a vegan onion is a tough one."

"No freaking kidding." This just gets more and more bizarre, and as I fight off a bubble of laughter, I can't help but enjoy the fact that my life is no longer dull.

All thanks to my boss being a vampire.

CHAPTER 22
CALEB

Jet lag finds you even if you fly first class, and even if you're a vampire.

I struggle with keeping my eyes open and the screen of my cellphone isn't enough to perk me all the way up. My assistant is the in the restroom and I sit with all our luggage at a row of chairs in the Barajas airport. The driver is waiting for us and I plan to nap really hard on our way down to Cordoba.

An incoming call from Dad is almost powerful enough to clear the fog from my brain, but some of it remains and I slur my greeting. What should sound as hello sounds more like hewo.

"How are your travels?" he asks, as if he didn't know the toll a trip like this takes.

"Doing okay. Our suppliers don't want to drop us and I got us a few discounts."

Dad chuckles. "Your assistant sent me the data and you're putting it mildly. A purchase volume improvement of fifteen percent and an estimated ten million savings at the end of the year, *after* a PR crisis?"

I shrug, but since he can't see me I say, "Yeah, well. Isn't this why you forced me back to work?"

"Imagine what you could accomplish if you *really* wanted to." He clicks his tongue. "Anyway, I'll have a reward for you once you return home."

That does perk me up some—until I remember that often what Dad considers a reward ends up being more like a punishment for me.

"What kind of reward?" I ask.

From the corner of my eye, I spot Serena coming out of the women's restroom and wave at her.

Dad says, "The kind you can enjoy your entire life. But don't expect any more details from me or your brother until your return."

Damn it. I was gonna ask Daniel next.

"How am I supposed to deal with my curiosity now?"

"By working harder." He has the nerve to laugh and click the call off before I can retort.

I stuff my cellphone in the pocket of my jeans and grab my luggage. Would it be so bad if I block my dad's number? It would certainly give me some satisfaction.

"Ready?" I ask my assistant and she nods.

I suspect jet lag has rendered her speechless, because we cross the entire airport in absolute silence, just putting one foot in front of the other and wheeling our suitcases until we make it out of customs, and officially, into Spain.

"There's Paco," I say, recognizing him right away. He's the only one dressed in all black, with a blushing smile permanently etched on his face and thinning hair at the top that he combs over his scalp.

"Señor Caleb," he says as greeting and I pick him up in a bear hug.

"Paco, my friend. It's been so long." I set him back down and straighten his jacket.

"Just a year," he says in his thick accent. "I drove you around the Mediterranean, remember?"

Ah, yes. He drove me on land and I sailed us at sea. He translated everything for me and I got us drunk. And considering he's my blood supplier in the south of Europe, we have the perfect relationship.

Paco knew all the best spots for diving, surfing or sailing. He also made sure to find me the most incredible local restaurants with authentic food. And he had plenty of recommendations for good places to meet Spanish women, even though I'm not the biggest fan of travel flings.

Speaking of, he takes one look at Serena and his eyebrows go up. "And who may this lovely lady be?"

She extends her hand out for a shake. "I'm Serena Lossada, Caleb's assistant."

"Very pleased to meet you." After the introduction, she busies herself with her phone and the old man turns to me. "Just your assistant, huh?"

I roll my eyes. "Stop trying to pair me up with everyone."

"I'm just saying, you're young. Live a little." He raises his hands for a second. "Anyway, follow me."

My assistant struggles to wrench herself from her phone and eventually follows after us. I wonder if she heard Paco's comment, but if she did, it doesn't seem to matter much. Instead, she leans closer to ask, "Is he an onion?"

I have to bite my lip not to laugh. "No, he's definitely not an onion, but he does know about said veggies."

"Oh."

We climb onto the back of Paco's Seat SUV that he refuses to replace, even though I've offered to trade it for a fancier ride. The back seat feels like it remembers the shape of my body, though, and maybe Paco's onto something by keeping the old vehicle.

"Can we go over the final numbers?" Serena says the moment she's settled in, but my head rolls back and I clock out.

Distantly, almost dreamlike, I make out my driver say that I must be exhausted. I can't distinguish Serena's words the more my consciousness fades, but I feel her now familiar voice and somehow it comforts me. I fall deeper asleep.

*

I don't know how long I'm out but a jolt snaps me awake. It takes me a moment to recognize my bearings. For a second, I'm puzzled about the landscape that goes by from beyond the window. Then I glance forward and see the back of Paco's head, and am about to turn left to check in on my assistant when I find that I can't. Because my head is resting on hers.

Paco catches my eye from the rearview mirror and winks.

"It's not like that," I murmur. Serena would kill me if it was like that.

In fact, she probably would kill me if she sees the position we're in. Carefully, I lift my head. Hers rests comfortable on my shoulder and there's no way I won't awaken her if I move. So I stay like that. Forever.

Which lasts about five minutes until the car makes a worrying noise.

Serena springs awake. She gives me a look as if torn between embarrassment and the pressing need to tell me off. But her glasses and hair are askew and there's a distinctive trail down her lips.

"You drooled," I point toward her face. While she wipes herself with enough fury to chafe her skin, I ask Paco, "What's going on?"

"I'm not sure, Señor Caleb." Of course, the second he says that, the front of the vehicle starts smoking. "But it looks like there's an issue."

He parks the car on the side of the road and gets out to inspect it.

By this point, the sky is painted in hues of purple and blue and there's almost no light out. I glance around at the mostly empty road, with few cars coming or going. It's surrounded by a dark prairie and no population in sight.

"Oh, shit," I say.

"No shit," my assistant says. "What do we do?"

"Wait here." I unbuckle myself and get out of the car. "Need help, Paco?"

He's waving the smoke away, trying to see what's up with the engine. "No, my boy. I think this needs a professional. You should go back to sleep."

Scratching my head, I ask, "Are we safe here?"

Paco takes a look around and laughs. "What can get us here?"

Technically, he's right. There is absolutely nothing as far as the eye can see. So I head back to the car and deliver the news to Serena.

"Okay, can we take advantage of the occasion to prepare for tomorrow's meeting?"

I turn away from her and say, "Nope, I'm going back to sleep. G'night."

"Caleb."

Glancing over my shoulder, I say, "Wow, did you learn that way of saying my name like it's a reprimand from my dad?"

"No, I think you just inspire that out of people." When I turn my back on her again, she sighs. "Fine, get some rest. But you won't escape this conversation tomorrow morning."

I sure will try.

After a while, even though my eyes are closed and the car is quiet, I still find myself awake. Serena's breathing is deep and even, which tells me she was more successful in the endeavor of catching a second nap. Outside the car, I can see Paco on the phone, shaking his hand around like he wishes he could slap whoever he's talking with.

This has all the signs of not going according to plan.

Sure enough, the old man climbs back into the car and the noise wakes my assistant up. "The good news is that it can probably be fixed. The bad news is that my guy is about four hours away."

"Crap." I run my hand through my hair. "I guess we'll just have to wait here."

"There's another option," Paco says. "An old bed and breakfast less than five kilometers away."

Serena gives me a look. I give her one back.

The old man continues, "I can wait here and pick you up in the morning."

"Five kilometers," Serena says, her eyes lost in the distance. "That's a lot, isn't it?"

I ignore that and ask, "Does the bed and breakfast have actual beds and food? Because if so, sign me up."

"Are you out of your mind?" she asks, the words coming out in a hiss.

"Yup, you could say I'm batshit." I grin at her. "Let's go. Adventure awaits."

CHAPTER 23
SERENA

"Why are we doing this?" I wheeze, propping myself up by hands on knees and barely managing to maintain my balance.

"We're doing this so we don't become sitting ducks." Caleb glances at me over his shoulder. There's barely a sheen of sweat on his skin. "Which is what we'd be if we wait locked up in a car and get attacked."

"Do we—" I start saying but I have to pause to gulp for air. It's annoying that I'm so out of shape compared to his perfect shape. "Do we really expect to be attacked in the middle of nowhere in a foreign country?"

He shrugs. "Why run the risk? Also, you don't look so good."

I want to say no shit with my mouth, but only muster enough energy to say it with my eyes.

"Do you want me to carry you?" Caleb asks, and my brain malfunctions.

The wind is warm and soft, the only noise around us comes from it caressing the leaves of the trees and the weeds. There aren't even crickets around, and it was half an hour since we last heard the sound of an owl. We're truly alone on this road, only filling the silence with my panting. If it wasn't for the full moon high above us, it would be so dark that I wouldn't be able to see him in front of me, and I would feel even more alone. And much more scared.

"I'm very tempted," I admit but shake my head. "But it doesn't seem appropriate."

"Appropriate is a very relative term in these circumstances." Caleb shrugs out of his backpack and switches it to the front, before crouching in front of me. "Hop on."

"Uh…" His back looks very inviting. My legs and lungs are especially eager for a break.

My brain is still reluctant, though. Which boss carries his assistant around? This isn't some soap opera. This is real life.

Then again, it turns out that vampires exist in real life. Maybe I should shed my preconceived notions of normality for a bit.

Slowly, I lower myself onto his back. He grabs onto the back of my thighs firmly and tilts me forward. By instinct, I wrap my arms around his neck.

"Off we go," Caleb says like nothing's amiss.

I sag, too exhausted to even panic about everything my body's touching. Instead, I go back to my earlier question. "Why are we doing this?"

It tears a laugh out of him.

"No, seriously. Why didn't we fly in a private jet or something?"

His body is still vibrating with chuckles as he responds. "This is a company trip and we have policies about travel expenses. And especially considering our recent scandal, it would look really bad if I broke said policies."

I grumble, hating that it makes sense.

Low, since my face is right beside his ear, I say, "I find

myself irritated right this moment that you're not the spoiled brat people make you out to be."

"Why, thank you." His voice comes out too animated for someone who is climbing uphill with someone on his back, and battling jet lag on top. If I didn't know he's a vampire already, this is when I'd start suspecting that something about him isn't quite normal.

Something catches my attention from the corner of my eye —a small dot of light up ahead. "Do you think that's the place?"

"I sure hope so." Caleb grabs tighter onto my thighs and picks up his pace.

The only way for me to not bounce out of sync is to hold on tighter, and when I do, I catch the scent off his skin. There's still a soft trace of perfume under what's uniquely his own essence, and it sends a flash of awareness down my body.

This is definitely inappropriate.

Fortunately, it's not long after that when a building comes into view. A sign hangs over the front door and I make out the word posada.

I smack my boss's arm. "That's it! That's the bed and breakfast."

"Whew, good. I was low-key worrying about what we'd do if the place didn't actually exist."

I rear back just a bit. "And you tell me that now?"

In lieu of answering, he jogs the rest of the way. The building is modest in size and in decor. The walls are painted the same color of sand, peeling in places and stained by humidity in others. Some of the orange tiles on the roof are missing here and there, but the windows look clean and firm.

The front door is firmly closed, too.

"Crap, what if it's closed for the day?"

"We'll force it open." Caleb knocks on the wooden door.

"You can set me down," I say and I grab onto his shoulders

as he does. My whole body is flaming by the exertion and the heat in the air. A lot of the heat settles on my face, though. "Thanks."

"No problem." Caleb knocks on the door again. Louder. "C'mon, I want a bed. Open up."

As if on cue, the door groans and creaks as someone opens it. An old lady about half of Caleb's height squints up at him. "¿Qué quieres a esta hora?"

I bless my lucky stars that I forced myself to practice Spanish growing up. Elbowing my boss aside, I say, "Buenas noches. Disculpe la molestia pero necesitamos que nos aloje."

She turns her squint to me. "El sitio está lleno."

My heart drops. My stomach drops. My spirit drops.

"Hey." Caleb whispers at me. "What's she saying?"

I ignore him and instead, I grab onto the old lady's hand. "Por favor. Nuestro vehículo se accidentó en la carretera y no tenemos a donde ir."

She grunts but doesn't pull her hand away from my grasp. Maybe a good sign? I give her my best puppy eyes, which although very rusty seem to have some effect in softening her expression.

"Solo tengo una habitación pequeña con una sola cama."

"La tomamos," I say, shaking her hand, not even comprehending what she's saying in my excitement to just get some rest.

The little old lady checks us in and when I offer my corporate credit card, she tells me she only accepts cash. Caleb saves us from that pinch by taking out a wad of euros from his wallet and giving her at least twice more what she charged us for.

She leads us up a narrow, winding staircase—that threatens with being my demise—all the way to the attic. Before opening the door, she looks at Caleb and I, and mutters. "Buena suerte."

It's only after I open the door with her key that I realize why she said that.

The room is so small, it probably used to be a closet. The roof is slanted, reducing vertical space to half of what it could've been and giving even more of a cramped sensation. The sole window actually hangs over the bed, which is twin sized at best. And only one.

Caleb and I stand at the threshold, just staring at what his copious amounts of money could buy us.

Slowly, he asks, "Rock, paper, scissors?"

"Absolutely not." I walk into the room, dumping my backpack on the floor and myself on the bed. A yelp comes out of my throat because the mattress is probably harder than the floor. Biting back the literal pain in my butt, I say, "Ladies choice."

He puts his hand on his chest. "What about me? I carried you all the way here."

I shrug. "You offered, I didn't ask."

Caleb has enough mojo to smile. "But you didn't say no when I offered."

"You shouldn't expect rewards for good deeds."

He chuckles and when he closes the door behind him, the room feels even smaller. Never mind that he carried me on his back for a couple of kilometers, out of all the wild things that have happened around him, this feels by far the worst.

"What are you doing?" I ask as he dumps his backpack and heads over.

"I'm going to sleep," he says, pushing me toward the side of the bed against the slanted roof and laying down on the remaining space. "I'm not going to fight you for the bed, even though I'd definitely win. So let's just share."

I'm backed all the way up as far as I can go, but if I breathe too deeply I will touch him. I try to make myself smaller but he's so big that he takes most of the space.

"We can't." I swallow with even more difficulty when he turns his face to me. "This is *definitely* not appropriate."

Caleb snorts. "Don't flatter yourself, I'm not doing this to cop a feel or anything. All I want is to sleep in a horizontal position."

I bite my lip. I was also really looking forward to getting to the hotel and burrowing in between fifteen pillows.

But we can't. This isn't right.

"Won't you be more comfortable if you sleep on the floor?" I ask, not even trying to be sassy. "I mean, it's not just because of me. But this bed is so small you can't even stretch your legs all the way."

His knees are bent because there isn't any space at the end of the short bed. Even in this position, his toes are touching the wall. Meanwhile, I fit just fine.

"You must not have noticed how dirty the floor is, then." Caleb wrinkles his nose. "Nope, I'm staying put."

Gritting my teeth, I prop myself up. "Fine, then I'll sleep on the floor."

With one hand, he pushes me down flat on the bed. "Shut up, stop worrying, and let's just sleep, okay?"

"But—"

For the first time since I've known him, Caleb glares at me with full force. My lips clamp shut. It's like looking at a younger version of Cedric Oh.

"Sleep. Now."

I want to protest. Or at least my mind does. My body has a different plan, and it consists of melting on the hard bed. I blink, or at least that's what I intend, but my eyelids don't lift back up. Next thing I know, I'm out like a light. A low rumble almost pulls me back up, but exhaustion weighs me down and I stay in the darkness.

*

I don't know exactly how long passes before something stronger than my bone-deep exhaustion pulls me away from sleep. I fill my lungs with air and open my eyes. Light stabs my eyes, painful enough to almost make me shout.

But that's not the worst of it. It's the heat.

I feel as though I'm submerged in fire but without burning. Probably because the sun is high in the sky and the roof window is right above me. Strangely, I feel most of the heat beside me and not from above.

When my eyes grow used to the light, I find I'm on my side and the room looks empty. Then I try to look down at myself and that theory proves untrue.

It's Caleb. He's on the bed with me. Or more specifically, tangled with me.

His face is tucked right in the crook of my neck, blowing heat against my skin where the neck of my T-shirt sags. One of his arms is under me, around my waist. The other one is above, and either my T-shirt rode up or he sneaked his hand underneath and is now splayed over my back. Worst of all, my thigh is slung over his hip and his thigh is snug between mine.

My heart races like a rabbit's. Any scenario I envision of trying to untangle myself from him is going to lead to a disaster.

Caleb mumbles something in his sleep and his hand travels down my back, and I can't help it. I scream.

It's either that, or releasing an embarrassing sound that is lodged in my throat.

"Wha—"

As he startles and I try to push him away, Caleb's reflex is to hold onto me and we go tumbling over the edge of the bed.

There's an ugly thud even before we crash onto the floor. I hit my nose against something hard—the explosion of pain in my face so strong all I can do is lay there. It takes me a moment to realize that the groaning isn't coming from me.

I pull myself up and through the dancing stars in my vision, I find Caleb rubbing the back of his head. His face is scrunched up like he's in excruciating pain—the back of his head is at the angle of the bedside table, which means he probably hit it there.

"Are you okay?" I ask. All he can respond with is a non-verbal complaint.

I know it was my fault for pushing him. But ultimately it was *his* fault.

That's when I become aware of the position I'm in. Straddling his hips.

Caleb's wide eyes meet mine for a second before I'm scrambling back. My back hits the wall with a thud that knocks the air from my lungs.

He clears his throat. For the first time, Caleb is unable to produce any sass.

In an effort to focus my attention anywhere else, I glance at my watch. Seeing it's mid morning makes me gasp. "We missed our first meeting."

"Not my main concern right now." Caleb pulls himself to his feet, still massaging the back of his head. "Let's go see if Paco's waiting for us."

I press my lips tight. "Fine, we'll talk about this later."

But we never do, because after we find Paco waiting for us outside in his newly fixed car, Caleb and I pick our itinerary back up. We get so busy with work that this night almost feels like a hallucination.

CHAPTER 24
CALEB

'm thankful she didn't bring that little mishap up again during the rest of the trip. I guess she had more pressing concerns, what with one meeting after the next.

I tried to follow in her example and submerge myself in only work. It went well during the day, but not so much at night when I lay on a soft bed with plush pillows and only myself for company. My mind kept circling back to waking up snug against my assistant.

By the time we finally land back in Miami, I almost feel like dropping on my knees and kissing the floor, if only because picking regular life back up will help me forget that little bed in Spain.

After we clear customs, I ask Serena, "How are you getting home?"

"I'll call an Uber and expense it to the company." She lifts her chin up. "Is that okay?"

"Sure, but I could drive you home as well."

"No," she says too quickly to be polite. "Let's just... part ways here."

Also known as *let's keep our distance.*

I tilt my head. It's the first time she gives a hint after what happened, subtle as it is.

"Am I making you uncomfortable?" When she doesn't reply, I figure I am. I stuff my hands in my pockets. "I'm sorry. That's not my intent but I recognize it's the impact of what's happened. I'll strive not to be stranded in the middle of nowhere with only one bed available with you, ever again."

Her brow crashes like thunder. "What kind of apology is that?"

I do my best not to laugh and almost fail. Almost.

"Let me try again," I say, and she folds her arms as if to brace herself. "I'm sorry for my body doing what I said I wouldn't do, which was to cop a feel."

Like magic, red rushes up her throat and parks on her cheeks.

And because I'm nothing if not magnanimous, I add, "I also forgive you for coping a feel back and for almost giving me a concussion."

This is what finally makes her splutter out a curse. "Excuse me? I'm the innocent party here."

I cock an eyebrow.

Serena raises the palm of her hand. "I think it's best if we assume the entire situation was a mistake that won't repeat itself ever again. I would like to continue having a professional relationship with no hassle."

"Sounds reasonable. I, too, would like to keep it that way."

Serena grunts. "In that case, I'll see you on Monday at the office."

I fully support her plan of acting like nothing happened and decide to play along until the end of time. Or until the next reminder that my assistant is hot and I'm weak.

I wheel my suitcase a few steps behind her. My eyes stray down to the sway of her hips in tight jeans and I force them back up to the back of her head.

Pretty sure my hands would fit perfectly on her hips.

Everything she said is right, though. I have to continue working with her, seeing her everyday. And sometimes doing those things in front of my dad. The last thing I need is for him to see me salivating over a human girl.

The second we walk out of the gates, I spot a tall guy in a black suit holding a sign with my name, as if I couldn't recognize him without it. I'm too stunned at seeing Phelan Murray that I don't even notice when my assistant slips away.

"Mr. Oh," he says for a greeting.

"The hell are you doing here, Phelan?" I ask him. As I stand before him, I poke his cheek. "Wow, it's real."

He makes no other reaction but to blink his green eyes. "Do you have all your luggage?"

"I—yes."

He takes the suitcase from me and motions at me to walk.

"Seriously, man. Answer my question."

Phelan takes his sunglasses from the pocket of his jacket and puts them on. "Your father commanded it."

"No way." I laugh. "He wouldn't leave Daniel unprotected so you can pick me up at the airport."

"Your brother isn't unprotected," he says, with his characteristically quiet voice that sends shivers down the backs of friends and enemies alike. "He's been assigned a detail of five of my best men."

I pause, looking at the back of Phelan's head like it's multiplying before my eyes. "Five of your best men aren't half of you."

He glances back over his shoulder. "Stop dallying, your father wants to see you right away."

I groan and want to dally even more. But if I attempt that, Phelan will carry me on his shoulders if that means getting me in front of Cedric Oh. I climb onto the back of the black

Bentley Mulsanne that Phelan typically drives Daniel around with. And more than ever I wonder…

What is going on?

But there's no point in asking Phelan. Not only is he the most focused driver I know and will never tear his attention away from the road, but he's also a yes-man. Dad could ask him to jump from a cliff and Phelan will never even wonder why before he's jumping. He probably has no idea why he was switched from guarding the heir of the vampire kingdom to babysitting the spare.

The question is locked and loaded in my mouth by the time I enter my parents's mansion, but it poofs like smoke when I find the entire Oh family assembled in the living room. If that wasn't strange enough, the addition of someone else is just bizarre. Especially when I haven't seen said someone in a blessed long time.

"Welcome back home, Son," Dad says, coming to meet me halfway. He squeezes my arms. "There's someone who is excited to see you."

"Said no ever," I mumble.

He gives me a warning look before presenting me to his guest. "Vivienne, I'm so pleased to bring my son Caleb, your future fiancé."

Maybe it's me Dad is asking to jump off a cliff. Or at least that's exactly how this moment feels like.

I take one step back, which makes every eye in the room turn to me. "Uh, Dad. Can I have a word? In private."

His smile, which had come naturally a second ago, turns into something like a caricature. I can see the desire to throttle me and appear polite warring in his eyes.

He's actually saved by the newcomer. "Aww, Cedric. You shocked the poor guy. I was hoping he and I could grow closer before making any sort of announcement."

It's the look on Daniel's face the one that almost makes me turn on my heels and jump into the Caribbean.

Pity.

"Dad?" I grab onto his shoulder in a vise. "A word."

Finally, I get away with something because Dad says, "Diana, would you mind taking Vivienne on a tour of the property? We'll reconvene in a few minutes."

I turn and don't head out the door to plunge into the ocean like I wish. Instead, I head over to Dad's studio. His steps follow behind me and when he clicks the door shut, I explode.

"What the hell are you doing?"

All Dad does is fold his arms and sigh.

Meanwhile, I flap my arms and pace. "I go on a business trip and you take advantage of my absence to do this? I've told you time and again I don't want to marry anyone who asks for my hand like it's the middle ages. You can't just up and marry me off—"

"I can and I will." He slices through my arguments with words like a knife. "I've let you play around too much and maybe you started to think you were normal. But don't forget, I'm your father and your king. You will do as I say."

"It's *my* life. You can't just do with it as you please." I square up against him, and even though I look down at him, I feel smaller than a mouse.

"You're the son of the vampire king," he says, thunder laced in his voice even though it's low. "Didn't these recent attacks remind you of that fact?"

"What does that have to do with this?"

"*Everything.*" The vehemence in that one word echoes across the walls of the studio. Dad takes a deep breath. "I know I've neglected you for too long but I can't afford to continue that way. I must protect you by all means."

I take a step back, shaking my head. "Phelan? I sort of get it. But how is marrying Vivienne Astor going to protect me?"

"You're weak," Dad says, as though he's pointing out my hair color. "You haven't prioritized growing stronger the way your brother has."

"That's because he's the heir."

"That may be." He shrugs, his lips turning into a downward u shape. "But solely being the heir isn't the reason. He's put the effort into strengthening his blood for fifty years. He's built a career for himself and married into a strong family. In contrast, what have you done?"

I'm breathing fast, like I'm running instead of standing in a dimly lit room in front of a smaller and much older man.

But he's right. I'm weak in every sense of the word. And suddenly I hate what I am.

Dad shakes his head. "I love you, Caleb. That's why I can't let you continue down this road. If you won't grow up and protect yourself on your own, I'll do it for you. I'll assign Phelan by your side and I'll make you marry Vivienne Astor. They will keep you safe."

CHAPTER 25
SERENA

My boss is nowhere to be found when Monday comes.

I first go to the office, following what's now routine, until I make it to the parking lot and don't see the Lamborghini.

Right, it's probably not in driving condition after the damage it sustained from freaking vampires smashing into it.

I take public transportation to his apartment, figuring he has one car—or ten—I could use to drive him to the office. But now that I'm there, his apartment is empty and so is the second floor. Even the pool water is serene without anyone to disturb it.

I stand very far from the edge, which feels like the opposite metaphor for the moment.

"This freaking guy."

Still, in the odd chance he's still asleep or in his bathroom, I try calling his phone before I'm ready to give up. Five phone calls later, it's clear he doesn't want to be found today. Which means I absolutely have to.

Back in the living room, I call Jon. "Have you seen Caleb?"

"Good morning to you, too," he says, chuckling. "And no, I haven't seen him."

"Sorry, I'm just already not having a good morning." I sigh and splay myself on the sofa. "He was doing so well. Why is he acting up again?"

Then I sit up straight.

What if he's acting up because of the mistake-that-shall-not-be-named?

But why would that send him into a fit? If anyone has a right to throw one is me, the one who got thoroughly felt up and got her nose bruised.

"The good news is that he's a surprisingly boring guy," Jon says and at the same time I hear some tapping. "I just sent you an address. It's probably where he is."

My phone pings and I switch the screen from the call to the text that just came in. It has a location pin and when I click it, the maps app shows it's in the middle of the ocean.

"Is this a typo?" I ask him.

"Nope, he's probably in the water right now."

Staring out the window of his living room, into the vast Caribbean ocean where he might be, I ask, "And how do you think I can get there? I can't even swim."

"Leave that to me."

And by that, an hour later I find myself in a car with Jon and another guy on our way to the Keys.

"It's going to be a very long day, isn't it?" I ask under my breath.

Three hours later, I'm tucking into a fast food sandwich on a speedboat. Jon sits beside me, checking emails on his phone as though this doesn't throw a wrench in his work. The other guy who drove us here is the one who steers the speedboat and nothing about their expressions screams that this is abnormal.

My food smudges against my face as the boat jumps over a wave. When it smacks back on the water and I grab onto the railing for dear life, I make two decisions. One, I should stop eating. No matter how hungry I am, this is making me nauseous. Two, I will kill Caleb Oh.

I must have said this aloud because Jon chimes in with, "Don't be so hard on him today. He's going through a tough time."

Last I checked he was fine and dandy. Very fine and very dandy.

Jon doesn't tear his attention from his phone after dropping a bomb like that, even when the waves get harder. He also doesn't seem to be bothered by the constant up and down of the boat. For the first time I wonder if he's also one them. An onion.

I tighten my hold on the railings. "What do you mean?"

Before he's able to respond, the driver says, "I see it, the Bad Blood."

The what?

But when I face forward, I see a black yacht with the words Bad Blood written on the side in red.

Finally, this makes Jon pull his eyes away from the screen. A smile draws on his lips when he sees the enormous boat floating in the middle of the ocean.

"Fortunately we were right. There's Caleb's yacht."

I tense. "Does this mean we might have wasted an entire morning for nothing?"

"We might have, but we didn't." He stands up as the speedboat begins to slow down. "Call Joe."

The driver nods and reaches for the radio. All I hear is gibberish from the other side, until our driver explains, "Joe confirms that Caleb's on board. Well, underwater right now."

"Fantastic, tell him Miss Lossada will climb aboard."

Next I know, the driver steers the speedboat right under a ladder nailed on the side of the sleek yacht's surface. I glance up at it. Then at the water. Back at the ladder.

I swallow hard.

"Do you need help?" Jon asks.

"I—uh. Maybe." There's the fact that I have the wrong kind of shoes for this. In addition, I'm wearing a skirt. And if that wasn't enough, I really will die if I fall in the water. Never mind that I'm fitted with a life vest. "One second."

I take my shoes off and stuff them in my purse. Then, I lace the handle across my torso, so there's no way it'll fall. Together, they help me reach the ladder.

Once I have a decent hold of it, I say, "Please look away."

I hear Jon say, "All right."

My bare feet don't slip on the ladder but my arms are shaky as I climb for what feels like forever. Seriously, does a boat for a single person need to be this big? Or does he host parties here? Who else throws tantrums in a freaking yacht?

I'll kill him when I see him.

"Welcome aboard, Miss," a new voice says as I reach the top. A guy with serious mien and toasted skin offers me a hand and I take it, grateful for some help for the last leg of the climb.

Panting, I ask, "Who?"

"Joe Cabello, captain of the Bad Blood."

I shake his hand. "Were you the one who named it that way?"

"Oh, no." He's startled by the question. "Caleb did."

Of course. Only he would name a multimillion dollar yacht by a Taylor Swift song.

I peek back down to see if Jon is making progress quicker than me, but to my utter shock he's still on the speedboat—as it drives away from the Bad Blood. I shout after him, but they're already too far to hear me.

"Can I get you anything while you wait?" Joe asks. "We have plenty of food and drink—all vegan, I'm afraid. And the wi-fi password is the name of the boat in all caps, with the number two at the end."

I open and close my mouth. Open it again. Decide it's better closed.

"Actually," I say, rescinding that decision. "Where is Caleb?"

Joe checks his watch. "Hmm, it's past lunch time. He'll probably resurface soon. Please get some rest."

For lack of anything else to do, I follow his instructions. I sit at what feels like a fancy living room but is above deck. Beyond the railings there's nothing but the deep blue ocean, interrupted only by the line where the lighter sky begins. The day is clear without a cloud in sight and the sun feels scorching on my skin, but even more through my dark blouse and skirt.

"Uh, Mr. Cabello? Do you happen to have sunblock?"

The question catches him in the middle of bringing over a loaded tray. "I'm sure we must."

He sets the tray in front of me with plates full hummus, chips, stuffed grape leaves, olives and cheese that can't be cheese if it's vegan. My stomach rumbles and sun or not, I tuck in.

Of course, the moment I'm munching away is when Caleb hauls himself up by the same ladder I came from. Except he's wearing a snorkel and an oxygen tank. And that damn Speedo.

He tears the snorkel off to gape at me. "What the hell are you doing here?"

I keep chewing. It's either that, or gape right back at him.

Since I'm squinting under the relentless sun, I hope he can't tell where exactly I'm looking. Since he's breathing hard, the motions make his abs and the V that starts at his hips even more prominent.

Dang it, my boss is shredded and one way or another, he keeps reminding me of it.

After I'm done with my bite, I take a swig of club soda. "You didn't come to work."

Caleb pulls the thick straps of the oxygen tank off and I

enjoy the work of his shoulders there. I focus on the hummus, longing for the time when I didn't find Caleb attractive in the least.

"So you came all the way here?"

"I'm not going to answer an obvious question." I stuff my face with food as he plops on the seat across the table, limbs outward like a starfish. "The real question is why are *you* here?"

I don't appreciate how hooded his eyes are as he assess me. Or how his biceps bulge while he runs a hand through his wet hair. Or how the sunlight catches on the beads of water trickling down his bare skin. I really, really don't appreciate any of that.

And because it's obvious I'm staring, I say, "Wow, so the sun doesn't really burn you, huh?"

Caleb snorts. "Yeah, I'm not gonna burst into flames any time soon."

Sure could fool me, with how hot he is.

I shake my head. "Answer the question, Caleb."

With a sigh, he leans back and exposes his face to the sun. He stays like that for a good, long while. Finally, when he looks at me again he says, "My father decided that I must get engaged to someone I barely know."

It's almost as if an invisible hand plucked me from the Bad Blood's deck and dropped me in the middle of the ocean.

"What?" I blurt out.

Caleb takes a deep breath and leans forward, resting his arms across the table. He closes his eyes. A drop of water falls from his eyelashes and rolls down his cheek like a tear. Frozen like that, he looks miserable.

My hand reaches out to his but at the last second, I pull it away before it makes contact. That's not my place.

But what is my place? It's easy to forget it when he seems like such a normal, silly guy.

Except he isn't. He's a billionaire. Not even human. What

do I know about the life of someone like this? None of the hundreds of dramas I've watched have prepared me for how to console someone who lives in a completely different stratosphere.

And yet, I find myself asking, "And you don't want that?"

His eyes look like honey under the sunlight. "No, I don't. But Dad's right, on my own I'm weak. I can't even fight him for control of my own life."

"Why not?" I ask, tilting my head.

Anyone would think he's just turned into a statue, if it wasn't for the rapid blinking of his eyes.

"Listen, forget your dad hired me for a second. I'm going to speak candidly." I dust crumbles off my hands and hide them under the table. They wring each other as I gather all the fake bravado I have in me and say, "Your dad is trying to control you—and with good reason, because when things get tough you run and hide in the middle of the Caribbean. Instead, why don't you show him that you can be in control?"

His Adam's apple bobs with a thick gulp. "How?"

"Become boring." I say. "Be so dependable that you gain his trust. Then he'll be willing to reward you."

"By not marrying me off?"

I shrug. "Maybe. I can't promise results, but it's worth trying, isn't it?" Instead, what I wish to say is that I hope this works.

CHAPTER 26
CALEB

Bright and early the next morning, I text Serena that from now I'll head to the office on my own. Today in particular I need to not be distracted so I can mentally prepare for what I'm going to do.

Of course, the definition of *on my own* turns out to be loose. The moment I set foot in the lobby of my building, Phelan makes himself seen.

"How?" I ask, shaking my head. "Did you install a spy cam in my apartment or something?"

"Or something," he respond, which is the closest to a joke I've ever heard from him. "You won't escape again like yesterday."

Ah, yes. It figures it would rankle on the mighty Phelan Murray to have his charge slip right through his fingers. All I did yesterday was wake up before the crack of dawn and leave my apartment through the service elevator. It was surprisingly easy.

Then again, I don't need to run away anymore.

I shrug. "Fine, become my shadow."

He follows like one all the way to the parking lot. I veer

away from his Mulsanne and head toward a brand new Lamborghini Urus. Phelan catches the key I toss at him easily.

"Is this bulletproof?"

"Of course," I answer, climbing to the backseat. "It also has the usual compartment with guns and ammo, and bigger storage for the emergency blood supply."

Moreover, it has a better first aid kit in case it's ever needed for my assistant. He doesn't have to know that part, though.

"Besides," I add as we're on our way, "it's less conspicuous."

Of all the supercars that can be seen in the streets of Miami, a black Urus isn't the most special. The Mulsanne tends to catch more stares. My parents, especially Stepmother, enjoy making sure their status is known—but I don't care about that. Everything I have is theirs, and why would I flaunt something that isn't mine?

That's why I'm going to the office early today. To have a chat with my dear father.

"Phelan," I say and although there's no response, I know he's listening. "Have you ever felt the desire to defy my dad?"

"No," he responds easily.

Yeah, that seems to be exclusively a me-thing.

It's not like Dad is a despot. Anyone else running an underground kingdom of some hundred thousand creatures, plus a business empire, would turn into a megalomaniac.

Rumor has it that at the beginning of his tenure, he sort of was. But there were many factions vying for power among vampires back then, and some were eager to establish their superiority on humans. Dad squashed all of that over the course of fifty years of bloody fights sprinkled with diplomacy.

To humans in the newspapers, all of these events appeared as turf wars of mafia bosses, when it was just Dad cleaning up the mess that warring vampire families made across the globe.

Under his reign, vampires have experienced peace and

prosperity, and once he achieved all those things, he chilled down and turned to making a family. That's where control started slipping from his grasp.

He married Diana Mancini, heiress of a conglomerate and descendant from one of the oldest vampire families in Europe, like she was a spoil of war. It was an advantageous marriage, an alliance between European vampires and a king who originally hailed from the Korean peninsula, but settled in the new continent. There was no love involved, and I guess at some point Dad figured his biggest reward would be to find love.

And he met my mother. The biggest mistake of his life.

Then, I was born. The second biggest mistake of his life.

Phelan trails me to the top floor of the main Comed Solutions building. Marissa is already at her desk, and I notice how her heart beats just a bit faster upon seeing my shadow.

"Good morning, Marissa. Is Dad in his office?"

She fixes her hair before addressing me. "Good morning, Mr. Oh. Your father hasn't arrived yet."

"I'll wait for him in his office." Before I shut the door behind me, I say, "Also, just Caleb. I don't want to confuse myself for my dad."

She gives a lukewarm laugh, doing her best to avoid looking at Phelan. Either she really likes him or she really doesn't, it's hard to tell. It's also puzzling that someone would have any sort of strong feelings for an icicle on legs.

The lights in Dad's office flip on automatically and I look around. Where is the best spot for me to make an obnoxious greeting? Should I hide behind couch and jump the moment he comes in?

Nah, he'll smell me from a mile away. There's no other vampire with sharper senses than the king.

And so, I sit at his chair and lean back. The leather seems to absorb me and I don't know how I'll ever get up again, now that I'm one with the chair. His desk is in pristine order, much the same way he tries to keep every aspect of his life.

Except me. I'm the blip in his plans. And I'm here to make it all worse.

When Dad finally walks into the office, an hour has passed and I've rehearsed how the conversation might go a million times. He stands by the door, eyebrows high upon seeing me.

"You're late," I say, even though I have no idea what time he usually arrives.

Dad snorts and closes the door behind him. "By the time you woke up I already had at least three meetings. If anything, you're early."

That's true, but not the point of this conversation.

He pulls up a chair and sits across the desk, not asking me to get up from his spot. That's also not the point of this inter-action. We both know who's really in power here, regardless of which chair we use.

As usual with being in close proximity to him, a cloying heaviness settles on my shoulders like physical pressure. Some-how, it feels like being in the presence of Cedric Oh could lead to your demise, even though realistically I know Dad wouldn't hurt me—not physically. His words are a different story.

"I want to continue our conversation from Saturday," I say, resting my hands atop his desk.

"Very well." Dad unbuttons his blazer and gets comfortable.

For once, I lead with the truth. "You're right, for an Oh vampire I'm weak and without you I have nothing on my own. But I want you to be honest with me, is that why you're doing this, or is there something else?"

Placidly, he blinks. "What do you mean?"

I lean forward. "Is there another reason why you *have* to make a blood alliance with the Astors, or is this merely for my protection?"

I'm not expecting the long pause that ensues. But Dad remains silent, just staring at me like I'm a book he's trying to read, except I'm written in a different language. This reluctance to answer my question is puzzling. I've never seen my dad hesitate.

Finally, he says, "It's for your protection."

I can't help the frown that forms on my face. This is the best outcome from that question, and yet it doesn't feel like a victory. If there were external forces leading Dad to require a blood alliance with the Astors, there would be nothing I can do. But now I might be able to change the course of events, provided the real issue is just me.

"In that case," I say, taking a deep breath. "Is it truly because I'm weak, or because you are the one growing weak?"

Dad's eyes widen almost imperceptibly, but the surprise is there, etched on the lines of his face. "Caleb…"

"I didn't want to consider it," I say, rubbing the back of my neck. "But you've seemed more on edge than usual, especially when it comes to me. I haven't changed—I'm the same clown as usual—which means it's you who has changed."

Dad smiling is not the response I expected. On top of that, he says, "Sometimes I forget how smart you are."

I wince. "Is that supposed to make me feel better?"

He chuckles for a moment, before sobriety falls upon his face again. "There is some truth to this. It's definitely me who has changed. I'm old, Caleb, I won't always be here for you. While Daniel is fairly prepared for life without me, I don't think you are."

I might as well have been punched in the solar plexus, with the effect his words have on me.

Choked up, I say, "It's not like you're going to die tomorrow, Dad. You have what, like fifty more years ahead of you?"

"Perhaps. Perhaps not." He pauses, regarding me as though we're meeting for the first time and he's trying to figure out the kind of man I am. "It's that second possibility what has made me realize how unprepared you are."

"What if I start preparing?" I ask, leaning forward on my elbows. "I'm just twenty seven, a baby vampire for all intents and purposes. It's not too late for me to start growing stronger. Is that what I need to show you, so you understand I can be in control of my life—that I won't always need you?"

"Won't you?" he asks, his voice soft. So soft it doesn't sound like him at all.

I have a sudden fear that he's going to vanish before my eyes, so I get up from his chair and kneel before him, grabbing his hands. Relief washes over me when I feel them warm and strong in mine. My lungs feel like they're filled with water.

"I have to try," I say, squeezing his hands. "You have to let me learn to live my life so I won't crumble when one very far day, you're gone. You won't accomplish that by controlling every aspect of it."

Dad squeezes my shoulder. "Then try. Make me not worry about you a single time. If you succeed, I'll give you the full reins. And if you don't, I'll do things my way until my last breath."

CHAPTER 27
SERENA

'm on the bus on the way to Caleb's apartment when I see his text message. *From today on I'll head to the office on my own.*

Weird.

Also… is this even reliable? We'll see.

He should've told me yesterday and I would've set the alarm later today. Still, I look forward to not having to cart him around the city. With all the extra time I'm going to get from this development, I'll be able to sleep in later every morning and also arrive home earlier in the evening. I'll even be able to put a dent in my list of dramas to watch. I'll probably get some more cleaning done too.

It's all good things, and yet I feel like I lost something.

That feeling hangs over me like a cloud as I finally make it to the office. At the front entrance, I ask if Caleb has already come in and they confirm he has. I guess this must be what parents feel like when they send their kids to the kindergarten for the first time, a mix of sorrow with a lot of pride. Maybe my days of babysitting Caleb Oh are coming to an end.

Bueno, ver para creer.

I'm in the thick of drafting expense reports when I realize

it's mid-morning and my boss still hasn't shown his hide. I check with the front desk again, in case he's sneaked out from under my nose, but they say his badge must still be in the building. Before I'm able to start wondering what he's up to, someone clears their throat.

A supermodel stands in front of me.

No, a Barbie doll made human.

Scratch that, she must be a robot. No one can possibly look that perfect.

It takes me another moment to recover my cognitive ability in the face of all this physical perfection. "Um, hi. Good morning. What can I help you with?"

She tosses her blonde, straight mane back over her shoulder. Each strand is so glossy, it might as well be made of sunrays. Her eyes are as blue as the Caribbean and her lips some fashionable pink that comes in a tube. She leans over the counter and I can't help noting that not only is her face the pinnacle of what most people would consider all-American beauty, but her body is also carved by the hands of an artist.

"Is this Caleb's office?" she asks, her voice slightly raspier than I expected.

"Yes, although he's out at the moment." I stand up, if only because I don't know what else to do. "Do you mind me asking who wants to see him?"

She smiles and my eyes hurt from it. "Vivienne Astor, his soon to be fiancée."

All at once, the cloud hanging over me this morning releases a bolt of lightning that travels through my body. It scorches any sense of worth I had for myself until this moment, leaving me only as a pile of ashes.

I hate the feeling. There's no reason why I should compare myself to this woman, or anyone else. Not just because I'm lacking in every regard, but also because we're not trying to tread the same path in life toward Caleb Oh. She's no doubt a vampire and his apparent future fiancée, where I'm just his frumpy, human assistant until a better gig comes my way.

I know Caleb said yesterday that he doesn't want to marry this woman, but considering that he seems to be a straight guy there's no way he'll resist her.

Clearing my throat, I say, "Nice to meet you, Miss Astor. I'm Serena Lossada, Mr. Oh's assistant. He will probably return shortly, would you like to wait in his office?"

Vivienne Astor looks me up and down and I wish I could tell her that she doesn't need to bother. But that would probably lead to an awkward question of why I have to say that.

In the end, her Mona Lisa smile doesn't dim. "That would be amenable."

There's a distinct southern twang in her words that makes her even more charming. When I walk around my desk to usher her into Caleb's office, I get an eyeful of the dress she's wearing—a tight little number that won't offer much coverage when she sits down, with a golden zipper at the front that goes all the way down. It's the kind of dress that is like battle armor, and the reason she's wearing it is to attack Caleb. Or stake claim to the territory that he represents.

"Can I offer you anything while you wait?"

She sits on the couch and crosses her legs, and of course they're long and shapely. "Just some water will do, sweetheart."

"Right away."

My joints are stiff as I backtrack and close the door. I close my eyes and take a deep breath.

"Stop it," I tell myself. "You're overreacting."

"To what?"

I jump half a mile in my skin upon finding Caleb right in front of me. "Oh my word, would you please make noise when you walk—both of you?"

Behind Caleb stands the same guy who picked Caleb up at

the airport. The only acknowledgement I get from him is a slow blink.

"Maybe it's not that we're too silent but that you're too jumpy." Caleb cocks an eyebrow and I have to grip my hands in front of me to prevent any of them from smacking the brattiness out of him.

"Anyway, Vivienne Astor is waiting in your office for you," I say, which settles on his face with a frown. "Can I get you anything for your meeting with her?"

"Got some novocaine lying around?" he asks, sighing. "Never mind. A cup of really strong coffee will do."

"Very well."

To the other guy, he says, "Please wait outside."

The tall redhead stands beside the door like some sort of enchanted statue.

I ask him, "Would you like anything? Water? Coffee? Tea? Juice? A soul?"

Caleb barks a laugh that makes heat travel up my throat.

"Sorry," I say to the still guy. "I realize now that if he's laughing it means I was offensive."

The statue's lips twitch just a smidge. "It was kind of funny. And no, I'm good, thank you."

Caleb gasps. "Oh wow, Serena. You made *The* Phelan Murray smile."

I take a deep breath. "Stop making her wait and go."

Caleb's nose scrunches up. He glances at Phelan, as if seeking backup, but the other guy stares straight at the opposite wall. Sighing, my boss finally goes into his office.

"Geez, you'd think he's going in for slaughter," I murmur.

"More or less," Phelan says.

There are many ways his comment can be interpreted, and I decide none of them are my business. Instead, I take my sweet time in the kitchenette, brewing coffee strong enough to fuel a jet engine. I decide to bring Phelan some orange juice and some calming tea for myself.

It proves a good idea. Not only Phelan accepts my offering, but the moment I open the door to Caleb's office and see what's happening inside, I figure one cup of calming tea won't be enough. The contents of the tray in my hand teeter dangerously, and I have to stop breathing not to make a mess.

Vivienne Astor is kneeling between Caleb's legs, her hair brushed to one side as she offers her neck to him. Actually, she's offering more than her neck. The zipper of her dress is much lower than I saw earlier, and only the sheer suction of the tight dress prevents her from spilling all the goodies.

Since she's the one facing me, she's the first to notice me standing there. "Oh, thank you. I was getting a tad thirsty."

The way she says this is as if nothing is amiss.

Slowly, Caleb turns to me and he seems furious. A hairs-width away from exploding.

Even though he's probably going to bite my head off for interrupting at the good part, I set the tray down on the coffee table. Without a word, I turn around and basically dash away.

And I keep running some more. Past Phelan and my steaming mug of tea, past the marketing lobby and the elevators. I crash open the door to the stairs and run up until my lungs burn and my legs feel like lead.

I keep pushing, putting distance between me and a scene that looked right out of any guy's fantasy, putting distance between me and the fallacy that Caleb's a normal guy.

There's nothing normal about him. He's my boss. A vampire. A billionaire. We're not close at all. If I thought we were, I was wrong. Just like I'm wrong for feeling the way I feel right now.

Annoyed. Hurt.

Jealous.

Finally, I make it to the rooftop. In the course of the morning, the sky turned overcast to match my mood. The wind is strong enough to whip my ponytail on my face and I welcome that sting. It's better than the sting behind my eyes.

I force myself to take deep breaths, one after the next. But none of that changes the fact that I'm stunned by what I saw. Or the fact that I shouldn't care, but do.

I crouch down into a ball and allow myself exactly one scream. It turns into a yelp the moment a fat drop splashes on my neck.

It's raining. This morning has room to grow so much worse.

I jog back to the door, unable to avoid the quick shower of rain. And of course, I try the door and it's locked. I palm my clothes and *of course*, I left my cellphone behind.

"Mierda."

CHAPTER 28
CALEB

I grit my teeth with enough force to break through concrete.

For a second, I debate whether to scream at Phelan for help. He would come in, guns blazing, and the shock should be enough to make Vivienne jump away from me.

"What the hell are you trying to accomplish here?"

"Isn't it obvious?" she asks, glancing up at me from the corner of her eye as she exposes to me. "I'm offering myself to you, in more ways than one."

It's exactly at that moment that the door opens behind me and I freeze. Phelan wouldn't dare disobey direct orders. The only other person who would care to come into this place is my assistant.

No!

I want to scream at her to go back. This isn't something I want her, or even myself, to see.

But I can't do that. The moment Vivienne finds an indication that I care about my assistant, she will pounce even harder. That's the kind of person she is.

"Oh, thank you. I was getting a tad thirsty," Vivienne says.

In a way, it sounds like she's thirsty for something other than water.

Steps approach and I turn. Serena looks pale as she sets a tray on the coffee table. With my eyes I try to convey that she should run, and maybe she catches the message because she pretty much bolts outside of the office. My legs tense. They too want to follow.

But I also can't do that.

Vivienne settles back on the carpet and reaches for the chilled bottle of water. While she's distracted taking a swig, I zip her dress back up.

She pouts. "Aww, were you not enjoying the view?"

"That's right, I wasn't."

Vivienne tilts her head. "Oh, I didn't know you weren't interested in women."

"I am, but I'm not interested in *you*." Feigning a calm I don't feel at all, I reach for the cup of coffee and bring it to my nose. Serena really made it extra strong. Good. "I'm also not interested in drinking your blood, or giving you mine if that's what you're after."

"Why not?" Vivienne stands up with much more grace I would expect from anyone dressed in cling wrap, and sits beside me. Her hand runs through my hair like she has any right to do that. I bat it away. "Caleb, you're hurting my feelings."

I snort. "You have those?"

"Admittedly, no." She shrugs. "But you're one of the few people who understand that's just who I am. I thought you'd be more excited for our engagement."

I take a deep, deep breath, and release it slowly. "Just because our families have known each other all our lives doesn't mean I want to keep you in mine forever."

"Even if it means I can give you power?"

Her smile is sweet at a glance, but her eyes are hard as granite. I volley what I hope is a similar expression back at her.

"Are you sure it wouldn't be you who gains power by marrying into the Oh family?"

"Quid pro quo, sugar."

I mumble. "I hate it when you call me sugar."

"How would you prefer I call you? Baby? Daddy? Baby daddy?"

I choke on my drink. "No. I would prefer if you don't call me at all."

"Husband," she says, ignoring me. "That's how I'm going to call you."

"Actually, thanks for coming and making my job easier because I was going to talk with you anyway." Setting the cup back on the tray, I face her squarely. "I'm not gonna marry you."

Vivienne's smile deepens. Did I tell her a joke instead of trying to ruin her plans?

This is why I've never liked her. She always gets away with what she wants, and until now I'd been content that it had never been me. In fact, I thought she hated me.

I enunciate every word with extra care. "I, Caleb Oh, am absolutely not in a million years going to marry you, Vivienne Astor."

Vivienne chuckles, which is terrifying enough when it's also not catching me off guard.

The next second, she leans forward lightning quick and kisses me. I pull away before she's able to deepen the contact and push her away with a hand against her stomach, her cling wrap dress forming a barrier. The way I wince seems to deepen her amusement.

"Are you struggling for hearing comprehension?" I wipe my mouth with the back of my hand. It comes out smudged in lipstick. "Vivienne, stop this shit."

The worst part is that the more uncomfortable I am, the more she seems to take it as a victory.

"You say that now, but soon you'll be begging for more." With that, she grabs her purse and gets on her feet. "I'll be seeing you around—or I should rephrase that, you'll be seeing *a lot* more of me, Caleb."

"No, thank you."

I wait for a few minutes after I last hear her laughter fade away, just composing myself after whatever that was. Sexual harassment? I wonder if anyone would even believe it.

And my parents expect me to marry that freak?

I head into the bathroom of my office and wash my face with cold water. If I was in the least bit attracted to Vivienne I might have enjoyed that show, but all I want is to bathe with bleach now. I have to find a way to make Dad see that making me spend my life with Vivienne is the opposite of giving me strength. She saps my will to live.

It's always been like that. Every time our families met at some gala or other bullshit, running into Vivienne turned into the worst part of those events. She's a bully of a similar nature to my stepmother. Why would I want to marry someone like that?

That's when I think of Serena and the stricken expression on her face.

If Vivienne's antics are shocking to me, I can't imagine what's going through my assistant's head right now. Especially with the optics of the scene she walked into.

My face is still dripping wet when I find Phelan standing guard outside my office. "Where's Serena?"

"She ran off a while ago."

"Where?"

Phelan's eyes narrow just a tad. "That way."

I glance where he points, which can lead to exactly anywhere. "Can you be more specific?"

"I can't," he says, easily. "I wasn't paying attention to her."

"Wow, you're as useful as paperweight." I pull out my cell-phone and call her, but a second later the ringtone comes from her desk. "Well, at least that means she can't be too far, right?"

I take one step and he follows. But I don't have much energy left in me to argue about not needing his company. First, I check out the Marketing floor because it's where we are. Then I go to Purchasing, in case she's out there. But I don't spot her.

Clicking through my phone's contacts, I call someone else. "Hey, Marissa. Have you seen Serena?"

My dad's assistant's assistant responds with, "Not today, no. Is something wrong?"

"No." Yes, but I don't want to explain. "She just left her phone at her desk and I need to ask her something. If you see her, can you please let her know?"

"You got it."

I hang up and call the front desk, but all I can glean from them is that she hasn't left the premises. Comed Solutions main building has thirty floors, though. Where do I even try next?

"Try leisure areas," Phelan shocks me by suggesting.

I stare at him. He shows no further reaction and it makes me wonder if I hallucinated the comment. Still, it's a good one so I take the elevator down to the main cafeteria.

There are already a few people assembled for an early lunch, but none of them are a short girl with light brown skin, long hair and black rimmed eyeglasses.

I run a mental inventory of the other areas someone might take a breather in. There are a number of sitting areas and a library, but if she's in the women's restroom there's nothing I can do.

That's when two neurons rub together and I have a eureka moment.

It hasn't been extremely long since I've known Serena

Lossada, but I don't think she's the kind of person whose engine would grind to a halt easily. She's someone who takes action. And if she's not taking action right now—like for example, reporting what she saw to HR, in which case I'd already gotten a call—then it means she literally got away as far as her feet could take her. Which, still staying inside the building, leaves only one option.

I snap my fingers. "The rooftop."

It's the only place I can think of that would hold her up for this long. Everyone knows the door only opens from the inside, and if you want to go up there for a smoke or for some alone time, you have to use a stopper to keep it open. She's new to the company and probably doesn't know.

"Here goes nothing," I say to myself as I press the elevator button.

It makes all the stops as people get in and out, until it finally dings that we've made it to the top floor. I veer away from Dad's office and take the stairs. Something like white noise rings in my ears along with Phelan's and my footsteps, and I realize it's raining.

"Great." To Phelan, I say, "Wait here."

He nods. I push the door open and a rush of wind splatters me with rainwater. I can't spot anyone right away, so I take one step onto the rooftop and then hear a gasp.

The handle of the door slips from my grasp and it closes.

"No!" There's Serena, running toward me from under the negligible shelter of a decorative plant. "Damn it, you let the door close."

Despite how ugly this morning turned out to be, finally finding her and seeing her sopping wet again steals a laugh out of me.

CHAPTER 29
SERENA

'm working really hard not to hit you right now," I say, gritting my teeth against the onslaught of rain. I glance up, trying to determine if the clouds are any less dark than before, but I can't make them out through my wet glasses. The only reason I can tell it's Caleb is because of his obnoxious laughter that doesn't stop.

"Why are you angry at me? You're the one who got locked out in the rooftop in the middle of a rainstorm."

I stomp my foot. "And you're laughing at *me* when you just did the same?"

Caleb doubles over because he's laughing so hard. But then lightning streaks the sky and it kills his amusement.

Next thing, he grabs my wrist and pulls me up beside him, against the wall. This is exactly what I was doing before he burst in through the door, giving me hope that I might finally escape this form of torture I inflicted on myself.

"This is certainly helping me cool my head." His voice isn't loud over the crashing rain, but I hear every word just the same. We're so close that our arms are glued to each other, and his hand is still a hot brand around my wrist.

All of this disconnects the filter between my brain and my mouth, and I ask, "Why? Was it hot?"

He snorts. "Yeah, with volcanic anger."

"I saw that," I mumble. I also saw a lot of other things. "Sorry for interrupting."

Caleb catches the hint right away, but not because of what I expected. "Let's be honest, if anyone should be apologizing it's Vivienne, but that's not gonna happen. So I'll say it instead, I'm sorry you saw all that. That's unacceptable in the workplace."

In the workplace. It's definitely acceptable outside of it.

I can't help copying and pasting the same image in his living room instead, and it makes my stomach queasy.

While, yeah, that scene had definitely not been safe for work, it was his office. In what is essentially his company. If it had been worse and I marched straight to HR to report it, he wouldn't face any consequences.

I pull my wrist free and hug myself against the cool rain. "You don't need to apologize, I should've knocked first."

"That's not the point." Caleb lets out an exasperated breath. "The point is that I wish none of that had happened, and I hate that it did."

The same anger as before is reflected on his face. I process his words for much longer than I should have, until I realize that his ire isn't directed at me. But at his to-be-fiancée.

"Wait." The word pulls his attention down to me. "So, like. You weren't all over that? Actually, never mind. It's not my place to ask."

"But you're curious, huh?" A note of amusement leaks into his voice and chafes me. "I'll answer anyway. No, I wanted to gouge my eyes out and dip them in bleach."

"Why? She's freaking gorgeous."

To take a page from his book on gory metaphors, I wish I could chop my tongue off and toss it out the rooftop.

His face has the same expression as someone who just took a morsel of real unsavory food. "But she's evil, and I'm not attracted to evil."

Butterflies flutter in my stomach. I clear my throat, trying to settle the hell down. I shouldn't be feeling this happy.

I shouldn't be feeling at all.

In an effort to focus on something else, I face forward and note that the rain has been waning. The first patches of blue sky start to appear in between the grey clouds.

"Well, that won't get the door to open but at least we'll be able to start drying soon." I glance at my boss from the corner of my eye. "Hold on, do you have your cellphone with you?"

"Nope," he says, rocking on the balls of his feet. He looks pleased by that blunder. "I take it you didn't bring yours, either."

I wipe the hair that has glued to my forehead away, wishing I could hit both of us for doing the same thing. "Do you think anyone will hear us if we scream?"

"Nah, let's just wait it out until someone comes to find us." He has the gall to chuckle. "Look at it on the bright side, at least your clothes haven't gone see through this time."

I don't have enough willpower to stop myself from landing a good smack on him. And because all this causes is another bout of laughter from him, I land a couple more strikes as well. I'm pretty sure the one who will be hurting from the blows is me, because his back is as solid as a wall.

"Geez, you should've been a boxer."

"If you report me to HR for hitting you, I will report you for what you just said about my clothes." I try to fix them, which isn't easy as the fabric keeps sticking to my skin. I'm glad they're different shades of brown today, and that even though I'm sure to turn heads for being sopping wet, at least it won't be for giving everyone a peepshow like I accidentally did to my boss a few weeks ago.

The smirk on his face tells me he's thinking precisely about that incident. Caleb leans one shoulder on the wall, facing me, and folds his arms. With water dripping from his bangs, trickling down his skin and gluing his now transparent shirt to his skin, he looks like an apparition from a dream. And the only thing saving him from giving me a thorough eyeful is that he's wearing a blazer.

"We would have to mutually report each other for too many things, don't you think?"

A shiver travels down my back and I can't hide it before he notices it. I wrap my arms tighter around me. "Uh, yeah. Maybe let's not go down that route."

"Which one should we take instead?" he asks, and what was left operating of my brain ceases activities. "We're not a conventional boss and assistant."

I mumble. "No, you're a freaking vampire and I'm not."

As his eyes darken, the smile on his face sends my heartbeat from human to rabbit.

I take a sharp intake of air and follow it by stepping back, away from him. Even though every cell in my body wishes for the opposite. And of course, that step makes me lose my footing.

I yelp. My arms shoot out grabbing at anything to keep me upright. But all I find is air. I close my eyes and brace for impact, but it never comes.

Instead, I feel Caleb's arms around me and he catches me a second before impact. The rain stops beating my face and I crack an eye open. From through the drops on my glasses, I find Caleb's face hovering just above mine. He has me firmly in his arms, like he's some kind of hero in a melodrama and I'm the hapless damsel in distress.

I open my lips and only a thread of voice comes out.

The smile from earlier is gone from his face, replaced by

something much more terrifying. Something that looks a lot like hunger.

"Are you okay?" my boss asks, his voice thick with something I can't fathom.

I nod. That's all I can do. If I open my mouth again I'm afraid of what might come out.

Caleb helps me back on my feet and it might be because my knees have gone weak, but I slip on a puddle of water again. He hasn't let go of me and instead, he tightens his arms around my waist until I'm pressed up against him. His face is so close to mine, even with my soggy glasses I can make out the freckles on his nose.

"Serena." My name on his lips wraps around my body like a second embrace. If he lets go of me right now I'll collapse on the floor. "Do these things happen on accident or are you trying to tempt me?"

I gasp. No longer caring if I slip again, I push him away. I'm breathing fast and I wish I could run away if that damn door would open.

I toe around the puddles carefully and try tugging at the door, but of course I have no luck. And because I can't face him, I lean my forehead against the cool metal and pray for earth to swallow me.

"Allow me," he says, pushing me away with a gentle hand. I can't even tell him he's going to waste his efforts too, because I no longer have command of my tongue.

But then Caleb grabs hold of the handle and pulls so hard, the metal door sags like rubber. Still he pulls, until the handle makes a sound like a snapping cracker and comes off altogether. With that, he opens the door and motions to the other side.

"After you."

I gape. "You could've done that all along *and didn't?*"

His lips lift into a smile that doesn't reach his eyes. "What can I say, I was having fun."

That's the moment when I officially start hating him with all I have.

CHAPTER 30
CALEB

My attention keeps going to Serena's turtleneck sweater. Which she's wearing in the middle of summer.

Granted, we have air conditioning in the entire building and I'm wearing a whole three-piece suit, but most of the day I take off the blazer and unbutton my shirt not to break into a sweat.

Meanwhile, my assistant is straight up mopping her forehead in the middle of this meeting, but she still made this sartorial choice for today. And I just want to know why.

The other executives are giving Dad their monthly update, while we sit at a massive conference table. A couple of them are abroad and their faces appear in the screen at the opposite end of Dads seat. But I can't focus much on any of that while Serena sits on my left, trying to discreetly let some air in from the neck of her top.

What's worse is that she won't even make eye contact with me, almost making me think this is my fault somehow.

But it's not like I got her soaked in the rain on purpose yesterday, and I can't see why a little bit of clingy clothes as a result would now lead her to this drastic decision. Especially when it's already been a month or so since the pool incident.

Now *that* did give me an eyeful.

Oh, maybe that's why she's wearing this turtleneck. She figured yesterday's incident would remind me of that other one.

I give her a raised eyebrow that she ignores. I'll have to tell her that vampires don't have X-ray vision.

"Your turn, Caleb."

My brain flips to my dad in an attempt to not make a fool of myself by blurting out how literally hot my assistant looks, and instead talking business.

I speak without a hitch. "The main update as acting Purchasing Director is that the internal audit has been completed."

This raises a ripple of murmurs across the table. Dad quiets it down with his voice. "Any significant findings?"

"Three minor ones that are being corrected with the development of a new process." I pause to motion at my assistant and she fires off emails to the entire board with the details. "Thanks to that, I'm confident to say we're prepared to begin the external audit."

"How long is that going to take?" Steph Banks, the top boss of the Legal team, asks me.

"Starting next Monday, it will take an entire month."

"Good. Keep us posted of any eventuality." Dad leans back in his chair. "Now, what about our suppliers?"

"I visited the three main suppliers who would've been affected. Fortunately, the relationships weren't harmed."

Frank Gutierrez from Quality cuts in. "I actually heard you got some good deals out this?"

I smile. "To put it politely, yes."

In more specific terms, I kicked ass.

To Serena, I say, "Please send them the report."

"Yes, sir," she responds with all propriety.

"In addition," I continue. "An important part of the damage control we have to do is when it comes to our image. Internally and with our suppliers, the situation is now under control. But we need to reassure our customers and the public that we're still the most reliable and ethical brand of medical supplies."

"That's a good point," Steph says.

One of the guys abroad nods. "Agreed."

Dad swivels his chair to fully face me. "What do you have in mind?"

"There's an opportunity right in our noses." I enjoy the puzzlement in all their faces, despite the answer being very obvious. "Our annual benefit."

"But, like, that's not until the fall," Sheila Brown from Accounting says.

I shrug. "Why wait? Let's move it forward and be very blatant about recognizing we're trying to do better. Being painfully transparent is exactly what we need right now."

Steph snaps her fingers. "I like it, shamelessness definitely gives people what to talk about. Let's use it to steer the conversation to our advantage."

Frank winces. "Is that the argument about bad press is good press anyway?"

"There's already bad press about us right now." I lean back. "Let's use *that* press to send a positive message."

"Pulling the benefit forward will be a major task," Dad says. "Who will take care of that?"

No one responds, but I was expecting that.

And this concludes the first portion of my plan to show Dad I can be trusted. Which is why I say, "Marketing, obviously."

Every eye turns to me, including my assistant's.

I wave a hand. "Yes, I mean me."

"I definitely have no problem with that." Frank grins at me.

"Are you sure you can handle all of this?" Chris O'Donnell from HR looks like he's worried I'm going to crumble to dust in front of him.

"Yup, I'm sure. I have a very capable team." That said, I give Serena a pointed glance and when she finally looks at me, I mouth, *we'll talk after this.*

She gulps and looks down at her device screen.

"Very well, send me a quick proposal by the end of the week." With that, Dad turns to legal topics and my turn is done.

By the time the meeting is done, I have a pep in my step I would never have got before at the thought of working harder. I'm pretty sure Dad will have no choice but to at least admit I have potential after this. Why would he worry after someone who can weather a crisis like this, right?

"Follow me," I tell Serena once we're in the lobby of my office. Phelan stands guard outside the office.

Once we're inside and the door is closed, she takes a deep breath and says, "Have you lost your mind?"

I remove my blazer and hang it from the back of my chair. "Not sure what you mean."

"Let me help you understand what I mean." She puts her hands on her hips. At least the glare is directed right at my face and not at an inanimate object this time. "No event getting pulled forward does ever go well."

I plop on the chair and volley, "Well, this one will have to because it's your first assignment."

"What?"

Leaning back, I lift my feet up on the desk and cushion the back of my head with my hands. "Is that why you're sweating or is it because you're too hot?"

"*What?*" This second iteration comes out as a screech.

I put a hand on my chest. "Because of your sweater, you perv. Get your mind out of the gutter."

Serena purses her lips. "I would like to make an amendment to my contract right now to clearly state that I'm allowed to hit you any time, inside or outside the office."

"I'll talk with Legal about it. Although, I would have to add a few more clauses regarding physical contact." I grin wider the more her expression darkens.

"Let me get you a refreshment to cool your head." Then she adds, in a very pointed manner, "Sir."

I snort. "Get something for yourself, too. Before you get dehydrated."

If we were outside of the office, I have a feeling she'd have flipped me the bird. Maybe we should add that clause to her contract too—she can flip me whatever she wants.

"Shit," I say aloud, despite being alone in my office. "Maybe she's right. I'm really losing my mind."

Is this why people say the apple doesn't fall far from the tree? Because the attraction I feel for this woman is hard to deny—and it's not like I have tried much.

I run my hands down my face. Even so, I have to be professional. This is a workplace and I'm her boss. I don't want to join the douchebag club of men hitting on vulnerable women. The last thing I want is to be the Vivienne in Serena's life.

She comes back into the office with a glass of juice and some snacks on a tray. Her expression is still dark like a thunderstorm, and that's when I know I've definitely overstepped some boundaries.

Everything else before yesterday was an accident, but I'm not innocent for yesterday's comment or today's.

"Listen," I start as she approaches my desk. I stand up and circle my desk to meet her halfway, but my right foot catches on something and this time I'm the one who loses my balance. "Whoa!"

Serena tries to avoid me but it's too late. The tray and its contents fly out in one direction while her body moves the other way. I find my footing, but the juice splashes me and the plate smacks right into my chest. The cookies it had contained rain down on the floor.

She stands before me, mouth as wide as it can go. I don't even assess the damage because I know it's going to be bad. Instead, I look down at my feet and find one of them tangled in a tie. I toss my soggy chest and put two and two. Looking at Serena sweat during the meeting was contagious, and I took the tie off and stuffed it in the pocket of my blazer. It must have fallen when I removed it.

"Oh." She covers her mouth.

I raise the palm of my hand. "My bad."

"I mean, yes, but I'm sorry for—" she motions at the mess down my clothes.

"Don't worry about it."

Fortunately, the disaster zone doesn't extend to my pants. It's an easy fix.

I march back to the shelves behind my desk, where among my blood supply and other essentials, I keep several changes of clothes for all occasions. I peel the soiled vest off and toss it on the floor before working on the buttons of my shirt.

"Can you please bring me a towel from the bathroom?"

She clears her throat. "Yes, right away."

I run a finger across my skin. "Make it damp, please."

When she returns with the damp towel, I've already removed my shirt and am folding it along with the vest. I take the terrycloth and run it across my chest and stomach quickly.

"Believe it or not, before this little accident happened, I had just been about to apologize."

Serena blinks really hard but doesn't say anything. I toss the towel on my chair and shrug into the sleeves of the first shirt I find in the closet.

"And I also know the fact that you've seen me half naked more times than you should have is probably not making my case." I turn my back to her as I button the shirt up and tuck it into my slacks. "But uh, I just wanted to let you know that if my comments yesterday or today have made you uncomfortable, I'm sorry and I'll strive to behave appropriately."

Once I'm presentable, I turn back to her. Her eyes fly up to mine quickly.

Still, no response.

"Serena?"

"Is that what you meant yesterday?" she asks, stretching the neck of her top. "When you asked if these things were accidents or meant to tempt you? Because I'm wondering the same thing about you."

A flash of heat travels through my body.

"I can assure you it has all been accident from my side," I say.

Serena nods. "Same here. Which means *nothing* should happen *on purpose*."

I know exactly what the pointed look in her face means. Still, I say it aloud, "In other words, everything until now is forgiven as long as nothing else happens in the future?"

She gives a grim smile. "Smart guy."

"Sure am," I murmur, wishing I could play a fool because not so deep down, I want more accidents to happen.

CHAPTER 31
SERENA

sit on a bench, just existing for a bit.

In the past month, I've managed to plan and launch what I've called Operation Warp Speed in a Black Hole of Doom. It has meant consecutive workdays of minimum twelve hours long and no weekends—a major effort to coordinate the company's benefit event two months earlier than its usual timeline.

All without knowing jack shit about organizing events, or even knowing jack all about Comed Solutions' history of benefit events.

I take a deep breath. This place is not the kind where I should have these thoughts.

But nope, I still hate my boss.

And yep, at the same time I also want to pour any liquid on his shirt *by accident* and force him to remove it right in front of me. Again.

"Ugh." I hang my head. I came here precisely to not think about him and here I am, failing spectacularly.

Squeals and a battalion of footsteps distract me for a second. From between the strands of my hair, I catch sight of a small army of kids of all ages and sizes, running this way and that behind a ball.

Ah, to be that young and innocent. To only care about a ball.

"Why are you sitting here instead of playing?"

The familiar voice makes me turn. Sister Emilia walks over, wheeling a massive cooler along. I know exactly what it contains. "Can I have one of those?"

"Of course, dear. You bought them in the first place." I open and close my hands at her like I'm a kid, and she takes a seat on the bench beside me. "But perhaps you should wait until the kids are done with the game."

"Hmph, I was looking forward to some favoritism."

The wrinkles in the corners of her eyes deepen with a smile. "Were you, now?"

Well, no. Sister Emilia is the blueprint of fairness. She has to be, considering she's the head of the orphanage. Keeping about fifty kids in check would be impossible if there was a pecking order.

"I should be an exception," I argue half-heartedly, folding my arms. "It's been six years since I left, and I brought the goodies."

She pats my shoulder. "You shouldn't expect rewards from good deeds."

Dang it, didn't I say this to my boss a while back?

And there it is, the image of Caleb Oh changing his shirt in his office, engraved in my mind for posterity. Along with every time he's come out dripping from a body of water, dressed in essentially only that water.

I flop on the bench.

"What's worrying you so much, dear?"

How could I even explain this?

"It's work," I say, because yes, that's how it starts. "Things have changed ever since I started working at this place."

"Like what?"

Even though I know I have her full attention, her eyes are focused on the kids playing in the patio. A couple of the other nuns play with them, and three more keep an eye on the kids who aren't interested in chasing the ball.

I almost feel bad for keeping Sister Emilia away from them, but I'm glad she doesn't turn me away—probably never will. No matter how many years pass since I last lived in this place, she's the only constant in my rudderless life.

"Everything." I kick the dirt under my feet. "The world isn't the same it was before."

For once, now I know vampires are real.

For two, my boss is one.

For three, I don't mind it.

For four, I do mind that he's going to be engaged to a gorgeous specimen of his kind.

She casts a worried glance my way. "Are they mistreating you?"

"No." I sigh and push my loose hair behind my ears. "I mean I do have a project right now that is working me to the bone but that's not it. It's my boss. How to explain it…"

"Is he bullying you?" She pushes her sleeves up her small arms, making me laugh. I would love to see Sister Emilia in her tiny sixty-year-old glory, squaring up with Caleb Oh.

"Not at all." It takes me a moment to recover from that imagery. "It's more or less the opposite? He's too…"

Sister Emilia sucks in a sharp breath. "He isn't coming on to you, is he?"

I wince. "We might sort of be coming onto each other?"

"Oh." As the fight leaves her, her chest deflates and she sits placidly for a second. The fight returns and puffs her up again. "He's not married, is he?"

"No." I wave both hands. "Goodness, no."

She blinks at me. "So if there's nothing inappropriate, and you like each other, what is the issue? Is he a bad person?"

"He's…" I look on as one of the smaller kids scores a goal and runs around celebrating as though he's Lionel Messi playing for the Inter Miami. "He's sort of like that kid. Silly, full of much more joy than I feel on my best days. Because he's lived a very privileged life I can't even imagine. And I guess that's the issue?"

Something lodges in my throat and I swallow it down with difficulty.

I twist on the bench to face her fully. "Yes, that's the crux of it. It's not just that he's my boss and I'm essentially his secretary, which is already a weird power dynamic. He just lives in an entirely different world."

So different, I can't even explain it in words without sounding more unhinged than I already am.

I lower my face to my hands and just stay like that for a while. "But I think I like him."

And now I can't stop talking.

"I know I shouldn't," I say, facing Sister Emilia again. "This is my first job out of college and I have to do well. My future hinges on it. I can't mess it up because of silly things like this."

There's a crease between her eyebrows. "Feelings aren't silly. You have to acknowledge them properly so they don't hurt you or others down the road."

"But Sister Emilia, I have no time for feelings." I have to bite my lip to stop it from trembling. "I'm not like other people. All I have to rely on is myself, I can't get distracted from that fact."

The void in my chest that I try to avoid makes itself known—the place that wouldn't hurt if my parents were here to tell me that I can always count on them, no matter how tough things are.

But they're not. It's only me, fending for myself. And it's worked well enough for the twenty-four years of my life, but not right now. I'm torn between wanting something I shouldn't, and the lonely path I *must* continue on.

"Child, that's not true." She brushes my hair away from my face and sets her hand on my head. It makes me feel like I'm seven again, when I was left at the orphanage's doorstep after losing my dad. "You're never truly alone."

As she extends her arms, I go in for a hug. After a moment, I mumble, "Maybe I should quit."

Half of the kids forgot they were playing soccer and started chatting in the middle of the patio, and it's kinda funny to see the serious players continue around them. I wish I had either of those attitudes. The fresh carelessness or the fierce determination to keep pushing on.

"Serena Maria Lossada Martinez," she says, hands on hips. "Your parents didn't make a quitter, and I didn't raise you like one."

The way I cringe turns me into a human raisin. I've grown so used to projecting a self-sufficient aura for the past six years, I forgot what it feels like when someone—this very specific someone—whips out my full name.

"Arturo was a hard-worker who never gave up, and from what I heard from him, so was Esperanza."

"I won't quit," I mumble.

I'm luckier than a lot of these kids. While I never knew my mom, since she died while giving birth to me, I did live with my dad for the first seven years of my life. And Sister Emilia is right, dad was always working. Always busy. Making sure we had a roof over our heads and food in our bellies.

Sister Emilia got to meet him, since Dad belonged to the parish where her congregation has their church. Thanks to those infrequent interactions, she's able to give me glimpses of what I lost.

She reaches into the cooler and finally gives me one of the popsicles. "I still remember how excited he was when he got that job at a big company, he said it was all so you could have the life he never had."

I sniffle but keep eating my treat. "Silly Dad, my life was always going to be up to me."

"But he didn't know that." She smiles, serene even in her sadness. "He thought working for Comed would solve all your problems."

The popsicle slips from my grasp and falls on my lap with a splat. "Wait, what? Where?"

"Comed? You know, that big company." She picks the popsicle up and returns it to me. "Oh, that might leave a stain now."

I close my mouth with a snap. "That's where I'm working now. Comed."

She blinks a few times really fast. "Well, what a coincidence."

A shiver goes down my back.

I know this place brings out the vulnerability in me that I keep under tight wraps everywhere else, but I can't help feeling like there's something fateful about this. Like everything that happened in my life led here, to this moment—and to Comed. But where's the connection?

With my luck, it'll be Caleb Oh. And instead of being able to keep a respectable distance from him, I will continue to be drawn to him by forces beyond my control. And that... is the scariest thought of all.

CHAPTER 32
CALEB

"Shit." I'm on my knees, leaving a puddle of sweat on the mat beneath me. "Won't you give me an opening?"

"No," Phelan says, not even producing a drop of sweat on his temple. He looms over me like the blueprint for most comic superheroes.

I sit on my haunches just trying to catch a breath. He's been pounding me like a punching bag and throwing me on the floor like a sack of potatoes. Every time I try to defend, deflect or attack, without fail, Phelan thwarts my plans and gains the upper hand faster than I can process.

"Have you ever been defeated?" I ask, expecting he'll say no but hoping there's at least one instance.

"Once. By your father," he says, looking down at me in a clear show of superiority.

I sound like a robot when I say, "Ah."

Chuckling behind me reminds me we're not alone. Daniel sits on a bench, munching on carrot sticks and producing the same amount of noise as a trash compactor. "Best abandon all hope, Caleb."

"Consider it done." I run my hand through my sweaty hair. "Doesn't mean I should stop trying to get stronger, right?"

"Of course not." A few seconds of my brother chomping carrots go by before he speaks again. "But why are you doing this in the first place?"

Slowly, careful of the sores all over my body that will go away soon but still throb like toothaches, I lean down until I'm flat on my back. A vampire-shaped starfish on the dirty mat.

"Trust me, if I could do something else I would," I say, blinking against the harsh white lights above me. "But I made a deal with Dad. Also, when are you going to stop eating?"

Daniel ignores that last part. "What kind of deal?"

I lean my head back to look at him, and it's kinda funny to see him eat upside down. "More or less, if I show him that I'm self-sufficient, I won't have to get engaged with Vivienne From Hell Astor."

That finally does it and Daniel sets his snack aside. "Whoa, really?"

Pulling energy from my reserves, I haul myself back to an upright position and motion at Phelan to help me stand up. The guy pulls me back up to my feet as though this wasn't the two hundredth time today.

"Let's do this again." I lower my center of gravity and raise up my arms.

Phelan stands like a mannequin, not putting up any guards or making any attempts to come at me. That's the annoying thing about him, he never initiates engagement but he always finishes it. It's the other guy—me right now—who has to put all the effort, only to land ass first on the ground.

So far I've tried attacking his face, his gut, his knees, and his sides. Nothing works. All I'm trying to do is learn how to react, how to fall, and where I'm most vulnerable.

The answer to the latter is: everywhere. Phelan hasn't a single opening, but I'm a walking opening.

I start by an easy jab. Phelan's head jerks out of the way. My goal here is to be annoying enough that he has to lift one arm to block. I give a combo that's worked for anyone else not named Phelan Murray. Jab, counter to the gut, a twist, and elbow to the jaw.

He sees me coming from a mile away and uses my elbow to twist my arm. I spin with the same motion and get out of the lock before he can tighten it. But all he has to do is sweep his leg under my most unstable one and I taste the mattress. Literally. I fall with my mouth gaping open and now there's a lot of salty goodness all over my taste buds.

"Again," I say, getting back up on my feet like a newborn foal.

"Your footing's unstable," Phelan explains, widening his stance in an exaggerated manner so I get the point. "Be one with the floor."

I bark a laugh. "Haven't I become intimate with it already?"

"Not in that sense." He points at his feet and knees. "Make it so these always know where the floor is."

"Is he speaking English?" I ask my brother.

Daniel shrugs. "I think he means you have to learn not to fall so damn much."

Deadpan, I say, "Gee, thanks."

"Let's do the same combination again." Phelan motions at me to start. "I will sweep your leg again. Don't fall this time."

"Okay." Somehow my heart is beating even faster this second time around. I want to succeed, if only so I don't feel like the past two hours of torture have been for nothing.

I go at it one more time. Jab, counter, elbow. Phelan twists my arm and I don't resist. As I move along with his motion, I know he's about to sweep my leg. Which one had it been? Left or right?

Shit, does it even matter?

Then I feel it. My left was unstable as I tried to recover from the twist. He sweeps it and the world starts to tilt. At the last second I push at the earth with my hands, arms working as springs. Rather than tasting salty mattress again, I jump back to my feet and lift up my guards. Too late, because Phelan lands a punch at my chin that rings my bell.

Once I'm able to clear the blinking lights in my eyes, I find Daniel hovering over me. "Wow, that was awesome, Caleb."

I groan. "What was, aside from Phelan massacring me?"

My brother offers his hand out to me. "You made him get serious."

"Go me." I accept his help and even lean on Dan for a second before I gather my bearings. Phelan comes into view, wiping one bead of sweat. "Oh yeah, look at him. He struggled so hard to defeat me just now."

"You didn't eat the floor again, though," Phelan says.

"Can you please just let me punch you once? For free?"

The top bodyguard of the Oh family's security forces snorts. "No."

"Party pooper."

"I brought you some blood to help you recover," my brother says as he walks me back to the bench he vacated. "Drink it to the last drop."

I wince. The taste of blood mixing with sweaty gym floor is the last sort of cocktail I want right now, but Daniel is right. Unless I want to spend a really crappy rest of my weekend with bruises everywhere the eye can and can't see, I best feed.

I take a deep breath before starting on the first bag of blood.

"You must be really serious about not marrying Vivienne, huh?" Daniel says, going back to his snack and crunching like a rabbit.

Pausing the feeding, I gag on air and it takes me a moment

to recover before I'm able to speak. "Yeah, I'll do all I can to not marry her. Including getting pummeled by Phelan."

Daniel munches in silence for a while, his eyes lost in the distance. "I'm sorry, little brother. This is my fault," he murmurs at last.

"Huh?" is all I manage to utter before the urge to puke my guts out hits me. I close my yap and lean my head back to force the contents of my gut to stay down.

Daniel continues as normal. "You might not have been forced into these circumstances if I hadn't married first."

When the first bag is finished and I toss it aside, I say, "Ugh, this one tasted extra bad. I want to barf."

From across the room, Phelan pauses from cleaning the equipment we used and commands, "Drink another one."

"But—"

He narrows his eyes. "Another one."

I scrunch my face up and pick up a second bag from the cooler. To my brother, I say, "Anyway, it's not your fault. It's Dad's, and maybe your mom's. They think I can't survive on my own unless I have the backing of the Astors."

Both of them give me very meaningful looks that aren't accompanied by words.

"You assholes. You agree with them."

"I don't necessarily agree that it has to be the Astors." Dan raises his hands in the air, forming an invisible barrier between us. "But, yes. If these attacks continue and get worse, you'll be in trouble by yourself."

"And I get that, which is why I'm asking Phelan to kick my ass everyday from now on." I drink some more blood before continuing, "But that's another strange thing. Why, all of a sudden, is Dad concerned his protection isn't enough? I know I've been lucky in the past attempts to my life, but not only is Dad the strongest vampire on earth, he also has the best trained fleet of bodyguards. Why is my safety suddenly an issue? What's happening that I don't know about?"

The fact that Daniel stays silent as a tomb tells me I'm on the right track. There's something. He knows it, but he can't tell me.

"Fine, don't spill the beans. But at least support me on my quest to keep Vivienne the hell away."

"I will." My brother squeezes my shoulder. "I'll do everything in my power to help you. Including signing up for the let's-beat-Caleb-up club."

"Membership's closed to only one Phelan Murray," I say.

"Hey, I may be not as skilled as Phelan's pinky finger, but I'm definitely better than you."

"I hate that you're right," I tell him, drinking the last of the second bag of blood. "Wanna go?"

Daniel tosses his carrot aside. "Let's go, little bro."

CHAPTER 33
SERENA

The Serena Lossada engine is powered entirely by coffee. Like oil, the thicker it is, the more energy I glean from it.

It's been two months of working non-stop and the benefit is tonight. I am both relieved that this torture will finally end, and terrified that something will go wrong and I'll be blamed for it. Never mind that I had to come up with the concept, calculate the budget, book the venue, invite the guests, press and partners, align the calendars of the entire upper echelon of Comed Solutions, draft speeches, oversee the decorations and catering, book the entertainment, arrange transportation and overnight stays for anyone out of state—and not die in the process. If something goes wrong, every effort will be in vain.

There were a few close calls along the way. A month ago, the band I had contracted cancelled after one of the members got into an accident. While looking for a replacement, I discovered that one of the hotel bookings for a visitor didn't actually get processed, and also that the caterer I had selected didn't have a good selection of vegan options.

Somehow, through lots of tears, I managed to get through

all of the crises. The days propelled forward at the speed of a rocket even though they were all the same—just me sitting at my desk, tapping on the keyboard, or having phone calls from seven in the morning until midnight.

But here we are. At last.

I'm trembling from head to toe as I tick items off the list on my iPad. The temperature is cooling down and there's still enough sun out that as the guests arrive, they can admire the way we've dressed this little corner of the Bahia Honda State Park. Soon, the sky will start turning to the beautiful dusk hues that will make the perfect backdrop for the pictures.

We're almost ready to get this event started.

"Press is here," Marissa says to my ear piece.

Even though it's good news, my heartbeat spikes. "Excellent. Is everyone else in position?"

"Yep, we're good to go."

I'm in the middle of doing some breathing exercises when another voice sounds from behind me. "Everything under control?"

"Absolutely." I turn to face my boss. In my mind, I add the word *not*. "All players are in position. We should get started."

Caleb's garbed along with the dress code, in a soft blue linen shirt and tight white pants that piss me off. Because not only he looks incredible enough to belong in a pictorial, it's clear to me that while I was working like a horse, he had plenty of time to work out.

He's buffer than the last time I saw him wearing little—and trust me, I *remember*—whereas I feel like I've gained weight from stress eating, and there are dark bags under my eyes that not even concealer could hide. It's unfair.

Caleb stuffs his hands in the pockets of his pants, checking out the crowd milling around the stage, the catering team fluttering about to see to their expensive needs.

"You've done an outstanding job in such short time."

Pushing my glasses up my nose, I say, "I'm glad it's obvious."

His eyes positively twinkle at my sass, which is annoying because it makes me want to say something that will cause an even bigger reaction. I keep my mouth pressed firmly shut.

Caleb's smile turns enigmatic. "It is, and it won't go unrewarded."

As we stand there, staring at each other, it's not the humid air what's making me break into a sweat. The way he looks at me makes ideas pop into my head of how he might be planning to reward me. None of them can be considered safe for work.

Which is the opposite of what I've sworn to strive for. Career over bros.

I clear my throat. "I won't accept any reward other than a raise and extra vacation days."

Caleb's eyelids are half mast. "What kind of raise?"

"Ten percent," I blurt out, without even thinking about it, anything to move the conversation past the unspoken tension.

"Deal." He shrugs. "And what about vacations?"

"Two weeks right after this event," I say. This, I did think about previously. In fact, the paid time off request is already on his inbox.

"Anything else?" Caleb asks.

Someone says something in my ear piece but I can't hear anything over the rushing of my blood to my face.

Yes, I want to say. *So much more.*

"No," I squeak out. "That'll be all, *sir.*"

Caleb's expression sours a bit at the emphasis I put in the last word.

I guess I shouldn't blame him for making me work so hard for the past couple of months, when that provided an excellent respite from him. Since he started showing up to the office regularly every morning, I spared myself from having to see him working out or swimming in his apartment facilities. And it was hard to moon over him when my entire attention was dedicated to work. If anything, I should thank him.

"Now, would you please join your father on stage?" I ask, ushering him in that direction. "It's time to begin."

Caleb gives me one last look before heading over to the spotlight. With a few strategic directions from me to the team, the event finally kicks off with a short speech from Cedric Oh, thanking everyone for joining. I don't pay much attention to his words as I busy myself working behind the scenes.

When it's Caleb's turn to speak, I'm with the catering team running inventory. His voice sounds clear over the noise, but I wonder if it's just because I've grown so attuned to him.

"We're not perfect," he's saying as I count champagne bottles. "But today we want to show you that we don't have to be perfect to do the right thing."

Oh, that's a good soundbite. Did he write it? Because I didn't.

That thought distracts me and I lose my count. I have to start over again to realize we're short on bubbly. I'll have to send someone from the catering team to buy more. Thankfully, Joe is on standby with the Bad Blood to assist.

"And the right thing," Caleb continues saying. "Is that we try to return to nature what it gives us. Which is why this year's theme is reforestation. Comed Solutions will strive to plant three trees for every one tree our supply chain uses in our products, starting today."

I peek out from the catering tent to catch Caleb as he descends the stage. It was a massive ordeal to get the park administrators to agree to us planting a ceremonial tree, but there's very little the Ohs can't accomplish with money. Like we rehearsed, Caleb poses for a few pictures as he plants a tree just a few paces beyond the stage, going as far as shoveling the dirt himself.

His shirt tightens around his arms and shoulders in a way that is guaranteed to gather a lot of funds. Especially since he's one of the main items for the charity auction to gather funds for reforesting the Amazon. I still can't believe he and his father agreed to that idea when I tossed it after days of sleep deprivation.

That's precisely the next part of the event. Top executives from the company, including Cedric and Caleb, offer a couple of hours of their expertise in auction to the public. Daniel earns a cool five grand from a local university that wants to pick his brain on hematology research. Cedric earns half of my yearly salary from a politician clearly looking to score points for his next political campaign. And then, it's Caleb's turn.

The MC, who is actually the singer from the band I hired, motions at Caleb as the younger Oh climbs back on the stage. "And here we have Caleb Oh, the young heartthrob of the Oh family. But don't let his looks fool you, Caleb has one of the highest IQs in the country. What are a couple of hours of his time worth? Do we have any bids?"

"One thousand dollars," someone shouts from the crowd. As it parts, a very old lady raises her number high in the air.

I have to stuff my fist against my mouth not to laugh. But that mirth vanishes in thin air as another voice rings.

"Ten thousand dollars."

A newcomer emerges from the crowd. Vivienne Astor shows up like a vision in a white empress cut dress that emphasizes her attributes in a very suggesting, but still tasteful way. She waves a plate with an auction number lazily.

The MC whistles low. "Ten thousand! Do we have another bid?"

The old lady harrumphs. "Fifteen thousand."

Murmurs ripple across the attendants. From my broke-ass

corner, I'm rooting for the old lady. Judging by the way Caleb frowns at Vivienne, I have a feeling he's on the same boat.

The blonde woman smiles. "Twenty five thousand."

"Twenty five going on once, going on—"

"Thirty thousand!" the old lady shouts, and I have to admire her for putting up a good fight.

But it's all over when Vivienne says, "Fifty thousand." That's higher than the bid for Cedric's time.

I shouldn't feel bothered that Caleb's fiancée won a bid for two hours of his time, so as soon as she's declared the winner I focus my attention back to making sure everything runs smoothly.

The band is now playing some ambiance jazz in the background of many conversations. I catch Caleb giving statements to the press and get distracted by a couple of suppliers who recognize me from our visit what feels like ages ago.

I take a glass of cool lemonade with me to the pier just to catch some air. It's mostly empty, except from a couple of attendees who had the same idea, but they're quiet and don't bother me.

I stare out at the ocean as it merges with the purples in the darkening sky. I'm glad I'll be able to take a couple of weeks off, not just because I need to catch up on sleep—but because I also need a break from Comed. And Caleb.

Feeling foolish for not being able to bid for his time *is* foolish, when what I need to do is spend less time around him.

"What was your name again?"

I startle and spill some of the lemonade on my iPad. As I turn, I try to clean the device with my dress. "Oh, hi, Miss Astor. I'm Serena Lossada."

With the fair lights all over the pier railings illuminating her, she looks like a fae come to life. Also, she's a bit too close for what I consider polite. I take a step back and my back ends right up against the railing.

Vivienne Astor looks me up and down. I feel inadequate standing in front of her in my H&M dress. "I saw the way you looked at Caleb earlier."

Every cell of my body freezes.

I can't even come up with a blanket statement in defense, because I don't feel innocent anyway.

"And I feel so sorry for you." Vivienne leans closer to me, resting her hand against the railing. "It's like looking at the moon from earth, right? You can admire its beauty all you want, but it'll never be within your reach. That's what Caleb is like for you, right?"

Nailed it.

Still, I muster enough annoyance to say, "Excuse me?"

There's a crunching sound I can't explain, especially since it sounds very close to me.

Vivienne's smile widens. "Let this be a warning, Miss Lossada. Don't get any inappropriate ideas about Caleb in that pretty little head of yours."

Then, before I'm able to react, I pitch backwards and I'm falling.

CHAPTER 34
CALEB

sweep my eyes among the crowd, trying to find my assistant. I want Serena to be in some of these pictures because without her this whole event wouldn't be happening. But she's nowhere to be found.

Marissa and Jon are nearby, so I join them. "Have you seen Serena?"

"She was here a second ago," Marissa says, glancing around her as though that will materialize the other girl.

Without looking up from his phone, Jon says, "I saw her head toward the pier."

"Thanks."

One of the suppliers stops me on the way, but she realizes pretty soon that I have somewhere else to go and I promise to find her again later. Dad makes eye contact with me and when I veer the opposite way, I come face to face with Phelan.

"Your father wants to see you."

"Let him wait." I walk around the bodyguard. Although his footsteps follow, I know he's not going to haul me on his shoulder and present me before Dad without my willing consent. At least not in front of everybody.

My loafers dig into the sand, slowing down my walk toward the pier. There's a couple of people chatting on the east side, and two women on the westside. One of them is obviously Vivienne, with her mane of hair glinting like strands of gold in the sunset. In front of her, against the railing, is my assistant.

"What the hell are they doing?" Of course Phelan doesn't respond behind me, but I can't help wondering what this unlikely pair is doing together.

That's when Vivienne snaps the railing with a simple push like it's made of crackers, and tips Serena over the edge.

I freeze for a precious second, the image replaying in my head.

Did I hallucinate that?

Then the other bystanders notice and turn to the scene of the accident. And then I remember that Serena doesn't know how to swim.

I kick my shoes off and break into a sprint. Pebbles dig into the soles of my feet and I kick my legs harder. There's roaring in my ears and that's all I can hear. Not the crashing waves. Not the wind. Not the couple making a rucks as Vivienne leaves the scene. I pass her by on the pier, if only because I can't dally by throwing her over the railing like I wish.

"Out of the way!" I shout to the other two and peer down at the water. It's dark under the waning light and I can't see any signs of my assistant.

I jump. I'm only conscious of my heart hammering hard against my ribcage. I wish I could see half as well in the dark as Dad and Daniel can, because it almost feels as though I'm floating in a dark void. I flap my arms about, trying to bump into something, until eventually my eyes get used to the dark.

There. Serena is sinking in the water, unmoving. I don't know if it's because she stopped fighting or if she's unconscious already. I swim toward her as fast as I can and grab her in my arms. Kicking my legs hard, I pull us to the surface. While I immediately gulp for air, she's limp in my arms.

Cursing, I wade through the water until I make it to the shore. "Hang in there, Serena. Please."

Serena is slumped on my arms and I can't make out whether she's breathing. As I set her down on the sand, I start praying that it's not too late. Because if it is, I'll become a murderer tonight.

I start compressions, counting each one to the rhythm of the word *please*. But they don't kick off her breathing right away. Leaning her head back into the sand, I plug her nose and breathe into her mouth. I notice her chest rise, but even after pausing, her lungs aren't kick-starting.

A bolt of ice-cold fear stabs through my chest.

"Please, Serena. You can't leave like this."

I start compressions again, unaware of the people gathering around us. All I focus is on her. On how pale her face looks. On her terrifying stillness.

And then, just before I'm about to start crying, her body jerks with a spasm. She coughs water violently, sending her glasses flying from her face. They held on through all of this ordeal until this point, and the second she comes to, Serena starts palming around to find them.

Trembling, I reach over her to retrieve and put them in her hands. With a soft voice, I say, "Welcome back."

I want to hug her. I want to kiss her.

More than anything, I want to kill Vivienne.

"What?" is all Serena is able to say while a coughing fit takes over her. I pat her back, trying to help her work it all out of her system. Once the worst has passed, she sags and I catch her before she collapses. "What happened?"

"You were pushed into the water," I respond, without further ado.

"Are you okay, dear?" a woman asks. I look up and through

the dim lights of the decor around us, I make her out as the woman who'd been on the pier. She saw the whole thing.

As Serena is unable to respond, I say, "She'll be fine."

I'll make sure of that.

I gather her in my arms and pick her up. She makes a sound almost like mewling.

Phelan is right beside me in a heartbeat. "I can take her."

"You won't," I say, and he leaves it at that.

He does help clear the path from people as I set course to a staff tent. I glance down for just a second and catch Serena's eyes squeezed shut. I suspect that she's trying to keep reality at bay.

"Phelan," I say.

"Yes?"

"Secure the witnesses." He freezes, probably torn between his real duty of staying by me the whole time, and doing as I say. "Go. Nothing's gonna happen here."

"Very well."

After he leaves, I turn to the staff. "You, find a towel. You, get a warm drink, preferably not coffee. You, make room over there."

They move to follow the directions with various degrees of enthusiasm. Someone brings a foldable chair and that's where I settle Serena. Her dress is stuck to her frame like a second skin, the skirt riding up too high up her thighs. I kneel down before her and push the soggy fabric down to cover her.

Looking up into her eyes, I say, "I'll take care of this."

I'm not sure if she's crying, with drops of water trickling from her face and hair, but her eyes are definitely scared and sad. I brush hair away from her forehead a second before someone comes with two towels. I wrap one around her shoulders and the other one I stretch over her lap.

"Um, what about you, sir?" the guy who brought them asks.

"I'm fine."

But I'm not fine. I'm so volcanically pissed, I'm pretty sure the water from my clothes is starting to evaporate.

Just outside the tent, I find Dad and Daniel about to come in. A few paces behind them, Phelan ushers the two witnesses toward us.

"What did you do, Caleb?" Dad asks, sighing as he sees my wet-rat look.

I have to take several deep breaths before I'm sure I can speak without screaming. "What did *I* do? More like what did Vivienne do. She tossed my assistant into the water for no reason."

Daniel gasps. "What the—"

"What reason would Vivienne have to do that?" Dad asks, frowning.

"Hell if I know. What I do know is that Serena can't swim. She could've died."

Dad shakes his head. "I'm sure it was an accident."

"Was it?" I ask the witnesses as they stand behind my dad.

The two of them, a human woman and man somewhere in their forties, glance at each other as if they'd rather magically teleport anywhere else.

"Well, I can't be sure," the man starts saying.

Less hesitant, the woman adds, "But it didn't look like an accident. I mean, one second the railing is in one piece and the next it breaks, and the girl falls into the water. It's strange."

It's even strange to me, knowing how incredibly strong Vivienne is. I can't fathom why she'd target my assistant like that.

"Thank you," Dad says to them, motioning to Phelan with his head to take them away. Back to me, he continues. "Regardless of what they think they saw, I'm sure it was an accident. Vivienne's a smart girl, she wouldn't do anything to get us in trouble."

I note how he doesn't defend her character, but only her intentions. Dad himself must know that Vivienne is a shitty person, but has wits to commend her.

Maybe she wanted to scare Serena off for whatever screwed up reason she got in her twisted head, thinking Serena would swim back to shore and would just spend an embarrassing night explaining to people that she took a swim in her clothes. But even if she pulled this prank only out of pettiness, it could've been lethal. For that alone, I can never let this go.

I lean closer to Dad. "Maybe their testimonies are negligible, but I know what I saw. Vivienne pushed Serena into the water and could've killed her. How can I be fine with that? How can *you* be fine with that?"

"Be rational—"

"No." I'm shaking from head to toe. "I'm not going to be rational about this. I'm going to be very, very emotional. And despite that, I won't regret what I'm about to say."

My brother puts a hand on my shoulder. "Hold on, Caleb—"

I bat his hand away and tell Dad, "I'm never going to marry Vivienne Astor. Mark my words."

CHAPTER 35
SERENA

When I thought the benefit might kill me, I didn't mean it in a literal way. All I thought was that it would put me through the figurative wringer, and I'd spend the rest of the weekend in a deep sleep.

Instead, I almost died. Literally.

It was Marissa who later told me what happened. She didn't witness the rescue, but she heard it from a woman who did. My boss dove into the water and fished me out, then gave me CPR and brought me back to life. In front of a bunch of people.

The next day, the picture that appeared in the news wasn't of him planting a tree or of the elaborately decorated venue. It was of Caleb Oh, walking out of the water like some sea deity, with a passed out blob of a woman in his arms. The press ignored the event or the reasons for it, instead putting the spotlight on the billionaire heir who risked his life to save someone else.

I mean, I guess it's good press for the company, which was ultimately the goal of the event. So thanks to me it was successful—just not in the way I planned.

The shot of adrenaline stayed in my blood much longer than caffeine, and despite barely getting any sleep last night, this morning I'm jittery with nervous energy. I know if I stay in bed, all I'll do is marinate the worst of the events last night until I become even more of a wreck. That's why, even though it's my first day off in months, I'm kneeling in the bathroom scrubbing the tile grouting.

Behind me, I hear giggling. Karyn says, "Wow, that's a really flattering angle on you."

I stop moving and count to five. Tossing the dirty brush at her smug face will probably lead to a lot of drama I'd rather not deal with, despite how much I'd like to snap.

Instead, I say, "Yup, I know I have a great butt."

She snorts and a second later I hear her footsteps fade away.

That's not probably what she meant. I'm sure she was just referring to me on all fours, cleaning. It's not the first time she makes a comment alluding to her belief that this is what I should be doing with my life, cleaning after hers.

I make a pause to pull out my cellphone from the pocket of my ratty jeans and check out my bank account. It's definitely healthier than it's ever been, but I'm nowhere near close enough to clearing my credit card debt or paying off my astronomical student loans from business school. It'll still be a while yet until I'm able to free myself from Karyn's tyranny.

My phone pings with an incoming message and my heart skips a beat when I see the sender. Caleb Oh.

You up?

I scrunch up my nose and reply back. *Who isn't up at ten in the morning?*

Normally, me, he replies. His three dots work for a couple of seconds more before another text comes in. *But anyway, this is good because I have an emergency and I need you.*

I'm on vacation, I respond and put my phone back in my pocket. I would rather keep unearthing questionable dirt from the bathroom than consider the fact that Caleb gave me CPR.

Of course, my butt starts buzzing with an incoming call. I sigh and don't even have to look at the name of the caller to know who it is.

"What?"

"Good morning," Caleb says. "I'm downstairs."

"*What?*"

That much louder question prompts Karyn to shout from the living room, "Keep it down! Richard and I are trying to watch something."

Rolling my eyes, I ask my boss, "What do you mean?"

"Coral Breeze Apartments, right?" he says, making me freeze. "If so, I'm downstairs."

"What the hell are you doing downstairs?"

"Waiting for you." There's a short pause. "Should I come upstairs?"

"No!" I scramble to my feet and look at my reflection in the mirror. My cheeks are flushed from the previous exertion, or from the fact Caleb Oh is freaking here. "Why are you here on my day off?"

"Because it's an emergency and I really need you."

I whine. "You're not going to let me off the hook, right?"

"Nope." Why does he sound almost happy? Then he adds, "I'll give you ten minutes, but after that I'm marching right up to unit one six nine and banging on the door until you come out."

"You will pay for this," I say, despite having absolutely no means to follow through with that promise.

"Ten minutes," is all he says before hanging up.

I dash past the living room, where my roommate and her boyfriend are making out on the couch, rather than watching the TV. In my room, I change out of my slightly sweaty clothes and grab my purse. I don't even bother fixing my hair out of the messy bun at the top of my head, because I have to make it downstairs in less than the allotted time. The last thing I want is for Karyn and her greasy boyfriend to see who I work for, deduce I make more money than I actually do, and demand a bigger cut.

"I'll be back later," I say, although they don't pay attention to me since they're busy with each other.

Outside, I spot Caleb leaning against the Lamborghini SUV. He wears a pair of aviators that shade his eyes from the relentless Miami sun. A hot breeze picks at the edge of his white linen shirt, giving me a glimpse of cut abs for a hot second. The pair of jeans he wears hug his figure in all the right places.

I can understand why a girl would lose her senses over a guy. Caleb is the visual example why.

Alas, I do have self-restraint.

I stomp across the parking lot until I reach him. "Let's go."

The corners of his lips draw into a smile as he opens the door to the backseat for me. I'm glad that my roommate and her boyfriend are busy and can't see this bizarre scene unfolding in the parking lot. The median income of residents in this place is probably around thirty grand per year. No one can afford a car like this.

Caleb climbs in behind me, and it's because Phelan Murray sits at the driver's seat.

"So, what's going on?" I ask. The only sort of response I get is Phelan passing a paper bag to me along with a drink.

"First of all, I got you some breakfast," Caleb says as the other guy drives us away from my apartment complex.

I peer down at the contents of the brown bag and find a wrap sandwich that smells delicious. "Um, I already had breakfast, though."

"Eat again, you'll need the energy." Caleb reaches for a drink of his own, some sort of green juice.

Side-eyeing him, I ask, "Why is that?"

He looks at me, expression all innocent-like as he sips his juice. And he says nothing else during the entire ride, no matter how many questions I make. Phelan is impenetrable as a wall, as usual. I eventually eat the meal, if only because the smell makes my stomach rumble and because there's nothing else to do.

Gradually, we progress through the intense traffic until I start recognizing the streets. "Wait, are we going to your place?"

Even though it's pretty obvious, Caleb still says nothing. He checks his phone and hums the song in the radio, sipping juice very slowly.

As we get out of the car in his building's parking lot, I ask, "Can you finally tell me what the emergency is?"

"You'll see."

The two of them tower over me in the elevator. What could these huge onions need from me on a weekend?

Somehow, I expect Caleb's apartment to be a total mess but everything looks normal the second the elevator spits us out. Phelan motions at me to follow him, and we head toward the guest room. Whatever I could possibly expect isn't what I get—he opens the door and shows me the bed completely covered by a pile of clothes.

"Please wear whichever is most comfortable," the man says before vanishing.

"Huh?" I take a step into the room and squint at the garments. They're swimsuits. Of all shapes and forms. "What the…"

The door closes behind me and muffled, Caleb's voice comes from the other side. "You're not getting out of here until you're wearing one."

I try pulling the door open, but he's either holding it firmly shut or he locked it from the outside. Knowing him, he's very likely going to follow through on his threat.

Sighing, I pick up the first swimsuit I find. A thong.

I hurl it across the room, cursing my boss in my mind in every way imaginable.

CHAPTER 36
CALEB

My shoulders shake with a silent laugh. As much as I wish to see Serena in a barely-there swimsuit, I only put a few R-rated options in there for fun. I know exactly which one she's going to go for and sure enough, some minutes later she emerges in a full-body neoprene suit that covers her from neck to ankle.

By far the most conservative of the choices, it still outlines her every curve in a way that makes me a very thankful man.

"I demand answers," Serena says as soon as she stands before me.

I bob my head. "And thou shalt get them. Follow me."

"Caleb…"

I ignore the warning in her voice. "Yeah, yeah."

Phelan stays in the kitchen like I ordered, sipping orange juice from a fairytale princess sippy cup I put out for him. I snap a picture on the way down to the second floor, because it's an image I want to preserve forever. Daniel will enjoy it too.

"You're so mean," my assistant murmurs behind me. "And immature."

Her bare feet pitter patter behind me as we traverse the

gym, and they stop when I open the door leading to the pool. Her eyes are wide as saucers.

"C'mon," I say. "In you go."

But she doesn't.

Serena stands, frozen, watching the water as though it will rise from the pool basin and swallow her whole.

"Don't make me pick you up."

The threat works to at least get her into the premises, although she glues her back to the glass partition between the pool and the gym.

As I unbutton my shirt, I say, "Listen, I know what happened is traumatic, but I think if you don't face this early on, it's going to grow into an even bigger monster in your mind than it already is."

Her voice comes out as a thin thread. "This was your emergency?"

"No." I shrug out of my shirt and the movement tears her eyes away from the pool. "It's your emergency, although you may not recognize it right now."

Serena shakes her head. "I'm not doing this."

"Trust me." I kick my loafers off and pop the button of my jeans open. Her eyes fly down and I have to use my entire willpower to behave. Clearing my throat, I say, "Remember when I said I'd take care of the situation? Well, this is part of that."

"You can't be serious."

"Oh, but I am." I'm also growing so hot that I need to hurl myself at the water soon. I turn away from her and march over to where I collected some supplies. "I prepared a swimming cap, goggles and a kick board for you. Come here."

"Nope." If anything, she glues herself to the glass even more.

I pull her wrist and as she resists, I bend over and press my shoulder into her stomach. Next thing, I carry her over my shoulders like a sack of potatoes.

"I will kill you!" she screeches.

"Sure, do it when you're able to catch me." I deposit her by the edge of the pool and press the floating board to her chest. "But first, I'm going to teach you how to swim."

Serena trembles like a leaf so I rub her upper arms. I start a breathing exercise and encourage her to follow suit. It takes a moment until she joins.

"Good, that's it." I continue rubbing her arms. "I'm not going to let anything bad happen to you."

Her lower lip trembles. "I will kill you if you do."

I smile. "Then I might truly become undead, huh?"

Serena glares at me.

After a few more minutes of coaxing her, she finally allows me to help her into the water. We're at the shallow end, where the water probably reaches her chest if she stands up. And still, just being in the water paralyzes her.

"Breathe," I say, standing in front of her. I hold her eyes with mine until she's able to breathe normally again, then I wade backward. "C'mon."

She shakes her head.

"Hmm, what can I give you that will encourage you to wade into deeper water?"

"More vacations?" she asks.

"Sure." I motion her over and very slowly, she takes a few steps further. "Have you always feared water?"

"It's not that I fear it," she says, her voice low. "It's just I prefer to drink it than to have it in my lungs."

I grab hold of her floating kick board and bring it to me gently. "Fair. I personally love being in the water much more than out of it. It's calming."

"That's only because you know how to survive in it." She

winces as her feet start having difficulty reaching the bottom, and starts clinging to the board.

"I'm pretty sure it's going to be calming for you too, once you learn how to swim." She latches onto the board for dear life as I pull her deeper into the pool. "Kick your legs."

She opens and closes her mouth. "I don't know how."

"Imagine it's my face you're kicking."

The fact that the idea has the immediate effect of making her kick furiously at the water makes me laugh. But there she goes, awkwardly propelling herself forward without me helping along.

"Look at you, you're swimming already."

"I am not," Serena says firmly. "I'm just kicking your face."

"And what a fine job you're doing." I swim beside her.

Pretty soon, she grows tired and stops kicking. When she realizes she's deep enough that she can't touch the floor, she yelps and starts flailing about. I wrap an arm around her and keep her upright. Serena grabs onto my shoulders like I'm her new kick board.

"Alright, our first step is to help you lose some of the fear." I smile down at her. "If you're a good student and graduate from this first lesson, we may begin with the next one today. Otherwise it will take us many more days to practice. Perhaps your entire vacation."

Serena's eyes are wide as saucers. "No thanks."

I ignore that and pry her hands from me, turning around until she's behind me. I circle her arms around my neck and start swimming. "I figure this is way more fun than the alternative."

"What's that?" Her voice right behind my ear makes my skin break into goosebumps, but if she notices she doesn't comment on it.

"Suing Vivienne," I say, taking an easy lap around the pool. "Which is probably what you could be doing instead."

She snorts. "Oh yeah, because not only am I too poor to sue anyone, but I could also see that going very well. Yes, your honor, this vampire broke the railing of the state park's pier and pushed me into the water for no reason."

"If you really want to sue her I'll bankroll it." I make a pause. "Was it really for no reason?"

It takes a moment before she responds. "Yeah, I think most people call that an accident. That's why suing isn't viable."

"Too bad," I mutter. "I guess we're doing the best we can, then."

"You're not serious about teaching me how to swim, right? Specially not during my time off."

I shrug. "It doesn't have to be during your time off, but yeah, I'll make sure you can swim. Didn't I tell you I'd keep you safe?"

"That was from blood-suckers, not from bodies of water."

I chuckle. "Add bodies of water to the list. I can't help you about mosquitoes, though."

She gives me a smack on the shoulder, which underwater has no sting at all. I'm conscious of the fact that sometimes, as I swim and her body bounces with the water, her chest presses against the top of my back intermittently. Since it's not glued to my back all the time, it means her body is mostly floating on the surface.

Too bad. I wouldn't mind it if she wrapped herself around me like a koala.

"How are you doing?" I ask after a while.

"Uh, hanging in there. Literally."

"Ready for me to let go?"

"No." She gasps. "I can't float!"

"You've been floating all this time, though." I stop in the middle of the pool and glance back at her over my shoulder. "There's the proof. I can see your butt from up here."

"What does my butt have to do with anything?"

I say, "It's not underwater."

There's no comeback after that little fact. I pry her arms loose. "Just relax and let your body do it."

Either she's petrified or willing to try, because she doesn't protest and I'm able to wade out from the circle of her arms. I flip around and see her floating, her nose just over the water and her eyes squeezed firmly shut.

"That's it, you're doing it."

Instead of encouraging her, my voice makes her lose the precarious balance she's gained and she sinks. Immediately, she starts flailing around and socks me a good punch in the chin when I try to fish her out of the water. I have to wrap my arms around her tight to stop her from struggling. When we break into the surface, she splutters for a good while until she wails.

"Oh, no! Where are my glasses?"

I sigh. "Don't worry, I'll find them."

But now that she can't see, she grows even more desperate and wraps her four limbs around me. "Don't you dare let go of me!"

As much as I enjoy the position, I need to calm her down before it becomes any fun. I swim us backwards and say, "I won't, I promise."

When we reach the edge of the pool, I have to tear her limbs apart as though they were glued to me with velcro. She latches onto the edge, blinking her eyes rapidly even when it doesn't improve her eyesight.

"Wait here."

Through gritted teeth, Serena replies, "I'm not going anywhere."

I dive into the pool. Unlike the beach at Bahia Honda, the water is lit up from underneath and I spot her glasses at the bottom right away. I regret not being able to take my time in my favorite place, because I don't want to make her panic any further than she already is.

Breaking out into the surface, I say, "I got them."

I rub my face and comb my hair back as I approach her. She clings to the edge with so much strength, it's a wonder the tile doesn't break under her grip. I offer the glasses to her, but she can't even move to retrieve them so I put them on for her.

"Can you actually see through all those water drops?"

She swallows hard. "Yep, crystal clear."

"Oh yeah?" In that case, with how close we are, she can probably count the freckles on my nose. "What do you see?"

She doesn't answer. I grab onto the edge of the pool from either side of her. Her knees knock against my thighs and I let the rippling water push me closer against her. Her lips part in a gasp, absorbing my entire attention. The world can be crumbling to pieces but all I care about right now are Serena's lips, so close to mine.

CHAPTER 37
SERENA

Every square inch of my skin feels like it's on fire.

While the water slows down our movements, it doesn't prevent me from feeling every ridge of Caleb's body as he presses up against me.

I should've never got in this pool with him. There were two very dangerous lines I've been toying since. One, drowning. The second, this—not being able to avoid the magnetic attraction that pulls me toward him against my better judgement.

I'm frozen, grabbing onto the edge of the pool because it's my only lifesaver. If I could pull myself up and out of the water without his help, I'd contemplate doing it—even though I don't really want to. There's nowhere else I'd rather be.

Caleb's eyes are half mast as he runs his hands down my arms, gently prying them away from the ledge. Before I start sinking like a rock, he cinches them around his neck again and now our bodies are fully aligned. I inhale a sharp breath when it's clear there's not even a molecule of water between us.

"Caleb, we shouldn't."

"Why not?" he asks, his deep voice rumbling through his

chest and through to mine. My entire body breaks into goose-bumps and a shiver runs down my spine.

One of his hands follows the sensation until it settles at the small of my back, pulling me flush against him. It makes me forget reason. I know there's more than one why we shouldn't, but I couldn't conjure them if he paid me a million bucks per.

His lips stretch into a little smile, and then they're a hair's width away from mine. I can feel his breath, the heat of his skin and the softest, butterfly touch against my lips.

"Can I kiss you?"

Caleb's eyes are intent on mine. The question causes the slightest friction against my lips, and it undoes me. A low moan is all the consent he's going to get from me and throwing caution out the window, I pull his head down until our lips meet.

I don't know how I manage to stay in one piece once his lips close over mine, stroking in a way that makes my eyes roll back and my eyelids close, and I abandon myself to his touch. The humid friction sends a bolt of awareness down my body.

With one hand, Caleb holds the back of my head and tilts it back for better access. His mouth opens and closes in languid motions that provoke little sighs out of me. Once my lips part, his tongue sweeps over them in a hot stroke that ignites a fire underwater.

And the fire is me.

I run my fingers through his wet hair and close my fist, making sure he can go nowhere else. His chest vibrates with a chuckle in response, but pretty soon the amusement is gone.

There's only heat as his tongue caresses mine, exploring deeper until I wish that there were no barriers between us.

I don't know if it's me or him, but one of us moans so loud, it echoes across the walls. That's what awakens my brain from the spell he's put it under. But even awareness isn't enough to make me pull away. It's only until we both need to gasp for air that we separate.

Caleb breathes just as hard as I do. Maybe he's as unstable too because he clings to the edge of the pool, his knuckles turning white from the effort. But even then, he doesn't put any distance between us.

With a raspy voice, I say, "We shouldn't have done that."

"You're right." His voice is just as gravely. After a pause, he adds, "Let's do it again."

Before I can react, he's kissing me again.

This time he pulls me away from the edge, his hands sliding down my sides until he grasps my thighs and wraps them around his waist.

If the first kiss was fire, this one is like taking a dip into the sun. I clench my legs tighter around him and he grabs my butt with two fistfuls to bring me closer against him.

But right as I'm enjoying this a little too much, my mind wonders how this would look like to a bystander. A boss and his secretary eating each other's faces in secret is such a cliché.

There's a loud, sucking sound as I pull away from Caleb and reach backward to the edge of the pool. Maybe he's finally regained some of his composure because he lets me go.

With difficulty, I haul myself up over the edge and crawl back away from it.

When Caleb tries to follow, I hold a hand up. "No, stay there. I need to think."

He scrunches up his face. "Thinking is more boring than what we were doing."

"But much more necessary." I breathe like a truck for a while, fighting really hard against the impulse to reach for him and do something I'll regret. My lips feel swollen—and that's what tells me I'm in real danger here. "This was a mistake that can't happen again."

Caleb props himself up against the edge, resting his chin against his forearms. "Why not?"

"Because—" I interrupt myself with a nervous laugh. "Shit, where to begin? There's a million reasons."

His eyes are still half mast as they sweep up and down my body, and even though I'm fully clothed I don't feel like it. I raise my knees up and wrap my arms around them.

"First of all, you're my employer."

"Technically," he says in a drawl. "It's my dad who is."

I wave a hand. "Regardless, we're not on even ground here."

He smiles a little. "No, you're on a higher ground right now."

I frown.

"Okay, I'll be serious." He runs a hand through his hair, leaving it a spiky mess. It reminds me of when I had it in a fistful. "I won't let him or anyone else jeopardize your livelihood."

"No, but that's the thing," I say. "The fact that you won't *let* it happen means you have that power. I don't."

Caleb expels a breath he can't recover from right away, so I soldier on.

"Second, we're not even the same species."

He groans. "Foul. It's not like I'm a wild beast."

"But you're not entirely human, either." That shuts him up, and by the way he looks at me I can tell it hurts him. Not my intent, but maybe it'll help my case. "Third, you're going to get engaged to someone who is, and I'm not going to become the other woman."

"No." Caleb all but barks the word. In a fluid push, he lifts himself out of the water and he's so beautiful that I have to fist my hands hard enough to hurt so I don't move a muscle. "No matter what, I'm not marrying her. I don't care if Dad disowns me and throws me in the streets, I won't marry someone who did what she did to you."

I shake my head. "You say that now."

"I'll say it now and I'll say it always."

"Fine, but that can't erase the fourth thing," I say, and Caleb grimaces.

"Shit, there's more?" As he bites his lower lip, I can almost feel the scrape of his teeth against my own skin. "What's the fourth thing?"

It takes me a moment to pluck it from the back of my mind, where it fell after the reminder of his kiss. The power he could have over me if I let him is terrifying, and that fear gives me the power to speak.

"Me," I say, my voice barely a whisper. "I won't betray my hopes and dreams for a moment with you."

The words hang heavy in the damp air between us. Caleb is almost as still as a statue when he asks, "And what are your hopes and dreams?"

"A stable future." I hug myself tighter. "A career. A respectable reputation. Being able to sustain myself and surpass my background. I can't do any of that with you in the way."

The light is almost gone from his eyes. "What makes you think I'll be in your way?"

"Experience. It's me against the world. I don't have room for anyone else." I take a deep breath. "The real choice here is between you and my career, and... I will choose my career—myself."

Caleb sucks in air, so sharply it has to hurt his throat. For a while, all he can do is stare at the wet tiles between us until he lifts his eyes back to me. "I understand. I'll never get in the way between you and yourself."

There's a sharp pain in my chest, at odds with the victory I just got. Nodding, I say, "Thank you."

After that, he pledges to sign me up for swimming lessons

with a professional instructor. And I don't see him again for two weeks until it's time for me to return to the office.

I spend the rest of my vacations under the bedsheets, crying intermittently.

CHAPTER 38
CALEB

After that, the two weeks without seeing Serena become a punishment.

On the one hand, I'm so hungry for her that my dreams are plagued with fantasies of what I wish would've happened after those red hot kisses in the pool.

Not long into the fun, I would wake up and remember her words. Between her career and I, she would always choose the former.

Crap.

I want to seduce her as much as I need blood to survive. And I could.

Even with that poker face of hers I suspect she enjoyed the glimpses of my bare skin—at least because if she didn't, she would've complained. And after Vivienne's noxious visit to my office, Serena seemed slightly jealous.

I could chalk all of that to my own need for her to see me in that light. But if I had any doubts about how she felt before, they vanished the second she grabbed a fistful of my hair and pulled my head down to kiss her deeper. There was fire in her and instead of putting it out, I stoked it with those kisses.

I crave her lips and her skin, and her hair cascading over me, and her hands on me. I crave much more.

But, damn it, she's right. All her four reasons are right and knowing that makes me unreasonably upset.

Even if we'd met somewhere in the streets of Miami, and we had no need to keep our relationship professional, it still wouldn't change the fact that she's a human and I'm not. Dad would still be against me being with a human, just as he's been my entire life. He doesn't care if I screw around with vampire women—as long as I don't make his mistake and make babies when I'm not supposed to—but human women are off-limits.

Actually, to start with if he finds out Serena knows what we are, it might be enough for him to kick me to the curb. If Serena and I got tangled with each other? He'd kill me.

Okay, I exaggerate. He'd torture me until I swear to never approach another human woman again. He has seriously done this to vampires toeing the line between the vampire and human world, because the less humans know about us, the safer we all are.

Even worse, he'd fire Serena on the spot.

She's right. Nothing can happen between us.

She's right. I repeat the sentence in my mind like a mantra, to the beat of punching a bag in the gym. I pick up the pace. *She's right, she's right, shit, she's absolutely right.* I do some of my favorite combinations using my fists, elbows and kicks. I wish she wasn't right. I wish we were the same. Two humans. Two vampires. Equally poor. Equally rich. Anything, so there wouldn't be this chasm between us.

I punch the bag even harder. More than ever I wish Dad wasn't interested in marrying me off to Vivienne. He will always consider her the better option for me, no matter who I bring to him instead. If not for that, I might've stood a chance at begging him to turn Serena—assuming she would even want to. And assuming Dad can move past what happened to my mother.

I snarl, kicking the bag so hard that my foot sinks into the fabric and tears it. A rush of sand pours out, but unlike some of the previous times this happened, I manage to keep my balance and pull my foot out of the broken bag without landing on my ass.

Right then, Phelan pushes the broken bag away with his shoulder and on the same rail where it hangs, he loads up a new one.

"This is the last one. Make it last," he says. Behind him, there's a graveyard of broken bags from today's session.

"If I break it I'll just punch the wall."

Maybe with my head, so I finally stop thinking about something I can't change.

I'm only able to land a couple of blows before a question rings behind me. "What's going on with you?"

Since I don't want to answer, I keep unleashing a flurry of punches, elbows and kicks.

"Babe, I think your little brother broke," Lara, the asker, says to an obvious person that can't be Phelan.

Without glancing their way, I ask, "Hey Dan, if I break this one will you become my new punching bag?"

My brother snorts. "As if you could. But seriously, what's got your panties in a twist?"

"First of all," I say, making a pause to glare at him. I'm breathing heavy but I feel the burn in my chest only now that I've stopped. "I'm wearing lycra and shorts, none of which can ride up my ass. Second, I'm pretty sure I can give you a run for your money now."

Dan cocks an eyebrow at Phelan, who says, "If he's having a good day and you're having a bad one, the probability of him giving you a run for your money is about fifty percent."

"Gee, thanks." I turn back to working the bag. My limbs

are heavier and slower after hours of this. After hours of swimming laps in the pool to stave off the frustration.

With a deep breath, I release a heavy punch that echoes like a car crash around the gym and its high ceilings. Sure enough, the punching bag tears in half as if I'd sawed it instead, raining down a torrent of sand that covers me above the ankles.

I stand there, working my lungs until gathering air is no longer such a harrowing task. I'm aware of my hair matted against my head and forehead, of my entire body dripping sweat like someone poured a bucket of water on me.

"Ignore these two." My sister-in-law is somewhere behind me, clear from the path of destruction. "But seriously, what's wrong? I've never seen you like this, Caleb."

"Nothing's wrong," I say.

Everything's wrong, I mean.

I'm wildly attracted to my assistant, who won't succumb to my charms because she's a human who knows I'm a vampire, and because Dad is the final boss I can't possibly defeat in the quest to getting together with said human assistant.

"You say that, but this entire mess paints a different story." Lara motions all around me, at the mounds of spilled sand from gutted punching bags. I probably look even worse than those deflated bags.

"Blood," Phelan says, shoving a bag of it against my bare chest.

"Don't tell me," Dan starts, making a pause. "Did Mom say something again?"

I shake my head as I suck on the blood through a straw. Even though this one doesn't taste as revolting as others, it still triggers my gag reflex.

After brushing a mound of sand flat with the sole of his shoes, Daniel stands before me. "Then, was it Vivienne?"

The gag that comes after that is so hard I nearly turn into a red fountain all over him, but at the last second I clamp my mouth shut and swallow it all back down.

He jumps out of the way into safety. "Was that reaction because you saw my face or because you heard the name of she-who-shall-not-be-named-again?"

It takes me a moment, but after a coughing fit I manage to say, "All of the above."

"Oh, so that's what this fit is about, huh?" Lara snaps her fingers. "Vivienne."

Sort of. If Vivienne hadn't almost drowned Serena, I wouldn't have attempted to teach her how to swim. I wouldn't have felt her body against mine. And I definitely wouldn't have kissed her and driven myself useless for two weeks.

But I can't even blame Vivienne for that when it's my own damn fault that I couldn't resist the temptation. Now, resisting is going to be even more difficult because I know how good succumbing feels like.

I glance around but like Phelan said, there are no more punching bags. Should I hit the weights instead?

Dude might be a mind reader, because the bodyguard stands in my way. "Stop. You've done enough for today."

I press my lips into a tight line, considering whether I could barrel through him.

The answer is no. He would knock me flat on my back in a second even if I was full of energy.

"Isn't the engagement on hold, though?" Daniel asks, falling into step beside me as I make my way out of the mat area. "Especially after the mishap with your assistant."

I freeze. "What mishap?" Does he know that Serena and I kissed?

"You know, when she almost drowned."

Oh, that one. Right.

Running a hand through my wet hair, I sigh. "I guess so, but I don't know how long that will last."

"Should we help you find another girl?" Lara laughs. "It shouldn't be hard if you show all those new guns."

Daniel laughs. "Gross."

I almost want to tell her that strategy backfired with Serena, but then explaining why my assistant has consistently seen me in various states of undress is the worst way to spend the rest of this Sunday evening.

Once I reach the kitchen, I grab a bottle with a sports drink and drain it in two big gulps. "No, thanks. I have enough on my plate with the women already in my life."

The wording catches Dan's attention. He gives me a long look, trying to pluck the answer to an unspoken question right from my mind.

"Anyway, why are you here?" I finally ask, now that I'm more recovered.

Daniel puts his arm around his wife's waist. "We haven't seen you in a while and want to have family dinner, but just the four of us."

Phelan doesn't even react at being lumped into the word *family* by Dan, and neither do I. Having grown up around him, the bodyguard feels more like family than my stepmother ever will.

Lara wrinkles her nose. "But first, you need to shower."

I'm thankful for the distraction they provide, but for the rest of the night I say not a peep more. The last thing I want is to give Dan more clues he could put together before he gets the full picture of how pathetic his little brother is.

CHAPTER 39
SERENA

t's Monday morning and I'm the first one in the office. Every time someone steps out of the elevators, I feel my blood pressure spike to the ceiling. At the fifth such occurrence, I figure I don't necessarily have to sit nice and pretty to welcome my boss for the day. For the week. For the rest of our lives together as nothing else but boss and employee.

I lock myself up in a bathroom stall and just breathe. Fortunately, the women's bathroom is spotless at this time of the day and there's nothing noxious coming into my lungs. But I still have trouble taking in air, and it might or not be linked to the water threatening to spill from my eyes.

As if I haven't cried enough for two weeks, there are still tears left to spill over circumstances I can do absolutely nothing about.

This is the right thing to do. I have to draw a line and force myself to stop feeling what I have no business feeling.

"It's not like I like him," I tell myself, for once hoping that lies have the power to erase truths.

Groaning, I hang my head. I do like him. Somehow, during the course of about four intense months, Caleb wormed his way past my defenses and made me feel something for him. If that isn't unforgivable enough, he had the nerve to do that while being a vampire. Romeo and Juliet could never.

Or maybe it wasn't him who did it. Maybe I just let him.

As the even more horrifying realization hits me, my work phone buzzes in my hands. It startles me and I almost drop it on the floor, but I manage to catch it in midair.

Jon's name appears on screen. In lieu of a greeting, the second I pick up he says, "Cedric wants to see you right now."

The small victory from catching the phone a moment ago fades. Something tells me a much bigger catastrophe might be on the way.

I run out of the bathroom and don't even bother to glance in the direction of Caleb's office. It's still probably too early for him. My heart races through the elevator ride.

I feel like prey running straight up to a predator as Marissa opens Mr. Oh's office door for me.

"Good luck," she murmurs. She must know or suspect that something's up.

"Coffee, Miss Lossada?" Mr. Oh asks upon my entrance. He sits on his lounge area with a steaming cup in hand. Since I'm frozen like a statue, he motions at Jon to run along. "Please take a seat."

My consciousness must have faded for a second, because next thing I know I'm sitting across from him with no recollection of how I got there.

After savoring a sip of his coffee, Mr. Oh says, "You must be wondering why I called you over."

"I—yes." I clasp my hands tight over my lap.

My mind isn't exactly blank trying to come up with reasons. The problem is that all of the options are terrifying, as most of them involve various compromising positions between his youngest son and I.

"I trust you had a good break."

Is he torturing me on purpose?

I clear my throat. "Yes, excellent."

The little smile on his face tells me he sees right through my impatience. I try to dial it down but I can't help myself. I need to know if he's about to take out some secret pictures of me making out with his son in the pool, or of any of the many times I've embarrassed myself in front of Caleb.

Before he takes me out of my misery, the office door opens and in comes Jon carrying a tray with a cup. He settles it on the table in front of me. "Enjoy."

The coffee does smell incredible, but I won't be able to enjoy it. Not as long as so many things weigh on my conscience —and definitely not while Mr. Oh sits there, reading my mind.

It's only when Jon leaves us again that Mr. Oh speaks. "I debated whether to talk with you about the events from two weeks ago right away, or if to let you enjoy your time off. In the end, I chose the latter."

Events from two weeks ago.

Which can only mean the kiss with Caleb.

A small sound is all my throat is able to conjure.

He sighs. "I see you're still visibly shaken. Maybe I shouldn't have waited this long to apologize."

"Huh?"

"I'm very sorry for the circumstances that led to the accident." I still have no idea what he's talking about until he adds, "Fortunately, Caleb was able to rescue you before you drowned."

"Oh."

Oh.

Warmth returns to my body when I realize he hadn't just been about to talk about the time Caleb and I slept in one bed and woke up as intimately tangled as a real couple would. Or about the many times I've devoured his son's form with my eyes. Or worse, about the time I *felt* his son's form against me.

"Yes, thank you," I say, my voice choked up. "I appreciate it."

Mr. Oh sets his cup of coffee down on the table. "I investigated the incident and it turns out the pier's railing was rotting in places. Unfortunately, one of such places was where you stood."

Although I stay silent, I bristle at the implication that the accident was in any way my fault. Even if the railing had been on the verge of collapse, I wouldn't have tipped into the sea if it wasn't for the handy help of Vivienne Astor.

He must have prepared for this train of thought, because he continues, "And I spoke with Vivienne as well. She said she merely intended to grab onto your shoulder and miscalculated."

Yeah, I'm sure.

She must have miscalculated when she said *let this be a warning* right before *accidentally* pushing me into the water.

"I'm extremely glad Caleb knew you don't know how to swim," Mr. Oh says. The little smile is still on his face, but it doesn't do much to warm me. "Although, I do wonder how he came about that knowledge."

I suck in a sharp breath, imagining myself telling him the reason. *You see, Mr. Oh. That's because when I was pretty much new to employment, I fell into your son's pool and almost drowned, and when he plucked me out from the water my clothes turned completely see through and I gave him a full boob-eyeful. I doubt he could forget that little trivia after that.*

Instead, I say, "I must have mentioned it in passing."

He hums from his throat. "Could it have been that time on his yacht? Jon told me he took you to the Bad Blood one time that Caleb was throwing a tantrum."

No, it definitely wasn't that time. That time all I did was ogle Caleb as he climbed back aboard, dripping water down his Speedo-clad body. That was it.

"It could have been, I don't recall the particular moment."

The blatant lie rolls off my tongue with the same ease as when, two weeks ago, I told Caleb I would choose my career over him.

Just because saying the words was the right thing to do, doesn't mean my heart is behind them. But if I want to survive, I have to do what I have to do. And unfortunately, this time it also won't pay off to be honest.

"I believe we established a very transparent relationship from the beginning, Miss Lossada, which is why I need to say this." Mr. Oh pauses, almost giving me heart failure in the process. "While I fully support your commitment to bringing Caleb to task, I must make sure that is all there is to this."

I stay still, not moving a single muscle to not betray myself. Maybe he has proof or maybe he doesn't, but with this it's obvious that Mr. Oh suspects something's up between Caleb and I.

And since I stay quiet, then comes the sledgehammer. "Caleb is going to marry Vivienne and I don't want your proximity to distract him from that fact. Make sure of that."

"Of course, sir," I say, with much more firmness in my voice than I feel inside.

He picks up his coffee again. "I hired you to be Caleb's assistant and yes, a sort of babysitter as well, but don't forget that I'm the one who employs you. Not him. As fond as he may grow of you, it's me you have to respond to."

Pulling strength from my reserves, I say, "You have nothing to worry about, sir."

"Good." After taking one more leisurely sip, he says, "You may go now. Have a good day, Miss Lossada."

I don't dally for a second. I leave the untouched cup of coffee on the table and march right out, somehow holding my shit together until I find the nearest women's bathroom. After making sure the coast is clear, I empty my heart out through my tear ducts. Only when I'm sure I have no further tears left in me, and no feeling at all, do I emerge back into civilization.

From this moment, the lie I told Caleb will be true. I will not choose him over my livelihood. No matter what it takes, I will amputate the tiny part of my heart he had taken over.

CHAPTER 40
CALEB

I am professionalism. Professionalism is me.

That's what I repeat to myself as Serena walks into my office with her iPad in hand. We haven't made eye contact a single time today, but when she's not paying attention I steal glances that don't give me any clues as to how she's feeling. Is she struggling like me? Or am I just making her uncomfortable?

None of them are things I want her to feel. Which is why I have to be professional.

"You have a meeting in the afternoon with the Marketing team." She flips through the screen of her device, never once lifting her eyes. "I heard through the grapevine that the main point is finding out if you're going to continue overseeing the division or if you're going to stay full time in Purchasing."

"I don't make that kind of decision. But you have a good point, I should give the employees some clarity. Book me for at least ten minutes with Dad beforehand."

"I'll try."

I almost want to joke that there's no trying, but doing.

Except here I am, trying to pretend like we're perfect strangers who have never kissed.

"In other topics," Serena says. "The expenses from the event have all been approved safe one."

I frown. "What's that?"

"The extra champagne I had to order on site." She squints at the screen. "It's only five hundred and twenty dollars, I don't get it."

"I'll override it and approve it myself. If they want trouble over pennies I'll fight them. Anything else?"

"Yes, I received an invitation for you to be the keynote speaker at marketing conference next month."

"Next month?" I ask, snorting. "That obviously sounds like someone more important dropped out at the last minute."

"I figured as much when I saw the invite, so I did some research and that's exactly the case."

I lace my fingers against my stomach and lean back. "But then again, it sounds like a great excuse not to work for a few days."

"Caleb." For the first time in this fine Monday morning, Serena makes eye contact—if only to fulminate me with the power of her displeasure.

"Anyway, don't respond yet. I have to think whether it's going to benefit Comed or not."

When she focuses back on the screen, I feel the severed connection like a hollow in my gut.

"Those were all the updates. I'll be at my desk if you need me."

With a low voice, I say, "Okay."

Serena turns around and I force my attention to stay glued to my computer screen. Otherwise, I know exactly what I'd be doing instead. Admiring her retreating shape and daydreaming of what it felt like in my hands for those few precious minutes while we kissed.

I hear the door open as she's about to leave, but then there's a yelp and a bang.

When I glance up, I find Serena pressed up against the closed door, on the opposite side of where I'd have expected her to be by now.

"What's wrong?"

Slowly, she turns around, pale as paper. "Vivienne Astor is outside."

The horror in her face migrates to mine. In the next second, I leap above my desk and land just before the sitting area. I run over to the door, lock it, and grab Serena's arm. She's about to protest, and I signal for her to stay silent.

I bundle us into my office bathroom and lock that door too, and it's only after getting the shower running that I speak again.

"Sorry, she has ridiculous hearing." And even this I say in a whisper. "Try to keep your voice down."

She nods. "Okay, but what do we do? It's not like we can stay huddled here forever."

"Can't we?" I run a hand through my hair. "Don't give me that look, I know we can't."

But for the life of me I can't think of why she'd suddenly show up again, unless it's to terrorize me. In which case, she's being very effective already.

The striking thing isn't so much that Vivienne freaks me out, but that she has the same effect on my assistant. Serena's mind is probably reliving the moment Vivienne pushed her into the water, considering how she's hunched over trying to make herself smaller. Her skin is pale and she keeps worrying her lower lip.

I can't let them be alone in the same room.

"Serena." I don't even know how to broach this in a tactful manner, so here goes nothing. "Why did she push you? You never did tell me."

In all honesty, I'd been hoping to talk about that with her after our swimming lesson, except the whole thing got derailed.

She rubs her arms. "I think it's because of you."

I let out a sharp breath. "Wow, so she's been trying to stake a claim in all sorts of misguided ways, huh?"

"Do you think she'd try to do something to me again?" Serena pauses, looking down at her shoes. "I mean, there's *nothing* going on between us, and people might start to suspect her if she attempts something again, right?"

"In theory," I say, hating everything about this situation. "But don't forget, she's filthy rich. Much richer than me as an individual. And she's also a lot stronger than me. She could get away with a lot."

Well, honesty doesn't reassure her, going by the way she looks about to cry.

"But it seems what she wants is me, which gives *me* the upper hand." *For now*, I add in my mind. And who knows for how long. "So, I think the best approach is to dangle the carrot in front of her but never give it to her."

Serena winces. "Is that some sort of innuendo?"

I have to bite my lips not to bark a laugh. "That's not what I meant. I think I need to keep her sort of happy, but never give her the alone-time she wants."

"Oh, so I guess I shouldn't turn her away saying you're busy, or something."

"Correct." I tap my chin. "I'll meet with her, but we have to sabotage the meeting until she gets annoyed and leaves."

Serena's eyes narrow. "That might work."

After a brief brainstorm about how to proceed, I turn off the shower and we emerge from the bathroom in a cloud of steam.

I go back up to my desk and wait until Serena ushers the most undesired guest in.

Today she's in a silk button up shirt, done up precisely to

the level between her chest, and the shortest shorts I've ever seen. As she walks, the shirt flares and shows bare skin where most people typically don't show bare skin.

Even though it's a very Miami outfit, it's part of Vivienne's technique for seduction. It boils down to dazzling men with her astounding looks, which works for absolutely anyone who doesn't know her personality. Unfortunately for her, I do know her well enough by this point.

"Can I get you anything?" Serena asks her, standing at a polite distance from the other woman.

Vivienne tosses her purse on the couch and folds her legs as she sits, fanning her neck. "Just an iced water, sweetheart. It's really balmy today."

"Right away." My assistant turns to me. "And you, sir?"

"Nothing," I say. "This won't take long."

Serena leaves at a pace quicker than her usual, keeping her back ramrod stiff like a server at an expensive restaurant. I give her a minute, tops, before she comes back.

Vivienne flashes me a hurt look that is almost convincing. "Aww, love. I make all this effort to visit with you and you don't spare me a moment?"

I make a point of typing nonsense on my computer. "Not my fault you came unannounced when I'm busy."

"I just had this urge to see your pretty face in person, so here I am. Will you show it to me?"

Without making eye contact, I say, "You're seeing it."

"But you're too far."

The door opens and Serena comes in. She places a chilled water bottle on the coffee table before heading over to my desk. She was even smart enough to bring props, and she pulls out her iPad with great fanfare.

"I was able to get the appointment you requested. From two oh five today."

"Ten minutes?" I ask.

"Five." She taps on her screen a few times. "The audit team needs your approval on a couple of important topics, I have forwarded them for your perusal."

Sure enough, a couple of emails hit my inbox.

Damn, she's good. She found actual topics to discuss about, instead of making some shit up.

Then Serena emphasizes, "They're urgent."

I could kiss her. But of course I won't, especially with that murderous audience.

Speaking of, to Vivienne I say, "Sorry, I won't be able to talk."

"In that case, I'll have to use the ace up my sleeve."

Serena and I can't help but glance at Vivienne. The other woman gets up on her feet.

"I bought two hours of your time, and if you want to get out of that commitment I will tell your father."

I press my lips into a thin line. Vivienne's eyes are as cold as ice while she stares me down, despite the fact that the sitting area is a level lower than where my desk sits.

This could be worse. She could've threatened with tattling to my stepmother.

"Serena," I say to my assistant. "How's my lunch hour?"

Vivienne gasps.

Over that sound, Serena says, "It's clear today, but you're booked the rest of the week."

Smiling to Vivienne comes easy after that, especially seeing angry color rush up her throat. I tell her, "There you go, one hour is all I have. Take it or leave it."

CHAPTER 41
SERENA

Being in the presence of this woman feels a lot like drowning in the ocean, with salty water burning through my lungs and no one to hear my screams. And that's precisely what I want to do. Scream.

How can someone so stunningly, impossibly beautiful, be so terrifying?

"Fine, but I'll choose the place," she finally says, shrugging her purse back on her shoulder. There's no way Caleb is missing how the fabric of her blouse clings to her figure, when it even has *me* blushing.

"Make the reservation for four people," Caleb says, nonplussed by the whole spectacle. "Unfortunately, I'll still have to work during our lunch appointment."

The woman's expression sours even further. "Four?"

"You," Caleb starts, ticking his fingers slowly. "My assistant, my bodyguard, and I."

The force of her glare turns to me for a single second, but it's enough to send a shiver down my spine.

"Very well." With that, she storms off.

Caleb raises the palm of his hand to stay me for a longer

moment. It stretches until it's uncomfortable, but I don't dare to even breathe loudly until he signals it's okay to do so.

As I sigh, he drops his face on the surface of his desk. "Shit, what am I going to do?"

I shouldn't be bothered, but that's exactly what I sound like when I say, "Gouge your eyeballs out?"

"Get me a spoon," Caleb mumbles before sitting back straight. "Call Phelan in."

I reel back. "Not for him to really gouge your eyes out, right?"

"It's a good idea but I don't really enjoy pain." He wrinkles his nose and purses his lips in a way that makes him look too damn adorable for the context.

I turn around sharply and march like a robot to just outside the door. Phelan stands like a statue, the only signs that he's alive are the occasional blink and the barely discernible rise and fall of his chest.

"Hey, the boss wants to speak with you."

Wordlessly, he follows me inside. We catch Caleb as he's tugging his tie off and I don't know why, but that movement sends a bolt of heat down my body. I clear my throat, but as Caleb pops open a couple of shirt buttons I'm rendered as still as Phelan was a moment ago outside the office.

"Vivienne's up to something," Caleb says, pacing back and forth in front of us. "We're giving her just a couple hours notice to prepare for this appointment and that's probably going to derail her plans a bit, but I don't feel much safer."

"But it's going to be at a restaurant—a public place, right?" I ask, glancing between both men. "It's not like she's going to pop open her blouse and sit on your lap in front of others."

Caleb makes a sound like he wants to agree but something holds him back.

"She'll probably book the whole restaurant and pay off the staff." My boss rubs his neck. "I'm pretty sure her intent is to get any sort of proof that I welcome her advances to seal the deal. I can't give her that."

I raise my hand up to my face on the pretext of pushing my glasses up, but I'm worrying my lip. I have firsthand experience of how red-blooded my vampire boss really is, and I don't have a lot of trust in his body's capacity to not react at Vivienne's blatant seduction. If a natural reaction gives him away, that will be all the proof she needs.

"Here's what we can do," Caleb says, squaring up to Phelan first. "You, be on the lookout for any paparazzi. If you find one, destroy their equipment."

"Roger that." Phelan nods.

"And you," Caleb says to me. "Interrupt as many times as you possibly can. If there's no actual work event to use as an excuse, make something up. Pretend to be choking, spill a drink on me, fake a fictitious friend's death—anything."

I click my heels and salute. "Sir, yessir."

I can't help but feel like by doing this we're pushing the needle of the doomsday clock closer to midnight on our own.

*

My heart hammers in my throat as Phelan takes us to Vivienne's restaurant pick. I can't look at Caleb, because I'm afraid of what my face might reveal. It's hard to believe it was only this morning when Cedric Oh pointedly reminded me of my place. Yet, here I am, hoping his son doesn't succumb to the charms of this woman.

The restaurant turns out to be no other but the top Michelin-rated place in the whole city. It sits at the penthouse of a building. The whole top floor rotates slowly so every customer gets a three sixty view of downtown Miami. I've only ever seen it in news articles, but it's even more stunning in person.

And Caleb was right. The whole place is empty except for the table where Vivienne sits at.

She's changed outfit since earlier this morning. This time, her top is white and strapless, the cleavage so low she's one millimeter from a wardrobe malfunction. Which is probably the point.

Only when Caleb is a step away from her table does she stand up, and my jaw drops. It's not a top, but a dress anyone else would wear as a top. It's so tight, the vacuum is the only reason it holds in place. The skirt is so short that at just a slightly different angle she'll be showing Caleb everything her momma gave her. Also very likely the intent.

She and my roommate are from the same school of fashion, except that money makes this look work on Vivienne. There are gold bangles around her wrists and a necklace of gold chainlink hangs from her neck and falls all the way down to her lap. The look is something straight out of a magazine.

If this is what she prepared on short notice, what would she have worn for a date with more time in advance?

I shake my head against the mental image as I join Phelan at an adjacent table. While I feel like my safety is in danger around Vivienne Astor, it's Caleb's who is truly at risk. I wish him luck.

She attacks right away. "Do you like my outfit?"

Caleb pars with, "Guys, you can order anything you want. The meal's on me, since I'll be disturbing your lunchtime."

My back is to them, but I glance at the polished window glass to catch Vivienne's reflection. Like a mirror, I catch her annoyed expression, and I have to pinch my thigh not to laugh.

Back to her, Caleb says, "Sorry, you were saying?"

It's nice to see his obnoxiousness unleashed on someone else for a change.

"Is this not enough to impress you, Cay Cay?"

I choke on the water I was drinking. Relaxed, Phelan passes a napkin to me.

A server joins their table first and launches on a long speech about today's menu and how it pares with the wine selections of the house. Caleb declines the wine, since these are business hours, but Vivienne selects different wines for all the courses of her meal.

In contrast, I ask for an unsweet iced tea and Phelan asks for just water.

Right away, I pull out my iPad from my purse and twist on my seat. "Excuse me, sir. I need your signature urgently on these documents."

"Absolutely."

I make a heck of a lot of noise pushing my chair back to stand up. As I join his side and present the iPad to him, I catch from the corner of my eye how Vivienne is mad enough that a muscle in her jaw keeps jumping.

Meanwhile, Caleb takes his sweet time pretending to sign a blank note I opened up beforehand. He even goes as far as checking the news before handing the device back to me.

"Wait," he says and I retrace my steps. "The conference."

"The conference," I repeat.

Caleb's eyes are shining like I haven't seen them at all this morning. He's enjoying this.

"It'll be good for the business. Say yes."

"Very well." I make an unnecessarily long pause. "I will email them right away."

I return to my seat with a smile. One of Phelan's eyebrows goes rogue and rises just a notch.

"Anyway," Vivienne says, huffing. "I paid for your time, not theirs."

"That's too bad, I'm pretty much booked for the rest of the year."

From the window reflection, I see Vivienne lean forward,

one hand extended out as if to grab Caleb's. At the last second, he picks up his glass of water instead.

"You might think you're being clever, sugar. But I enjoy the chase, and I always catch my prey."

That causes a pang to stab my chest. While her voice has a flirtatious tone, the threat isn't disguised with it.

She's the huntress and Caleb is her prey.

To my shock, Phelan loudly says, "Excuse me, I'm using the restroom."

His chair also makes a racket as he stands up, and in his wake a tense silence falls over the three of us. Phelan isn't the type to attract attention to himself at all, which means he's following Caleb's previous orders and must have seen something suspicious. I have to follow mine.

"Sorry to interrupt again," I blurt out before I even have an excuse.

Vivienne snarls. "What now?"

"Your brother is calling me," I say to Caleb. "It's probably because you turned off your phone for this appointment."

"True," he says, tossing his napkin on the table and getting up. "I was expecting this call about his project. I need you to come with and take notes. Vivienne, excuse us."

I grab my purse and follow Caleb to the lobby. Out there, I ask, "Are we doing okay?"

"Yep, she's furious." He sighs. "Can you find an excuse to end this lunch early?"

I think about it for a second. "Do you have any relatives I can kill off?"

Caleb snorts. "Unfortunately, she knows all of them, so no. Maybe we can kill off one of Phelan's relatives?"

"Oh, good idea." I can't help mirroring the smile on his face for a second, before reality comes crashing back to me. "Be strong."

Resist her.

Don't let her seduce you.

Don't look at her boobs.

Or anywhere else.

Because, sadly for me, I care if you do.

Caleb's dark eyes are intent on mine in that loaded pause. I wonder if he catches onto what I'm trying to convey without words.

Then he mutters, "Don't worry, I don't have eyes for her."

CHAPTER 42
CALEB

An entire month went by with me playing cat and mouse with Vivienne. Never in my life did I have to be as creative in coming up with excuses to get out of having to share the same air as someone. Whether it be family dinners, events, and even at work, I ran from it all.

That's why normally I wouldn't be caught dead at a conference like this—for people who talk, breathe and live marketing —when my reason for being here is just to put as large a stretch of land between Vivienne Astor and I.

It's not impostor syndrome if you're really an impostor, right?

Which is why I make the last of my presentations precisely about that, how I got a huge leg up in this industry because of my family, and how we should have less people like me in positions of power or as keynote speakers for these events. I finish the panel up by promoting a few emerging marketers from underserved communities and announcing a grant to five students from those communities, from my own pocket.

And when I say my own pocket, I mean from the rent I earn from the apartments in my Brickell building. Which is about five percent of my income. The rest comes from Comed, also known as Dad.

It's around noon while we drive back to our hotel in an upscale area of Chicago, when my assistant gives me a long look I couldn't decipher if I had the Rosetta Stone of facial expressions.

"What?"

"That was actually pretty good," Serena says and folds her arms. "What you did back there."

"Thanks, I'm occasionally able to do something decent." As her expression turns sour, mine goes the opposite way. "Also, I'll need your help to coordinate the logistics of the grant."

Is it just me or do her eyes look shinier than just a second ago?

"Yes, I would love to."

And I would love to see her this happy more often.

That's when Phelan, our driver, jerks the car abruptly and sends us tumbling to one side. As I recover, I ask, "What the hell, man?"

"Apologies." After a too-long pause, he adds, "We're being followed."

"Not again!" Serena cries out, as Phelan jerks the car again.

I turn around. Behind us, there are three black cars swerving in and out of the traffic lanes, following Phelan's erratic driving pattern to a T.

I pull out my cellphone, scrolling through my contacts list until I find the one I need. "What are our coordinates?"

Phelan gives them to me and I parrot them to the operator. The Oh family has private suppliers, mainly of blood but also of other service—like security—all over the world. While they might not always be located exactly where we are, someone will be nearby enough to assist. That's what I'm calling for help.

"Okay," I say after hashing out the details with the operator. "There are some guys in town who can help but it'll take them about twenty minutes."

"I will stall them. Hold tight," Phelan says as all warning before he starts doing his job, which is saving our lives from whoever is after us—by first giving us a heart attack.

All around us, drivers honk at the reckless way we're driving and Phelan caused a car crash a block ago. It didn't seem life threatening, but I'll have to follow up to make sure everyone's okay and compensated.

Meanwhile, my assistant is full on praying in Spanish again.

I don't know who this is going to comfort the most, but I reach out and grab her hand tight as our car swerves again.

"I have to prepare you both for the worst scenario," Phelan says, which is not at all something I'd ever thought I would hear from him. "If I'm unable to keep a good distance between these cars and ours before support arrives, I will have to take extreme measures."

"What are they?" Serena asks, her voice coming out as a squeak.

"I will get us in a controlled accident." The way he says it sounds like it's no big deal. But our speechlessness must give him a clue. "Caleb, you'll have to protect Miss Lossada so she doesn't get hurt."

"Uh, roger that."

"But—" she starts.

"Then you two have to get out of the car and blend with the crowd." Phelan continues like we're having a conversation about the weather over tea, despite our breakneck speed in downtown traffic.

Phelan brakes without warning. We whip forward as the pursuers swish past us. Before they can react, Phelan turns the car sharply into a corner and drives diagonally away from them. This works for a solid five minutes before two of the cars are on our tail again.

Shit, where's the third?

"Caleb," Phelan says as a last warning. "Whatever happens, don't let them drink your blood."

Serena gasps. It's the first time Phelan slips like this.

But right now, who the hell cares?

"What about you?" I ask him.

He glances at me through the rearview mirror. "I'll do my job."

Which means no matter what, blood is gonna spill. And it's not gonna be his.

At that moment, the third car appears in front of us from a block away and this is it. I don't need any warning to pull Serena toward me and cover her with my body.

The sound of crunching metal and plastic comes before any impact. Shielding her becomes my priority as we're jostled around. In only a few seconds, I'm banged up more than if I'd been put on a blender.

There's only calm for one second as the car settles, before Phelan barks, "Go!"

I'm slightly disoriented as I rip my seatbelt off of me. Serena looks okay, and when I say *okay* I mean she doesn't seem to be bleeding or concussed. I rip her seatbelt off and take one second to check the perimeter. The nearest car has its doors open, but no one seems to come out yet.

Shit, I hadn't thought about this but—what if they have guns? It's not like I'm immune to bullets.

But if we stay here, we're sitting ducks.

"Let's go," I say, pushing my caved in door open with strength a human can't muster.

Sure enough, there's a popping sound. I push Serena in front of me to shield her. Even amid the chaos, she keeps her head firmly screwed on and runs with all her might. There are a couple more popping sounds and I feel a sting, but I keep running.

Phelan staged the crash in a busy area. The accident stopped traffic in the street and the shooting sends people in the sidewalks running in all directions.

I keep my hands firmly in Serena's shoulders as we blend with the crowd—I don't want to lose her. There's no doubt these assholes are here for me, but if I lose sight of Serena and they catch her, they'll use her to get me.

I have to protect her.

"That way," I wheeze, pushing her into a department store. I check behind us and there are three guys following us.

I crash into a clerk and can't catch her in time before she falls. My legs tangle for a second, but I tuck and roll at the last minute. The contact with the floor sends a flare of pain on my shoulder, but I can't stop to analyze it.

"Serena!" I call out.

Her hand reaches out to me and I grab it. We run through the store without any sense of direction other than away from our pursuers. At least they have the sense not to shoot at us in here.

I see a sign above us for the parking lot exit, and pull my assistant that way. She resists for a second and says, "No, we should stay among people!"

I pull at her harder in that direction. "They're only three, I can take them."

"But you're injured."

We weave through clothing racks until we find the exit. A couple coming into the store almost get ran over by us, but we veer away in the last second. Serena's breathing has got progressively harsher the past seconds, and I stop us between a column and a parked car.

Putting my hands on her shoulders, I say, "Listen to me.

You can't let them see you even if they kill me. They have to think we ran in different directions."

Serena's skin is so pale that her lips have turned blue. It fills me with enough rage that even if they were fifteen men, I could kill them all.

"Get back to the hotel. If I make it, I'll meet you there." When she doesn't respond, I put my hands around her cheeks. "That's an order."

All she can do is nod.

I wish I had more time to give her assurances, even if they're false. But I need to take care of these guys before their buddies find us. I send a prayer to the heavens that this isn't it for me, before coming out of hiding.

CHAPTER 43
SERENA

I want to barf. And cry. And scream. I also want to attack. But I don't want to die. And I also don't want Caleb to die, which is what is going to happen if I don't do something. But what can I even do?

Crouching behind the pillar, I poke my head out to see. At that second, Caleb jumps from the hood of the car with so much force it sends its alarm blaring. He makes an arch in the air before dropping his elbow on top of a guy's head. Two more pounce on him as their buddy falls.

Last time he took on as many guys on his own and won. The reason my heart is lodged in my throat is because this time, he's been shot.

There are two crimson splotches on his shoulder, back and front, growing larger by the second. That he can still move with a hole in his body is proof that we aren't the same.

"There!" someone screams, and five more guys dressed in similar fashion burst in through the door to the parking lot, just as Caleb was done knocking a second guy out.

Now there are six.

A small peep leaves from between my lips, and one of the

men turns his head in my direction. I recall a month ago, the moment when Caleb locked us up in his office bathroom because of Vivienne's super hearing. This jerk must have the same super hearing.

I bite my lips hard. Try to temper my breathing. Does any of that matter when I can't even move? If six vampires get the better of my boss, what do I do? I don't even have my phone or my wallet. More importantly, I don't have any stinking superpowers.

All I can do is pray and watch Caleb pummel someone and take a kick, send someone flying and get the same medicine in return. He lands hard on the windshield of a car, cracking it. As the alarm goes off, Caleb looks so out of breath that he's probably about to pass out from the pain.

Survival instinct must be what's keeping him going. He rolls out of the way with a lot more speed I would think possible, avoiding a point blank shot from one of the assailants. I press my hands against my mouth.

Of course they'd play dirtier. It's six against one, and they still need to use guns?

"Shit!" Caleb's curse carries all the way to me as he miraculously gets out of the way from another bullet. He takes off at breakneck speed, heading exactly opposite of me. The six guys sprint after him and then—

Caleb vanishes. Straight up jumps over the fenced edge of the parking lot.

My mind blanks. I can't process for a good moment. When I come to, I catch the last of the pursuers following suit until they all disappear too.

The scenes in my head reel back to the desperate sprint from the car crash to the department store. We started at ground level. We followed the crowd. The busier it was, the more that led our sprint. We came out from the electronics section, which wasn't on the ground floor.

It's only several minutes later, when no more people burst through the doors, that I dare move from my hiding spot. There are blood stains across the length of the parking lot until the edge, but it could be Caleb's as much as the guys he was beating up.

Then I peer over the edge and my vision swims. Somehow we made it to a fourth floor. And my boss just jumped from here!

But there are no gory scenes on the asphalt. He must've landed and kept running, and so did the other men. Which means, first, they're still after him. Second, there's nothing I can do.

A sob tears from my throat.

"¿Qué hago?" I ask myself, glancing around. My eyes catch on all the blood on the floor and I recall what Phelan said to Caleb. *Don't let them drink your blood.* I don't know why, but I at least can help in this.

I take off my jacket and use it to mop up the blood, mixing it all up among the different puddles, and scooping up some car grease to add in. I gag several times, but that's nowhere near as bad as the torrent of tears that starts falling from my eyes.

What if something bad happens to Caleb?

What if he dies?

The gaping hole opening up in my chest at that thought makes me stagger. I fall on my ass in the middle of the parking lot, and that's how a group of people find me.

I put my hands up to shield my head, but one of the newcomers says, "Um, we're not the bad guys, Miss. We're the store's security."

Another one adds, "We saw what happened on camera but everything happened so quick."

No shit.

"Are you okay?" they ask and all I can do is shake my head.

It takes what feels like forever before I'm able to talk, but I don't even know what to say. *My vampire boss was being chased by bad vampires? And I'm not one of them? And I don't know if he's even alive anymore?*

In the end, all I can tell them is that I need to get back to my hotel. Instead, I end up dealing with the police too and it's well into the night when two cops drive me back to the hotel, promising they'll check in with me in the morning.

I don't even hear the tail of that sentence before I'm running into the hotel. The front desk employees look at me like a dinosaur just strolled into the lobby, but maybe they recognize me from the past week because they don't stop me.

My entire body quakes during the elevator ride to the penthouse. I have no idea how late it is, but it's deep into the night. I don't even know if Caleb is back in his suite or in a hospital, or somewhere worse. But this is where he said we should rendezvous, so it's where I try first. I run out of the elevator before the doors are finished opening and bang on his door.

It's not long before it opens, and there's Phelan.

He looks disheveled and his clothes are torn in places, but other than that, he's not worse for wear.

"Where is he?"

All Phelan does is step aside and usher me in. But I stand there like a fool because my eyes fall on the sofa, the television, a lamp, the kitchen, and a series of closed doors. And I don't spot my boss right away.

"Follow me," Phelan says.

It's almost like I'm walking through a dream, or a nightmare, and I'm not conscious until the moment Phelan opens the bedroom door and there he is—Caleb, lying in bed. And he doesn't react upon the noise.

I gasp. "Don't tell me he's—"

"He's just asleep," the bodyguard says.

The relief that falls upon me threatens to topple me over. I only keep standing because Phelan holds me up by an arm.

"Sit," he commands, dragging me to a chair by Caleb's bed. Maybe where he'd been sitting before I arrived. As I melt against the chair, he says, "You look unharmed, are you?"

I swallow with difficulty and say, "Traumatized only, thanks."

I guess that's no biggie because he nods. "Good. I will go find us food. Don't let anyone else in."

I almost want to beg him to not leave us alone, but the truth is that even if another contingent of men invades the hotel in search of Caleb, a single Phelan would probably not save us.

And my stomach is rumbling. I haven't eaten since breakfast. I can't believe that I can still be hungry in these circumstances.

Through that and Phelan closing the door on his way out, there's no reaction from Caleb. His skin looks pale even under the yellow light of the bedside lamp.

Phelan must have done first aid on Caleb, because my boss's torso is bare safe for bandages around his shoulder and waist. There is a lot of red in the gauze strips. One of his pant legs is torn clear from the knee down, and there's another bandage from there until halfway through his calf. His feet are bare and dirty, as if somewhere along the way he lost his shoes.

Why is he here instead of a hospital?

I hiccup through ragged breaths, and it's finally what makes Caleb's eyelids flutter open. There's no light in them, maybe he's still unconscious.

Carefully, I climb on the bed to sit beside him. I brush the matted hair off his forehead. "Caleb?"

It takes another moment before his dull eyes find me. His voice is pure gravel as he asks, "Are you okay?"

And that—

Is when my heart shatters to a million pieces.

"You fool," I sob the words. My hands hover in the air, an inch away from his bruised skin. "I'm not the one who's a beat up mess."

Caleb grunts as he props himself up with his elbows, trying to sit up.

"No, stop. Stay down." I almost push him until I remember his left shoulder has a bullet hole. I freeze as he works himself up to a sitting position. The effort must pain him so much that he squeezes his eyes shut for a long moment.

Oh my word. His back is a mess. It's even more scratched up and bruised than the front. Then I remember how hard he landed on that car's windshield. It's a miracle he can even move.

"I—what can I do for you?"

"Blood," Caleb rasps out. "Give me blood."

I look around, almost hoping there's a fountain of the red fluid. All I see is furniture and decorations.

"Um." Shaky, I present my wrist to him.

Even in his state, he has enough energy to wheeze a little laugh. "Not yours. In the freezer."

I scramble out of the bed, looking for one of those hotel refrigerators stocked with little alcohol bottles and overly priced snacks. I find it, and it's filled with the usuals. Glancing back at him, I shut down the impulse to ask him where this freezer is when I catch him holding his head with both hands. Instead, I open and close every cabinet door and drawer until I hit the jackpot.

The freezer is in the closet. I open it and sure enough, it's stacked with bags of blood. I bring one back to the bed and Caleb fumbles with trying to get it open.

"Here." I take it from him and peel the seal off.

He can't seem to grab onto the bag firmly enough to

convince me he won't make a bloody mess. I hold onto the bag, gently tilting his head back.

"Open your mouth."

I feel like this is the kind of thing where Caleb would normally make a childish joke, but he's too far gone for that. Instead, he obeys. I get on my knees and from the higher vantage, position the opening of the bag on his mouth and squeeze.

There's a part of me that is thoroughly weirded out by everything about this, but all I focus on is on not spilling a single drop of what will keep him alive. I stop when it's obvious that he's having trouble swallowing, and he convulses with a gag. Before he can react, I press his jaw shut with one hand.

"Swallow," I say. There are tears rolling down his closed eyes. "I know you hate it, but you need to keep it down."

We repeat the operation once more until the bag is drained. I leave it on the bedside table and help Caleb lay down again. There's a drop of blood on his lip and his tongue sweeps it clean.

A shiver runs through my entire body and he catches onto it.

"I'm sorry… for all of this."

Another tear rolls down his temple and I wipe it away. "Why? You kept me safe, even at this cost."

Caleb closes his eyes. "It's the least I could do."

As his consciousness fades, I sit back on my haunches, my heart squeezing at the implication.

As if somehow, my life was more valuable than his.

CHAPTER 44
CALEB

When I wake up, I'm not in Kansas anymore, Toto.

Not that I ever was, actually.

But I recognize the cream colored ceiling with exposed wooden beams, the heavy drapes blotting the sunlight from massive windows to my right. Even the soft mattress that sucks me in like quicksand is the same. And although I can barely move a muscle, it doesn't take glancing around to know I'm in my childhood bedroom.

How did I get here?

With the drapes drawn across the windows, I have no way to tell what time of the day it is. And since I'm alone in the room, I have no one to tell me what day it even is. I try to pull myself up, but there isn't enough mojo in me for even that much, and I collapse back on the mattress.

Flares of pain explode everywhere. There's one in my left shoulder competing with my ribs. The shoulder one I remember—it's not everyday a person gets shot. But what the hell happened to my ribs?

I groan, remembering the last guy. Out of the six on my

tail, he was by far the strongest. Every time he hit me, I felt like one of the punching bags I blew apart in the gym. Did I even manage to defeat him? I can't remember anything that happened after he slammed me against a wall.

Crap, did he drink my blood?

The door opens and in comes my brother. I don't even have to say anything before he realizes I'm awake.

"Dad, Caleb's awake!" he shouts out into the hallway.

"I was hoping for more peace and quiet." My voice sounds like someone tenderly caressed my throat with sandpaper.

"You've had enough of it." Daniel marches into the room with his medical suitcase and pulls up a chair by the bed. "You've been out for a week."

"Whoa." A burst of energy helps me sit up, but it vanishes the second that pain intensifies. "What happened?"

Daniel gives me a funny look. "There's a lot to unpack from that question. Where do you want to start, the extent of your injuries? Who attacked you? Whether we caught them? How the others are doing?"

I wince. "Yeah, one of those."

My brother props up a mountain of fluffy pillows behind me and pushes me back against them. I stay still as he runs a quick check of my vitals, wishing he'd at least start giving me answers at the same time.

There's something about his face, though, that doesn't want to make me press him. I think he's angry at me.

"You got a concussion, cracked two ribs on your left side, got a hairline fracture on your right tibia in addition to extensive bruising all over your body. And oh, that's also excluding a through and through bullet wound on your left shoulder, and also a grazing one on your left thigh."

I open and close my mouth.

Well, shit. No wonder everything hurts and I feel like dying.

Daniel's face is pinched like it gets when he's grumpy. "I

need you to drink three bags of blood per day for a week and
to rest for one more."

"What?" I shudder. "Three bags of blood per day?"

He shrugs. "Unless you want to take as long to recover as a
human, then yeah. Three damn bags of blood per day."

My jaws clamp shut, making a snapping sound.

"You scared us all, Caleb," another voice says. Dad walks
in through the open door.

Behind him is Phelan. I'm both relieved and annoyed that
there isn't a single scratch on him, but at least that partially
answers one of my questions.

To the bodyguard, I ask, "How's my assistant?"

"Safe and sound at her home," he says.

Every muscle in my body relaxes.

My dad sits at the foot of the bed, arms folded. "Phelan
says there were a total of ten men. Four went after him and six
after you. The four men he defeated confessed the target was
actually you."

I bob my head. "Makes sense."

"They did not say why, specifically, they were after you,"
Dad adds and I give him a condescending look I have no right
to produce. He waves a hand. "Aside from the obvious. But
clearly there's someone targeting you with their full intent."

Daniel says, "I don't think this is like any of the previous
kidnapping attempts for ransom. Do you think something
leaked?"

The way Dad looks at Daniel is almost as if he could
throttle him any moment. Weird.

"Anyway," Dad says, facing me again. "The support team
captured the other six and rescued you in time before any of
them could drink your blood."

"Where's my confetti?" I ask, and they ignore me.

"But none of them are saying who sent them, even under
torture." It shouldn't weird me out that my father is talking

about torturing someone, despite twenty seven years of history with him, but here we are. "I've been trying to compel them to talk, but whoever recruited them must also have compelling abilities because they immediately shut down."

Daniel frowns. "Not that many people have such powerful abilities or the money to carry out an operation like this."

Dad nods. "There are only a few families who fit the profile. I'll investigate all of them and find who did this to my son."

He reaches forward and pats my good leg, and I ask, "But why me? Not that I wish Daniel was being attacked at all, but why would anyone target *me*?"

The silence that falls between them is extreme. Even Phelan, standing in a corner as still as a marble statue, seems more animated than my dad and brother.

I narrow my eyes. "You guys are acting so suspicious, it makes me suspect you suspect something very specific."

The last family member waltzes in through the door. A glass of champagne is in her hand and she's dressed for a cock-tail party. I mean, it's not like I expect Diana to be dressed in all black, with bags under her eyes from sleepless nights worrying about my condition, but I also didn't imagine she'd come here looking like she's celebrating.

"I heard you're up," she says, stopping a few paces from my bed and sipping on her drink. "I guess we should be glad you don't die easy, huh?"

"Mom," Daniel warns.

"Well, it's the truth. This is what, like the eighth attempt on his life?" She shrugs.

My eyebrows go up. "Wow, you've been keeping count?"

"Don't flatter yourself. You've simply been the most prob-lematic child in this house."

"All right, that's enough." Daniel ushers his mom outside the door. "He needs to rest, Mom."

From outside the door, her voice carries clearly as she says, "Are you siding with your half-brother instead of with your mother?"

"I'm siding with my patient." Daniel shuts the door with her outside and if seeing that interaction with Diana Mancini-Oh wasn't bizarre enough, it absolutely freaks me out when Dan glares at Dad and says, "Until when are you going to let Mom keep saying things like this?"

Dad takes a deep breath and his voice is dangerously shaky. "One more word about this from you, Daniel Oh, and there will be consequences."

"Fine," Daniel all but barks. "Let's go have those consequences at your studio."

"What the heck is happening?" I ask, and when both of them ignore me I glance at Phelan who, even if he had answers, would never share them without my dad's explicit approval. "Why are you all acting like you're the ones who got whopped up the head?"

Phelan gives me a look as if to say *not me*, and I almost want to laugh. Almost.

"Tell you what," I say, pulling the bed sheets up to my chest. "Dan's right, I need to rest. Go take your business elsewhere."

"C'mon, Dad. Let's finish our conversation." With that, Dan leaves the room.

Dad closes his eyes, taking a moment to collect himself, and I interrupt. "I don't know what's happening between you two, but don't kill him. He's your heir."

"Thanks for the reminder," he mumbles, standing up slowly, exhaustion lines etched on his face. As an afterthought, before he leaves my room, Dad says, "I'm glad you're back safe, Son."

"Ah. Thanks, Dad."

He takes one more second to look at me before closing the door behind him.

Phelan's about to follow him but I clear my throat. "Not you. You stay."

The bodyguard turns like a soldier and clasps his hands behind his back. I narrow my eyes at him.

"What do you know about all of this?"

"What specifically?" he asks, and I grow even more suspicious. It's the first time I don't see him give a direct response to a command.

"Why are they fighting?"

A long, silent moment passes until Phelan says, "I cannot say."

I make a sound from deep in my throat. "Hmm, so you do know the reason but Dad forbade you from speaking, huh?"

Phelan's eyes shift in my direction for a second. That's all I'm going to get out of him.

"Fine, then answer this instead." And really, this is what I'm most curious about. "What happened with Serena?"

"She was unharmed in the attack, although she is shaken."

"Still?" I ask. "A week later?"

Phelan gives me a look of pity. "Wouldn't you be, if you were a human and went through all of that?"

"Crap, you're right."

"She seems to know you're a vampire." His eyes narrow.

"Double crap," I say. "Don't tell Dad. Or anyone."

"Very well," he says, although for the first time I think he actually would rather defy that order. "I trust you know what you're doing."

That's when I know he doesn't trust me for shit. I reach for my cellphone on the bedside table, gritting my teeth through the pain, because if even Phelan thinks I lost the plot, what must Serena be going through after all of this?

I need to reassure her somehow. The problem is that I don't know how, when I'm so freaking helpless.

CHAPTER 45
SERENA

Anyone would think that if a team of men attempted to kidnap the son of a billionaire in downtown Chicago, it would be all over the news, right?

Pues no, nada.

There's absolutely no information to be found. I've tried all keywords and all search engines and got the same grand result of zero. All Caleb's name produces is the old tabloid articles describing him as a womanizer or unhinged, none of which I know to be true now.

Caleb's somewhat eccentric, with his penchant for being underwater as much as possible or with his sense of humor fitting a teenage boy. But he's not any danger to society. He's also not with a different woman hanging from his arm every week. In fact, even sans kidnapping attempts, he doesn't have much time to fool around—with a few exceptions, namely the one that involved kissing me. And even then, it's not like he's a sleaze the way some of these articles paint him.

If any of these reporters knew the truth, the articles would say he's a vampire. A hero. So ridiculously sweet that he's making his assistant's heart beat a million per minute even when she's alone in her room.

I stare up at my ceiling. Bone-deep exhaustion hasn't let me move a muscle ever since I returned from swimming lessons this morning. The reason isn't that, though. It's been a week since the attack in Chicago and I haven't heard any news about Caleb, which is why I've been obsessively trying to find something about him in the news.

When I close my eyes, I can still see him in the hotel bedroom, wounded in ways a human being wouldn't endure. I can still remember how I cradled the back of his head to feed him the blood he needed to survive. And how his eyes, at half mast, looked at me when he asked if *I* was okay.

"Ugh." I put my hand on my chest, willing my heart to beat slower. "Serena Maria Lossada Martinez, we said we weren't going down this path."

Rolling on my bed until I'm facedown, I stuff my face against my pillow and release a series of high-pitched whines.

None of those circumstances have changed. He's still my boss, still a billionaire, still a vampire whose father wants to marry him off to a woman with the same specs. I'm still living from paycheck to paycheck, my student loans are still massive, and my credit card debt is still almost intact. Moreover, I'm still a human with no connections other than to an orphanage.

So why am I yearning for him? Or is this actually survivor's guilt?

Caleb said he would protect me and he did. Almost at the cost of his life. I wish the attack hadn't happened—not just so he wouldn't be injured—but so I also wouldn't feel this way.

I owe him my life and there's nothing I can do to possibly repay him. But I sure want to kiss him.

Fortunately, or unfortunately, my roommate chooses that moment to burst into my room. "Aren't you gonna clean?"

I roll my head to glance at her, but I'm not even wearing

my glasses. With a grunt, I reach for them on the makeshift bedside table—which is actually the cardboard box our blender came in—and put them on. I regret it immediately. She's in her underclothes.

"Aren't you going to put on any clothes?" I volley back.

Karyn rolls her eyes. "This is my house, I can do whatever I want."

And she does. Routinely.

"Ditto, and what I'm going to do today is rest." I make a pause. "Because this is also my house."

The smile she gives me has nothing of amused and everything of evil. She leans her shoulder on the doorframe and folds her arms. "Funny you should say that, because last I checked this place is sixty percent mine. And unless you plan to start paying up for my extra ten percent, you should start cleaning when I say so."

"What's going on, babe?" Richard walks by and smacks his girlfriend's butt so hard that it makes her jump.

I don't know why she doesn't imprint her hand on his face in return.

Karyn pouts at him. "My roomie's being a brat, boo. She doesn't want to do her chores."

Over her shoulder, her boyfriend glares at me. "Do you want me to do something about it, babe?" The fact he says this *about me*, as he continues to feel his girl up, makes me want to puke right then and there. But then I'd have to be the one to clean it up.

"Okay, that's enough." Awkwardly, I get up from the bed and shoo them out of my space. "Go do your thing out of my sight."

Karyn laughs at me. "Why? Are you jealous?"

"No, I'm just barely swallowing my bile back down."

Richard forces the door back open when I attempt to shut it. "So, aren't you gonna start cleaning up this pigsty then?"

As Karyn starts giggling, something inside of me snaps.

"Aww, boo," she says, leaning her face into his neck. "Looks like we made her angry."

"Get the hell out of my room." I grind my teeth so hard that it makes my jaw hurts, but that's nothing compared to the hurt I wish I could inflict on them.

"Or what?" Richard asks. "You gonna kick us out with your forty percent stake in the lease?"

"That's still forty percent more than you pay."

The second those words tumble out of my mouth, Karyn stops her playfulness and jumps out from her man's hold. Before I can react, she slaps me across the face and sends my glasses flying out of my head.

I stand there for a long moment, stunned.

Nothing like this has ever happened before. They're rude, gross, and thinly veiled racists. But they've never been violent.

"How dare you," Karyn says, as if *I* had been the assailant. "This is my house. I can bring whoever the hell I want to live with me if I want and you have no say in that, you damn housemaid."

Even though I want to cry—even though I want to scream and rage, and throw fists and kick them where it hurts—I don't. I will never stoop to their level.

My roommate jabs her index finger against my shoulder, hard enough it'll leave a bruise. "So you better shut the hell up and start cleaning, or else I'm going to demand you pay me back your ten percent for all these years. Should we do that instead? It's the only way you won't keep being my personal cleaner."

I rub my jaw where she hit me. Is she a boxer? Why does it hurt so much?

Pushing my hair away from my face, I smile at her. "No, don't worry. I'll start cleaning right away."

"There." Karyn tosses her hair over her shoulder. "Was it that hard?"

Without waiting for an answer, she turns around and saunters away. Richard's eyes follow her for a moment, before he focuses back on me.

"Don't make me be the one to hit you next time."

I slam the door on his face and lock it. A shiver goes through my entire body and I collapse on the floor, hugging my knees tight against my chest.

If living here has always been uncomfortable, now it's straight up dangerous. I have to get the hell away as soon as I possibly can.

To prevent any further drama for today, I start cleaning the bathroom—using their toothbrushes to clean the dirtiest areas—and promise myself from today on, I will start looking for a place to move. I'll just add the penalty for breaking my apartment lease to my credit card debt. Anything is better than staying here any longer.

Luckily, Richard has a late shift at the supermarket and stays there pretty much for the rest of the day, and Karyn decides to go out with friends tonight. In the calm that remains after they leave, I grab my laptop and start looking.

That's when my cellphone pings with an incoming text message. Seeing Caleb's name on the screen sends my heart to a gallop.

Are you doing okay?

And because I'm not, and I know he also isn't, I burst out into the kind of ugly sobbing I never show anyone else.

CHAPTER 46
CALEB

The security compound of the vampire king is in his basement.

I know, not terribly exciting. Unless you see it.

When Dad bought this private island all those years ago, all the curious public could see were the efforts to build the gothic mansion on its surface, with slanted roofs, dark hues and straight up gargoyles. What they couldn't see, is that the house sits over a subterraneous bunker that is larger than the surface of the island. It contains enough self-defense weapons and IT systems to make Iron-Man weep with joy, and enough getaway cars and airplanes to make Batman jealous.

Not to mention, it's where we have the dungeon.

The place is cinematic, with steel walls and doors, and biometric readers at every corner. It's a geek's dream as much as it is a murderer's. The latter is why I hate it.

I understand that the title of king to the vampires comes with a lot of responsibilities, the main one being keeping the peace among families that have historically feuded, and keeping unruly vampires in line who threaten to topple the precarious balance of our secretive world—but I wish having torture chambers wouldn't be necessary for this.

Call me ethical, but if I can't stand cruelty to animals, I don't know why I should stand it against those of my ilk.

But also, call me a hypocrite because that's exactly what I'm doing right now.

I stand between Phelan and Daniel in a grey room, behind the protection of a one-way mirror. On the other side, a shocking scene: Dad and Diana working together. To torture ten men.

Well, not to torture them anymore, after Phelan took care of most of that. Stepmother's never liked getting her clothes dirty. Instead, as the king and queen of the world's vampire population, they're combining their compelling powers to try to extract any useful information out of the men about who was behind this operation. But so far it's been an hour of both of them trying, and there's been only silence from the captives.

I sigh. "At what point do we give up?"

"Never," my brother says. "Not until we catch the mastermind."

Almost as if to contradict him, my stepmother gets up from her chair and marches out of the room. Her steps echo across the hall outside our door, but continue past it until they fade away.

A good while later, Dad also lets up. He walks into our room shaking his head. "I hate to say this, but either whoever compelled them is too strong or did it in layers. No matter how much we dig, there's nothing we can find in their minds that's worth a damn."

Well, that makes me feel warm and fuzzy.

"No middlemen?" I ask Dad as he takes a seat. There are dark circles under his eyes I don't recall seeing earlier. "I'm sure whoever planned this sent someone else on their behalf. Or even hired them through some shady means, you know."

Dad shakes his head. "There's nothing. The only thing in their minds is how they have to kidnap you and call a phone number once you were in their power. They can't even remember their own names."

"And I assume the phone number doesn't exist anymore?" Daniel asks.

Dad gives him a finger gun. "Bingo."

I run a hand through my hair. "So, a dead end."

"Not entirely," Phelan says. "I have the Midwest team looking for physical clues. They might have cleaned these guys' heads up, but someone must have made a mistake somewhere."

"Good call." Dad turns his eyes to me, they glow as red as streetlights. "You can go drink their blood now."

If I could shrink like a raisin I would. "Do I have to?"

"Yes." Daniel smacks me on the back so hard I lurch forward. "Nothing will help you finish healing faster than the blood of your defeated opponents."

"Am I the only one bothered by that vaguely medieval notion?"

"Yes," Phelan says.

"Only you," Dad adds, snorting.

Daniel points at the door. "Stop dallying. Go feed."

I dally some more by dragging my feet in a way that could shave off layers of the metal floor. I almost want to ask them if I'm the only one bothered by the fact that I'm going to feed on a bunch of men who are tied up, beat up, and on their way to starvation.

But I did defeat five of them, fair and square. The proof is in all the badges of honor they left on my body, which I've been recovering from not with three bags of blood per day, but four.

Even that doesn't make me acquire a taste for the thick, coppery liquid. I have to take deep breaths to not gag as I stare at the first guy's wrist, tied to the armrest of the chair. I lift the sleeve from his arm and bite it. On top of blood, there's the salty taste of sweat and dirt accumulated for days, ever since the security team captured them in Chicago. After this is all said and done, I'll probably have to chug a bottle of Listerine.

Once I'm done feeding on the guy, I wipe my mouth with the back of my hand. "Dude, stop smoking. You taste like an ashtray."

While my parents aren't compelling them, their minds are lucid enough that the guy glares at me. If it wasn't for the gag in his mouth, he'd probably be spitting verse at me.

I pause for a moment, absorbing his blood into my system. It'll take a few minutes until I can figure out what his mutations contributed to mine but if I wait, I'll probably be here the whole night until I reach the last guy.

With that in mind, I move to the second guy and repeat the operation. While this guy's blood tastes like pure sugar, his skin has the addition of mosquito repellant. If it wasn't for the overwhelming desire to throw up, I would laugh.

The third one must be some Don Juan, because even though he was sent out to kidnap someone, he took the time to spray cologne all over himself. That taste makes me even dizzier than a third different type of blood roiling in my stomach.

"You're doing well," my brother's voice comes from the speakers. "Keep going."

All I can respond to him is via groan. I sit back on my ass, gulping for air and tilting my head back to keep the bloody bile down. If I puke, I'll have to start all over again and that would be even worse.

After a moment, I move onto the fourth guy. This one is a more normal one, where the only disgusting thing is the natural taste of his blood. Although it's a little thin. And sure enough, as I finish feeding on his wrist, the punctures of my teeth don't close up as quickly as the others. Not as common on vampires as on some humans.

"You may need to take some antifibrinolytic medication."

The only response the guy can manage is to fight against his bindings.

The fifth guy's blood almost makes me spill my guts right out. It's the most iron-rich blood I've drank in my life. I might as well be drinking a melted down hammer.

When I'm done, I spread on the floor like a starfish and close my eyes.

This part would be better if someone could knock me out cold, but while my stomach feels like a blender at full power, I can feel the mutations traveling through my own blood like a billion ants inside my skin. I grit my teeth not to cry out as my limbs spasm.

Shit, I've never drank so many different vampire bloods at the same time. Normally it doesn't feel like this—like I'm being ripped apart and sewn back together at the same time. There's liquid fire in my veins and I can't help the scream that tears out of my throat.

After a while, I'm only conscious of the sensation fading when it's almost gone. I'm breathing as hard as my lungs can, and even then I can't take in enough air to weather this crisis. I'm drenched in sweat and when I find the energy to sit up, I leave a wet puddle on the floor behind me.

"Halfway there, son," Dad says through the speakers.

His voice tilts my consciousness. It sounds loud enough that I almost pass out at the echo it leaves.

One of these guys has super sharp hearing and now so do I. That'll be an adjustment.

I shake my head, plugging and unplugging my ears with my fingers until the ringing stops. "No, that's it. I only defeated five."

"It doesn't matter," Dad says. "I say you feed on all of

them. That will be their punishment for threatening the royal family."

"No," I say. The silence that falls in both chambers is almost deafening. Slowly, shaking, I pull myself to my feet and turn to the mirror. Through my reflection, I see my eyes are the same neon crimson of Dad's earlier. "I won't feed from all of them. Not until I defeat them all."

There's a brief interference sound before Dad's voice sounds again. "Fine, we have all night."

And unfortunately, that's as long as it takes until, exhausted and nauseated from fighting each and everyone of them off, I start feeding on guy number ten.

CHAPTER 47
SERENA

s this what freedom tastes like?

I lean back on my chair and allow myself a little spin. The Oh men are absent from the office, on the pretense of taking a family vacation. I know otherwise, thanks to Caleb's occasional updates via text message. He's been in recovery from his extensive injuries for the past couple of weeks, sequestered away in his parents' home, where Cedric and Daniel also are.

Why all of them need to be together for Caleb's recovery is a mystery, but their combined absence is a fact that has lifted the spirits of every Comed Solutions employee. Everywhere you look, people walk with lighter steps. There are more smiles —partially thanks to longer lunches, later arrival times, and earlier departures.

It is wonderful. And so very boring.

I hadn't realized until now how much I depend on Caleb's chaos to drive my day. Without him, I've been able to file all expense reports, start drafting the plan for the grants that Caleb offered, and I've even had enough time to clean my entire work station and Caleb's office.

On top of that, with management meetings suspended for the Oh family vacation, there are no fires that need urgent putting out either. Thus, everyday has become the exact same. Come to work, scrounge up anything to do, go home to continue looking for a new place to live.

I narrow my eyes at my computer screen, showing a very quiet inbox this morning. Maybe I should take advantage of the lull to keep looking for apartments here.

The moment I open an incognito window on my browser, someone clears their throat above me. As reflex, I jump half a mile in my seat.

"Hello there, you cutie." I recognize the face smiling down at me, with bronze skin framed by brown hair in perfect beachy waves.

"Uh, hi, Mrs. Oh. Or is it Mrs. Khouri? I'm sorry."

She waves a hand decked in colorful jewelry. "Ugh, no. That makes me sound like my mother-in-law. Please call me Lara."

I smile. "What can I do for you, Mrs. Lara?"

She bursts into a laugh. "Mrs. Lara? Oh, the hoops you jump to stay polite. *Just* Lara."

"In that case," I say, biting the inside of my cheek. "What can I do for you, *Just* Lara?"

Chuckling, she says, "Ooh, I can see why he likes you."

The smile on my face freezes.

Her eyes take on a sly glint. "Anyway, since I know things are slow around here for *reasons*, I'd like to take advantage of them and ask you for help."

"Of course," I say immediately, as though there's actually anything I could do for a woman married to the firstborn of a billionaire, probably with a comparable fortune.

"Excellent, grab your purse and follow me."

Without waiting for my response, she twirls around and heads over to the elevators. I hesitate only for a moment, but it's not as if anyone will need me to be at my desk when the mood in headquarters is a mixture of *screw it* with *let's nap*. I grab my purse, phones and the essentials scattered across my desk, and follow Lara Khouri.

As we stand waiting for the elevator, I'm able to observe her through the reflection on the closed doors. She's taller than me by two or three inches, and although she doesn't have the unreal beauty of a Vivienne Astor, the happiness radiating from her every pore makes Lara ten thousand times more beautiful. She's the kind of person whose very presence makes you want to smile, and I have to put a lot of effort to keep my face straight.

I follow her all the way out of the building, to a Rolls Royce parked out front. A man opens the door for us and she motions for me to climb in first. If the day wasn't packed with enough surprises, there's one more inside the car.

"Marissa?" I ask, as if my eyes could betray me that way.

She twiddles her fingers at me in greeting. "Hey there, Serena! So glad you could join us."

As the three of us strap on our seatbelts and the driver sets the car in motion, I ask, "Where are we going?"

"To my studio," Lara says, fixing the skirt of her flowy summer dress so it sits comfortably over her legs. "My models for today bailed and you guys will substitute them."

"Whoa." I reel away from her. "I can't model."

Lara pouts. "Why not?"

Marissa ignores us. "Last time was so much fun! I'm looking forward to it again."

I stutter through my words. "I—um, I'm not at all like a model. In any way."

"Exactly." Lara grabs my hands. "That's what I'm looking for."

I make two more attempts to convince her that I'm not

right for the job, but the car keeps moving and in a short few minutes, we're at her studio.

If that's what you want to call a whole freaking building.

Her name is on the facade of the building, an art-deco style with at least twenty floors. Everyone greets her with smiles, and some even with hugs, as she makes her entrance with Marissa and I in tow.

"Basically," she explains while we walk. "This is my first everyday-wear clothing line. I'm looking for models just like the target customers. You know, the women you can find in the streets of Miami."

I push my glasses up. "Uh, I don't know if you've noticed but generally speaking, the women of Miami are lookers and I'm well below that average."

Lara stops abruptly and I almost crash into her. She gives me a look of pity. "Aw sweetie, you're stunning. All you need to show it is a change of clothes."

Marissa hooks her arm with mine. "It'll be fun, I promise. Lara's clothes are like magic, they'll make you shed all your inhibitions."

Somehow, at that moment, the word choice doesn't worry me. Curiosity propels my feet one after the other, until Lara directs us to her personal studio at the top floor.

If I could describe it with a single word, it would be chaos.

Swatches of fabric of all colors hang from every available surface. Walls are covered from floor to ceiling in sketches in various degrees of completion. An entire shelf is filled with trophies, pictures and plaques. Opposite to the entrance, massive windows offer a view to the business district, and the mess of downtown Miami looks orderly compared to Lara's office.

"This way," she says, taking us all the way to the back. Here, rows of tables with material and sewing machines precede a room that ends with heavy cream curtains.

The president and head designer of the world-famous *Lara Khouri* brand turns around, clasping her hands. "Here's how we're gonna do this. Marissa, I want you to try on the tops and bottoms combinations, and Serena, you'll try on the dresses."

Marissa salutes. "Roger that."

I cringe, but follow my fellow assistant as she disappears behind the curtains. The nook is divided in two by more drapes. Behind me there is a mirror large enough to capture the reflection of the entire room. And beside me, a rack full of dresses of all colors, shapes, and lengths.

"Um, where do I start?" I ask.

Lara laughs. "Why, by undressing, of course. And then try on any of the dresses."

"Right."

Marissa immediately gets to rustling in her dressing room, and I realize I'm truly trapped but no longer bored. Might as well contribute.

Carefully, I remove my clothes until I'm down to my skivvies. The first dress that catches my attention is a sensible black one. There's no sizing tag but when I put it up against my frame, it seems to be around my size. I walk into it and slide it up my body—and gasp.

"I can't go out in this!"

"Why not?" Lara's voice comes right from outside the curtains.

Even though I can't zip the dress all the way up by myself, just looking at the front is a hard pass. "It's too… revealing."

Which naturally makes Lara say, "Let me see."

"Me too," from Marissa.

Without further ado, the designer opens the curtain and lets out an extended o letter. "Va va boom, mamacita. You look hot."

Marissa was in the middle of changing, because she appears behind Lara with a fancy top on, but with her own pencil skirt still on the bottom. Her jaw drops. "Damn, you were hiding all that?"

I put my arms over my chest. The black dress isn't so sensible after all. It's cinched around the torso, with a cleavage that plunges to the middle of my stomach. If it wasn't for my bra, I wouldn't know how to hold the fabric in place.

"Here," Lara says, zipping it up all the way. Like magic, the fabric tightens around my body and no longer sags at the front. "You'll have to wear this dress with some lacy lingerie to catch the eye."

"Lacy lingerie?" My voice comes out in a screech. "Try more like a turtleneck."

Both women laugh, but as Lara turns me around and moves my arms away from my chest, she says, "If a certain someone saw you wearing this, his tongue would turn into a tie."

Marissa nods. "Caleb would absolutely lose his mind."

I freeze into a statue. "What?"

"Don't worry about it. It's not like people are talking about you and Caleb." Marissa shrugs. "I just happen to be very close to Lara, who happens to be way closer to Daniel Oh, who is very close to Caleb Oh—who apparently has been asking about your wellbeing a lot."

"And when you put two and two together," Lara says as she fiddles with the dress I'm wearing. "It's pretty easy to see why the boy has his eye on you. You're smart, funny, and hot."

I open and close my mouth. Not a sound comes out— which is good, because anything I say will incriminate me.

"Anyway," Lara continues. "If you're not a hundred percent comfortable with this one, I'm sure there's another one that will feel more you. Why don't you try the candy red one?"

I shake my head robotically. "That one has a bare back."

Lara puts her hands on her hips. "You're a Miami girl! You should learn to have some fun."

"Think about it this way. Imagine the expression on his face when he sees you flaunting what your mama gave you." Marissa wiggles her eyebrows.

"No." I push them out of the dressing room. "That's too dangerous."

"Why?"

"What do you mean?"

Because I may like it.

Because it may lead to even more fantasies than those already living rent-free in my head.

"Fine, try the mauve one." Lara takes it out of the rack. "I think this one will definitely be your style. And you, Marissa."

The other girl smiles. "Yes?"

"Let's find you something to dazzle that stoic bodyguard you fancy."

The way Marissa's eyes go as round as saucers almost makes me laugh. Almost. But I'm much more stunned by putting two and two together and I blurt out, "Phelan?"

Marissa's cheeks turn as red as tomatoes.

Lara giggles. "Let's find you both the perfect outfits to make those silly men faint."

CHAPTER 48
CALEB

wake up in the morning to a text message from my sister-in-law. It reads, *did you see this* and includes a link.

Unfortunately, I can't dismiss it as spam because I recognize the URL. It's from one of those local tabloids that love to shit on anyone deemed famous in the South of Florida. While I don't consider myself famous per se, they took an interest in my business since a couple of years ago. Seems like they're back on their bullshit.

Taking a deep breath, I brace myself and click on the link.

A blurry picture of me sitting across from Vivienne at the restaurant appears under a bold headline: *HOT HEIR AND HEIRESS IN MARRIAGE TALKS?*

"What the hell?"

I kick my bedcovers away and jump from my bed, scrolling through the article in the dark of my room. I don't even feel the coldness of the floor on my bare feet or the blasting air conditioning against my skin, because the rage coursing through my veins is hot like lava.

The first thing I do is forward the link to Phelan, and the second is to call him. "What the hell, man?"

He sounds as confused, saying, "I took care of the photographer's camera, there must have been someone else."

I run a hand through my hair. "Of course there was. It's Vivienne."

"My apologies." After a pause he adds, "Should I take care of the newspaper?"

His definition of taking care of someone isn't to send them a gift basket, but beating up a bunch of human civilians from a trashy news outlet won't be the solution here.

"No, there's nothing we can do."

That's the kicker. If I put out a counter article, it'll only drive interest up in this topic and that's exactly the opposite of what I want. The best alternative is for me to grit my teeth and let this blow by—with the public.

I do have to give Vivienne a little phone call to express my displeasure, though. This was so not how I expected my first day back in the office to go.

When I finally get to the headquarters building of Comed Solutions, the only thing that's changed from this morning is that I'm fully dressed. I remain just as pissed, though. Every step I take echoes across the halls of the company and employees give me a wide berth.

When I step out of the elevator, I spot Marissa leaning against Serena's desk. Her voice drifts over to me as she says, "So, what are you going to do for your birthday, then?"

I freeze. Phelan halts beside me.

"Nothing much." Serena sighs. "Since it's on Saturday, I guess I'll have to spend it cleaning or my roommate will throw another fit."

I make a mental note and resume the walk to the office.

Serena scrambles to her feet the moment she spots Phelan and I. "Good morning to you both. It's good to see you've recovered well."

"Good morning, Serena." I say, then glancing at the other woman. "Marissa."

"Um, good morning to you both." Jon's assistant tucks a curl behind her ears. She turns to Serena and says, "I'll talk to you later then!"

Walking around Phelan, she trots back to the elevators.

And then, because Phelan's presence feels the same as a museum statue, it's just my assistant and I.

I stand in front of Serena for a moment, imagining an impossible scenario where Vivienne isn't in the picture, and where I can run up to Serena with my arms wide open. I would lift her in the air before kissing her like no one's watching, but the entire office would witness the event and cheer for us. Then I would lock us in my office so I can show Serena just how recovered I truly am.

Alas, I guess fantasies exist only as escape from realities that are completely different.

Clearing my throat, I say, "Please bring me coffee as strong as tar. I'm going to need it."

"You got it." She turns to my body guard. "What about you, Phelan?"

"I'm fine, thank you."

She nods. "Orange juice it is."

That puts me dangerously on the edge of developing a good mood. Serena's always taking care of everyone, even the people who don't want to be taken care of. Exhibit a, me. Exhibit b, Phelan.

Dude never seems to eat, drink or sleep, and yet he must. Vampires need to do all those to survive. Even during that wretched lunch with Vivienne, Phelan refused to order any food so Serena did it for him, and because Phelan Murray's only known preference is for black clothes and for using as little words as possible, he ate everything without complaint. It's also why I'm able to get him to drink from fairytale princess sippy cups. He doesn't give a rat's ass about optics.

As Serena walks around her desk, I grab her arm. "Wait."

Her eyes meet mine and send a bolt of electricity down my body. Maybe she feels it too, because her voice is airy when she asks, "Yes?"

It takes me a moment to remember that we're not alone and I can't follow through with my fantasies. Or that even if we were isolated from prying eyes, I still shouldn't follow through with the overwhelming desire to kiss her again.

"Give Phelan a silly glass," I say, releasing her arm and stuffing my hands in the pockets of my slacks, lest I grab her again. "I need a pick me up this morning."

Serena blinks fast. "Uh, I'll see what I can find."

I watch her go until she disappears in the kitchenette. Why does she have to have common sense? If it wasn't for that, she would probably agree to go out with me.

But then again, I probably wouldn't like her as much. It's the combination of her many qualities—the wits, the integrity, the determination and yes, the devastating curves—what drives me wild about her. It's precisely the lack of such qualities what repels me about Vivienne.

Once I reach my desk, I take off my blazer and tie, and roll the sleeves of my shirt up to my elbows. I almost feel like I should be wearing firefighting turnouts as I dial Vivienne's cellphone. I set it on loudspeaker so I can pace, and do precisely that as it rings.

She lets it almost go to voicemail before picking up. "If it isn't my future husband, finally calling me of his own free will."

At that moment, the door opens and Serena comes in with a tray. I could cry at the smell of strong coffee wafting my way.

To the phone, I say, "I'm not calling you because I want to but because I have to. Were you the one who got them to publish this bullshit article?"

Serena's eyebrows are as high as they can go when she places the steaming cup of coffee on my desk. I watch her retrace her steps back out of the office through the plumes of stream, and it almost seems like she's a mirage and I'm in the desert, dreaming about her and thirsty for her lips.

Meanwhile, Vivienne says, "It's not bullshit, sugar. I'm just trying to get you used to the facts."

"The only fact in that headline is that I'm hot," I say, snorting. "Everything else is a fallacy and I'd like you to get used to *that* fact once and for all."

This somehow makes her laugh. "Wow, I've never actually liked you much, Caleb. But the more annoyed you pretend to be, the more I want you."

I grind my teeth. "First of all, I'm not pretending, and second, I'm not an object no matter how much you try to treat me like one."

Vivienne has the gall to ask, "Are you sure you don't like it? Men like to be seduced a lot more than they let on. You wouldn't be pitching a hissy fit if you'd just let me show you a good time."

That catches me in the middle of sipping my coffee and the hot liquid goes down the wrong pipe. In between coughs, I say, "When will you catch a hint? I'm not interested in you—not now and not ever. Not even if you parade naked in front of me."

Vivienne hums. "Should I try that next time I drop by your office? I bet that would be a real eye popper."

"Stop, this isn't funny. If the situation was reversed you'd be calling the police."

"Actually, no." She laughs. "I would love to see that. You've grown up pretty fine for someone who doesn't even feed properly."

I take a deep breath. "Listen to me, and listen to me well.

You need to stop this shit. If I see any other articles like this I will sue you."

"Fine," Vivienne says, which is the opposite of what I expected. But then she adds, "I guess I'll have to do all the seducing in private."

"Go seduce a lamp post."

Her lilting laugh makes me grind my molars. "I would probably get more of a reaction out of it. Are you sure you don't have some deficiencies in your family jewels? Or do you bat for the other team?"

As someone who is an expert at offending other people with the things that hurt them the most, I'm not the slightest miffed by her implications about my sexuality.

Instead, I imbue as much sarcasm to my voice as vampirily possible. "Is it that hard to accept that I'm just not into you?"

There's a heavy pause that tells me I hit the nail on the head.

I sip from my coffee and fight against a smile. Vivienne Astor always gets what she wants, whether it be men, cars, land or businesses—but she's not gonna get me. Vivienne's seduction techniques may work on every other guy on this planet, but it's not *her* I bat for.

"We'll see about that," she says, hanging up the call.

I might not have been the one to get the last word, but it sure feels like it.

CHAPTER 49
SERENA

There's a video from a Venezuelan comedian in the US, who parodies how long the birthday song is in the culture of my parents's home country. As a nod to them, I watch it from bed on Saturday morning.

I wear my headphones and hide under the bedsheets, just in case my asshole roommate and her even more despicable boyfriend barge in. Pretending to sleep in is the best gift I can give myself on this fine September thirteenth morning.

After the video ends, I toggle back to browser to look up a cool bakery I can hit up later today, but the browser is still open with the tabloid article about Caleb and Vivienne Astor, and my brains become scrambled eggs. Whoever took this picture, captured her in a moment when she was leaning over the table to reach for Caleb.

From the angle of the picture, the edge of the table hides her dress altogether almost making her look naked, which I'm sure is selling copies. Right behind her, I can spot my pony tail and I'm glad that my back is turned toward the camera, but that's as far as my good feelings go.

The captions under the picture read, *Vivienne Astor, heiress to the most powerful bourbon family in Kentucky, and Caleb Oh, second son of Comed Industries. Who knows what was happening under that table?*

"I can tell you," I murmur to the screen. "Absolutely nothing."

No matter how long Vivienne's legs are, there's no way she could reach Caleb from such a distance. And as for him, I wouldn't blame him if her cleavage awakened his interest—but if it did, he didn't show it.

I drop my phone on my bed and peek down at my chest. It's as gravity-defying as Vivienne's, but Lara's creations show that I do have something to flaunt.

"Ugh. What am I thinking?" I turn until I bury my face in my pillow. As if I'd ever wear something like that in public—or have an occasion for it.

Buzzing suddenly explodes against my stomach and I yelp, but it's only my phone with an incoming call. I can't think of a single person who would call me today, and I'm doubly shocked when I see it's my boss, the *hot heir.*

"Um—"

Before I get another word in, Caleb says, "I have an emergency."

"I am not going to take swimming lessons from you ever again."

"No, this is a real emergency," he says.

I huff. "Nothing in your voice leads me to think you're in any sort of pinch."

I should've stayed mum and hung up instead, because Caleb deepens his voice in a way that does something to my hormones. "Oh but I am, and I need *you,* Serena."

Goosebumps break all across my skin and I have to toss away the bedsheets. The feel of them against my limbs is suddenly too much. I press a hand against my rapidly beating heart, willing it to slow down.

Trying to sound annoyed, I ask, "What now?"

"Well, I need you to come with me."

"To the office?" I can barely stifle a groan at the thought. Although, actually, that might be better than spending my birthday cleaning up after Karyn and her boyfriend.

"Nope, I'm downstairs."

"You what?" I screech.

"But you don't need to hurry." Caleb chuckles. "Just make sure to wear comfortable clothes and shoes."

"Caleb Oh, what are you plotting?"

He ignores my question. "And also, I got you breakfast. So maybe you do want to hurry after all."

With that, he ends the call.

I get up from bed and find my reflection in the mirror. My hair is a tangled mess tumbling down my back, and all I'm wearing is an oversized T-shirt that saw better days five years ago. A laugh threatens to escape at the thought of showing up in front of my boss like this. Taking a shower and dressing presentably will take a good moment.

And then what excuse can I give my tormentors for having to ditch a cleaning day?

But then again, I bought a baseball bat since the previous little incident.

"Wait a second," I tell myself, folding my arms. "I shouldn't be doing any of this."

I have to keep my distance from Caleb, and tagging along to whatever shenanigans he wants to rope me into is the opposite of that. In contrast, I also want to stay the heck away from Karyn and Richard. The lesser of the two evils is definitely Caleb.

And it's my freaking birthday.

With that in mind, I take a quick shower. I spend most of the time contemplating what to wear and what to do with my hair, but in the end I go for a simple white T-shirt, boyfriend jeans and white sneakers. I do my hair up in a half ponytail and pack up my essentials in a mini backpack.

A final inspection in the mirror confirms that no one would post a picture of me in a tabloid, and I decide that's a good thing.

Richard's in the kitchen, drinking orange juice directly from the carton. "Where are you going?"

"I need to shop for tampons," I say, effectively shutting him up. That allows me a smooth exit without further questions.

Downstairs, I spot the Urus among the modest cars of the residents. I climb onto the backseat and Caleb offers me a paper bag right away.

"Congratulate me," he says. "It was really hard to not to eat it, but I held back."

I take the bag from him, shaking my head. "Congratulations, I guess. But this better not be another silly ploy of yours."

Caleb's brown eyes shine like amber stones against the sun. "Why, but it is. Hit the pedal, Phelan!"

I jerk back as Phelan takes the order a bit too literally. Before they get me killed on my birthday, I fasten my seatbelt. "No, but for real. What's the emergency?"

"It requires a bit of travel, but you'll understand when we get there."

A bit of travel ends up being three hours on the road, which clearly indicates this isn't work related. But no matter how many times I try to coerce explanations from Caleb, he's as tight-lipped as his bodyguard typically is. I spend the biggest portion of the drive dozing off, which already makes this the best birthday I could've got.

"We're here," Caleb's voice says right next to my ear. When I shift around and open my eyes, I find his face very close to mine. His eyes lower and for a second I'm sure he's going to kiss me, but then he pulls away. "Welcome to Universal Studios in Orlando!"

My jaw drops. "How is this in any way an emergency?"

Caleb opens his door and gets out of the car to stretch. "I debated whether to fly you to Barbados or Costa Rica, but I figured anything over a day trip would annoy you."

Phelan opens my door and stands there, silently pressuring me to step out of the SUV. I do and Caleb bounces over. The way excitement drips from his every pore puts me even more on edge.

"Problem is, I spent so long debating it that the day almost went by—hence, this turning into an emergency," my boss continues saying as he stuffs his hands in the pockets of his jeans. "If I didn't do anything to celebrate your birthday, I would be even more annoyed."

I open and close my mouth. "What?"

"I overheard you and Marissa." He rubs the back of his head. "Happy birthday, Serena."

Something hot takes over my chest, expanding across my body and settling behind my eyes. I look down at the asphalt of the massive parking garage until I know I won't start crying in front of Caleb Oh.

"Thank you."

There's a clapping sound. "Now, let's forget everything that sucks about the world and have fun."

Clearing my throat, I say, "And you're covering all expenses right?"

Caleb does a flourish with his hand and bows. "It would be my honor."

Since it's noon in a weekend, the park is packed with people as far as the eye can see. But Caleb buys fast passes for all three of us so we can skip the lines.

"First we start there," I declare, pointing at the biggest

rollercoaster. I've only seen it in pictures and I really would like to celebrate today from new heights.

"Really?" Caleb asks, eyebrows raised. "I'd have figured you were a teacup kind of person."

I toss my hair over my shoulder. "If I didn't have any adventure in me I wouldn't have taken on the job as your assistant."

Caleb nods. "Good point."

We manage to sit at the very front of the rollercoaster, Caleb beside me and Phelan behind us. I nudge my boss with my elbow. "What's that? Are you nervous?"

"Me?" Caleb blows a raspberry. Then wipes a bead of sweat from his forehead. "I've survived worse."

Once the ride starts, he's the one who screams the loudest.

Once the ride ends, he's also the one Phelan and I need to drag away.

We make a stop by the souvenir shop and as Caleb recovers his breath, I wait around to see if they took any good pictures of us.

My patience is rewarded. There, in the middle of the screen, is our picture. Caleb's hands are hiding his face from the camera and I remember the precise moment. It was during a sharp drop, when covering his face muffled his screams. Meanwhile, I'm captured in an instant where I laughed my head off. In contrast, Phelan looks like he was taking his passport picture.

The scene makes me burst out laughing and I have to buy the picture. Best birthday present ever.

CHAPTER 50
CALEB

Who would've imagined that my sensible, strict assistant, is a rollercoaster fiend?

Not me.

But after the third rollercoaster, I start dragging her to the nearest teacups. She laughs at me as we spin and I can't even be annoyed, because on my left Phelan sits ramrod stiff and *that* makes me laugh. It also almost makes me upend my stomach.

"I thought you'd be the one dragging me to the biggest rides," Serena says later, as she takes an ice cream cone from the seller.

I eat a spoonful of lemon sorbet and freeze, not because of how cold it feels in my mouth, but because Serena licks her chocolate ice cream, and I feel it viscerally—the severe envy over an innocent ice cream cone. The only thing that saves me from letting out a groan is a choking fit.

Since Phelan is closer, he interrupts eating his own popsicle to pat my back.

"Thanks," I tell him in between coughs, with tears trickling down my eyes.

He surprises me by murmuring, "You're too transparent, you perv."

Clearing my throat, I glance at Serena from the corner of my eye, but she's too focused on her treat to have noticed what a perv I am.

"So, what next?" I ask her as we resume the walk across the park, sorting through throngs of people moving in all directions.

"I would like some Marvel souvenirs."At my obvious surprise, Serena adds, "What? Shocked that I'm also a super-hero fan?"

I grin. "I'm starting to think the real onion here is you. You're full of layers."

She gives an exaggerated sigh. "You have no idea."

Only because she walks a step before me, I allow myself a quick glance down her frame with the fervent wish I could be the one to peel all her layers off. But damn it, alas.

I buy her enough souvenirs to fill up four shopping bags. They're stuffed with small items like keychains, stickers, pins, and pens. I don't understand why she needs so many, but I also don't question it.

After I'm done paying, I hand the purchase to Phelan. He looks really funny carrying bags with Captain America's face on them. They kinda look like cousins, one blond and one ginger.

To Serena, I say, "You're not gonna tell me your burning birthday wish was to have enough keychains to use a different one every day for a year."

"No, it's for the kids in the orphanage."

I stop in the middle of the walkway.

She must have felt me not following, because she also pauses and turns. "What?"

I tilt my head. "Orphanage?"

"You didn't read my file?" Serena asks, scratching her elbow. "I was raised in an orphanage."

"Whoa, I had no idea." My jaw drops for a second. "And believe it or not, I've never read your file. In fact, Dad never gave it to me."

"Oh." Serena looks down for a second. "Well, does this change anything?"

"Of course it does," I say, which immediately turns her expression sour. I grab her wrist and pull her back to the store. "We should buy more stuff."

The smile that blooms on her face makes my day. I would ride fifteen aggressive rollercoasters, back to back, for that smile.

One hour later, I buy so much stuff from the store that they agree to ship it for me, and Phelan's arms get freed up again. There's a pep in Serena's step I've never seen before. For the first time, she looks her age. A twenty-something year old girl without a care in the world, whose eyes shine at the wonders around her.

Rather than being pleased, I'm angry that it's taken this long for anyone to give her this joy.

She finally steers us in the direction of a restaurant. There's a massive line we won't be able to skirt with fast passes, and all three of us go to the end. Serena is drenched in sweat after running around the parks in the scorching late summer heat and, frankly, I'm not faring much better. I use my grey T-shirt to fan myself and the movement catches her attention.

"So, onions sweat too, huh?"

We're surrounded by tourists who speak other languages, so as long as we don't use the V word, we should be fine.

Phelan gives us a weird look, but of course he says nothing.

Both of them make me grin. "Yes. We also get stinky after sweating too."

"But you don't get tanned?" Serena eyes my arms before

comparing them to hers by lifting the sleeve of her T-shirt just a notch. There's a distinct tan line on her skin and I wish I could run my finger across to test how soft it is.

"Uh, yeah." I run a hand through my damp hair. "We don't. No matter our skin color, we stay pretty pale."

Serena leans closer to whisper. "I wonder if that's where the writer of Twilight came up with the idea that onions glitter under the sun—because you're always pale?"

I have to stuff my fist against my mouth to resist laughing, and also because she smells so good that I want to lick her like she did her ice cream cone earlier. There's still a lingering scent of soap in her skin along with the sweat, and also something unique that makes my blood tingle.

"Maybe," I say. "But rather than having diamond skin, we just don't need sunblock."

Serena shakes her head. "Even after all of this, I still can't get used to it."

"Don't worry, neither can I." I shrug.

A half hour later, the three of us are finally sitting at a table in an enclosed place with air conditioning. I could probably melt on the chair.

"Thanks about earlier, by the way." Serena says while looking at the menu.

I position my chair to better catch the flow of air from the vents and ask, "About what?"

"The gifts for the kids." She takes a deep breath that she lets out slowly. "I've been meaning to buy them something nice, now that I have a full time job. But all I could afford was snacks."

I pull up my menu and spread it open to hide my face. Phelan is probably right about how transparent I am. I'm sure if she glances up she could see how I'm on the verge of sliding over the table to kiss her.

But that would shatter this delicate truce.

Instead, I ask, "So, feel free to not answer but, why were you raised in an orphanage?"

Her eyes shift to mine over the edge of her menu, then back down to it. For a moment, it seems like she's going to choose not answering the question, but she closes the menu and sets it on the table.

"My parents migrated from Venezuela as soon as they married," she says, pausing to track a drop from the wall of her water glass with her finger. "They were very poor there but that didn't stop organized crime from targeting them. Coming here was probably the best they could do, but it didn't end well for them."

I frown. "What happened?"

"I think they had maybe one good year together here before Mom got pregnant with me." Serena takes a sip of water before continuing. All throughout, she makes no eye contact. "She died while giving birth to me. So, today is my birthday and also the anniversary of her death."

"Oh."

I'm as still as Phelan, wondering if I should change the topic. But I guess I want to know more, because I don't try. And Serena wants to share, because she continues speaking.

"Dad raised me on his own after that." A little smile forms on her lips. "I actually heard he worked at Comed during that time."

I lean forward. "No way. What was his name?"

"Arturo Lossada," she says, the smile slowly fading away. "He died when I was seven. And since we had no one else here, Dad had listed Sister Emilia as my next of kin, and I was delivered to her after that. She's the headmistress of the orphanage and more or less became my parent after that."

"What would you like order?" a waitress says, appearing by our table as if by magic.

"Um," Serena's voice cracks as she changes gears. "May I have the shepherd's pie, please?"

"You got it." The girl turns a blinding smile at me. "And you sir?"

"The vegan burger, please." I hand her our three menus and add, "And this guy will take the regular cheeseburger."

"With fries?"

"Yes, please." I gesture with my hands. "A whole pile." And *I* will eat them all. I need an outlet for my sudden stress.

After the server leaves, everything in Serena's postures screams *uncomfortable*. Gone is the easygoing mood she had earlier. I wish I could reach for her hand. I have to sit over mine to not follow through.

"If it makes you feel better, my family's far from perfect." I shrug. "My dad and brother are okay, a bit out there at times but nothing terrible. But my dad's wife hates me because I'm an illegitimate child."

Serena's jaw drops.

I snort. "Bet you can't find that in the tabloids, huh?"

"I—no. I had no idea." She shakes her head as if to clear it.

"It's not common knowledge. My stepmother hates people finding out about the infidelity even more than she hates me."

"She hates you?" Serena smacks the table. "But it's not like it's your fault."

I throw my hands up in the air. "Exactly. But I guess I must remind her too much of my mother or something."

"Wait." She tilts her head. "You guess?"

I grimace. "Ah. I'm just realizing that we have that in common too. My mother also passed away."

Serena lets out a long exhale. "You're right, in a very strange way I do feel better."

"Misery loves company?"

She shakes her head. "No, it's more like… finding *one* thing we have in common is kinda comforting."

The reminder of everything else we're different in hangs heavy over us. The money, the position, the sub-species. I'm suddenly glad there's something I can grasp onto, any excuse no matter how painful, so I can keep her by my side.

"So." I clear my throat. "Does this mean we can be friends?"

She pushes her glasses up her nose and her eyes get lost in the distance. "Only friends?"

No.

More.

Much more.

But that answer would make her run away. Instead, I say, "Yes."

I bet Phelan can read my mind, but somehow Serena doesn't. Her eyes focus back on mine, shining with a tentative smile. "In that case, yes. We can."

Simultaneously, it feels like the biggest victory of my life, and also the biggest defeat. But for now, I'll take it.

CHAPTER 51
SERENA

Finding a decent place to live in at a cost that isn't astronomical shouldn't be so hard, and yet that's the state of affairs in the city of Miami. Every time I find a place where bacteria don't crawl from the walls, it's well out of my means. Every time I find a place within budget, just looking at the pictures makes me want to wash my eyes with bleach.

The only feasible option really is to move in with roommates. But after the experience I've had with Karyn, I'm not eager to gamble my peace of mind with someone new who might turn out to be worse.

I groan and lean back, resting the back of my head against the chair and closing my eyes. Since work hasn't been too action packed this morning, I was able to dedicate some time to looking at apartments for rent online. I might as well have thrown that time down the toilet, considering all the luck I've had.

"What are you up to?"

I jump in my skin. Marissa stands in front of me, blinking as though my reaction was disproportionate. Caleb and Phelan have been upstairs with Mr. Oh for a good portion of the morning, and since Caleb texted me saying they'd grab lunch with his dad I wasn't expecting anyone around here.

"Uh." I low-key switch tabs from my browser to a random Excel sheet just in case. "Nothing much, slow Monday. And you?"

"Same." She leans on the counter above my desk. "Which is why I want to take you out on a long lunch to celebrate your birthday belatedly."

A smile blooms on my face. "You don't have to."

"But I want to." Marissa snaps her fingers. "So pack up your stuff. I've already got permission from our supervisor to play hooky to our hearts content."

"Really? Jon is on board?"

She bobs her head while I collect my things and stuff them in my purse. "He probably would be joining us if that meeting wasn't running long."

"What even is the meeting about?" I ask as we get on the elevator together.

She hums from her throat. "I don't know the details, but it's something about Daniel's classified research project."

My eyebrows go up. What can be classified about anything the Oh men are doing, unless it relates to vampires?

And then I put two and two. Daniel is a hematology expert. And a vampire. Whatever he's working on is about blood and not anything I'm supposed to be privy to.

As we walk onto the massive parking garage for Comed employees and visitors, I change the focus of the conversation by asking, "So, what's the plan?"

Marissa clicks on her car key and a sensible Toyota blinks nearby. "We can go wherever you want. There are some really good restaurants nearby. Cuban, Mexican, a couple of decent American grills, Italian—"

"Oh, yes. Pasta, please."

She laughs. "As the birthday girl desires."

The drive is short enough that we probably should've walked, but mid September is still pretty balmy and I'm thankful for the air conditioning of her car. The restaurant is decorated in a style that makes you feel like you're a Tuscany villa, with terra-cotta tiles, rough walls, and iron appliqués with real wax candles. I immediately know I can't afford it.

"Uh." I lean closer to Marissa as we wait for the host to grab menus for us. "Can we go somewhere cheaper? I'm kinda tight this month."

And every month until I'm able to move out.

Marissa smacks my arm. "Don't you worry about that, it's my treat."

She leaves me gaping like a fish out of the water to follow the host. I'm too happy to continue protesting by the time we sit at our table. It's right by floor-to-ceiling windows and a view into a gorgeous garden, and for a moment it doesn't feel like we're in the south of Florida.

A waitress sets a little tray with soft, warm bread and olives and I'm in love.

Just as I start thinking this would be a great place for a date, Marissa sets a small gift box before me.

I cock an eyebrow. "You're not about to propose, are you?"

She grins. "Not me. This is from Lara. She wanted to congratulate you in person but she's in New York on business."

"You guys are ridiculous." I push the box back to her. "None of this is necessary. We're practically strangers."

"I would like to think accidentally seeing your employee file and finding your birthday that way is the perfect excuse for us to become friends." That said, she places the box on my hands. "And after the fun we had with Lara, I'm pretty sure she feels the same way, so open it, woman."

Friends. What a concept.

If I look back at my low-key but bizarre life, I can't find a single person I can call a friend. Sister Emilia is more of a parent figure I still occasionally run to for comfort, but it's not like I always share the reasons why I may need comforting.

Growing up in the orphanage, it wasn't like things were hostile among the kids. We did our chores, went to school, tried to fit in despite being round pegs in a square world. Some of them did, and established bonds with other orphans or with kids at school. But I never could. I was too busy pouring my entire attention on schoolwork, thinking of the next stage.

Then when I was in college, I did the exact same thing— studies over relationships with people. As someone who was several steps behind everyone else, I had to focus on catching up rather than getting distracted with relationships that would make me hang back. Even when there was someone I liked in my major, I ignored that and kept my nose in the books.

I open the gift box. Inside, there's a pair of dainty earrings made of gold threads into the shape of a daisy. They're the cutest thing I've seen with my four eyes.

"I can't accept this." I sigh. "It's way too pretty."

"You'll accept them even if I have to put them in your ears myself."

That tears a short laugh out of me. "Sheesh, I didn't know you could be so forceful."

Marissa leans her chin on her hand and bats her eyelashes. "I wouldn't have to be if you weren't so stubborn."

"Good point." I put the gift box in my purse. "And I'm really touched by the gestures. I'm just so unused to this."

"To gifts?"

I gesture around us. "To everything."

"Hmm." She picks up her menu and peruses it for a moment. "I hope you get used to it quickly because we like you."

I duck my face behind my menu and stay like that for as long as I can. Between Caleb declaring that we're now friends to this, I may start to think there are actually people out there who can tolerate me. Another concept I've never had the opportunity to explore.

We place our orders. Since we can't decide between pasta and pizza, we order one of each to share along with side salads.

"Even if there's no room for dessert after all of this," Marissa declares while munching on bread. "We should still get that chocolate bomb from the last page."

It looked like a lava cake inside of a chocolate globe. Just thinking about it makes my mouth water.

"Oh, absolutely. We must."

"So, what did you do on your birthday?" she asks, setting the bread back down on the tray. "I gave you a call to see if you wanted to hang out but you wouldn't pick up."

"Oops."

The word comes out from my heart because, yes, I did see her missed call—about two hours after I received it, while I was hopping back in Caleb's car to start the long drive back down to Miami.

"I, uh." I clear my throat. "I was out with a friend."

Marissa draws in an exaggerated gasp. "What kind of friend?"

"Just a friend I've made recently." I wave my hand, but that's not enough to disinterest her from the topic.

She leans over the table. "Is it... a male friend?"

Responding honestly would be a trap, so I say, "No, just a friend who isn't going to be anything more." No matter how much I think about kissing him.

Marissa gives me a look that makes it clear she doesn't believe a single word I said. "Does that mean you aren't interested in anyone at the time?"

Oh, I am. I'm very interested in someone. But he happens to be wrong for me in every possible way and I'm trying to train myself into looking at him only through a professional lens. Like I should have, all along.

"Nope." Diversion is the only solution, so I ask, "And you?"

Her demeanor shifts, first by the subtle pout that bows her lips, then by the way she can't stop tearing pieces of her bread portion.

"You don't need to say anything if this makes you uncomfortable," I say.

"No, it's not that." She dusts flour off her hands and sighs. "It's just sort of a lost case. He's just like… in a different realm altogether. Every time I look at him my heart beats a million per minute. I'm pretty sure he can hear it from the distance. But there's no reaction. Nadita de nada. Like he doesn't care about anything."

I'm frozen between wanting to scream again and laughing. It takes me a moment to compose myself. "Don't take it personally, Phelan is just like that about… everything, really."

Marissa puts her hands on her face. "You also think it's impossible, right?"

"I—honestly, it might just take some work." Laughter bubbles to the surface until it bursts out. Instead of being offended, Marissa joins and next thing, starts telling me all about how she developed a crush on the stoic, but very good looking bodyguard.

For the first time, I'm making an actual friend. It's the best birthday gift I could've ever got.

CHAPTER 52
CALEB

f I look like a million bucks it's because I'm wearing just as much. On my top half alone.

The diamond cufflinks keep catching on the fabric of my tux, and my stepmother sends me a glare when she catches me fidgeting.

"You best not act like a nervous little child in front of all those people," she says from her spot in the back of the limo. Beside her, Dad's stare is lost in space, somewhere between the back of the driver's head and the alternate reality we all would rather be in.

Across from me, Daniel and Lara sit together. My brother also looks like a million bucks. His wife looks about ten, give or take. I like that the handkerchief in Daniel's pocket matches the emerald green of Lara's dress. My pocket has a white handkerchief that matches the emptiness on the seat beside me.

I don't bother stuffing the sigh that will no doubt bother my stepmother. Glancing out the window, all I see is darkness. There are so many places I'd rather be, but the top choice is going back to an amusement park with Serena—

and Phelan. Even his company is more enjoyable than these affairs.

Yet, here I am, on my way to the Gonzalez-Blackwell banquet. Every so often, one of the more affluent vampire families will throw a party we have to attend for unity's sake. Which means an evening of blood-thirsty hypocrites, vying for the king and queen's attention.

Diana loves them. Dad, Daniel and Lara tolerate them. I abhor them.

Today, I especially do, because Vivienne informed me in advance that she'll be in attendance.

"How long do I have to be at this thing for?" I ask, running my finger across a cufflink sharp enough to draw blood.

Rather than answering my question, Stepmother says, "Don't you dare leave before we do. The Oh family has to show a completely united front."

With a deadpan voice, I reply, "Yes, *mother*."

She hates it when I call her that way, but it's also how she wants to be addressed in public. With her arms crossed, she squeezes her own flesh so hard that her nails will leave marks under the dress. No doubt she wishes it was my neck instead.

When we finally reach the old Blackwell manor that sits in a densely forested area in upper New York state, my step-mother emerges from the vehicle like blood personified. With her paper-white complexion and blonde hair, it's impossible for the eye not to be drawn to the way her crimson dress flows around her. Dad is a spot of darkness beside her in his black tux, shirt and tie. His black hair is sleeked back in a severe wave. Despite being several steps behind them, even I'm intimidated.

Between that couple and I, is another one. Daniel and Lara walk arm in arm, and the newlywed atmosphere between them hasn't vanished after twenty years of marriage. Their easy smiles and even the colors they chose, speak of hope and kindness in a way my parents don't. Daniel and Lara will be a great king and queen in the future.

Closing rank is me, the black sheep of the family. Far more eyes than makes sense turn my way upon our entrance. I run a mental inventory of myself. Hair, on point. Zipper of slacks, closed. Holes in my clothes, none.

So why are they staring?

Stevie Blackwell, the matriarch of this clan, parts the crowd on her way to Dad. A few paces before him, she bows low enough for her nose to touch her knees. "It is such a great honor to have you grace our halls, Your Highness."

One by one, all the vampires in attendance bow to Dad.

It's easy to forget what he is when no one at Comed is allowed to curtesy to him, lest the humans start suspecting something. But as Dad bids them to rise, I get the reminder that nothing about my family is normal.

"Thank you for your hospitality," he tells Stevie, now that she's upright. "I trust that you and your family are well?"

"All thanks to you." She smiles, motioning at someone at a distance. "Marissa speaks nothing but praises of working at Comed. Roberto and I are so proud she can assist you—Honey, come greet the royal family."

Roberto, Marissa's father, appears beside Stevie. He repeats his bow and starts talking with Dad about business. The Gonzalez-Blackwell family is the result of two oil dynasties, one from South America and the other from North America. Naturally, Dad has stakes in the business and seems almost glad to have an excuse to extricate himself from Diana's hold.

Now bored, Diana latches onto Daniel's arm. "Come, Son. Let's greet your future people together."

The fact that she doesn't invite Lara or I to join would annoy us—if we were entirely different people. Instead, my sister-in-law and I make a bee line for the bar.

"Are you thinking what I'm thinking?" Lara asks me as she picks up the front of her long dress to hurry up.

I chuckle. "If what you're thinking is that we should get plastered, then yes."

We down a whole champagne bottle together as we watch my parents and brother work the room. Clusters of people follow them wherever they go. Every so often, Daniel casts a look at us that begs for rescue, and every time, Lara and I raise our glasses to him and don't move from our spots.

If the whole evening continues this way, it won't be so bad. I set my empty glass on the bar behind us, about to ask the server for a refill when a commotion by the entrance catches my attention—and in the next second I wish it didn't.

Vivienne walks into the Blackwell manor wearing something that can only be defined as a gown by the long skirt, but is otherwise paper mâché. The top has to be glued to her skin because there's no law of physics that can explain it.

Lara whistles. "Ballsy of her to wear one of my gowns."

I raise my eyebrows at my sister-in-law. "You designed that?"

"Yup." She shrugs one shoulder. "Although it was meant to be for that famous actress in those superhero movies, what's her name?"

I don't answer. I'm too busy looking for the exit signs.

If there's such thing as battle armor, this is the kind Vivienne would choose. She's determined to make others catch us in a compromising position that will set her claim over me in stone, a very Victorian scheme for someone using very little clothes to achieve those means.

My stepmother greets her halfway, pulling Vivienne into a big hug that signals to the entire audience that Vivienne Astor has moved up the chain, and now has the interest of the queen.

That's sort of when I notice they're like two generations of the same woman. Blonde, beautiful, and cold-blooded.

The realization makes me like Vivienne even less than I already do.

"No matter what," I say to Lara. "Please don't leave my side."

She sneaks her arm around mine. "You got it, little brother. I'm not gonna let that throne digger put her claws on you."

"Throne digger?"

Lara laughs. "Well, she has plenty of gold already so what else could she possibly be after? No offense, but it's probably not your heart or body."

I let out a brief hum. "None taken. You have a good point."

Diana sweeps the younger woman with her. As they head in my direction, my body fills with dread. If they both worked together to kill me, they would absolutely succeed. Fortunately, my stepmother dislikes public drama much more than she dislikes me, so the only one I really have to look out for is Vivienne.

"Caleb," she says, in a tone of voice that makes several men nearby turn. Vivienne sweeps her eyes down and back up my frame. "It's so good to see you."

"Can't say the same," I mumble.

"Lara," my stepmother says with a smile that has nothing pleasant. "Why don't we leave the two lovebirds alone?"

I choke on air. "The—what?"

Of course, a ripple goes through the people all around. Even if not every vampire has augmented hearing, Diana said it loud enough that a human across the massive manor would probably hear it.

"Aww, thank you so much for looking out for me, Diana." Vivienne gives the queen an air kiss. "I would so love to spend some alone time with my future fiancé."

For someone with such a high IQ, it takes me far too long to realize that this was a setup. They both orchestrated this moment and I wouldn't be surprised if the reason why we joined this random gala was for this very reason.

Nothing pisses me off more than being played like a toy, though.

As if nothing was amiss, I turn around and grab a new glass of champagne for Lara and one for me. To my sister-in-law, I say, "Future fiancée? That's funny, I thought you were married already."

An abrupt laugh rises from Lara's throat, in conflict with the champagne she was drinking. I busy myself patting her back and ignoring the fuming women.

"Obviously not her," Vivienne says through a smile made of gritted teeth. "You."

"Me?" I put my hand on my chest. "I'm sure you have the wrong person. Trust me, I would've noticed if I'd asked anyone to marry me."

"Stop this babbling," Diana says to me in a hiss.

"I would, if you both would start making sense." I nudge my sister-in-law. "Now, if you'll excuse us. I promised Lara a dance."

I spend the rest of the night avoiding the two blonde women, but unable to hide from the stares of Dad's court. Somewhere in the back of my mind, there's the certainty that I'll pay for this. But for now, I'll enjoy my little victory.

CHAPTER 53
SERENA

Watching old Venezuelan soap operas is one of my favorite pastimes. It's the only way I have to reminisce about Dad's accent.

I used to speak Spanish with a heavy Venezuelan accent at home and Spanglish at school. My mix of colloquialisms from classmates of Boricua, Dominican, Cuban ascent and more, used to clash with Dad's. He would tease me for changing r's into l's, and I would tease him for saying *mira vale* every other sentence.

A soap from the '80s sounds in the background from my laptop. Comforting noise over the ruckus that Karyn and Richard have in the living room. I did all the cleaning and a fair bit of cooking in the morning, which fortunately has bought me plenty of alone time this afternoon to start packing.

Not that I've found a new place to live yet, but with the way things are deteriorating here, I may have to make a dash for my life at some point. Which is why I'm sitting on the floor by my closet, classifying everyone of my belongings into two piles: keep versus discard. The latter I will then sort into things to donate and things to trash.

"Te amo," the male lead tells the female lead in the background, and I shake my head. It only took him fifty three episodes to be able to admit it.

"Pero yo no te amo," she says, drawing a gasp from both the actor and me. I pause from folding up a sweater and turn back to watch the action.

I laugh—not loud enough that my roommate will catch a whiff of any joy. But the way the actor cries is way too exaggerated, yet I can imagine everyone who watched this thirty years ago suffering along with his character. A converted player, eating his own medicine.

My brows crash. Why does that remind me of my boss?

I blow a raspberry. It's not like he said he loves me or something ridiculous like that. He just kissed me and I said we had to stop. Now that we have agreed to stay friends, I don't understand why my chest squeezes at the thought of him.

"Mira vale," I tell my chest, channeling my best impression of Arturo Lossada, though I no longer know if it's accurate. "Quietecito te ves más bonito."

But nope, it keeps beating at a faster gallop than usual for a moment longer. I vanish the thought of my boss from my mind by focusing on the task at hand. A pair of shorts goes into the discard pile; it's been years since I could last squeeze into them. Broken flip flops follow suit. An oversized T-shirt with holes goes onto the keep pile because it's one of my favorites.

The farther I dig into my closet, the more items I'd forgotten about are unearthed and the activity becomes an archaeologist expedition. That's how I find, at the very bottom, a shoebox I haven't seen since I moved into this place.

I draw in a sharp breath. It's as ratty as almost anything else I own, and there's nothing valuable in it to anyone else. But inside are the vestiges of a life I couldn't have. The only mementoes I have from my parents.

My hands tremble as I pick it up and set it on my lap.

Every single thing inside is definitely going on the keep pile. Maybe I should get a nicer box, though.

I lift the cardboard lid up and like magic, my eyes well up instantly. At the top of the contents, there's a picture of Dad and I. The grin on my face isn't one I've sported since the day this picture was taken. Not once since have I been so happy.

"Shit," I say, lifting the picture. It's a little blurry but I can make out the Comed Solutions logo on Dad's polo. This was taken on the day he started his new job, the one that was supposed to change our lives for the better.

Under this one, there's another picture. The only one ever taken of both my parents and I. Arturo Lossada and a very pregnant Esperanza Martinez de Lossada pose for the camera with wide smiles. I turn it around and find the date scribbled at the back, roughly a month before I was born and Mom died.

I put the pictures back in the box and close it. There are other pictures and trinkets inside, but every time I peek inside I get this feeling like my lungs are being squeezed by a vise. No matter how much I gasp, I can't gather air at the rate I need it.

Fortunately, Karyn and her gross boyfriend are entertained by the TV in the living room, and they don't see me rushing to the bathroom with tears streaming down my face. I take a moment there to let it all out before washing my face.

My reflection shows my skin with red splotches across my cheeks and nose, and my eyes are already as puffy as if I'd spent the whole night bawling. Sighing, I put my glasses back on and push my hair behind my ears.

"Well," I say, smacking my cheeks. "No one said life was easy."

But it sure has been hard to me, huh?

Hopefully things will look up when I move by myself. With that thought in mind, I walk back to my room to continue working.

And find Richard crouching over my things.

Several things about the image are offensive. First, that he dared cross the threshold of my door without my permission. Second, that his shirt went missing somewhere along the way. Third, that he's rifling through the shoebox with my little family heirlooms.

"What do you think you're doing?" I ask. Or more like, yell.

He turns around, holding up the picture of my dad and I. "What's this old thing here? Did you steal it from a museum or something?"

I grimace. "Give me that."

Of course, he holds it as high in the air as he can, which is considerably higher than me. I try to jump for it but Richard moves out of the way.

Laughing, he says, "So I guess it's something important, huh? How much are you willing to pay to get it back?"

"Why would I pay to get back what's mine?" I push my hair away from my face and extend my hand out. "Give it to me while I'm being nice."

"Or else?" His face morphs into a mockery of a smile. "What are you gonna do, call your daddy? Oh, wait. You don't have one."

Something hot inside of me bursts from the pit of my soul. I grab the baseball bat I hid behind the bed frame and brandish it. For the first time, uncertainty flashes in Richard's eyes.

"Give me the picture." My voice comes out a lot calmer than I feel. By contrast, my heart beats so hard that I can feel my pulse in the palms of my hands, where I grip the bat tight. "Or I'm going to get you acquainted with this bat."

"Fine, you damn pest." Richard raises his hands up in the air, still holding the photo. "Here, take it back."

Richard extends it out but right before I can grab it, he rips the photo in half.

As the pieces flutter to the ground, he strolls past me and out of my room.

Outside, I hear him say, "Babe, I'm hungry."

"For food or for me?" she responds from the living room.

His laughter is the last thing I hear before I close the door and lock it. Dropping the bat, I rush to the pile of things that was messy even before Richard, but is now worse.

My vision is blurry as I pick up the broken picture. In tearing it up, the asshole also wrinkled it. I do my best to stretch it back to flatness while I tape it up, but my dad's face can barely be recognized anymore.

Sister Emilia's voice rings in my head, telling me not to hate anyone despite the very strong urge I feel to do the opposite. Richard and Karyn are heinous and they deserve each other—very far away from me. That's the least I could wish them.

I put the box under my bed and make a plan to bring it to the office with me next Monday. It's going to be safer there.

In the meantime, all I can do is work through the rage. The rest of the night goes into sorting out my small life in piles, and browsing real estate websites in search for a new place to live.

CHAPTER 54
CALEB

f I wasn't a vampire with fast recovering abilities, I would be sporting a bloody claw mark on my face where my stepmother slapped me. Her nails were sharp as needless as they cut through my skin.

"Can't you just shut up and be useful for once?" she said right after, as I wiped my own blood from my cheek.

Of course, she chose the right moment to pounce. We were already back to our New York mansion after the banquet, Dad was in his room, and Daniel and Lara in theirs. I should've known the knock on my bedroom door would be suspicious after everyone had retired.

Even though my cheek throbbed in pain, I smiled at her. "Too bad. I wasn't born to be your pawn."

The look on her face when I shut the door was priceless.

Two days later, I still feel the slice of her nails in my skin, though. I inspect my face on the mirror of my office bathroom, but the skin is unblemished.

Clearly the scars run deeper.

Sighing, I leave the bathroom and head outside the office. The first person I see is Phelan, standing guard by the door.

And then my eyes fall on the one I really want to see. My assistant.

"Serena," I say, and two abnormal things happen at once.

The first one is that she jumps so high, her chair topples over and crashes on the floor with a deafening bang.

The second one is that she takes off. Just straight up runs away.

"What the—"

The fact those two words come from Phelan, and not from me, are a testament to the bizarre nature of the scene.

Glancing at the bodyguard, I ask, "Did I do something wrong?"

"Not this time."

His response makes me frown. "When did I do something wrong?"

Phelan blinks, still staring straight ahead. "Is this a rhetorical question or do you really want me to give you the accounts?"

"Anyway," I say, closing my office door. "I'm gonna go see what her deal is. You can stay here."

As if being contrary is part of his job description, he follows me. I get déjà vu from that time when I searched up the entire building for Serena, only to find her in the rooftop getting soaked to the bone.

I give her a call, expecting no answer like that time, but she does pick up.

In my surprise, I forget how I can use my vocal cords and she hangs up.

"What the hell?" I say, at last relearning how to speak. I call her again and when she picks up, I repeat, "What the hell?"

She clears her throat. "I'll be back to my desk in a minute."

I press on the elevator button and it opens right away. "Is there something wrong?"

"Nope, nothing's wrong." The way her voice is pitched a

few octaves higher smells of a lie. "What makes you think something's wrong?"

Also, I can hear the wind whipping in her phone's microphone, so I press the button for the top floor.

I snort. "Well, I dunno. Something about the way you bolted upon seeing my face was kinda odd. Don't you think so, Phelan?"

On cue, he says, "Very odd."

I have to stuff my fist against my lips not to laugh.

"You're just imagining things," Serena says, before hanging up.

"She says," I murmur, putting my phone in my pocket. "As she acts so completely out of normal that I start contemplating calling an ambulance."

After we reach the top floor, I walk by Dad's office and go straight to the emergency stairs that lead to the rooftop. I had the door fixed since the little incident there, so I can't pull the same trick as before—which also means she's a flight risk again.

Just before opening the door, I tell Phelan, "Stay here this time."

He does. I guess he's not as curious as I am to see what the deal is with my assistant.

I find her pacing on the rooftop, knocking her phone softly against her forehead over and over. The second she spots me coming her way, she screeches, "Stop!"

I freeze. "What? *What*?"

Serena's almost on the verge of tears and I'm starting to freak out.

"I—" she starts but her voice breaks. Slowly, she shifts around until the wind is against her. "I don't want you to come closer today."

"Why?" I'm still as a statue, but high-key panicking. "Did I do something?"

"No." She cringes. "I just… I'm on my worst day."

In the ensuing pause, all that can be heard is the wind whipping against us. Finally, I scratch the back of my head. "Worst day of what?"

Serena gives me A Look. Eyes as wide as they can go, lips in a straight line. As if I was foolish for not getting the message she's not conveying clearly.

"Of my period, you jerk!"

She gasps in open shock—as though she wasn't the one who just shouted against the four winds—and covers her face with her hands.

The laughter that comes out of my throat is explosive. It racks my whole body until it threatens to topple me over like her chair did earlier. I bend over my knees, gasping for air because I can't stop laughing. Tears stream down my face.

"You're… doing all this"—A wheeze makes me pause and I stand up straight to help my lungs—"Because you're on your period? And what, you don't want me to smell it?"

The groan that comes out of her mouth makes me laugh harder.

"Stop laughing at me."

"I can't help it." I wipe the moisture off my face. "It's not like it's the first time you get your period while working for me, so what's the big deal?"

"Somehow I was lucky before." Serena folds her arms, but her foot stomping the ground doesn't really help her look too stern. "My worst day always fell on a weekend or while you weren't in the office."

I put my hands on my hips and take one step forward. She moves one step back. I try one more time, but she widens the gap again.

"What's the big deal?" I shrug. "It's not like you're the only person with their period today."

"Oh, no." Anyone else who hears her might think she was just given the worst news. "You can smell everybody else too?"

"Yes, but it's like white noise." I wave a hand. "I could zero in on specific smells, just as if you were watching a landscape and concentrated on a single item."

I continue walking toward her but while she tries to keep against the wind, she hasn't realized that I'm quickly cornering her against the fenced edge of the building.

"Especially," I continue saying. "Why would I focus on this?"

A little yelp escapes her lips as she finds herself trapped between the fence, and me. "It's embarrassing."

"It's normal." I lean closer to her, placing my hands on both sides of her so she doesn't have an easy escape route. "I promise you I hadn't even realized it until you screamed it at me. But, if I focus now——"

Lightning fast, she reaches up and pinches my nose. Her eyes blaze like fire as she glares up at me. "Don't you dare, Caleb Oh."

"Exactly the wrong words to say to me," I say, which even without the context makes me laugh at how strange my voice sounds. Pulling her hand away, I say, "Okay, okay. I promise I'll just focus on how your hair smells."

"Oh, no," she says again, putting her hands over her head. "I didn't wash my hair today."

"Stop." I grab her wrists and pull her arms back down. "Why are you being so self conscious?"

Serena's mouth opens and closes, but not a peep comes out.

In suppressing a full grin, a corner of my lips goes up. "If it makes you feel better, your hair smells amazing."

Her face scrunches up, as if disbelieving.

So I tilt my face down until my nose almost touches her

hair. "Lavender shampoo, right? But it's mixed with your own scent, which is even better. It feels like sunshine in my nose."

She pulls her wrists away from my grasp to push me away. "This is what I was trying to avoid."

Chuckling, I lower my head to her level. "You can smell me as much as you want."

"No, thanks." She points a finger in my direction. "No sniffing me, or else."

"Or else?" I ask, stuffing my hands in my pockets. "Because if the threat is that you'll run away again, I'll still chase after you."

Serena sniffs. "Do you realize how creepy that sounds?"

I think about it for a minute. If it was Vivienne saying that to me, I'd be jumping over the fence.

"Ah, yes. I can see that." I retreat until she has enough space to walk away comfortably, but she doesn't. "Do you also realize how strange your reaction was?"

"Yes." She frowns at the floor. "But I can't help occasionally freaking out when I remember what you are."

And there's the real wedge between us, the reminder that we're different. A vampire and a human. Two different subspecies that can coexist, but not mingle. Even though I really, really would love to mingle with her.

Suddenly overwhelmed by it, I take so many steps back it's as if I'm the one running away.

"Anyway." Serena clears her throat. "Please keep a cup of coffee beside you all day today, it neutralizes scents. And also communicate with me via phone only."

"What about Phelan?" I ask, folding my arms. "He was a few steps away from you but you were fine with it. Why is it only an issue with me?"

"That's because I forget he's there half the time." Without making eye contact, she says, "But it's not like I can *not* notice you when you're there."

And with that, a bright ray of sunshine pierces through my heart.

"Ooh," I say in a singing voice. "You can't ignore me."

"Ugh, stop."

Serena walks away from me toward the exit, and I keep teasing her until we stumble upon other people on our way back to our office.

She makes me forget all about my stepmother and Vivienne, and I realize Serena has quickly become the brightest spot of my life.

If only she could stay shining beside me forever.

CHAPTER 55
SERENA

Going through my morning routine everyday helps me emotionally brace myself to see Caleb's face. Anyone else would probably be used to it after spending the better part of the year in his employment, but his good looks still hit me like a physical blow.

Which is what I get—and straight to the solar plexus—when I walk down the stairs of my apartment complex and find him right there, in his smart business attire that probably costs as much as this entire building and its contents.

"What are you doing here?" I ask, struggling through my galloping heart as I descend the final steps.

"Good morning to you too."

The way he smiles entices people to commit crimes. Namely, public indecency.

Hoisting the strap of my purse on my shoulder, I walk out into the parking lot and he follows. The Urus sits all shiny and eye-catchy. Without a doubt Phelan watches us from the comfort of the driver's seat.

"Hop in," Caleb says, motioning toward the car.

I pause. Would I rather walk two blocks to the bus stop,

wait for the public transport to arrive possibly in the company of at least one smoker, to then ride the overstuffed and certainly stuffy bus? No. I would rather not. But I'm also not entirely on board with this surprise.

Squinting against the morning sun shining from behind Caleb's head, I ask, "Why are you picking me up now?"

Something about the overly innocent look on his face puts me on edge.

"I don't know about you, but I'm in need of a pick me up." He shrugs those wide shoulders of his. "And I thought a good deed before starting the day would improve my mood."

I narrow my eyes. "And that's it?"

"Yes." He nods solemnly, and I believe him.

Or maybe I just want to. As I strap my seatbelt on in the back of the car, I relish in the air conditioning and the lack of body odors.

Good morning, indeed.

Except, a good while later Phelan drives us well past the Comed Solutions headquarters. My jaw drops as I watch the building disappear behind us.

Meanwhile, Caleb is checking his phone like nothing is amiss—and maybe to him nothing is. He might not have noticed that we just missed our stop. But Phelan also isn't the kind of person who would make a mistake like this, especially because I often doubt he even is a person and might be a robot in disguise.

"Wait," I say, breaking the easy quiet in the car. "We just passed the office."

"I know," Caleb murmurs, still scrolling through his phone screen.

I take exactly three deep breaths.

"Caleb Oh." He flinches almost imperceptibly at the tone of my voice. "Where are we going?"

"Today we're working offsite." Caleb's expression seems

serious as he adds, "I packed up your devices before picking you up."

I sit back, not just because I stand no chance at convincing him to return. But also, because he said we're *working* offsite, which means we're not just going to play hooky. I check my phone to scan this week's agenda for any supplier or customer visits that would justify a field trip outside the office, but there's nothing.

And then I remember what he said earlier. Leaning back against the seat, I ask, "So, why do you need some cheering up?"

Caleb props his chin on his hand and looks out the car window. I almost want to ask him if he's recording the music video for a sad ballad or what. He certainly looks like a celebrity.

A long, intense sigh deflates him. "Things have been… kinda rough lately."

"Hmm, I'll agree with that."

I copy his posture and look out my own window. There's something soothing about watching the streets go by, of letting my eyes get lost in passing cars, palm trees, and a sky so blue it looks like it was painted by an artist. My eyelids grow heavy, and before I know it I doze off.

*

"Serena," a voice brings me back to the waking land. "We're here."

An uncivilized sound comes out of my mouth as I finally snap awake. Even worse, I feel a trickle of drool down the corner of my lips. I wipe it as discreetly as I can and take a look around.

I recognize the place, but it's so unexpected that I wonder

if I'm still asleep. After rubbing my eyes, the image of the pier is still crystal clear.

"What are we doing here?" I sound more asleep than awake, but the shock is getting me there.

Caleb's cheeky grin makes him look five years old. "Today we're working aboard the Bad Blood."

"What?"

But it's like that old question, if a tree falls in the forest and there's no one to hear it, does it actually make any sound? My question has the same effect in the pier, with only Caleb, Phelan and Joe, to hear it *and* ignore it.

I stomp my feet as I follow after my boss, grumble some colorful language that makes Joe choke on air as I'm outfitted with a life vest. He helps me climb onto the Bad Blood, Caleb comes up after me and last is Phelan, carrying a large duffel bag.

The bodyguard sets the bag on top of the table and opens it. Out comes two laptops, iPads, other office equipment, as well as swimwear.

"No, you didn't." I point at Caleb's face.

He laughs. "No one said we have to work in business suits."

"Caleb Oh!"

The spoiled brat snatches his swimsuit off the table and disappears downstairs. I sit by the table, breathing hard. One thing is bracing every morning to see his face, another one is preparing myself to see his body.

By the time he climbs back upstairs, I have my nose firmly in my email inbox and I'm firing up emails like I'm a human cannon. I'm well aware of his presence from the corner of my eye, but I refuse to look.

"You have a half-hour meeting in fifteen," I tell him. Caleb sits across the table from me and I dig more into my screen. "It's with the Marketing management team."

"And after that?"

I check his calendar. "After that, your next meeting is after lunch."

"Excellent, suit up while I talk with the Marketing guys."

That tears my eyes away from the screen and I regret it right away. His arms are extended out over the backrest of his side of the booth, and again he's not wearing a T-shirt. It gives the illusion that he's sitting there in the buff.

"You're not serious," I challenge.

But he nods. "I am. If you're not suited up by the time I'm done with this meeting, there'll be consequences."

I fold my arms. "I have the right to refuse."

"Always." He tilts his head. "But do you really want to get your clothes wet?"

I pinch my lips and I can tell he's enjoying his victory.

A few minutes later, as he takes the call with his team, I follow Joe as he leads me to a room below deck. This thing is basically an apartment, each room of a comparable size to the one I currently rent, but with furnishings straight out of a catalogue. Folded on the bed is a swimsuit the kind surfers use, and I'm glad that at least it isn't a barely-there bikini I'd never be caught wearing.

Once I'm done, I climb back upstairs and take my seat. Caleb gives me a thumbs up when he sees me, and continues with the meeting.

It's pretty impressive how he can go from complete goofball to serious businessman in the span of a second, and that's exactly what he does right now. Unless he's sharing the camera of his laptop, his subordinates would never guess he's on a boat in a swimsuit.

When the meeting ends, Caleb snaps his laptop shut so hard that it's a wonder it doesn't break.

He jumps on his feet, hands on hips. "Are you ready?"

"No." I shake my head.

Not only am I not ready for whatever he's cooking, I'm also

not ready for the jammers he's wearing. While they offer far more coverage than the ridiculous Speedo he tends to favor, they're so tight on his skin that I have to force my eyes to stay above his waist level.

Caleb motions for me to get up. "Chop, chop. We don't have all day."

Slowly, I stand up. "To do what?"

"We're going diving."

I blink once. Twice. Scratch my head.

"Uhh. I've barely learned the basics of swimming." I shake my head again. "What makes you think I'm ready to dive?"

Caleb points both thumbs at himself. "You got me."

Before I can protest, my boss launches into a passionate lecture about scuba diving. From the proper way to breathe with the equipment, to what each device is for and how to operate it, including the basics of topography and why this area is one of his favorite diving spots.

His eyes shine not just from the sun high in the sky, but because this is the pick me up he was looking for. It wasn't so much about being far from the office, as it was about being close to the water. And while I'm no longer as daunted by it after taking swimming lessons at the community center, I'm not as alive as Caleb is at the prospect of being underwater.

"And if that isn't enough," he says, now fully decked in his equipment. "I'm a certified scuba diver and so is Joe. And we can both remain without oxygen underwater far longer than a human, so you're safe with us."

I feel far from safe as I wear heavy equipment I'm not used to. Additionally, I can't even walk well with the fins on my feet.

"I have my doubts."

Caleb extends his hand out. "Trust me."

Those two words feel a lot bigger than what he probably intends. I swallow with difficulty.

"You do know we're not talking about trying some new

food dish, right?" I motion up and down at myself. "We're talking about my life, here."

"When have I let you come to harm?"

I give him a side eye. "Never, but it's been close a few times."

Caleb opens and closes his hand. "It'll be fun, I promise."

I waddle slowly over to him like the most graceless duck to ever exist. "If I die in the middle of nowhere, I will haunt you forever."

"I'm sure you will," he says with a laugh, and down we go.

CHAPTER 56
CALEB

Serena trusts water even less than she trusts me, and it takes several tries until she's comfortable keeping her head under the surface and breathing with the oxygen tank. I keep her hand in mine at all times, both for her to feel anchored and also for simple ulterior motives.

I don't feel the cold underwater like a human does, which is why I can even dive in a Speedo, but where my skin touches hers it feels like fire.

This area has plenty of sand banks and coral reefs where she won't feel too far from the surface, and since we're far enough from land we can still find a lot of life for a relatively low depth.

The first fish sighting, a smooth trunkfish, sends a ripple through her body and I pause, trying to determine if it's from fear or excitement.

Clumsy as someone without much swimming experience, she tries to follow the fish and that gives me my answer. She's at least curious. I pull her along and we follow the fish as it makes a slow perusal of the sandbank. Serena jolts as the fish blows a jet of water at the sand.

A small bank of French grunts floats in figures nearby, and I wave at Serena to direct her attention to it. We swim at a slow pace, watching the fish weave in and out of the swaying flora. In my opinion, this is way better than watching any TV show. I wonder if Serena feels the same.

After a while, I help her swim back to the surface. The sun feels hot on my skin, and while I won't burn from it, Serena might. I lead her back aboard the Bad Blood and when we're safely on deck, she removes her mask and snorkel, and gasps.

"That. Was. Amazing!"

I can feel my grin push against my mask. "Wasn't it? I told you so."

Serena clears her throat and folds her arms, attempting to look like the stern assistant and not like she's about to burst at the seams. "But we still need to work."

"Can we maybe…" I pause, lifting one shoulder. "Reschedule my meeting for another day?"

For a while, all she does is stare off into the distance until a sudden spring comes to her body. "Okay, I'll see what I can do."

I can't help chuckling. While she towels off and installs herself back at her computer, I join the other two men in the captain's cockpit. A deep silence that would be uncomfortable is instead de rigeur amongst these two. Joe's attention is on the yacht's controls, with as much intent as Phelan's is on the horizon.

"You guys good?" I ask them.

"Yes, sir," they respond in unison. Weirdoes.

Snorting, I say, "Let's grab some lunch together on the deck."

"The usual, sir?" Joe asks and I give him a thumbs up.

I snatch a towel on the way back to where my assistant sits. She's typing on the laptop with even more vigor than earlier. I almost feel bad for the keyboard. "Everything okay?"

"Yes," she says, keeping her now bespectacled attention on the screen. "I was able to move the meeting, but there are a few documents you need to approve today. They're in your inbox."

And because I'm not a complete fool, I know the success of this expedition hinges on keeping Serena happy. Which is why I do a bit of work until Joe and Phelan come in with trays of food and drinks.

And blood.

Phelan places a cold bag of the red liquid on the table before me, and says, "Drink."

"But—"

That's as far as I can complain before he starts glaring. I deflate and grab the bag.

Ever since I started the quest to get stronger, Phelan's been acting like both a nutritionist and a babysitter. Aside from grueling gym sessions with the bodyguard and night escapades hunting for vampires I can defeat, he's also taken it as his role to make sure that I consume blood at the rate of a normal vampire. Which is about five times more than I'd prefer.

Crying would probably not be a good look, so I squeeze my eyes shut and just swallow the blood without tasting it. Even then, the gag reflex is strong.

Once I'm done with the bag, I whine. "Why?"

Phelan must not have detected the rhetorical nature of the question, because he replies, "Because you hadn't fed in two days."

I glare at him.

"Um." Serena points at the corner of her mouth. "You have a little, uh…"

"Oh." I lick the corner of my lips and pick up the taste of iron. "Done?"

Her brow is furrowed as she grabs a napkin and passes it onto me. "No, you made a bit of a mess."

I look down at my chest, and sure enough there's a red

trickle that's made it all the way down to my stomach. I mop it all up with the napkin, conscious of her attention on me.

"Well, I hope that didn't ruin your appetite," I say without looking up.

Her voice comes slightly deeper than usual. "Nope, appetite's just fine."

Catching a double entendre from that answer and acknowledging it is the surest path to sending my pledge of friendship overboard. Instead, I tuck into the food before us. The assortment of high nutrition snacks is what I usually keep the kitchen stocked with, and I wolf it down with a lot more gusto than what I actually need to survive.

Joe and Phelan are less enthusiastic with their meal. I don't know there's anyone in this world who could cheer these two stoic suckers up, but I try by saying, "You can just drink blood instead if you want. Serena knows what we are."

Joe perks up. "Oh, bless. I'm tired of hummus."

"Me too," Phelan says.

I frown. "Hey. Hummus is delicious."

The two men leave their meals on the table and trace their steps back to the kitchen, where the blood stock is.

Movement from the corner of my eye catches my attention, and it's Serena shaking her head. "I don't think you realize just how truly strange you are."

I fold my arms and lean back. "Trust me, my stepmother makes sure I'm very aware of that."

"Is that why you needed a pick me up?" She sets her fork down, giving me her full attention. "Family issues?"

"Damn, you're smart," I mutter, running a finger over the rim of my glass full of carbonated water.

"What happened?" she asks, biting her lower lip. "If it's something you can share."

I prop my elbow on the table and hold my face up with my

hand. "Sure, it's not like you haven't seen me at my worst before."

As much as I wish I could only show my cool side to this girl, there's no hiding that I'm very much the opposite: a weakling vampire, a mistake, and a spoiled brat. She's seen it all.

I give her the gist of what happened at the Gonzalez-Blackwell banquet, sans the bloody slap later that night. That is a detail too raw for me to want to rehash it. Besides, it's just a consequence of the real issue.

"I mean," I start. "I knew my stepmother hated me, but not enough to make a pact with Vivienne."

Serena cringes. "I wish the soaps I watch equipped me with the means to give you some advice, but I'm at a loss."

"You watch soaps?"

She ignores that. "This is probably a silly question, but what's the worst that can happen if you refuse to marry Vivienne?"

I shrug. "I'd probably be kicked out of the family and stripped of everything I have, and while we're far from perfect, I don't relish in the idea of being completely alone."

"Can't blame you," she says.

A massive cringe takes over my body. "Wow, I've reached new levels of insensitivity. I'm sorry."

"No, I understand." Serena waves a hand. "I, too, would rather have a flawed family than none."

Groaning, I drop my face on the table. "Kill me now."

To my shock, this makes her chuckle. To my even bigger shock, I feel her hand patting my head. "There, there, little onion."

Even though I feel worse than gum under her shoe, she makes me laugh. I peek at her from over my arms and her smile pierces through every negative feeling roiling in my chest, making them scamper away.

Oh, shit. Not only am I embroiled in my stepmother's plot

to marry me off to the highest bidder, but I've also fallen for entirely the wrong person.

The realization robs me of air for a moment, and though the surface of the water is far below us, I feel like I'm drowning —in Serena's eyes, and smile, and the scent that clings to her skin and hair that she'd hate to hear about.

I'm drowning in her.

CHAPTER 57
SERENA

"**I** need your help."

I pause typing up an email the moment Caleb's voice sounds in front of me. He leans against the counter, sporting something that looks a lot like a pout. My first impulse is to tell him he's too old to pout, but I surrender to my second impulse. Which is to admire how damn cute he looks.

Taking a deep breath, I ask, "What can I help you with?"

"Well, it's not really a work topic." Caleb raises an index finger before I can make an obvious comment. "However, it's definitely distracting me from work. Thus, I believe it needs to be resolved."

I press my lips real tight. "Are you trying to play hooky again?"

Caleb gasps. "You wound me! But also yes."

"At least you're honest," I say, shaking my head. "What is the important issue we need to solve?"

"It's Lara's birthday soon and I don't know what to give her."

With a surge, I stand up. "When?"

"In two days, but her birthday party is this weekend." His

face lights up all of a sudden. "Oh, by the way, I almost forgot to tell you. She wants you to come to the party."

"Why did you wait until last minute to tell me all this?" Self-conscious, I latch onto my earlobe sporting the earrings she gave me. "Now I won't have time to find her a present."

Caleb cringes. "Yikes, sorry. I've been kinda busy."

I fold my arms. "Anyway, what's your budget for the gift?"

"No budget." He runs a hand through his hair and it falls back perfectly in place. "The difficulty is in *what* to get her. There isn't anything Lara technically needs, and she doesn't value commercial brands because of their unethical practices."

An idea pops into my head almost immediately. "How about something artsy?"

"Hmm, that might work."

And that's how, instead of working at the office like we should, Caleb, Phelan, and I end up driving around town on the quest to find two perfect gifts for Lara.

Courtesy of Google, the first option is a bohemian art gallery that's been gaining reputation in town. Its website attributes the inspiration to most pieces to the art deco popularized in Miami Beach.

"This place sounds promising," I say as the three of us walk up to the gallery. "Not only is it very Miami, but all the pieces are made by local artists."

"Strong points in favor," Caleb agrees.

But upon entering the gallery, my eyes fall on a small vase with a five hundred dollar price tag. The fact that it says, at the bottom of the sign, that clients can pay in bitcoin, makes me think this place is well out of my budget.

It's not even that pretty, anyway. Aside from catchy colors, its shape is so strange there is nothing in this material world that can stay inside without falling off. I glance around at other pieces nearby and they're all a lot more creative than my square mind can comprehend.

Turning to Caleb, I say, "See anything you like?"

The answer is written on his face by the way a grimace distorts it. "Do you think she'd like something I don't?"

It's very hard to resist the temptation to laugh, but I also don't want to get us kicked out of the place.

"You know her better than I do," is my diplomatic response.

With that, Caleb turns on his heels and leads Phelan and I out. Only when we're back in the car, does he say, "I can do math in my head as well as a calculator, but I can't wrap my mind around what I just saw."

"To be honest, same." I do a double take. "Wait, is that true? You can calculate in your head?"

"Yep," he says as he fastens his seatbelt.

While I follow in his example, I ask, "How much is pi?"

The answer comes out of him automatically. "3.14159265359."

"You could have memorized that." I pull out my cellphone and without showing him, I make a quick division I wouldn't be able to respond to without a calculator. "How much is seventy three divided by five?"

"Fourteen point six." Caleb grins at my obvious shock. "I can do more complex math too."

I take a sharp breath and tap on my phone's calculator. "Okay, how much is ninety divided by six times seven?"

"A hundred five." He chuckles. "We can do this all day, but Phelan's waiting for the next address."

I face forward and sure enough, Phelan's been looking at me expectantly all this while. Except, I'd never have noticed if Caleb didn't point it out. I wish Phelan made noises, geez.

"I'm sorry. Here's the next place." I show him the address and he speaks it to the car's GPS. Once we're safely on the road, I ask Caleb, "What other talents have you been hiding?"

He smirks. "Well—"

I lift the palm of my hand to cut him off. "Never mind that. Tell me about Lara's party instead. Is there a dress code or something else I should know about?"

"I left your invite home, but let me get the details from her."

A few minutes later, he texts me the information and we arrive to the next destination. This one is also an art gallery with local roots, but most of the artists are still college students. Right away, I find that the prices are more affordable and I like the pieces better, but I wonder if this is up to the calibre of someone like Lara Khouri—fashion designer, famous, incredibly rich, and a vampire.

Although if the latter factored into the situation at hand, I'd just give her a bag of blood and called it a day. Alas.

Since I'm only on the lookout for something small, a vase catches my attention again. A plain glass vase sits inside an intricate work of wiring that simulates the bloom of a flower. It's so realistic that it almost seems alive.

And even better, I can pay for it.

A second after I put my hand on it, someone else does the same. I trace up the arm until I find a familiar face. Not one I expected.

"Serena?" he asks.

Shocked as I am, I don't lose sight of my mission and snatch the vase from him. "Hi, Fernando."

Saying his name gives me flashbacks of college that aren't entirely pleasant.

We were in the same major, and often we'd end up pairing together for projects. That closeness, and the fact that he's pretty easy on the eye, made me wonder for a bit if I should let the little butterflies in my stomach be free. But I killed each of those butterflies the second I caught myself in class staring at him instead of paying attention to the lectures I was getting indebted for.

And he never treated me the same once he realized that I didn't want to get together with him.

"Wow, it's wild to see you here." Fernando glances at the vase again, but must figure I'm not going to give it up because he stuffs his hands in his pockets.

"Sure is," I say.

Beyond him, Caleb stops checking out a painting and sets his attention on my ex-classmate. Somehow that makes me want to end this conversation quicker.

"Anyway, I have to—"

"You know," Fernando says, giving that easy smile I used to stare at. "Maybe this is serendipity because I was thinking about you the other day. Why don't we get together to catch up?"

Caleb pivots and starts heading this way.

I clench my teeth into a tight smile. "Actually, I'm pretty busy right now."

"It doesn't have to be right now." Fernando shrugs. "We can get together for coffee or dinner. Do you still have the same phone number?"

Shit, I do. I should've changed it.

"What did you find?" my boss asks, appearing beside me like magic. Naturally, Phelan is right behind him and I angle closer to them. As if noticing Fernando for the first time, Caleb asks me, "And who is this?"

Fernando seizes Caleb up and I can imagine what he's thinking. Who's this pretty boy who oozes money from his pores? Because if I hadn't looked Caleb Oh up before starting to work for him, that's exactly what I'd have thought upon first impression.

But Caleb is more than the rich kid from the tabloids. Even though I know Fernando would never hurt me, it's Caleb's closeness what makes me feel like the situation isn't dangerous.

"An ex-classmate," I say, glancing up at my boss. "And I'm getting this vase. What about you?"

Caleb tears his eyes away from the other guy for a second to check out my find. "Nice, I think she'll really like that. I also found a painting that would look great in her studio."

"Great!" My voice is several octaves higher, but I don't care. "I guess we're ready to check out, then. It was good to see you, Fernando. Bye."

I push Caleb away and he has no problem following. A quick glance back reveals Fernando giving me a weird look, as if he was appraising me like the art around us. Maybe, as if wondering what the deal is between me and the rich guy I'm jostling around.

It turns out what Caleb said wasn't a lie, and he did purchase a massive painting that will have to be delivered directly to Lara's studio. Meanwhile, the wrapped up vase is in my arms as we head back to the office.

"I don't need to be a math genius to put two and two together." Before I can ask Caleb what he's talking about, he adds, "There was something between you and your ex-classmate, right?"

Oh.

Is that jealousy?

Nah, I must be imagining things.

I look outside the window. "Not really."

Caleb hums a clear sound of disbelief from deep in his throat.

As much as I wish to tell him that friends don't get jealous of who their friends hung out with—or didn't—in the past. Not so deep down, I'm happy that he's bothered.

And in turn, that bothers me.

CHAPTER 58
CALEB

To compensate for losing the security of a one-man army now that Phelan has become my shadow, Daniel and Lara's home is guarded by a detail of about fifty people. Most of her guests can't tell that the waitstaff is part of it, but I've caught them routinely canvassing every corner of the mansion at the same time they hand out canapés.

With how high-keyed they are, you'd think an attack is imminent.

Sipping from a glass of chilled champagne, I murmur to my brother, "Isn't this going a bit overboard?"

"I know." He sighs. "But Dad wouldn't have it any other way."

Speaking of, the vampire king mingles with Lara's guests like he's running for office, smiling, chit chatting, posing for pictures with babies. Although this might all be a pretense to be away from his wife, who is nestled in a group of the most powerful matriarchs of the worldwide vampire kingdom. Deals will be made tonight.

Which is fine, as long as none of them are about my marital status.

Unfortunately, I don't have high hopes. One of the men beside Dad is Ernst Astor, father to the current bane of my existence. And if the father is in attendance, the daughter must not be too far.

The thought puts me on edge, even before I remember that Serena's coming to the party too.

I down the rest of my drink. As much as I'd like to drink about five bottles more, I should probably stay sober for whatever may come.

"Where's your wife?" I ask my brother. He checks his Omega Constellation for the time.

"Should be coming downstairs any minute."

As if on cue, a ripple washes over the attendees as Lara Khouri descends from the stairs in such a regal manner, I almost start thinking she's the queen. Lara waves at people and blows kisses, her yellow dress flutters behind her like liquid gold.

"Am I drooling?" Daniel asks me. "I feel like I am."

I can't help laughing.

But then I feel exactly the same, because among Lara's entourage following her down the stairs, is my assistant. The blush color of her dress no doubt has to be matching my face, especially when I catch all the cleavage she's showing.

Aside from the little pool incident, I have never seen Serena's goods this clearly—and I want more. But only for myself.

"Shit." I tug at my tie. "Am *I* drooling?"

My brother blinks at me. Then back at the women around his wife. "For which one?"

I debate whether to tell him, but I know exactly how the conversation will go. Daniel will call me names for having the hots for a human, even more for one in our employment. And he'd be right, but the facts would still piss me off for going against what I want.

Serena. In my arms. By ourselves.

A security guard disguised as waiter walks by with a tray full of more champagne flutes, and I snatch one. Downing it in one go causes temporary burn that distracts me from the direction of my thoughts.

I follow Daniel along toward the birthday girl. He tells me, "You go first, I'll take a while."

"What are you talking about?"

But he pushes me toward his wife, who is all smiles upon seeing us. "The Oh brothers suited up is the best birthday gift ever!"

"Happy birthday, you weirdo," I tell her, giving her a big hug.

Behind Lara, I can't help making eye contact with Serena. She looks gorgeous with her hair down. I wish I could run my fingers through it.

I pull away from my sister-in-law. "My real gift to you is in your office, by the way. You'll see it on Monday."

Lara beams. "I can't wait. I heard Serena here helped you find it."

"It's not a big deal," Serena says under her breath.

"And you, Daniel," Lara says, walking by me. "Aren't you going to wish me happy birthday?"

Transfixed as I am by Serena, I barely register Daniel sweeping his wife off her feet and kissing her in the middle of their living room. The attendees break into cheering, as loud as the audience in a sports stadium where the home team just scored.

How I wish I could be the one to score instead.

I jam my hands in the pockets of my slacks and leave the commotion to stand in front of Serena. She tucks a strand of her hair behind her ear, avoiding my eyes like it's her job.

"Hi," I say.

She clears her throat. "Hello."

Even from three paces away I can feel her heat, strong as a

furnace. Far stronger than if she was a vampire. I close my eyes for a second and concentrate on the beat of her heart. It pumps blood at a fast pace, maybe she's nervous.

It prompts me to ask, "Are you okay?"

Her dark eyes finally find mine. There's a question in them, but I can't decipher it from her body's clues. She's still as a statue, not quite to Phelan-level, but more than her normal restraint.

"Yes, I'm fine. Why do you ask?"

Behind me, Daniel and Lara must have finished making out, because my sister-in-law declares, "All right, let's get this party started!"

Music starts playing, the kind two to three hundred years newer than what my stepmother prefers.

Abruptly, someone pushes me from behind and if not for my improved reflexes, I'd have sent Serena and I crashing to the floor. I collide with her, and before she loses her footing I wrap my arms around her and spin. By bracing my legs, I prevent an accident.

Lara stands where I was a second ago, laughing. "Go on, dance you guys."

"Geez, are you turning five years old or what?" I ask Lara, rolling my eyes.

The way her eyes twinkle worries me. Especially as they stray down. In following her line of sight, I realize that Serena is really snug against me.

She looks at me with eyes as wide as saucers through those glasses of hers. This close I can see black specks in the warm brown of her irises. Her lips are just a shade or two darker than the dress. I lick mine, remembering her taste like it was just a minute ago when we last kissed.

Even worse—no, better—is that I can see *and* feel Serena's curves pressed up against me. In this position, her cleavage disappears between our bodies.

Before I embarrass myself, I jump away from her.

"Uh, that was entirely an accident not of my doing." I keep my hands up in the air as I retrace another step. "But I apologize anyway."

"D-Don't worry." Serena glances away. "Oh, Marissa's calling me. See you later."

To her credit, she's not just running away from me. The other girl appears genuinely eager to welcome Serena, who now keeps her back firmly turned my way. From this side, her dress would be less heart attack-inducing, if it wasn't for the dip of her small waist down to wide hips. The itching in my hands reminds me of how they felt.

I need air.

I don't make it outside, though. Lara intercepts me on my way to the gardens and pulls me into a conversation with her friends. It gets painful pretty quick because I've never been interested in the fashion world, but at that moment Vivienne walks into the place and I'm thankful to appear occupied.

"Why is she here?" I whisper to my sister-in-law.

"Who?" Lara glances around until she finds the target, who is hard to miss in a dress that shows one hundred percent of her legs. "Damn it, she's wearing another one of my dresses. Do you think she's doing that on purpose?"

"There's nothing casual about Vivienne." From the corner of my eye, I make sure Serena is far away. The last thing I want is for Vivienne to try something again.

"Are you sure?" Lara shakes her head. "Because she just casually invited herself to my party."

Sighing, I ask, "Do we ignore her or kick her out?"

Lara pushes the sleeves of her dress up her arms. "Definitely the latter. I don't want her to ruin this extra happy occasion."

I tilt my head. "I know it's a happy occasion, but extra?"

And because, by contrast, there's everything casual about

Lara, she says, "Oh, it's because Daniel and I are going to announce that I'm pregnant."

The way I suck in air catches many eyes. "Get the heck out of here!"

Probably not the polite comment anyone would expect, but it makes Lara laugh. I pick her up in my arms and twirl her around.

"No wonder he looks more besotted than usual." I set her back down.

Lara's giggles don't abate even as she says, "I think he's just shocked."

"Seriously, let me be the first to congratulate you." I open my arms and Lara gives me a hug so tight that I forget how to breathe for a moment.

In my ear, Lara whispers, "Now, go kick out the mean girl so you can spend your evening with the one you like."

When I pull away, my sister-in-law gives me a sly look that speaks volumes. Lara wouldn't have invited Serena if she didn't like her, but that show-stopping dress? It screams Lara's machinations. And boy, am I thankful.

I give her a kiss on her cheek. "Yes, sister."

Whistling a jolly tune that doesn't match the ambiance music, I weave my way through the crowd until I spot Vivienne. I smile at everyone, as though nothing about me pulling Vivienne away from them was abnormal. I hate that my hand falls on bare skin as I push her back.

"This is a welcome change of pace," Vivienne says, letting me guide her outside.

"Is it?"

"Yes." She lets out a twinkling laugh. "I have to say I very much enjoy your skin on mine."

I let go of her, which is a shame because we're not outside yet. "And I have to say this is a new low for you, showing up uninvited."

"Sugar, who says I'm uninvited?" Vivienne stretches a hand out. Only because there are guests nearby do I not bat it away. I stand still as she fixes up my tie. "Your mother extended an invitation to me. Said it was an important family event I couldn't possibly miss, since I'll soon be one of y'all."

"Get out." I glare down at her, regardless of whose eyes might be watching. "I don't care if my mother invited you. You're still not welcome here."

Vivienne sticks out her hot pink bottom lip. "But I just arrived."

"Too bad you just had an emergency to take care of, huh?"

"Oh, Caleb." In one long step, Vivienne wraps her arms around my neck. "The more you resist me, the more I want you."

Just before she kisses me, I jerk my face away—

And come face to face with the last person I want to see this. Serena.

CHAPTER 59
SERENA

Like a reflex, I turn around and mingle among the other guests.

The image of Vivienne Astor leaning up to kiss Caleb is engrained in my mind, though. Despite Caleb making a good impression of Phelan on an average day, surely he had to be tempted by someone as beautiful and provocative as Vivienne in her skin tight, fashionable little dress.

Not only am I not some fantastical beauty in the flesh like she is, but the much more modest dress Lara lent to me for the occasion already feels like it's too much. My heart hasn't stopped racing ever since I tried it on. Earlier, I had the impression that Caleb liked what it showed—but now? How can I possibly compare?

Ugh, I shouldn't compare in the first place. I don't want to be that person. But the second I saw Vivienne walk into the room, I felt myself becoming green.

I don't even have a right. Didn't I draw a firm line between my boss and I?

Why does it matter who he kisses or not? And why does it matter if who he kisses is incredibly freaking hot?

My chest squeezes painfully and the only way I can ease the knot is by chugging an entire flute of champagne, bottoms up. A second one improves my mood dramatically. I'm interrupted on my way to grab a third.

"Easy there," a warm voice says behind me. The loud noise should make it hard to distinguish the owner, but my body knows. It's in the way my skin breaks into goosebumps all over.

Feigning ignorance, I turn to face him. "Caleb, what are you doing here? I thought you were busy."

Yeah, in the preludes to *getting* busy. I hate how imagining that makes my eyes sting.

He shrugs. "Now that I have removed the uninvited guest, I'm pretty free."

The what?

It takes me another second to figure out that he means Vivienne. And the relief that washes over me is embarrassing.

So is the fact that, without glancing at a clock, I say, "Oh, look at that. It's getting pretty late and I should head home."

I dodge Caleb once more. My pulse skyrockets in the course of that one minute conversation, and ironically it's the climb upstairs what calms me down. I retrieve my purse and a shopping bag with my own clothes from the room where Lara, Marissa, and some of their other friends made me over. But when I open the door and find Caleb leaning against the wall beside it, I almost get heart failure.

"Why are you here?"

"Waiting for you." He cocks an eyebrow. "Did you forget who drove you over?"

I totally did. But in theory it was Phelan who drove *us* over.

Clearing my throat, I shoulder my purse and say, "You don't need to take me home. I'll just call a taxi."

"Taxis don't come around here." As he stands up, he takes his car key from his pocket. "People in this community don't appreciate giving others the freedom to come in and out, you know."

By community he means an exclusive neighborhood littered with vast mansions, sitting quite remote from the rest of civilization.

I bite my lip. I could ask Marissa to drive me home, but I also don't want to pull her away from her best friend's bash. The second option would be asking Jon for the favor, but he seems to still be on the clock with the way he's always one step behind Cedric Oh. I don't really know anyone else I would ask.

"Stop thinking so hard and let's go." With that, Caleb walks to the stairs and begins the descent. I have no choice but to follow him, even though he's the last person I want to be with right now.

We bid a discreet farewell to Lara and Caleb's brother, and the moment our feet hit the lawn outside, Phelan appears behind us like a shadow.

Just to avoid Caleb, I ask the other guy, "Were you enjoying the party?"

In his characteristic way, Phelan responds with a simple, "No."

Caleb and I break into chuckles at the same time. We make eye contact and butterflies explode in my belly. Just a glimpse of his eyes sends me free falling into an endless abyss. I look away and keep my attention firmly away from my boss, for as long as it takes us to find the Urus and be well on our way back to the city.

In the heavy silence in the car, I'm even more thankful for Phelan's unassuming, steady presence. If he wasn't here, the space between Caleb and I would feel even smaller, more suffocating.

Also, because I'm just a regular human and I can still smell his perfume. And it smells so damn delicious that it's making my mouth water. I push up against the door and glue my eyes to the dark outside. It makes for a very long ride back.

"Um, can we play some music?" I ask a long while later. Phelan turns on the radio, and the song that plays is very descriptively celebrating the horizontal tango to a very Caribbean tune. "Never mind, silence is better."

Without further ado, Phelan turns the radio off.

A high pitched noise catches my attention, and I find my boss curled up into a ball. Shaking.

With laughter.

I harrumph. "Grow up, Caleb."

"I refuse." His voice comes choked up, preceding an outburst of cackles.

When I feel mirth threatening to come out of my throat, I squeeze my hands tight and remind myself that I'm supposed to be the mature one here. Fortunately, my suffering starts coming to an end as Phelan pulls into my street.

"Can you drop me off here?" I ask while we're stopped at a red streetlight.

"No!" Both men say in unison.

"Are you kidding?" Caleb all but cries. "We're several blocks away from your apartment complex and it's the middle of the night."

I lift my hands in the air to pacify him. "I just don't want anyone to see me coming out of this car, especially my roommate."

While the light turns green and Phelan sets the car in motion again, my boss continues his outrage. "I've picked you up several times, what's different now?"

Me. I'm the one who's different now. Brimming with embarrassment and anxiety, and an urge to pull him up against me that I can barely control anymore.

"I was lucky no one saw any of those times," I say, folding

my arms. "Besides, the walk wouldn't be far from here and it's pretty safe. I do it plenty of times."

"That's it," Caleb says, his voice low. "I'm getting you a car."

"No thanks." I snap. "Phelan, please stop the car."

The equivalent of a trained puppy, Phelan obeys the second it's safe to stop the car. I unbuckle myself and jump out.

Not a second later, I hear another door slam closed and steps follow. I don't have to turn to know it's Caleb, and in addition he asks, "Why are you upset? I'm honestly at a loss here."

I grit my teeth until my jaw hurts. The truth wants out but I swallow it back down. I can't tell him that it's because I'm jealous of how good he looks with Vivienne. Or how I wish he would just hold me tight against him, like he accidentally did earlier. Or how I want to wrap my arms around his neck and pull him down for a kiss fit for scandal.

Voicing any of those things would justify the yearning I feel for him—that I shouldn't. That I said I wouldn't. And so I can't tell him the truth.

And in grasping for straws, instead I spill a different truth. "Because it's really annoying how easy it would be for you to fix the problems I can't. I have to walk in the dark and in the day because I'm dirt poor, you know? That's my reality and I'm not scared of it, but you made me feel ashamed just now."

In the ensuing silence, I stew over my excuse. It's not a lie, I'm also upset about this. It's another reason why I can't just surrender myself to the desire I feel for him—I'm just nowhere near his league.

Suddenly, I regret every single second of today. From the excitement in my stomach at putting on this dress, to this very second.

My steps echo with his, even after what I said. "Why are you still following me?" I ask.

Caleb lets out a shaky breath. "You're right, I'm an ass. But I couldn't live with myself if something happens to you because I turned away to lick my wounds."

I freeze.

He stops right behind me, so close that if I lean just a bit, I will touch him.

After a moment, I hear him step away.

"Please be honest," he says, his warm voice chases away the ice in my chest. "Would it be so bad if I use my money to help you?"

"Yes." I glance at him over my shoulder. "It has to be my accomplishment for it to mean something."

Caleb's stricken. He can't stop blinking.

"Well," he finally says. "As someone who is absolutely unaccomplished on his own, I think I understand."

Occasionally, Caleb will make a self-deprecating comment here and there, but this is different. This is a raw nerve I poked in my desperate attempt to push him away. The regret I feel at hurting him is the same as a knife through my heart.

With a thread of voice, I say, "Goodnight, Caleb."

This time he doesn't follow me.

With every step I take in the quiet night, the wound in my chest grows deeper. I hope it isn't as big a deal to him, that I'm the only one who will cry herself to sleep tonight.

Two minutes later, I finally make it to my building. My feet are like lead as I climb up the stairs. By rote, I unlock the apartment door and—

Every feeling inside of me gives way to a single one. Horror.

The scream that comes out of my throat pierces the night.

CHAPTER 60
CALEB

My body springs to action before I can even think it through.

Serena screams only once, and as my feet pound the pavement I fear the worst—that she can't scream again because something horrible has happened. I pray like I've never prayed before that the conversation we had a few minutes ago wasn't our last. That this isn't another assault by vampires of dubious loyalties.

I reach the parking lot of her apartment complex. My eyes immediately go up to the second floor, where her apartment is. Serena stands outside her door, clutching at her head.

Pulse skyrocketing, I jump on the hood of a car and launch myself in the air. In a smooth arch, I vault over the second floor railing and I'm beside her.

"What's wrong?"

She jumps like I'm the scary one. "Caleb, what—"

I can't see anything in the hallway that would be a threat, so it must be coming from inside the apartment. Pushing her behind me, I grab the doorknob and—

"Stop," she says behind me, clutching my clothes. "Don't open the door."

My heart still throbs in my temples when I ask, "What's inside that made you scream bloody murder? Don't tell me it's *actual* bloody murder."

"No." Her voice comes out raspy. "It's a few steps less severe."

Thoroughly confused now, I turn around to face her. "What in the actual hell can make someone scream like that if it's not a gory scene?"

"My roommates screwing each other in the middle of the living room, that's what." She cringes until she looks like the human version of a raisin. "Ugh. Why did I have to open the door to that, *why*?"

With an exhale, my entire body deflates out of energy. I stagger and have to brace myself against the railing not to fall on my ass. "You mean I almost got a heart attack and it was because of this?"

Before she can respond, heavy footsteps come pounding up the stairs and Phelan appears, gun drawn and pointed at us. The second he sees it's just Serena and I, he lowers it to the floor.

"What happened?" He has that expression on his face that means he can go from zero to bloody murder in a half second flat.

If Serena wasn't truly terrified before, going by the paleness in her face, she probably is now. I signal Phelan to put the gun away and he upholsters it back in the vest hidden under his blazer. I know if we'd been in real trouble, he would've used it or the one on the opposite side of his vest, or one of the two hidden under his pant legs, or the knives tucked up his sleeves, before using the truly nuclear weapon—himself.

Fortunately, he has better self-restraint than I do. If I'd been a walking armory, I probably would've ran to Serena's side all guns blazing—only to find the emergency was caused by an amorous couple.

Giving my assistant a side eye, I respond, "Serena just saw something traumatizing."

"Human or vampire?" Phelan asks.

"Neither." Serena mumbles before pulling me by the arm. "You can leave. I'll deal with this."

I fix up my clothes, rumpled now after the dash. "Are you sure? If you open that door, there's no guarantee what you'll see can make the Care Bears happy."

"Ugh."

Considering that she's keeping a wide berth from her door, and that her shoulders are up to her ears in an attempt to make herself smaller, I figure her saying that *she* would deal with this was an attempt to psyche herself up to do something she truly doesn't want to do. Which is to open the door.

So I do it for her.

I get a horrifying glimpse of what she must've seen earlier.

I close the door again.

The only sound in the hallway is that of the wind, rustling the leaves of trees. It's strong enough to muffle my laughter.

"I get it now." I say, clearing my throat. "Let's go."

"Where?" Serena looks on the verge of tears.

Steering her gently back down the stairs, I say, "You should spend the night somewhere else." That way she can try to get some peace of mind for a bit.

"But where?"

"I'll take care of that."

I rub her back in small circles, and she must be so shaken that she doesn't bat my hand away. Phelan parked the car just downstairs and in another minute, we're pulling back into the road.

I can tell that she's genuinely upset. It's in her drawn in posture, the way her bottom lip trembles and the watery eyes. I stuff my fist against my lips and look away, focusing on the streetlights beaming like lines in the dark as Phelan drives.

Stronger still, is the desire to pull her into my arms or compel her into forgetting the past fifteen minutes, but I can't do either. On the one hand, I don't want to take advantage of the occasion to force closeness with her. On the other hand, I'm not strong enough to have such compelling skills. Phelan probably can, but he doesn't use them unless Dad orders him to, and the king wouldn't concern himself with something trivial like this.

"We have arrived," Phelan says after a while, turning the Urus off now that we're in my building's parking lot.

Serena glances around, as if waking from a dream. "Your place? I can't stay here."

I unbuckle myself. "Why not?"

She splutters for a moment before clearing her throat. "I don't think it'd be appropriate, especially after what just happened."

I put my hand on my chest. "You honestly can't think I'd try to make a move on you after everything that's happened tonight."

"No, not you."

My head makes mental gymnastics around that statement, but like a complex math problem with many variables, I can't reach a single conclusion.

"What is that supposed to mean?"

She ignores me. "Phelan, can you please take me to a hotel nearby? Preferably a really cheap one."

My bodyguard glances at me through the rearview mirror, waiting for confirmation. Obviously, that's not gonna happen.

"Why don't you stay at my place and I spend the night somewhere else?" I ask my assistant.

Usually, I'd crash Daniel and Lara's place, but the party's going to continue all through the night and I'm not in the mood for that. The second option would be my parents's house, which would be safe if they stay at the party for long—except the probability of running into them in the morning and being embroiled in a conversation about Vivienne makes me almost break into hives.

That means Serena's idea is the winner. A hotel it is.

"Phelan," I say, leaning forward. "After Serena's safely in my apartment, take me to a hotel."

"I'm not going to put you out of your own home." She pulls out her cellphone. "I'll find a place I can stay at—"

"Then we're at an impasse." Folding my arms, I continue, "Because I'm not just going to drop you off at a hotel by yourself."

Our wills clash in a fierce exchange of glares. By now I recognize the stubborn set of her jaw that means she's not budging down. In contrast, I'm sure she recognizes my tell that I'm also not going to give in.

A long, suffering sigh interrupts the contest, especially since it comes from Phelan.

He doesn't say a single word, but the meaning is clear. We're acting like kids.

"Look," I say, breaking the silence. "Nothing good ever comes from testing Phelan's patience. Just let me help you this one time, no strings attached and no further questions asked."

"Fine." She's the first one out of the car, and I watch her stomp toward the entrance of the building for a moment.

I mumble, "Why is she so difficult?"

"You're made for each other," Phelan says.

Not only is that meant as an insult, but also a surprisingly optimistic take from the human statue he is. If Phelan can see that, then I might stand a chance at convincing Serena, right?

As I get out of the car and follow him, I ask, "Wait a second. Is the mighty Phelan Murray the captain of this ship?"

His expression is a blank slate that doesn't confirm or deny the question, but also doesn't show whether he understood it.

The three of us get on the elevator and Phelan presses a button a few levels below the penthouse.

"You, behave," he says to me. Then, glancing at Serena he says, "And you, don't kill him or I'll be out of a job."

"I always behave." Both of them ignore my comment.

Frowning, she says, "Don't worry, if I kill him I'll also be out of a job and I need the money to move out of that hell hole."

As the elevator reaches his floor, Phelan gives me one last sharp look before he steps out.

I fold my arms. "Here I am, trying to to do something nice and I get dragged through the mud."

With her eyes firmly focused on the floor count above us, Serena says, "Ever thought it's because your reputation precedes you?"

I gasp. "There's an implication there that I'm a bad boy, when I'm in fact, pretty much an angel."

The elevator opens on my floor. Before walking out, Serena shakes her head. "No, you're just a step up from a mosquito but just as annoying."

I should feel offended, but it's hard to feel that way when I agree. Unfortunately for her, I enjoy being annoying. It's precisely the skill I intend to use from this moment on, and for however long it takes her to realize that I really, really like her.

CHAPTER 61
SERENA

Contrary to my name, I am not serene. Even though my body is exhausted, my mind is as alert as though I'd drank an entire pitcher of coffee.

I was already in turmoil from Lara's birthday party forcing me to come face to face with the green monster residing inside of me. I enjoyed seeing Vivienne's arms around Caleb's neck just as much as I liked finding what Karyn and Richard were up to in places where I normally eat or lounge.

Even more painful than those events, is the way that green monster reared its ugly head out in front of Caleb, blending with every other worry and insecurity I carry on my shoulders everyday like a backpack. If it wasn't for my roommate and her boyfriend, that would've been how Caleb and I parted ways tonight. Regret would've kept me up all night.

That's not the reason why I can't give in to sleep right now, though. Every time I close my eyes, I see the way Caleb defied the laws of physics to come to my aide. My chest squeezes with gratitude, but mostly with a desire to kiss him I can barely rein in.

It doesn't help that there's just a wall between us right now.

Although realistically we'd have to walk around the entire apartment for one of us to get in the other's room, I can't help feeling like the wall separating the guest room from the main one is as flimsy as chiffon. On the other side, Caleb lies in bed just like me.

Turning, I pull the sheets up to cover my head and curl myself up into a ball. This is the problem with getting too close to Caleb. He makes me think all sorts of things I shouldn't, like how instead of Vivienne, I wish I had been the one pressed up to him, my arms around his neck pulling him down to me. How with him, I could probably gather the courage to explore a side of me that's been dormant until I met him.

At the thought, my heart pounds so fast that he can probably hear it. Heat radiates off my body until I kick the bedsheets away. The air-conditioning feels too cool but there's no way I can pull the sheets against my sweaty skin again. I fan myself with the T-shirt Caleb lent me and lay there, limbs spread wide across the massive bed.

I'm hot and cold at the same time and at this rate I'm never going to fall asleep.

In the privacy of my mind, I can admit that yes, I have the hots for my boss.

Caleb's silly and smart, capable of dashing kindness and terrible jokes, not to mention so intensely gorgeous he makes me question my four eyes. I wish I could march up to his room and do something that would offend even my roommate, but I can't. None of that changes the glaring facts.

"Maybe I'm just hangry," I say into the dark, rubbing my stomach. I didn't eat much at Lara's party, and a glance at the clock confirms it was ages ago.

As I pull myself up to my feet, I know what I'm feeling is a different thing, but feeding my stomach is the one need I can satisfy without ruining the careful balance I'm trying to strike with my boss.

Padding softly on bare feet, I peek out into the hallway and find only darkness in the apartment. I'll have to turn on the kitchen lights to find a snack, but hopefully that doesn't disturb him. The last thing I need is to see Caleb in the middle of the night. What if his hair is all mussed up, his eyes hooded, and cheeks flushed with sleep? I would die.

Holding my breath, I make it to the kitchen and flip on the light switch.

A blood-curling scream tears out of my throat.

There, crosslegged on a barstool, is precisely the person I wanted to avoid. He no longer sits, though, because after a scream like mine anyone would jump out of their skin.

"What now?" he shouts, his chest rising up and down rapidly. His *bare* chest.

"What the hell are you doing out here in the dark?" Pointing at him, I also ask, "And you're not naked under there, are you?"

All Caleb can do for a moment is blink.

All I can do is fix my eyes on his forehead, because even though the kitchen island hides anything from his waist down, what I can already see is far too tempting for my own good.

"I was having a snack," he finally answers. "And I can assure you I'm wearing clothes."

To demonstrate the point, he lowers a hand and the sound of a waistband snapping against his skin echoes in the kitchen. For my sanity, I decide to ignore this problem and focus on the other one.

"In the dark?"

Caleb shrugs, which in his chiseled body looks like poetry in motion. "I have night vision and didn't want to bother you."

My jaw drops. "Night vision?"

The corners of his lips draw up in a little smile, but instead of bragging like I'd expect him to, he goes back to his snack. Ice cream.

Maybe he was also too hot in bed.

I twirl around and focus on inspecting his kitchen. Everything is spotless, thanks to a cleaning crew that comes twice per week as per Caleb's instructions. Every edible thing is also vegan, per Caleb's dietary preferences. I wonder if vegan ice cream is any good and decide to join him with a pint.

At the first spoonful I can confirm the answer is yes. The flavor and the texture are exquisite, and the coolness helps tame some of the heat burning inside of me. A little groan escapes from my throat, and Caleb's eyes flash to me like attracted by a magnet.

Not good.

Clearing my throat, I ask, "So you can jump super high and have night vision, too. Don't tell me you also have some sort of natural sonar and can fly."

Looking away, Caleb licks his spoon and sticks it back in his ice cream tub. "I can't turn into a bat, if that's what you're asking."

He almost looks offended and it makes me want to laugh, but I know better. He juts out his bottom lip and it sends a bolt clear through my chest.

How can someone this hot also be this cute? I hate him.

I attack my ice cream. It's the only outlet I have right now.

In turn, Caleb attacks *me* by saying, "Are you going to move out of that place?"

The question catches me in the middle of eating an enormous spoonful of the frozen treat. I munch slowly until I say, "I've been looking for an apartment for a while now, but I can't seem to find anything decent that doesn't break the bank."

"And I assume you won't let me help you, right?"

All at once, the conversation preceding Karyn and Richard's little surprise comes back to me.

"I'm sorry for how I said things," I start, gnawing at my lower lip. "But the gist remains true. I already owe you a debt I can't even pay. You've saved my life more than once, you know? I can't depend on you for everything I may need."

Caleb pushes his empty ice cream carton away. "Accepting help isn't the same as being dependent."

For a moment, there's only silence. I make progress on my ice cream until eventually, it's gone. And so is my desire to stay aloof.

"You're right, it isn't. But I'm not used to having anyone who can help me." I lace my fingers over the counter. Holding my hands together is the only comfort I'm used to. "Ever since Dad passed away, I've basically been on my own. Sister Emilia, the head of the orphanage, always had too many kids to focus on. And after her, ironically the only person who extended a hand to me was my roommate. But that came with a lot of strings."

I tell him about Richard, the freeloader who pays for his room and keep by scratching Karyn's every itch, and how I turned into their maid so I could pay an affordable rent. The more I talk, the more Caleb tightens his jaw. Red blooms on his chest and expands up his throat, as though he's a volcano accumulating lava inside.

My bottom lip starts trembling when I recall the more recent incidents. A tear rolls down my cheek and I wipe it away with fury. "I think I best head back to bed."

"No." The firmness in his voice keeps me rooted to my seat. "Tell me everything."

My vision blurs as more tears threaten to fall, but I can see the lightning in his eyes cutting clear across the dark.

I don't want to tell him the rest… just as much as I do.

There's no one else I could say these things to. The only other person who really cares about me is Sister Emilia, and this would break her heart. Marissa and Lara are lovely, but I can't burden them with such a sour story when we're only getting closer now.

With Caleb, I'm afraid of what this will make him think of me. Maybe he's made a picture of me in his mind of a capable and confident woman, not at all how I really am—an insecure and lonely person, constantly in need of comfort I don't know where to get.

But he sits there, quietly waiting to offer it. And for once I take it.

So I tell him the truth about my home life, and everything else Karyn and Richard did to me that led me to purchasing a baseball bat and starting the search for an apartment.

When I'm done, his entire frame is trembling with the effort to control his anger. Through gritted teeth, Caleb says, "Should I kill them or only beat them up half dead?"

"Neither." I wipe my face with the collar of the T-shirt I'm wearing and sniffle a couple of times. "I think I'd rather you pretend this conversation never happened. Heck, pretend this whole night never happened."

"I can't do that." Caleb rubs his hair, leaving it a mess atop his head. "While I'm angry enough to punch a hole through the wall, I'm also sort of glad."

I do a double take. "What?"

He gives me a sheepish smile. "Because at least now you trust me this much."

My lips part and out comes a shaky breath. "You're going to be the death of me."

It makes his smile widen. "But at least don't die alone. Let me help you find a new place."

Slightly morbid, but sweet nonetheless.

Sighing, I say, "Fine. But first, put on a T-shirt."

CHAPTER 62
CALEB

Putting on more clothes doesn't figure anywhere in the list of things I want to do with Serena right now. I figure she won't let me do any of them, so it's either obeying her command or marching straight into a freezing cold shower.

"If that's the only condition for you to accept my help, I'll take it." I get up from my chair and before she can protest, I walk into my room.

For a moment, I just stand in my walk-in closet and breathe deeply. It's terrifying to not find her scent here, now that it permeates every other area of my home. I wish I could tell her to just move in with me on the excuse of an easier commute to the office, when in truth I just want to keep her with me at all times. That way I can keep her safe from everyone else.

Jerking a simple grey T-shirt over my head, I realize she wouldn't be safe from me, though.

I should at least be thankful for the rage coursing through my veins. It's helping keep my need for her at bay.

Serena sits on my couch, browsing on her phone. As she

hears me approach, she asks, "How are you planning to help me, then?"

All of the ideas that come to my mind would piss her off.

I vault over the backrest of the couch and plop to a seat beside her. "First, let's start by finding the perfect apartment and then we can talk money."

She freezes for a second. "And by money you mean a loan, right?"

"A loan." I nod very, very slowly. As if she were a wild animal I don't want to scare off. "Yes. With interest, even."

"Good."

With that, we start working like this is a project for Comed Solutions. I project the options on my TV screen and we discuss pros and cons of each place, charting them on Excel with my laptop. Eventually, the sky starts to lighten up and in contrast, my vision darkens, and my body grows slacker until I fall asleep.

For a while, there's only black. No dreams, no feelings. Only the heavy sleep that comes from pure exhaustion.

What disturbs it is a beam of sunlight piercing through my eyelids.

I groan and try to turn away from it, but I can't. My arm is trapped under something that doesn't budge. After struggling against the light for a bit, I open my eyes to find a mound of hair using my left arm as a pillow.

Serena's loose hair has taken over the world. It falls on her face and all around her, including part of me. I spit some of it out of my mouth and immediately clamp my lips shut so I don't start laughing.

Carefully, I pull strands of her hair away from her face. She wrinkles her nose a couple of times and a snore comes out. I could get used to waking up like this every morning, even if it means not having any feeling left in my arm.

Her own snore snaps her awake and she catches me biting my lips hard.

Serena yelps, and in trying to put distance between us she rolls over the edge of the couch.

Lighting quick, I wrap my free arm around her waist and pull her up against me. Even knowing how dangerous this is, I keep her there.

"Good morning," I say, my voice coming out raspy with disuse.

In contrast, her voice rivals a chipmunk. "Um, you're awfully close."

"Awfully?" I pout. This makes her eyes latch on my lips.

I must be dreaming. There's no way Serena Lossada, she who has told me to back off in all possible ways, is contemplating kissing me.

"Oh no, this is dangerous," she says under her breath.

The words travel down my spine, leaving flashes of heat and cold in their wake. I know exactly how dangerous this is, how much my blood is boiling with hunger for her, how my hands itch to explore her skin and sink into her hair. Only she can stop me, because with her body pressed against mine I have no self-restraint.

"Stop me," I say, almost in a growl. "Tell me you don't want me. Push me away. Hit me, if you must. Because if you don't, I'm going to kiss you."

Her mouth opens and closes, which in combination with her wide eyes makes her look like a fish out of the water. And even then I'm as attracted to her as if she were a north magnet to my south.

"I-I—"

With my free arm, I pull her flush against me until our noses touch. I can feel one of her hands curling around the fabric of my T-shirt, and I desperately wish her nails were sinking into my skin instead.

Through gritted teeth, I say, "Just say no."

"I—don't—"

Serena gasps as, in a smooth move, I flip her on her back and settle in between her legs. My arms strain with the effort it takes to hover over her, not because they're weak but because *I* am weak against the gravity she's causing. I brush the hair off her forehead, clearing the path.

"If you can't say no," I say, choked up. "Then say yes. Let me kiss you."

Drawing in a shaky breath, Serena's hands settle on my chest. She doesn't push me away, but also doesn't pull me to her.

Finally, she says, "I shouldn't, but I want it."

"Then, let me give it to you."

I lower myself all the way. The full-body contact draws a gasp out of her and while her lips are parted, I kiss her.

Fireworks explode inside of me as my lips close on her bottom one, every holiday of the year blending into this very moment. I slide her thigh up until there isn't a single molecule of air between us. The feeling of her tongue sliding against mine, of her hands traveling down my sides until they find the hem of my T-shirt, are almost enough to push me over the edge.

I want to rein myself in. I don't want to scare her off. But I also want to taste more of her, feel more of her. I want to know every plane of her body. I want her.

When breathing becomes too hard for Serena, I trail my lips down the column of her throat, paying special attention to the spots where her pulse beats harder. There, I place hot, open kisses. I let my tongue sample her skin at the same time as, with one hand, I push the collar of her T-shirt down, and with the other I caress the skin of her side higher and higher.

Before either front reaches the goal, Serena pulls me by my hair until I'm kissing her again. The sound that comes from my chest is something very close to an angry animal, but I'm not disappointed. On the contrary, I'm happier than ever.

"Serena." I growl against her lips. "You better stop me, or else I'm going to take you on this coach."

"I'm trying, Caleb. But you keep making me fail," Serena whines like I've never heard before, and pride explodes in my chest.

I kiss the spot behind her ear and the way it makes her groan, almost makes me lose the last thread of control I have left.

To her ear, I whisper, "That's because I really want you to lose this battle."

"Oh, it's a battle?"

I start chuckling, but before I can react the world is tilting and I slam on the ground.

The loss of air and the throbbing at the back of my head disappear the second Serena sits on my lap. Every one of my senses tunes to her hands as they pull up my T-shirt and I help her until it's off. We're both breathing hard as she stares down at me. At some point she lost her glasses or I pulled them away, and maybe it's her blurry vision what leads her to run her hands up my stomach and to my chest. My skin breaks into goosebumps.

"It's so annoying," she says out of the blue.

Panting like a lap dog, I ask, "What?"

"How freaking perfect you are."

Well, that's unexpected. But more so, is that out of her own free will she leans down to kiss me as though that is what she needs and not air. While she devours my mouth, I take advantage of the position to run my hands up her thighs until I find her butt. And squeeze.

"Caleb Oh!"

The protest doesn't come from her. After all, her lips are busy trapped against mine.

There's also no way her voice is quite that deep.

Gasping, Serena pulls away and even without glasses she must discern the figure of the third wheel. I tilt my head back only to see the upside down figure of my dad standing in the living room.

"Shit."

That word comes from me.

It triggers Serena into jumping as far as her legs can carry her. Which means that, in the blink of an eye, they take her as far as the guest room.

I sit up dazed against the instinct of following her to finish what we started—as if that way I could pretend that we weren't just found by the worst possible person—and the sense of responsibility I owe her. Instead, I palm the carpet around me until I locate my T-shirt. Best I put it on before facing Dad.

Once I'm somewhat presentable, I turn to him. "What are you doing here?"

"What am I—" Dad cuts himself off and I brace myself for the explosion I know is coming. "I should be the one asking you what the hell you think you're doing with your assistant!"

I cringe. The back of my neck tingles with the same feeling a prey gets in front of its predator. With the way the edges of Dad's irises start turning red, I think it's not just a feeling of danger.

I'm screwed. Not in the way I intended.

"Dad, I—"

"And you." He whirls around, and there she is. Serena in her own clothes, trembling from head to toe. "Didn't I warn you to stay away from Caleb?"

"You what?" Those two words from my mouth slice through the air.

Dad takes several deep breaths before facing me again. "I don't care if you hate me, but I won't let you make the same mistake as me."

"It's not a mistake." I take one step closer to him.

But his attention is back to Serena and he says, "You're fired."

Someone gasps.

Serena is frozen still, so it must've been me.

I grab Dad's arm and turn him around. "You can't do this."

But my voice sets Serena in motion. She scampers to the elevator and the moment I try to follow after her, Dad yanks me by the collar of my T-shirt like I'm a damn dog. He tightens the hold until I'm almost choking.

"Let her go. It's what's best for both of you."

I roll under his arm until either I dislocate his joint or he lets me go. He chooses the latter.

Choked up, I say, "I'm tired of you telling me how I have to live my life."

Dad's irises are fully red now, and even though I have a clear shot for the elevator I know he won't let me reach it. He's stronger, faster, and can compel me to kneel down for the rest of the day if he so desires. With the way fury radiates off him like heatwaves, I think he might do something worse this time.

"Then stop screwing around—especially with a human girl—and marry Vivienne."

"Turn Serena," I say, shocking both of us. But I know that's the only way out of this mess. "Then I'll be a good little boy and marry a vampire like you want. Only if it's Serena."

As if instead, I'd been the one to compel him, Dad stays rooted to the spot.

I run for the elevator in my bare feet and pajamas, counting my lucky stars that Dad didn't follow me. But when I reach the lobby, Serena is far gone.

CHAPTER 63
SERENA

I sit in a park bench for a very long time. All I can do is watch my shadow gradually shorten until it disappears beneath me, until it grows longer from the other side, until it starts fading after dusk.

The earth keeps spinning even though my world has come crashing to a halt. How cruel is that?

The enormity of what's happened crashes on me like a boulder, and I double over under its weight until I'm folded in half. I cry onto my lap, letting out big, ugly wails that drive even the birds away from me.

I can't stay in that apartment with Karyn and Richard anymore, not after the shitshow of last night. The one person who offered to help me is now no longer within my reach, because I just lost my job in exactly the way I tried so hard to avoid.

Cedric Oh's right. He did warn me.

He warned me and I forgot, consumed by my feelings for his son. I forgot who really was my boss here. And now I lost what little I had.

After a while, I'm too exhausted to continue crying. I grab my purse and the bag where I stuffed Lara's dress. I don't even know how I'm going to return it, because I don't have her address. It was Phelan and Caleb who drove me over to her house. And while I could ship it to her office, I don't even know how I'm going to wash it.

I can only stomach the thought of going into the apartment to grab my essentials and leave. But where?

Where can I go?

After calling an Uber, I wait in the parking lot of the apartment complex until it's deep into the night. According to Richard's schedule, he'll be working the night shift tonight, which means the probability of Karyn being asleep is high. I sneak inside, thanking my past self for having already prepared to move out. I carry all my bags with essentials, mementos, documents and some clothes, and leave everything else behind.

Never has descending these stairs been slower or more painful. It never was a home, but it was the closest thing to stability that I had. The farther I walk from the apartment, the more an icy hand cinches around my heart.

"¿Qué voy a hacer?" I ask myself. The lights from the parking lot posts start blurring as my eyes well up again. Tilting my head back, all I can see is a grey sky with no stars. "Help me."

That's when I remember. There's still one more person I can go to.

I sit on my bags as I wait for another Uber. Until I find a new job, it's clear my credit card debt is only going to keep rising. One night ago, I was contemplating a loan from Caleb so I could move into a place on my own. Tonight I can't even afford thinking about it.

And yet the earth keeps spinning…

The drive to the orphanage feels endless, especially as the driver tries again and again to establish an animated conversation in Spanish. Eventually, he gives up and turns on the radio. Merengue songs fill the silence, so jarring to my mood that it churns my stomach.

My phone starts vibrating in my hand. The screen lights up with another call from Caleb. The list of recent calls shows he's tried seventeen times. I wait until the Uber driver drops me off at the entrance to the orphanage before switching off the device. In the morning, I'll find the way to mail it to Comed. It's the only thing from work I have with me and once I return it, there won't be any connection any longer.

I fold up my legs and rest my arms on my knees. I'm not going to disturb the nuns and the kids in the middle of the night, so this is where I'll sleep. The suburban area is quiet enough that the only danger I'm running is from critters of the night.

Much better than the eyes of a vampire, flashing red in anger, trained on me.

Closing my eyes, I give myself to a restless sleep. In my dreams, I'm drowning in the ocean. Caleb floats above me, extending his hand to me. But he stays on the surface no matter how hard he swims, and I keep sinking no matter how hard I kick.

A hand touches my shoulder and I snap awake. Sister Emilia exclaims, "Serena! What are you doing here?"

I draw in a deep breath and open my mouth. Instead of words, a big sob comes out, followed by another until I'm full-on wailing.

Without minding the dirt on the concrete one bit, Sister Emilia lowers herself to sit beside me. She pulls me to her and I weep on her shoulder. She pats my head and that's it—that's all I really needed.

It takes me a long while to be able to breathe properly. Tears still roll down my cheeks, but at least I'm no longer sobbing.

"Tell me what happened," she says, her voice sweet but braced in authority.

And I spill all the beans. Including all the ones that make me look really bad. From Karyn and Richard, to Caleb… until the moment Cedric Oh walked in on *that* scene.

The only thing I hold back is talking about the onions, but boy it sure feels like someone is chopping some.

Once I'm done with my tale, Sister Emilia's mouth is open as though she's forgotten how to control her jaw.

I wipe my face with the back of my arms, but they too are wet from older tears. "I know, I've misbehaved and now I'm paying for it."

"It's true that I'm a little surprised," she says, offering me a sheepish smile. "But I'm not here to judge you. I'm here to help you."

"You can judge me." I sniffle. "If I were you, I'd be judging me so hard right now."

It makes her chuckle. "Well, not all is lost. If you regret some of your actions, it means you know they were wrong. You can always strive to be better from now on."

I hang my head. This feels even worse than being scolded. There's no defending against the truth.

I knowingly treaded on a minefield. It shouldn't come as a shock when I stepped on one. All I can do from now on is choose a path with no bombs.

"What do I do now?" I ask her, looking up at her to help me find answers.

She pats my hair again. "You can start by coming in and having some soup."

"And then?"

Sister Emilia smiles. "And then why don't you help me with the kids for a few days, until you find something you really want to do instead?"

It's not the clear blueprint I wish I had, but it's a much

better start than anything I could think of during the long hours after leaving Caleb's apartment.

*

Despite my protests, Sister Emilia helps me carry bags into the building. It's Monday morning, which means the only people we find on our way to the cafeteria are some of the other nuns. The kids are all at school.

I long for those days, when I was sure only everyone else could fail me—never myself. But now I know even I can screw myself over. All I needed is to fall in love with the wrong guy for that to happen.

I'd been right when I avoided dating all through high school and college. The second I graduated and thought I was finally an adult, that I could make my own decisions and I'd always be fine, was precisely the moment I failed myself.

While I can't turn back time, I have to find a way to face forward. Sister Emilia guides me to one of the small rooms meant for the nuns. My bags don't fit in the tiny space between the bed and the wall, and after pushing the smaller ones under the bed I conclude that I have to get rid of more stuff. That'll be today's project.

"It'll do for now," she tells me.

"Thank you." I sniff to prevent my nose from running. "It's more than I deserve."

"No, child." She wipes my face with her hands, rough to the touch but so warm. "You deserve the world, but maybe you don't get it in this life."

I give a watery smile. "As long as the afterlife is better, I'll soldier on."

"Atta girl." Sister Emilia pats my back. "Now let's go get you that soup. Today's menu is minestrone, one of your favorites."

On cue, my stomach roars loud enough to echo across the hall. My head and my heart hurt, but that little rascal stomach of mine is just fine.

I have to follow in that example. No matter what happens, I have to be fine.

CHAPTER 64
CALEB

After Dad finally leaves, I call Phelan up and the first place we try is Serena's apartment. Her roommates claim not to have seen her ever since we left last night.

"But who the hell are you, anyway?" the woman asks me, sizing me up with eyes that make me want to jump out the window.

I fish in my wallet for one of my nondescript cards that only have my first name and phone number, and give it to her. "If she comes home, make sure to call me."

"Why should we?" The man snorts.

Through gritted teeth, I say, "I will reward you."

Then I turn around and meet Phelan outside.

"I checked the perimeter and—" He cuts himself off to shake his head.

No other words are necessary. She's nowhere to be found.

In the car, I call her for what feels like a billionth time, begging her in my mind to pick up the phone. If she's not home, there's even less guarantee that she's safe. All I want is for her to be safe.

Phelan and I drive around the neighborhood for hours, waiting well into the night for her to show up, but there's no luck.

Pulling at my hair, I ask, "What if by any chance she's at my place? What if she's come back to talk or... or..."

I'm pulling at straws here, but I don't know what else to do.

"Let's try," is all Phelan says.

The streets seem to blend onto a single straight road that I desperately hope leads to her. I've kept my fists clenched so tight, by the time we make it to my place, I can no longer feel my hands.

But Serena is also not here.

I stand in my living room, gasping for air in an effort not to burst into tears. If Dad saw me, he'd probably think I'm just a big baby whose toy got taken away. Except it feels like an implacable hand tore through my chest and ripped out my heart.

"Phelan." My voice sounds so far away, for a second I wonder who spoke. "What do I do now?"

For a long moment, there's no sound at all. I'd think I'm alone if not for his steady presence behind me.

Finally, he says, "Keep looking or give up. Those are your only choices."

Cruel, perhaps. But actionable.

I kept looking for an entire week. Calling her phone didn't work the first days, and in the middle of the week it arrived to the office by post. Marissa didn't hear from her. Lara did, but only because she received a dress in the mail. No return address.

I didn't even bother speaking to Dad. There's no way he'd care to know the whereabouts of an employee he fired so easily.

Meanwhile, Phelan carted me across the city of Miami every day, several times per day. One day we started at her apartment complex before driving to the office or to my apartment, the next day we'd switch around the order. I spent most of the time camping at the parking lot of her apartment complex, to no avail.

One afternoon, I spot Serena's roommate's boyfriend getting out of a beat up Honda. Before Phelan can react, I jump out of my car like someone's chasing me.

"Hey." I call out to the other guy, who freezes upon seeing me. "Any news?"

"The heck, man. You scared me."

I'll do worse than scaring him if he doesn't start talking.

It takes all my willpower to not say that to his face, though.

"Whatever—No." The guy grabs a backpack from his passenger's seat. "If you see her, tell her rent's due in a week."

"Rent is not what you should be worrying about while a person is missing."

A hand falls on my shoulder, the fingers digging into my muscle enough to hurt. I don't have to turn around to know it's my bodyguard, actually extending his services to protect the dismissive asshole in front of me *from me*. The only thing preventing me from punching this guy in the teeth is the vise Phelan has on my shoulder.

"Let's go," Phelan says in his quiet voice.

Exactly a week after I last saw Serena, I lay awake in bed staring at the ceiling. At this point, I've already put a report to the police and combed through every spot of the city I've ever known her to be at.

There's nothing else I can do.

And that thought is more crushing than I expect.

In the middle of the night, I grab a duffel bag with basic stuff and leave my apartment. This must be the one night when Phelan is deep asleep, because for once he doesn't follow me right away. I get on the fastest one of my cars, a McLaren

F1 that even the second most powerful vampire in the world won't be able to catch up to, and drive off.

With the mostly empty streets, I reach my destination in record time. The marina is closed at this time of the night, but I jump over the fence and if the cameras catch me, Dad can deal with my mess later. I don't care anymore.

Since I haven't called Joe to prep the yacht, the Bad Blood sits empty at its dock, which is perfect. This wouldn't have worked as well if I'd planned it. I go through my mental checklist to prepare the yacht for sailing, and about two hours later I'm well on my way deeper into the Caribbean.

They'll find me. Joe will probably be the first one to realize that the boat is missing. Worse, Phelan will find me missing from my apartment and nothing on this earth will prevent him from locating me. Eventually, word will get to Dad and if he has to swim all the way to the middle of the ocean so he can tell me off again, he will. But he owns like fifteen more boats that will do the work for him.

At most, I have about five hours alone. Enough to have the emotional breakdown I've been postponing.

Through big, rough gasps, I unzip my duffel bag and pull out a full body diving suit. I'm going to swim until my lungs burn, until the ocean has absorbed all my tears and I'm able to come back on land—dry, ready to face a reality I don't want.

I barely hold on until the sunrise to jump in the water. It hits me as though I'm diving into a block of ice instead. The deep darkness underwater doesn't scare me. Instead, it makes me feel like there's nothing for a while, and that's comforting in itself.

I can't tell if I'm crying, but deep down I feel like I am. Like all that exists is the darkness enveloping me and the sorrow in my chest.

Underwater, my head quiets until it's empty, but every time I come up aboard the Bad Blood to change my oxygen tanks, my head fills up again. Where is Serena? Is she okay? Will I get to see her again? Will she let me apologize? When is Dad going to find me? Does he even care anymore?

And then I jump in the ocean again, and all is quiet.

The fourth time I come up to the surface, I find a speedboat beside the ladder leading to the Bad Blood's deck. I've finally been found. The sun is high enough that it's probably noon, which is later than I thought they'd locate me anyway.

By this point, my limbs are so exhausted it takes me forever to climb aboard. Daniel and Phelan stand by the ladder. Together they haul me up and drag me to the seating area. I'm there only for a few seconds until Joe appears with a cold bag of blood.

"Drink," Phelan demands.

I accept the bag, no longer feeling anything as I drain it.

"I heard what's happened," Daniel says, sitting across from me with a look on his face like he doesn't recognize the person he's talking with.

In a raspy voice, I say, "If you're here to tell me off—can it. Dad already did that."

"I'm not," my brother says. "Dad did wrong in firing Serena like that. And he's also doing wrong pretending everything's okay."

I drop my face on the table, overly warm in contrast to the ocean.

"But," he continues. "You're also wrong in not talking to him."

I snort. "I talked *back* at him, though."

"Caleb." Dan says my name in that way that sounds like he's teetering over the edge. "Why don't you ask Dad why he's acting like this?"

"Because he wants me to marry a nice little vampire of his choosing—who, by the way, isn't nice at all." I sit up straight and run my wrinkly hands up and down my face. "He also said he doesn't want me to make his own mistakes, which is rich coming from the only guy who can turn humans into vampires. If I had the power to turn Serena, would he still consider my feelings for her a mistake?"

My brother rubs his nape. "Listen, none of that is the reason why Dad's doing all this."

"No? Then why?" I scrunch up my face. There's only one other possible reason. "Is the Astor family threatening him, or something?"

But Daniel surprises me by shaking his head. His voice chokes up as he says, "No, Caleb. It's because Dad's dying."

It feels as if the boat is capsizing.

CHAPTER 65
SERENA

Laundry duty for an orphanage with fifty kids is a punishment. There's no other way to put it. Every day, I wake up to do loads upon loads of laundry in the two washing machines available. While they operate, I hand wash a small pile of delicates and almost the moment I'm done, the laundry machines are too and I have to start the laborious task of bringing hampers of heavy wet clothes out to the yard to hang them. Because of course there isn't a dryer in sight.

One day, while bending down to pick up bedsheets to hang, Sister Emilia drops by with one of the younger nuns, Sister Luisa, who joined the orphanage sometime after I left.

"How is it?" Sister Emilia asks me, smiling as though she can read the true answer in my mind.

I pat my achy lower back and straighten up. "Well, either this is truly back-breaking work or I'm not as young as I thought."

They chuckle at my pain—and they have a right. After all, they stand from the higher vantage of point of simply being used to these tasks that I instead consider a punishment.

"I brought Sister Luisa here to help you." Sister Emilia nods at the younger nun, who promptly dashes into the laundry room to collect another hamper of clothes. "And now tell me how you really feel."

I finish clipping a pillow cover to the clothesline before facing the closest person to a parent that I have.

"It's a loaded question." I run my damp hands against my sides, drying them with my own clothes. "But I'll admit I feel a lot of negative things right now. Against myself and against others."

"Forgive, before you do harm." She grabs my hand and pats. "Including to yourself."

I bite my lower lip hard the second I feel it start to tremble.

Sister Luisa comes bounding out of the laundry room with a hefty basket, which at once makes me realize she's stronger than me. I run over to help her, if only because it gives me a distraction from my thoughts.

Lonely laundry isn't good for that. While my body works to exhaustion, it allows my mind to wander. In the past week and some, I've ruminated over every moment where I acted out of line.

The worst part is knowing that while my mouth said what I knew to be true—that Caleb and I weren't on a level playing field—my heart still betrayed those words and pretended like we were. Otherwise, how dare I catch feelings for someone I had no business even calling by his first name?

And while Mr. Oh was right—about all of it—I still can't help the grudge tainting my insides.

At the end of the day, it might have been better to never be hired for that job. Never did I think I'd regret acing a job interview quite like I do now. I should've known it was too good to be true the moment I was offered the position at just the first interview.

If I hadn't signed a non-disclosure agreement as part of my

employment contract, I would've hopped online to warn future applicants to the position of assistant to Caleb Oh.

Be careful, you might fall in love with this gorgeous, adorable man, and lose everything you've built.

How would that look on a tabloid headline, huh?

"It's tough work," Sister Luisa says with a soft voice I barely catch. "But it will give you some certainty for a bit, and I think you can draw some comfort in that."

I smile. "You sound like Sister Emilia."

"I hope so, she said the same to me once."

Makes sense. Sister Emilia has a way of giving advice that cuts directly to the gaping need inside of you. I used to be afraid of her as a child, because it felt like she could always read my mind. In truth, she's just the most empathetic person I've ever met in my life. Very far from how I am.

Once I'm done hanging everything, Sister Luisa asks me, "Will you join us for mass at noon?"

I put my hands on my hips. It's either that or staying alone with my thoughts.

"I will," I respond.

*

Hours later, even as mass has concluded and everyone else is back to their daily duties, I sit on a pew in the chapel. My head hangs low and gravity pulls one tear after another.

I hope that one day the hole in my heart shaped like Caleb Oh will stop hurting. That day I might be able to lift my head here.

Quiet, shuffling steps sound behind me and I wipe my face quickly before Sister Luisa reaches my side.

"Excuse me," she whispers. "But you have a visitor waiting for you at the entrance."

My heart skips a beat.

It can't possibly be him, right? I did tell him I grew up in an orphanage, but I never said which one. And it's not like this is the only one in Southern Florida. What if he got the address from the receipt at the gift shop at Universal?

We do our reverences to the altar and the second I'm out of the chapel, I break into a sprint like a little kid about to get a treat. My heart pounds not from the exertion, but from the hope that it's Caleb. From the fear that it's actually him.

How should I react? I want to fling myself into his arms, but I also know I shouldn't. And if there's one lesson I've learned from all of this, it's that just because I *can* do something, it doesn't mean I *should*.

But all of that comes crashing to a halt the moment I reach the entrance. It's not Caleb who came to find me.

There, back turned to me, is someone with a cascade of blonde hair and the longest legs a woman can possibly have. As if sensing me, she turns around and gives me a smile.

Vivienne Astor.

I don't take one step closer to her, but she also doesn't walk into the premises of the orphanage. It's not like she physically can't, but maybe even Vivienne knows she shouldn't come anywhere near a holy place. And I'm glad for it.

"What are you doing here?" I ask her.

She takes off sunglasses that look more expensive than a car. Cherry red lips smile at me, but the gesture doesn't reach her eyes. "So it's true, you got sacked after being caught banging your boss, huh?"

Her voice carries far and the words reach one of the nuns nearby, who is sweeping leaves off the ground. I don't need to be a vampire to hear how loud this lie makes her gasp.

I squeeze my fists tight. "There was no banging, as you put it. But yes, I got fired. Which begs the question again, what are you doing here?"

Vivienne laughs in a twinkling way. "I came to see if the

rumors are right, or if you're still an obstacle I have to remove."

A shiver runs up my spine. Even the sunlight of a bright afternoon can't imbue any warmth to Vivienne's eyes.

I finally understand why Caleb fears her. It's not just because she's gone as far as sexually harassing him before, attempting to get a biological reaction out of him that will help her claim a stake on him. It's because she's capable of doing even worse things.

I never thought what happened at the pier was an accident. The railing had been sturdy when I leaned into it to watch the ocean. But the wood gave like a cracker after Vivienne appeared beside me. She might not have *known* I couldn't swim at the time, but it was a possibility she might've contemplated and didn't care about. To her, I was just an obstacle to get to Caleb.

The certainty that he's in danger washes over me, but there's nothing I can do to help him.

"Is that how you see anyone around Caleb?" I ask her, trembling with both rage and fear.

Vivienne's shoulder lifts slightly. "Put yourself in my shoes. Wouldn't you? Here I am, doing everything I can to marry the guy. Meanwhile, he's fooling around with his secretary. Who's the honorable one here?"

I draw in a sharp breath. "I'm astounded by your capacity to twist the truth around to serve you."

This makes her laugh again. "Is that what you tell yourself to sleep at night? Or is knowing you were actually *the other one* too hard to face?"

"Have a good day." I turn around and hug my arms around myself. A late October afternoon is still pretty warm, but I feel like I just walked out of a meat locker.

"Be a good girl and stay here," Vivienne calls out behind

me. "Become a nun, or whatever. As long as you stay away from my man, you'll be safe."

There's no need to ask her what would happen otherwise. The threat behind her words isn't veiled at all.

I could tell her that while I'm not quite nun material, she has nothing to worry about. Nothing more can ever happen between Caleb Oh and I—his dad will make sure of that with the power of his money.

But something inside of me doesn't let me put that final nail in the coffin and hand the victory to Vivienne. I leave her there, in the yard, letting her wonder if I have any moves left to do or if I'm completely out of the game.

CHAPTER 66
CALEB

Night falls by the time we finally get to my parents's mansion. I took a shower and changed into clean clothes while the Bad Blood returned to land. I spent the lion's share of the time sitting in my cabin, alone with my thoughts.

Dad has always been strict and what I know he's capable of, as the strongest vampire in the world, has always given me a healthy fear of him. But for most of my life, he hasn't hovered over my every move.

He was the parent who spoiled me, a radical contrast to the vitriol my stepmother felt for my very existence. As if the only way he could atone for his sin of falling in love with his human assistant, turning her, and having a child with her against his wife's back, was to pour all the love the world would deny that child.

Until recently, Dad had given me a long leash. When I said I no longer wanted to eat meat, he nodded. When I said I wanted to go into business and not medicine like Daniel, he said fine. When instead of going to the office I spent my days scuba diving, he said just don't drown.

Only when I did something truly bad—like that period of my early twenties with a revolving door of women—did Dad yank on my leash and force me back under his wing. But the way he's been shortening my leash these past few months was suspicious.

In the back of my mind, I knew it. I just refused to acknowledge it.

It was as if every plea Dad made for me to do this or that, was driven by fear.

In my small mind, I thought it was because someone was threatening him. That there was a power struggle I didn't know about, leading the king of the vampires to micromanage one of his sons for his safety. But I should've known better. Cedric Oh isn't afraid of anyone else, especially since we're all lessers compared to him.

There's only one thing in this world that is a certain threat to both humans and vampires, though. Death.

Part of me still refuses to believe it's his time. The truth is, Dad is three hundred and ninety two years old. In human years, that makes him about eighty three or so, but you'd never guess it from his face. People don't put him a day over sixty. Human employees at Comed gossip that it's because he's a fixture of the local plastic surgeons that make Miami Beach a sight for sore eyes, but that's not it.

Cedric Oh is the king of vampires. The only one alive who has drank the blood of every single vampire in the world. His physical strength, the unnatural abilities, all make him one of the healthiest creatures on this planet.

And yet, he too shall die.

I jump out and dash in the house the moment Phelan parks the car at the entrance of the Oh mansion. Lately my strongest sense is hearing, and I let it lead me across the mansion. I pay no heed to Diana in the living room, or Maria in the kitchen.

Instead, I follow the vague sound of a familiar grunt. I break out into the backyard, which is basically a golf field. A few yards into the field, Jon stands beside Dad, who is hitting one golf ball after another. He's always preferred golfing in the middle of the night, not just because he can see every nook and cranny even without the lamp posts around the field, but also because it's cooler at night.

I can't believe that the strange, remarkable man who is my dad, is dying.

Jon is the first one to catch sight of me. I hear him warn Dad of my arrival, but it doesn't stop him from swinging at another ball.

"Say it isn't true," is my greeting, still a ways away from him. But I know he can hear me.

"Leave us," Dad says to Jon. The assistant makes a short bow and trots back into the house. Dad takes off his cap and wipes the sweat of his forehead with the back of his hand. "Welcome home, Caleb. Have you finally come to your senses?"

"No, if anything I'm more senseless now." I stop before him, right under the beam of a lamp post. "But Daniel told me something that's making me lose my mind even more."

Slowly, Dad selects another ball and puts it on a tee. Getting himself in position to swing, he asks, "And what is that?"

"That you're dying."

The club makes a smooth swing in the air. The golf ball disappears into the night sky like a rocket. The sound of a perfect hole in one doesn't come this time.

"Ah, that." Dad uses the golf club as a cane and just stands there, as if I haven't just said something enormous. "I can't say it isn't true."

Air leaves my lungs.

"So that's why you're doing all of this? This intense worry you have over my future really is because you won't be part of it any longer?"

Finally, Dad turns around to face me. His expression is serene, as though we're talking about our next vacation or the weather. "You're not wrong. Time is now my enemy, Caleb. And I can't leave things to its whims anymore."

I want to laugh. I want to cry. I want to kick the grass until I'm so drained of energy that all I can do is lay on the ground.

With a shaky breath, I say, "That's so like you. Death doesn't scare you, but you're afraid *for* me."

His eyes light up with a smile. It pisses me off, because it means he's resigned to something I can't accept.

"I hope you understand now," Dad says, squeezing my shoulder. "Everything I do is for your sake. Even the things you don't like."

"I get it, but there's something you also need to understand." I grip his arm hard, wishing that it could stop him from fading into thin air. "Eventually, it'll all be up to me."

"I know that." Dad sighs. "It's why I'm trying to get you settled before I go."

"At the expense of someone innocent?" I ask, taking a step back and breaking the connection between us. "You will put me on the path you want for me, but let someone else careen from theirs."

I stuff my hands in the pockets of my jeans and tilt my head back. The sky is clear tonight and the stars twinkle as if they were happy—the little suckers. How dare they be bright when my entire world is cast in darkness.

"I won't turn her," Dad says. "For a human who drinks my blood, survival is a game of chance. Even if they do, there's no guarantee they'll be able to adapt to being a vampire. Look at what happened to your mother."

We don't talk about it often, especially anywhere within

earshot of my stepmother. This time, Dad also refrains from going into details.

All I know, is that Dad turned my mother and she made it to the other side. Dad was happy, finally the woman he truly loved could spend the rest of his life with him. And even though it was all wrong, he still welcomed the news of her pregnancy despite knowing it would be the end of his marriage.

What he didn't know was my mother's mind was gradually being consumed like the wick of a lit candle. The hunger for blood and the heightened sensations, added to the stares of natural-born vampires who questioned why Dad turned an average human woman, eventually burned her out.

Officially, her cause of death was a car accident. But I've always had my doubts.

In my selfish desire to be with Serena, I didn't even stop to contemplate what asking Dad to turn her could really mean.

He's right. Of course he is. Serena and I can never be together.

"I know that," I say after a while. "I wasn't in my right mind when I asked you to turn her. But it's not fair to ruin her life because of me."

Dad's eyes are devoid of anger when he says, "You should've thought about that before getting tangled with her."

"I know," I repeat, casting my eyes down to the grass I want to kick, but won't. "Punish me instead, but let Serena keep her job."

"You consider my best intentions a punishment?"

I lift my eyes.

Now that I know time with Dad is running out, I should say no. I should say I love him, that he's never wrong, that I can't imagine my life without him.

But while all of that is true, it still won't lead me to lie to him. So, I say, "The road to hell is paved in good intentions."

His brow creases. "Be that as it may, you will still do as I say, for her sake?"

"Yes."

"Including," he says, pausing to look me up and down. "If one of my orders is to get engaged to Vivienne Astor as soon as possible?"

I take a step back as if he dealt a physical blow.

Unlike Dad, I do feel plenty of fear, and this ranks high in my list of things I least want to face. I should've known it'd be precisely what he wants.

But that's why he's the longest serving king of vampires—because no one's been able to maneuver him out of the throne. And every choice I took led to his desired outcome, my options are to marry into the powerful Astor family, or refuse to do his bidding and ruin Serena's life.

He knows I will never do the latter, and the former won't entirely ruin my life. If the secret of me being illegitimate were to come out, the Astors would close rank around me because I'll already be one of them. In exchange for my safety, I have to forsake happiness.

For Serena, I will do that. And more.

"Yes," I say through gritted teeth. "As long as Serena gets what she wants, I'm fine not getting what I want."

As if sensing I'm about to crumble down, Dad pulls me to him and gives me a hug so strong I almost doubt he's declining. "I'm proud of you, Son."

With my face stuffed against his shoulder, I mumble, "That makes one of us."

"If you're able to put others before you, maybe I don't have a lot to worry about," he says, chuckling.

And then, because I'm still in his arms, I can feel his chuckles turn into the barest cough at first. In the next second, they rack his body with such violence I'm the one who has to hold him up.

All at once, I know it's true. How he hid the malfunction in his lungs is probably more a reflection of how weak my senses were before.

Dad's dying, and my world is about to change drastically as result.

CHAPTER 67
SERENA

bring some chamomile tea and crackers to Sister Faustina, who has been in bed with a stomach bug today. The cramps in my lower stomach, which aren't related to a bug, almost make me want a bland dinner like this too. Gathering my strength, I'm about to knock on Sister Faustina's door when heavy footsteps distract me.

"Juan Diego is missing," Sister Luisa says at me as she zooms by down the hallway.

Not even two weeks into rejoining the orphanage life, and I already know exactly which kid is the one missing. The one who always gives everyone trouble.

"How can I help?" I call out after her, before she disappears around the bend. For a second it looks like I'm too late, but then she pops her head around.

"Help us find him!"

I set the tray down by Sister Faustina's door. She's been refusing any food or drink today and I was meaning to oversee that she clears the tray, but now I won't be able to. I say to the door, "Try to nibble on some toast and have some tea. I'll come by later to see how you're doing."

I push my glasses up and roll up the sleeves of my sweatshirt. Right now, I have an unruly teen to catch.

Breaking into a sprint, I forgo checking the rooms in case he's hiding there. I'm sure the other nuns and staff have already considered that option.

When I was a kid here and wanted to hide, my favorite place was a nook between the back of the building and the HVAC system. It was hot and damp, but there was one shady spot where it wasn't unbearable. After jogging around the building and squeezing my way in between some hedges, I find my old spot empty. Maybe this generation of kids hasn't found it yet.

"If I was a tween, angry at a world that has abandoned him," I say into the night, my words almost entirely drowned by the noise from the HVAC. "Where would I go?"

Outside, of course.

I spent my entire time at the orphanage dreaming about the outside world. Surely I wouldn't follow so many rules if I had no one else to set them for me, right? In my childish innocence, I thought once I had a life outside, I could sleep in as long as I wanted, eat what I pleased, and not go to mass everyday.

I didn't know the outside world would be filled with uncertainty.

As I waddle in between the hedges, my sweatshirt catches on a branch and when I pull, it tears the fabric. "Darn it."

Something worse could be happening out there to that kid, though. I better hurry.

In the yard, I find old Francisco, the groundskeeper, calling out for the kid's name. When he sees me, he asks, "Any sightings?"

"Nothing yet." I put my hands on my hips and catch a breath for a second. "I'm gonna check around the block to see if he made it out."

The groundskeeper sighs. "I wouldn't put it past him to jump the fence."

We both look at the structure. It's at least eight feet tall and with barely any footholds. But I have no doubt that a determined boy can find a way.

The old man lends me the gate key and I walk outside. The neighborhood isn't entirely asleep at nine in the night. Nearby houses have lights streaming out of the windows and a few voices drift to my ears. But the streets are empty of any traffic, reducing the odds of Juan Diego hitchhiking. He must be around.

I make a pause after walking the perimeter of the orphanage and look up at the cloudless sky.

Is this my life now? Should I just become permanently employed at the orphanage, a place I wanted to escape as zealously as this kid? I certainly can't become a nun, I'm not that good of a person. But I can't see myself venturing in the outside world any time soon.

After I find Juan Diego, I'll run the plan by Sister Emilia and see what she says.

"Juan Diego!" I call out into the night.

Rustling sounds nearby.

I turn in time to catch some bushes move, even though there isn't wind strong enough to cause it. Which means one of two things. The thing behind the bushes is either one of Florida's animal species… or a runaway orphan.

Slowly, I approach from the side of easiest escape, praying that it isn't something that bites. And then—

My prayer is answered. Juan Diego crouches on the ground, his eyes going wide as saucers the moment he sees me. He tries to run, but I anticipate the move and throw myself at his back.

"Gotcha."

"Let me go!" He tries to weasel his way out of my chokehold, but I'm still bigger than him. How this scrawny kid a half head shorter than me jumped that fence, we'll never know.

"Nope, can't do." I drag him with me down the sidewalk. "You have the whole orphanage in an uproar, you know."

He sniffles. "Good. If they want peace they should let me go."

"You won't find peace outside, though." The moment I say that, his jaw clams up. "Trust me, I know."

The kid's eyes are watery as he says, "I just want… to be normal."

I rub his messy hair. "Sorry, kiddo. I'm not gonna sugar-coat it. You'll never be normal. But if you accept that, you might be happy. Which is much better, if you ask me. I wish someone told me this when I was in your position."

We walk in silence for a while, with only the company of our footsteps. We both know he's in for a world of hurt after we make it to the orphanage, but I trust relief at finding him will triumph over the stress he caused. It gives me an idea to pitch to Sister Emilia, about creating a program to ease the kids integration into society.

Because I know this firsthand: none of us are 'normal.' The grief, loss, and neglect we've faced in our short lives don't prepare us for the possibility of fulfillment and joy. I sure didn't recognize them for the short time I had them.

"Did you hear that?" the boy asks, stopping on his tracks.

"Good try, but you're not gonna escape from my grasp." Especially since I have a fistful of his shirt in one hand, and with the other I grab his arm in a vise.

"No, seriously." He sounds truly afraid. "I've been hearing it for a while. Listen."

We stop and do just that. Listen.

It takes me a moment to catch what he means. There's another set of steps.

"Maybe it's one of the nuns," I say, glancing back. We're

standing right under a lit lamp post, and it makes it harder for me to see out into the dark.

"Let's just go," the kid says, pulling *me*. Maybe this is why he looked so afraid when I found him.

We only walk a yard or so when the steps sound closer. I glance back again and this time I catch the shape of a man walking a distance behind us.

Okay, that's definitely not someone in the orphanage's staff.

Without saying anything, I pick up the pace and for once Juan Diego is compliant. Maybe this whole ordeal has been scarier than he was counting on. It sure is turning out that way for me, too.

I let go of Juan Diego's T-shirt to pull up my beat up cellphone. Unstable because of our hurried pace, I dial 911 without pressing the call button.

Another glance back reveals the man is closer. And that his eyes glow red.

Oh, shit.

Oh, shit.

"You shouldn't curse," Juan Diego murmurs, which means I spoke aloud.

"Listen to me." By this point we're full on running, and the mismatched steps behind us means the vampire is following. "No matter what happens, get to the orphanage, okay?"

"But—"

"Just run!" I order him.

I'm equally glad and horrified that Juan Diego is a lot faster than me. It means he'll make it to the orphanage safe, but probably means I'm going to get caught.

I can't think of why a vampire who lives in an underground society would risk his entire species to hurt an orphan. So, either this guy is a senseless murderer wanting to target a kid that not many people will mourn, or he's here for me.

The orphanage gate looms closer and I wait until Juan

Diego reaches it before I change direction. As I hoped—and feared—the vampire follows me.

Why hasn't he caught me? I've seen a vampire jump several feet in the air and run faster than a human can comprehend.

Is he just toying with me?

I fling myself out of the main path and roll into someone's backyard. Now that I know this is just a game, that he either doesn't intend to kill me, or not right away, I take a second to stop and take out my cellphone again. Trembling, I swipe through my short list of contacts and press the call button on the last person I ever thought I'd contact again.

But he said he would protect me. And I don't want to die just yet. Desperate times and desperate measures.

As the call rings, the vampire drops in front of me from out of nowhere. A sneering smile twists his face. Then the call connects.

Out of breath, I say, "Caleb, save me."

CHAPTER 68
CALEB

"Why didn't you tell me?" I ask, watching Dad pour two glasses of liquor for us in his studio. The bottle is nondescript but the smell is so potent it makes my eyes water.

Dad sets one glass before me and sits across the table, taking a hefty swig from his drink before speaking. "Don't be offended, I wasn't planning to tell anyone. But your brother's a doctor and he found something abnormal in my annual exam."

"What is it?" The question is both to his illness and to the liquor. I take one sip and—okay, I'm not a lightweight. After all, being a vampire means my metabolism is significantly faster than a human's. But this shit makes me cough and splutter, and my esophagus feels on fire. "Gah, is this kerosene?"

"A close cousin." Dad raises his glass. "Screw cancer."

Cancer.

My larger-than-life, king of vampires, father… has cancer.

I'm rendered immobile as he drains the rest of his glass and pours himself a second one. That's when I have to agree, the only way to swallow down these news is with whatever high-octane poison this is. I down the rest of my glass and just sit there, blinking through bitter tears that have nothing to do with the liquor.

"The only people I have confirmed this to are your brother, your stepmother, and you. Others might suspect, but they have no certainty." He leans forward to top my glass again. "But I worry the information has leaked. It would partially explain the emboldened attacks against you. That's why I have to ensure your future."

"Forget about me," I say, leaning forward. "I have many questions about you. How long have you been sick for? What is your prognosis? Are you looking for the leak? What are you gonna do when you catch them? Do you think the families are planning something?"

While my head churns with thoughts of a coup when the king is weakening, all Dad does is laugh.

"This is why I left giving you the news for last." Shaking his head, he runs his finger over the rim of his glass. "You're the only one who questions things. Daniel never does, he quietly accepts everything and keeps on keeping on. Your stepmother wants to question and defy, but she doesn't want to deal with the consequences. She's the kind of person who takes her frustrations out on her lessers instead.

"But you," he continues, his eyes crinkling at the corners as he regards me. "You've always been as curious as a cat."

I mumble. "Funny, I'm not the one dying."

"To answer some of your questions," Dad says, and I catch the subtle emphasis on *some*. "I don't exactly know how long it's been, but the liver cancer is progressing a lot slower than if it was a human's case. Which makes sense."

I swipe the liquor bottle from him. "What the hell, Dad. You shouldn't be drinking this."

"But treatment for human cancer also doesn't work on me." He leans forward and tugs the bottle free from my grip. "Which is why it's a losing battle. Also, this is my favorite moonshine."

A sound that is a cross between a snort, a laugh, and a cough erupts from my throat. "You drink moonshine? *You*? I thought your favorite drink was soju."

"I also quite like breaded pickles with ranch."

Sagging in my chair, I observe my dad like it's the first time. There are lines on his face I can't recall noting before, and his hair is streaked with more grey than just a year ago.

He's dying. There's nothing that can be done, but waiting. And he's totally fine with it.

My phone starts ringing and absentmindedly I pull it out of my pocket, my attention still on the old vampire across from me. "What about my other questions?"

"Don't you want to take care of that?" He glances at my phone.

"Dad." I narrow my eyes, but all it does is amuse him.

"Let's just say," Dad starts, slowly. On purpose. "That I'm working behind the scenes to dig up the traitors. And you'll help me, one way or another."

Why does that sound even more ominous than his impending death?

My phone keeps buzzing and I look down. It isn't a number I know, but I pick up anyway.

Right away, the voice I've been most wanting to hear says, "Caleb, save me."

I jump to my feet. "Serena. What's happening?"

Even Dad tenses at the tone of her voice.

"I-It's a vampire. A vampire found me."

My vision blurs for a moment. The way my voice comes out sounds far away. "Where are you?"

"The orphanage, I—"

And then the call is disconnected.

"Son! Snap out of it." Dad stands before me, squeezing my shoulders so hard it hurts. "She needs you right now."

I shake my head in hard jerks. "I don't know where to find her."

"I do," he surprises me by saying. He raises his voice so the guard outside the door can hear. "Phelan, get the car and set course for Sister Emilia's orphanage. Get Jon and Marissa to tag along."

Muffled by the barrier, Phelan responds, "Yes, sir."

"Go save her," Dad says to me, "but don't forget our deal."

How could I forget?

"Thank you, Dad."

With that, I turn and run out the mansion. Jon waits outside for me, with the door to the backseat of the Urus open. Phelan is in the backseat, and Marissa sits at the passenger's. The seating arrangement is not at all what I'd expect—Jon and Marissa must've been in the mansion for work related reasons —but that's not my pressing concern.

As Jon peels off the driveway, I ask Phelan, "Did you know she was at the orphanage all along?"

"No," he says. "It didn't occur to me."

And that's that. Anyone else would make excuses to clear themselves of culpability, but not Phelan. He speaks the truth as he can see it, in as short terms as possible. I have no choice but to believe him.

"She said she was being attacked by a vampire," I tell them. "But we don't know if there's more than one or…"

Or if she's even okay.

"The GPS says we're only fifteen minutes away," Jon says from the front.

Marissa turns around. "Wait, Serena knows about vampires?"

"Yes." I run my hand through my hair and pull at it. "Unfortunately, this wouldn't be her first encounter."

The drive feels incredibly slow even though Jon is breaking traffic laws left and right. He's going to end up with hefty fines that Dad will find a way to expunge. I've never been gladder for the Oh family money than at this moment.

Jon stops the car at an unassuming gate and I jump out of the car even faster than Phelan does. A couple of nuns stand behind the gate, their heartbeats so quick that they rival my own.

"Where's Serena?" I ask them.

The younger one says, "We don't know. We've been looking for her but—"

The older woman shushes her and turns to me. "And who are you, young man?"

"Her boss," I say. Shaking my head, I add, "A friend."

"Then help us look for her," the older nun says. "It's been an hour since I last saw her."

I nod and turn to the others. "Let's spread out."

"I'm coming with you," Phelan says.

"Fine."

I have no time to argue. I'm sure he'd find Serena faster if he went on his own. But I'm the one he's in charge of, and where I go he goes.

"She was last seen that way," the younger nun points to her right—our left—and that's where we head. Marissa veers left at the next intersection, Jon takes a right, and Phelan and I continue straight.

The myth of werewolves probably originated from someone seeing vampires sniff the air like Phelan and I are doing, thinking a vampire with highly evolved olfactory abilities got them from a dog. But I actually got this from a vampire named Jim, who also smokes like a chimney.

It's what helps me catch an almost imperceptible trace of

Serena's scent in the air. And she might not like this, but what's helping me the most is that she's on her period.

Phelan and I head down the same direction without the need for words. I can hear several sets of footsteps up ahead, all racing somewhere. We pick up speed and catch sight first of two men—vampires, by the rich iron in their blood.

Beyond them is Serena, running in the middle of the street like her life depends on it.

With a roar, I throw myself at one of the men.

It happens quicker than I can process it. We roll on the asphalt and I come out on top, raining a flurry of blows on the man's head that knock him out. In the back of my mind I'm confused that it's over so quickly, but that doesn't matter.

A yelp comes before a hard thud. I look up to find Serena crumpled on the road. I take off after her, half expecting a battalion of angry vampires to pop out of the hedges, but nothing happens.

Serena groans and pulls herself up on all fours. When she glances back and sees it's only me, she freezes.

Only our breaths echo in the night. As no one else is throwing themselves at us, I assume Phelan took care of the other man just as swiftly.

It seems... she's safe now.

"Are you okay?" I ask, my voice coming out in a rasp.

Serena's glasses are skewed on her face and she fixes them up. For a moment, that's all she manages.

Finally, she nods. "I think so."

As she tries to stand, her legs falter and I catch her before she hits the ground again. Air rushes out of her lungs while I hold her up against me.

Then I remember what I signed up for, as long as it means she's safe. That's the most important thing. Not the burning need to pull her to me and wrap my arms around her.

I take a step back. Without tearing my eyes from her, I ask, "Phelan, are we clear?"

"Yes," he says from behind me. I glance back and find the unconscious men on his shoulders like they're the straps of a backpack. "I can't detect any other threats nearby."

"Me neither." Taking a deep breath, I say to Serena, "Let's go. You're safe now."

CHAPTER 69
SERENA

tremble from head to toe as we retrace our steps back to the orphanage. Caleb walks ahead of me and Phelan brings up the rear with his cargo.

Caleb's back looks tense, as if he's still coiled to spring to action any second. To keep me safe.

Somehow, the vision is far more beautiful than his naked skin.

"How did you find me so quick?" I ask with a thread of voice.

"I didn't. I looked for you everywhere and couldn't find you," he says, jamming his hands in the pockets of his jeans. "But Dad knew exactly where you were."

That doesn't surprise me. Cedric Oh probably looked even my ancestors up before hiring me.

After a while, Caleb says, "Phelan probably knew too."

I jump out of my skin as the bodyguard behind me says, "I said I didn't."

Caleb tosses a grumpy look over his shoulder. "Doesn't mean I have to believe you."

And while the other man doesn't acknowledge that verbally, I do catch the way his eyes narrow just a tad.

A sob escapes from my throat that halts them on the spot.

Caleb's hands come up in the air but stop before touching me. "Um, it's okay, Serena. We won't let any more harm come your way, trust us."

I take my glasses off and wipe my eyes before any tears can escape.

Contrary to what he may suppose, I'm not crying because of what happened tonight. But because I missed them. I missed their polar opposite personalities. The way they'd become a comforting presence in my life.

"Thank you, both," I say, catching my quivering bottom lip between my lips. Before they can respond, I continue walking.

We make it to the gates of the orphanage pretty quick. There, I'm surprised to find a group I never would've imagined. There's Jon and Marissa on the right, and Sisters Emilia and Luisa on the left. The women sag in relief upon seeing me, but it's Marissa who breaks into a sprint and hugs me.

"I'm so glad you're fine!" She squeezes the daylights out of me. Pulling away, she inspects me from head to toe and gasps. "Oh no, your knees are skinned. And your arms are scratched up. Is there anything broken?"

"Only my pride," I say.

Sister Emilia is next on cue to hug me. "I was so worried, child."

"I'm sorry." I'm debating in which palatable way I can explain what happened tonight, but Sister Emilia's eyes stray to Phelan hauling two grown-ass men into the back of the SUV. "Um."

Sister Emilia blinks rapidly, but says nothing.

Meanwhile, Sister Luisa's jaw touches her chest.

"Would you all please come in for some tea?" Sister Emilia says, clearing her throat. "I'm afraid I need some, myself."

I probably need something stronger, but there isn't a drop of alcohol to be found in this building.

Out of all the possible ways tonight could go, the least likely scenario I would've thought of is how I end up. Sitting— unharmed—in the cafeteria of the orphanage I grew up in, surrounded by two nuns and four vampires.

The way Sister Luisa's lips keep moving and how she crosses herself, tells me she's deep in prayer. Meanwhile, Sister Emilia scans each of the vampires with that way she has of penetrating through people's innermost thoughts. Caleb keeps his eyes trained on his hands, neatly folded on the table. Marissa keeps glancing around, more or less in the same way I do. Jon and Phelan are silent sentinels in their own ways, Jon's attention fully focused on his cellphone and Phelan's in the ether that exists inside his mind.

I nurse my cup of chamomile tea, debating what to say and choosing silence in the end.

"Thank you for keeping Serena out of harm's way," Sister Emilia says. "But I have to ask, who are the men in the trunk of your vehicle?"

Caleb lifts his eyes to her. "I don't know, but I intend to find out."

Sister Emilia holds him hostage with the power of her gaze. "You look like a decent man, but can you keep my girl safe from the bad ones?"

"I don't know," he repeats, slowly. "But I'll do everything in my power to try."

Sister Emilia takes a deep breath and leans back. "Then, are you here to take her back?"

All eyes turn to Caleb. There's no response for a while, until he says, "If she'll have us."

Us. Not *me.*

"Serena is a valuable employee," he continues, to which

Marissa nods profusely. "We'd definitely love to have her on board again."

Under the table, I squeeze my hands so hard that I'll leave a bruise.

I want to scream that yes, I want to return. To pick my life back up. To not send my career tumbling down a cliff. But I also know I shouldn't. Not if it means staying close to Caleb.

"Um." I clear my throat and lift my head. "Do you all mind if I have a word with Caleb, alone?"

"Are you sure?" Sister Emilia asks me, uncertainty on her face at the prospect.

I squeeze her hand. "I promise nothing untoward will happen."

She shakes her head. "That's not what worries me."

Ah.

Maybe she doesn't know exactly *what* they are, but she has suspicions they're not normal. If not by how ridiculously beautiful they all are, but by how Phelan could carry two men at once without breaking a sweat.

"Yes." I smile to her and Sister Luisa. "He would never hurt me."

"Very well." Slowly, Sister Emilia gets to her feet. "But we'll be just outside."

Bless her. Even if Caleb was a bad guy, she wouldn't be able to protect me. I give her a big hug before she goes and in a short moment, it's only Caleb and I, sitting across the table without being able to meet each other's eye.

"What do you mean about me returning?"

He takes a deep breath, expels it. "It isn't fair that you're the only one punished, so I bargained with Dad."

I jerk back. "Bargained?"

"Yeah." The usual light in his eyes is gone, even under the bright lamps of the cafeteria. "Your career and your future will remain untouched."

"That's not how bargaining works." I lean forward, splaying my hands on the table to prevent them for reaching out to him. "What did you give in return?"

Finally, his brown eyes meet mine, lighter than mine in color but so sombre. "My future."

The two words sounds so abstract, I can't comprehend the message. Shaking my head doesn't make them magically fall in place in an arrangement of ideas that makes sense.

"What are you talking about?"

"I'm to marry Vivienne," he says, the words hitting me like bricks. "And keep a wide berth from you."

"What?" The question comes out in a whisper.

Caleb runs both hands down his face, hiding it from view for a long moment. "Here's how things stand. If I don't agree to marry her, you'll really stay fired and I'll still be maneuvered into marrying her, because that's Dad's plan for me. You might as well take advantage of that inevitability to stay employed."

I let out an incredulous laugh. "Are you expecting me to thank you for this? Especially because—"

Especially because we have feelings for each other.

I don't allow myself to finish that sentence. It isn't something that factors into Cedric Oh's plan, after all.

"How can I come back like this?"

In turn, Caleb asks, "How can I let your career goals evaporate when I said I'd never get in the way?"

"But Caleb," I sound almost like I'm crying. Maybe I already am. "Marrying Vivienne is too steep a price for *you* to pay for my career."

"It's not for your career." Caleb's voice is thick, like maybe he's crying on the inside. "It's for you."

I drop my head on the table and just cry there for a moment. None of this is what I want.

Yes, I still want a solid job, along with the financial stability that comes with it, and the feeling of being able to fend for myself.

But I also want him. With a fierceness that rivals my previous notions of happiness.

What I'm being offered is the career I've always wanted—provided I watch from the shadows as Caleb starts a life with Vivienne.

Vivienne, who might be one step removed from murderer, who stoops to sexual harassment to get what she wants, whose smiles never reach her eyes.

"How can you ask me to do this?"

"Serena." Caleb's voice is as warm as his hand, suddenly caressing my hair. "I'm not asking, I'm begging. If you don't do this, not only you'll lose what you've been working for, but we'll be kept apart... probably forever."

As I weep on the table, all Caleb does is run his fingers through my hair. It's probably the last time we'll allow each other any physical contact, because he's right. We're both doomed to follow Cedric Oh's command, no matter what.

But I feel the same way as Caleb. I'd rather observe him from a distance than through Google searches.

"Fine," I say, sniffling. "I'll return."

Not because I want to be an executive at Comed, but to be able to see him again.

Between Marissa and I, we take ten minutes to collect all my things from the room I was borrowing. We agree I'll stay the night with her, an option I never imagined I had.

It takes me much longer to tear myself away from Sister Emilia's embrace. She pats my back, trying to coax the sobs lodged in my throat. But I don't want to cry anymore. It won't change anything.

"Be safe, my child," she whispers in my ear. "From the world, from your dangerous friends, and from yourself, too."

She knows. I pull away and look into her steady eyes that see everything. Without having to explain anything to her, she knows exactly what's happening.

"Thank you." I swallow thick. "Am I doing the right thing or am I straying?"

"Neither. You're just finding your path."

I nod, and after one last hug I walk away from the orphanage again.

CHAPTER 70
CALEB

Call me a drama king, but I feel as though someone ripped my heart out and jammed it back in. Except now it doesn't fit quite the same way as before.

Now that Serena is back at the office, I often catch myself staring at her in silence. I fear that she's an apparition that can vanish into thin air. I watch her do mundane tasks like bring me coffee or give me a report, afraid that I'll blink and she'll be gone. Even more afraid that I'll blink and she'll be replaced by Vivienne.

Who I'll have to marry.

"Screw me," I murmur as I drop my head on the table.

"No, thank you," an unexpected voice says.

Without sitting back straight, I twist until I make eye contact with Phelan, the owner of the retort. Anyone who looks at him would doubt whether he spoke—or can speak—considering Phelan is what a wax figure from Madame Tussauds aspires to be. But he can't fool me.

"You know, for someone with such a sardonic sense of humor, I wonder if it chafes your throat to hold it back," I say.

He doesn't even glance my way and for a moment I think

that's the end of that conversation, but then he says, "Lozenges are for that."

"How dare you make me want to laugh."

I sit back like a normal person and run my hands through my hair. People often say that laughter is the best medicine, but all I can see myself really doing is moping. Forever. Three hundred years of moping and bringing everyone else's mood down. It sounds like the apt punishment for falling for a human I can't be with, and having to spend the rest of my life with someone I can't stand.

Speaking of, Serena opens the door to the meeting room and precedes a couple of the Marketing managers. She's speaking to them, "Would you like anything to drink before the meeting?"

"I'm good, thank you," Patrice from Strategic Marketing says, lifting her water bottle in view.

"Do you mind getting me a coffee?" Raul from Customer Focus says, and I want to tell him that Serena absolutely minds. She's the lead for this project and damn it—

But she did offer, so I stay silent.

Then Serena turns in my direction, and although our eyes never meet she asks, "What about you, Caleb?"

See, it's the little moments like this the ones that kill me. When she's so close, because there are only a few paces between us, but feels so far away that she can't even meet my eyes. Like there's an invisible wall to everyone else, but only she and I know we can never climb it.

Whoever said it's better to have loved and lost than never loved at all, can stuff it up their—

I clear my throat. "I'm okay, but maybe Phelan can do with a drink."

"I'm also okay," he says, and for the first time since her return I see Serena smile, and the kind of smile that would most typically be found on me.

It shouldn't surprise me when a few minutes later, she returns with Raul's coffee, plus orange juice on one sippy cup for Phelan, and another one for me. As the Marketing professionals look on in horror at the mockery of two grown men drinking juice from fairytale princess cups, I can't help but bursting out laughing.

Serena keeps her eyes downcast as she sits to my right, but her cheeks are flushed. "Sorry, it's become a bit of a running joke among the three of us."

Phelan's straw makes an awful noise as he sips and it makes my laughter become convulsive. At this point, Patrice and Raul join in, probably getting past the shock when they realize it's not something Phelan and I will be enraged about.

It takes me a minute, but when I manage to catch my breath and wipe the tears from my eyes, I look at Serena to see if she's managed to find some mirth in the middle of this mess. But she looks away as soon as our eyes meet.

I rub my chest, where the joy from a second ago has fled and left the Serena-shaped hole exposed again.

"Anyway," she says, looking at the screen where she's projecting a presentation. "Thank you for taking time out of your busy agendas to meet with me about this topic."

"This is so exciting," Patrice says with a smile. "And I'm sure you guys didn't plan it out because of this, but it'll go a long way to improving our image with customers and the public after the whole Purchasing scandal."

I nod. "That might or might not have been why I came up with it."

"Spoken like a true billionaire, huh?" Raul nudges me.

I smile and say nothing, because in truth I'm not a billionaire. But I still have enough millions that donating a few hundred Ks won't hurt me.

That's not the shameful thing, but rather that I didn't come up with this concept earlier.

"But," I continue saying. "I don't want people to think that's the reason, because ultimately this initiative shouldn't be about cleaning up our image. It has to be about really supporting the next star marketers from marginalized communities. Which is why we'll make this a yearly event. Serena, please show them the plan."

"Absolutely."

She picks it up from there and explains how we'll take a scaled approach. First it'll be grants to college students this year. Next year we will offer internships to those students, and at the same time select a second wave of grants. The cycle will repeat every year.

"In addition to that," Serena says, clicking on the next slide. "Caleb has pledged to financially support the grants from his own pocket for two years, and from then on will become a partial contributor."

Patrice tilts her head. "Who will provide the rest?"

"Comed." Serena smiles. "As part of the social responsibility budget,"

"Isn't that going to compete with the benefit we do every year?" Raul asks, scratching his head. "I'm concerned the team in charge won't want to approve this."

I wave a hand. "Leave that to me."

Dad will approve anything I ask for, now that he's got what he really wanted out of me.

"In any case, that's farther down the line." Serena clicks through to the next slide, showing the stats of applicants. "And this is where you all come into the picture."

We received thousands of applications for five grants of fifty grand each, and had to filter them through the tools HR uses for a standard hiring process. That narrowed it down to a couple hundred potential candidates, and for the first week since Serena returned to work, all we did was manually sift through each application until we narrowed it down to the top twenty five.

"So, brace yourselves, because these candidates are so amazing that Caleb and I couldn't discard anyone."

I tuck into my sippy cup as though it's the most important thing in the world, because just hearing the words *Caleb and I* makes me nostalgic for a time when that seemed like a possibility.

How am I going to be able to marry Vivienne and see Serena everyday like she's just another stranger?

I can't.

I absolutely can't.

As they study each of the candidates, I get up on my feet and pace across the meeting room, back and forth in front of Phelan. Over and over.

"Sorry," I say when it becomes apparent I keep distracting everyone. "I just have too much energy today."

Of the anxious variety.

"You must be excited," Patrice says and I give her a watery smile.

"Let's go with that."

That makes Serena break through the discipline she's held herself by, and finally her eyes make direct contact with mine.

They arrest me, ceasing every movement of my body. Only when she focuses back on the screen does my heart start beating again, and the itch returns to my limbs.

Yeah, I sure as shit can't function anymore.

An idea pops into my head, inspired by a conversation I had with Dad what feels like a different era ago. The Marketing team doesn't need me, it's been fully functional for a long time. The Purchasing team is well on its way to settling down, and soon we'll start recruiting for a new head of department.

Essentially, I'm not needed at Comed headquarters. Or

granted, anywhere else. Especially not after I marry she-who-must-not-be-named.

What's stopping me from packing up my shit and screwing off? My absence won't be felt in the company. Vivienne will enjoy having an absent husband. And since I'm not the heir to the vampire kingdom, I won't have any obligation to produce offspring.

All I need is to hold out until after the wedding, and more importantly, stay near Dad during his decline, and then I don't need to be seen again.

A world of distance is the only way I won't be able to keep succumbing to the feelings I have for Serena. That's probably the only way I can endure a life without her.

CHAPTER 71
SERENA

t took hours but we finally have the five grant recipients selected. I'm so excited that instead of packing up my things and leaving for the day, I go back to my desk to draft the final proposal for HR to approve, even if it means staying late.

Fortunately, Caleb has the opposite idea and goes home right after the meeting, which means I can finally breathe again.

Unfortunately, that's why I'm available when Marissa calls me. "So, um," she starts, giving me a strong hint that this isn't going to be in my favor. "Mr. Oh wants to see you right now."

I barely manage to swallow down the groan before it makes itself known. However, I do not manage to hold back the question, "What now?"

She chuckles. "I don't think it's that bad, he doesn't seem pissed today."

"Great," I say with a watery voice. "I'll be there in five."

It only takes one minute to ride the elevator up to the top floor, but I need five times as much to psyche myself up to face Mr. Oh. I haven't had the pleasure of encountering him face to face for over a week since my return to work, let alone one on one. I actively avoided all the common areas where I might run into him.

Even days of success haven't prepared me for this moment. What if he wants to talk about the moment he caught me redhanded, literally fondling his son while making out with him?

What can I possibly say about that?

While riding the elevator, I lean back against the wall and close my eyes. The only thing I can do for this meeting is take a page from the Phelan Murray book of behavior, which boils down to saying as little as possible.

Marissa gives me two thumbs up when I walk by her desk. Outside of Mr. Oh's door, I take a couple of deep breaths before knocking and making my way in.

As usual, Jon hovers around Mr. Oh, taking notes from whatever they were discussing when I came in. Jon motions for me to wait in the sitting area, and I park myself there. Their voices are too hushed to understand what they're saying and it's almost like I'm alone. It sends my pulse up to high speed, until I remember they're vampires and can probably detect that I'm freaking out.

I pull up my phone and find a gif that walks you through breathing exercises and follow it. I didn't even feel this nervous before the job interview, but that's probably because I hadn't done anything wrong at that point.

"I'll take care of it right away," Jon says in a way that sounds like their conversation has come to an end.

"Excellent." Mr. Oh pushes his chair back and stands, and I don't know if his footing caught on something but he falters. I flinch, anticipating a fall I can't do anything about. Jon is close enough, though, and he helps the older man stabilize himself.

They carry on without a hitch. Neither of their prides will

allow them to recognize the mishap. Or maybe it wasn't the first time.

Weird.

Mr. Oh appears fine as he approaches, but Jon stays close to him until the CEO of Comed Solutions takes a seat in front of me. Only then does Jon leave the office.

"Is there something wrong?" I ask before I'm able to catch myself. But it might have been even weirder if I didn't acknowledge what just happened, right? It's not like I can pretend things aren't what they are.

Mr. Oh displays all the diplomacy I wish I had and says, "Just tired today, thank you for your concern."

"What can I do for you, sir?" I clasp my hands together on my lap. They're so cold it almost feels like I'm holding onto ice cubes.

"I've been thinking about this long and hard," he says while popping open the button of his blazer and rearranging his tie. "And at first, I figured the message was clear and we didn't need to discuss the matter further."

I don't need to ask what specifically he's referring to. *I know.*

"But, things have changed."

I'm left at that cliffhanger as the office door opens and Jon returns with a tray in hand. "It's pretty late, so I figured refreshments will be welcome."

He sets the tray on the table, angling it so that the refreshments are clearly for me. There are sandwiches, chips, three different beverage choices and cookies. Nothing a vampire truly needs, but with the way my stomach clamors at the sight, definitely what I need.

"Please tuck in." Mr. Oh motions at me. "I already had a meal."

Probably blood.

"Ah, thank you." I pick up a sandwich and bite into it.

"As I was saying, I've decided that it's best I put the dots on the i's and cross the t's for everyone's sake."

I swallow my food so hard that it physically hurts my throat, so I help myself to a big swig of water.

Mr. Oh sighs. "Miss Lossada, I'm aware that you know what we are."

And of course I start choking.

He waits until I get through the crisis. My eyes water and my voice sounds like a chainsmoker. "The what?"

"Vampires," he says, as if it's no biggie. "This is the real reason why every employee working directly for the family has to sign a NDA."

Shit, and here I thought it was just because of Caleb's out-of-the-box personality. The truth was right in front of me all along, huh?

"I would never breach the contract," I say still with some difficulty.

"That's not my concern." Mr. Oh runs his hand through his hair in much the same way as his son. "What I want you to understand is that *that* is the reason why I can't allow you to get closer to my son."

"Oh."

"A human and vampire relationship isn't impossible, so long as both parties understand it's temporary."

He leans forward, which makes his bottomless eyes feel even more penetrating.

"Let's say you and Caleb got together. For the first couple of years or so, it will feel pretty normal. But before you realize it, you'll grow older than him. All of a sudden he'd look about thirty years old, but you'll be sixty. And then one day you'll pass away, and Caleb will be left with two to three hundred years more to live missing you. Does that sound appealing?"

"No." My voice is still choked up, but now it's from holding back tears. I push the tray of food away from me. "Of course not. How can I possibly want to inflict that kind of pain on him?"

His brow furrows. "It wouldn't be a bed of roses for you either."

Mr. Oh is right. It would be a bed of thorns.

I would watch myself grow older every day, and even if Caleb was okay with it, one day we'd be walking down the street looking very much like a mother and son, and that would be too weird to handle.

"So there are two ways to go about this," Mr. Oh says, snapping me out of that mental image. "But the best way is for you two to simply not start that relationship."

I cast my eyes down. My hands clasp each other hard enough to turn the skin paper white. "I agree."

"I'm glad you do." Mr. Oh sighs in a way that makes him sound bone-deep tired. "Now let me ask you, does this mean I can trust you to keep a professional distance from Caleb from now on, always?"

It feels as though I'm being asked if I want to join a cult. But it's not like I have a way out of terms I already accepted when Caleb convinced me to return to Comed.

With a deep breath, I say, "Yes, sir."

"Good. It will make the rest easier."

I tilt my head, but the businessman needs no further prompting to get to the point.

And the point is a sucker punch to the gut.

"Since Caleb probably realizes the same, he has agreed to marry Vivienne, and because I need someone I can trust to handle the situation and *him*, I want to ask you the very difficult task of planning the engagement party."

Did someone remove the floor from under me?

Or why do I feel like I'm in a free fall, with wind whipping at me, but with no oxygen reaching my lungs?

I open and close my mouth repeatedly, but nothing comes out.

"Yes." Mr. Oh nods, more to himself than to me. "I recognize it's an unreasonable request, but I can't trust him to participate in the arrangements without sabotaging them. And I also don't want to leave this affaire entirely to the Astors. I want someone who can keep me informed of the progress, and who can make sure Caleb isn't running away. You're very good at pulling him by the ear."

Inside, what I truly want to say is *jódete*. Why should I do this? I'm not employed as a wedding planner. I don't want to plan the engagement of the guy I've developed feelings for to someone else.

How can Cedric Oh ask for something so cruel?

But how can I possibly say no? I all but proclaimed I will squash any feelings I have and behave in a professional manner forever. My heart doesn't matter, that much is clear. And whereas Caleb's does matter to Mr. Oh, he obviously wants to erase whatever place I had in it. What better way than to stick me right where I will become the sorest spot?

I have no ground to stand on—partially because I'm still spiraling.

My words come out as if spoken by someone else. "Absolutely, you can count on me."

That's the moment I die on the inside.

CHAPTER 72
CALEB

'm being tortured.

To my right, Dad sits at the head of the table. Ever since our tête-à-tête I've alternated between wanting to scream at him, and sticking to him like velcro. Holding back from either settles like a log stuck sideways in my throat, which isn't conducive to amenable conversation at the dinner table or frankly, to eating.

On my left side, sits Vivienne. Next to her, at the opposite end of the table is my stepmother.

The only consolation I have is that every time I look up, my brother offers me a little smile of encouragement. Next to him, Lara keeps the conversation going and frees me from having to put an ounce of effort into being polite.

Like a robot, I eat one bite of my salad after another, busying my mouth with that instead of all the expletives that would rather come out.

"I absolutely love your designs," Vivienne says, leaning to treat Lara like her BFF.

"Thank you." Lara's smile is for all intents and purposes friendly, but I've known her almost my entire life and I know her ticks. When her lips quirk just a bit more on the right side, she's actually annoyed. "I'll admit my surprise at seeing you wear them on more than one occasion."

Vivienne gasps. "Are you kidding me? I could kill to be the first one in line any time your new gowns hit the stores. It's almost like they're made for me."

I chew on a cherry tomato with a vengeance.

"I hope not literally." Lara laughs.

"Actually," Diana says, picking up her glass of white wine. "Lara, you should design Vivienne's wedding dress."

"Oh my." Vivienne puts her hands on her chest. "I couldn't possibly ask that."

Then don't.

She continues, "But maybe you'd be open to at least designing my engagement dress?"

I mouth the words *engagement dress* to my brother, who shrugs. It takes me a second to understand that of course Vivienne will want to make a big deal out of our engagement. She won't settle for just getting a ring, when she could be professing to all the vampire families in the world that she's nabbing the last spot available as spouse of an Oh family member.

Sardonic, I ask Lara, "On the condition that you also design *my* engagement dress."

My sister-in-law stuffs her hands against her mouth. "Now that's a novel idea."

Stepmother sets her cup down harder than usual. It breaks and wine spills all over her hand and the table. "Why must you ruin everything, Caleb?"

"Diana," Dad warns.

Maria appears from out of nowhere. "Please, allow me to clean up."

But my stepmother waves her away. "Just bring me more wine."

In the mess she caused, wine spilled to Vivienne's lap and

soiled her cream colored dress, but if it bothers her she doesn't show it. Instead, she grabs onto Diana's hand to inspect it. "Are you okay? I hope you didn't get hurt."

Even my stepmother stiffens. No matter how much she loves this woman, Diana still pulls her hand away quickly. A single drop of blood from the queen of vampires could significantly increase a regular vampire's abilities, which is why it's royal family policy to not let anyone drink our blood.

"I'm fine," Stepmother says, casting her eyes on me. "If only your fiancé would show as much concern for me."

Nah, I'm too busy being concerned for myself and a future where family dinners now include Vivienne Astor. As if they weren't already awful events before her.

"I'm glad he at least is finally doing something good for the family," Diana says, and the words fall like an anvil on me.

While taking deep breaths, I close my eyes to try to block this scene from my consciousness. Maybe if I don't acknowledge the implication that my existence has been a hindrance to this family, then everyone else on this table will also ignore it.

But then there's something like a growl, and Daniel's voice is rough as he says, "Mom, stop it."

Of course, she doesn't.

"Stop what?" Diana asks. At the same time, she snatches the new wine glass Maria presents to her. "It's the truth. What has Caleb accomplished until he finally accepted to marry this fine young woman?"

I open my eyes. Daniel grips his fork hard enough to bend the metal. Beside him, Lara's mouth is set into a line so tight, she must be grinding through layers of enamel.

Finally, I glance at Dad. Although his eyes blaze hot-red like lava, he says nothing. It's not like he normally defends me in front of his wife, who he cheated on to produce me. He has no reason to start doing so in front of Vivienne.

It's entirely up to me to start a scene. And what else do I have to lose?

Nothing. I've already lost everything that matters.

Let's freaking go.

Calmly, I dab at the corners of my lips with the cloth napkin previously on my lap. I take my sweet-ass time folding it into a neat triangle before setting it on the table. The ordinary but deliberate motions capture everyone's attention, and I gift them a smile in appreciation.

That's the only politeness they'll get from me.

"So essentially, my value boils down to being cattle, huh?" I lean my chin on my fist and meet my stepmother's eye. "As long as I can be herded in the direction you want, I won't be considered a waste of space. And let me guess, the next thing you'll want from me is to breed like a seedstock bull? Or would that actually be a threat against the actual family lineage?"

With a roar, Diana tosses her brand new glass of wine at me. Not the contents, but the whole thing. I duck away from the flying glass but get splashed with wine everywhere. It burns my eyes, but still feels like a victory.

Dad slams the table. "Caleb, you can't talk to your mother that way."

As I wipe my face with the napkin, I say, "But she can talk to me like that?"

"I can talk to you however the hell I want," my stepmother says, her voice hissing the words like a snake about to bite. "You should be thankful I raised you."

I laugh. The sound is so jarring it makes everyone freeze. "I should be thankful I didn't take after you instead."

"Enough!" Dad jumps to his feet so fast, he'd have lost his balance if it wasn't for the vise grip he has on the table. "This is absolutely embarrassing and in front of a guest, no less."

"At least you got one thing right, Dad." I pick up my wine glass and raise it to him. "Vivienne really is just a guest."

My sister-in-law lets out a little squeak, also finding the hilarity in this mess.

"I certainly don't wish to become an apple of discord in the family," Vivienne says. "After all, we will soon *truly* be family."

I'm annoyed that she quickly scrambled to claim the spot in the family I just said doesn't belong to her.

"Maybe we should call it a night," Daniel says through gritted teeth.

"That sounds like an excellent idea." I push my empty plate away from me. "I'm full anyway."

Not of food. Of anger, and I hope they catch my meaning.

Vivienne turns up her southern charm to a hundred, and honey drips from her smile as though nothing unpleasant happened at all. "Thank y'all so much for having me tonight, I hope to join you again soon."

"You must." Diana lifts her nose at me, as if trying to pull it away from my stank. "And there will be ample opportunity, now that the engagement preparations are finally starting."

"Phelan," I say in a low voice, and in a second the man appears beside me. "Please escort Miss Astor to her vehicle."

And far away from me.

He turns to her and motions vaguely toward the exit. "After you, miss."

Before my parents can scold me for my impolite behavior, I push to my feet and beat them until I make it outdoors. I take big, gasping breaths into the night, but it doesn't help. It still feels as though there are two hands squeezing my lungs like sponges.

"Are you out of your damn mind?"

I wouldn't have to turn around to know it's my stepmother, but I do, in case she's about to throw worse projectiles at me. But she's stomping on the grass toward me, bare-handed.

Stuffing my hands in the pockets of my slacks, I shrug.

"Actually, yeah. I am. It's a side effect from being toyed with like a chess piece."

"That's exactly what you are." She points at me. "Which is much more than you deserve."

Behind her, still in the dining hall across the French doors that lead to the vast backyard, Daniel turns to our Dad. "Until when are you going to allow this?"

"Quiet," Dad tells him, which shocks me more than any venom my stepmother might hurl at me. Neither parent ever uses such cutting tone of voice to Daniel.

"I've had enough of being quiet." My brother stands up so fast that his chair topples over. The crashing sound echoes out into the night. "Can't you see your lies are gnawing at this family?"

What the—

My stepmother laughs. "More lies from Cedric? Color me shocked."

"This conversation is over." With that, Dad turns around and disappears down the hallway.

Lara rubs my brother's back, trying to bring his temperature back to normal. From way over here, I can hear his heart hammering hard in his ribcage, and the way he breathes is as harsh as if he ran from Miami Beach. Daniel runs a hand through his hair and pulls at it.

He locks eyes on me and says, "Hang in there, little brother. If our parents aren't willing to protect you, I will."

I stagger back, off balance by that declaration. I get the niggling feeling that Daniel knows something big, something Dad doesn't want me to catch whiff about.

And I wonder if it's something that might get me out of marrying Vivienne.

CHAPTER 73
SERENA

This is the third time this week I lock myself up in the bathroom at work to have a little cry.

The first time was after placing the order for engagement party invitations. The second time was after booking the venue. Today, I had to sit through a meeting that lasted the entire morning in the company of Vivienne Astor and a decorator, to select what they called the ambiance of the ball. Everything from the color palette, to the flower arrangements, to the type of music the orchestra will play.

For all intents and purposes, it's like planning a hasty wedding with only two weeks notice—with a broom who isn't interested in it at all.

Caleb's been conveniently missing from any of these preparations. It should annoy me because then I have to work harder on his behalf, but that's not how I feel. I'm glad for the rebel streak in him, so notorious since we met, that gives him ample excuses to recluse himself from the painful matter. And that way I also don't have to see him up close more than strictly necessary.

It would be exponentially worse if I had to sit through Vivienne's bullshit with Caleb beside her, agreeing to her every whim.

The good news is that with practice, I've become able to anticipate the moment of breaking point before the waterworks start. I politely excuse myself to go to the restroom and if they want to think I'm taking too long because I'm doing number two, I let them. Additionally, knowing I'm surrounded by vampires with uncanny hearing, I've learned to just let the tears roll without the heaving sobs or any of the wailing.

When my tears have finally dried, I step out of the bathroom stall and wash my face. I'm still in the middle of that when the door opens and the sound of clicking steps from stilettos tells me that Vivienne has come in.

Sure enough, she says, "There you are. I thought you flushed yourself down the toilet."

Is she implying I'm shit or something?

She's washing her hands on the sink beside me, which also feels charged with symbolism. "I'm so excited for the afternoon. We'll find the perfect ring, no doubt, but it's a shame I haven't quite found the perfect gown."

I say nothing as I blot my face with paper napkins and set out to clean my glasses. No matter what she says or does, I'm tired of crying for the day. She won't get a rise out of me anymore.

"But I heard something interesting." She shakes her wet hands in the air, splashing me and not apologizing for it. "It seems you've grown quite close with Lara Khouri? Maybe you can get her to design a dress for me."

I wouldn't say I'm close to Lara. It's not like we know each other's deepest secrets and have pajama parties where we paint each other's toe nails. If anything, now that I'm temporarily rooming with Marissa, I feel much closer to her than to Caleb's sister-in-law.

Speaking of, at that moment I'm saved from giving any sort

of response when my phone rings with a call from Marissa. The second I pick up, she says, "It's an emergency, I need you to grab your purse and meet me in the parking lot in five minutes."

"O-okay." She hangs up before I can even ask what's wrong. Vivienne no doubt heard every detail, and her eyebrows are sky high as I say, "You'll have to excuse me if I'm not able to meet you in time this afternoon. Have a good lunch."

I expect her to block my exit, if only because I haven't expressly agreed to her weird request. But as she starts reapplying her lipstick, I take that as a dismissal and leave.

A few minutes later, I find Marissa waiting for me in her car. Through the open window, she says, "Get in. We're going lunching."

I bark a laugh. "Is this the big emergency?"

"Well, yeah." She rolls her eyes at me in an exaggerated way as I sit on the passenger's seat and fasten my seatbelt. "I knew you would need rescue from the evil one. The key was to not trip up the trap of your sense of responsibility."

I look at her like it's the first time. Marissa has always been pretty, with a winsome smile that belongs to a toothpaste commercial, dimples on her cheeks, radiant dark skin, and tight curls that frame the face of a Barbie. But her kindness to me has officially transformed her into the most beautiful person on earth.

Sighing, I say, "How can I ever thank you for everything you've done for me?"

"By being my friend?" She shrugs. "Occasionally, I'll want consolation in return."

"You got it." After a pause, I ask, "How do you prefer consolation, though? Food? Movies? Makeovers? I have to confess I'm not very versed in this whole friendship thing."

"I sort of want to laugh but at the same time I want to cry." She shakes her head at me. "And yes to all of the above, but probably the best is to just talk about things until it almost becomes like beating a dead horse."

"Sounds lovely."

To my further surprise, when we arrive to the restaurant, Lara Khouri is waiting for us at a table. She gets to her feet to squeeze the life out of us in a massive group hug.

Grunting, I say, "Geez, lady. Why are you so strong?"

"You know why." She winks at me once we're sitting at the table. "Or at least I heard through the grapevine that you know why."

Marissa raises her hand slowly. "I was the one who told her."

"That's okay." I pick up the menu. "Even Mr. Oh knows that I know about onions."

The two of them ask in unison, "Onions?"

For a moment, I don't know how to react, but I end up bursting out laughing by myself. Through that fit, I tell them the story of how Caleb and I came to use that word as code name for vampires, back in the day when their existence seemed like the biggest threat.

After my tale, Lara's eyes are as bright as stars. "Oh, I love it. Some of us are really stinky, after all."

"Especially Vivienne," Marissa says, wrinkling her nose.

"I can't believe my father-in-law is forcing Caleb to go through with this farse of an engagement." Lara takes a big gulp of water and sets the glass down on the table with enough force to make it shake. "I mean, the boy is clearly smitten with you, for goodness's sake."

I cringe and hide my face behind the menu. "Yeah, but it's not like onions and non-onions can be together, you know?"

"Why not?" Lara shrugs. "You could be turned into an onion."

I freeze.

Marissa leans forward, her index finger against her lips. "Careful, you never know who might be hearing."

Following that advice, Lara leans closer to me and speaks so low I can barely hear her. "There's a way. It's not easy and it doesn't work every time, but if Miss. Haughty wasn't in the picture you probably could've stood a chance."

My mouth opens and closes like a goldfish.

All at once I recall the conversation I had with Mr. Oh in his office last week. I was so stunned by his request that I oversee the preparations for the engagement party, that I didn't even pause to consider how he specifically said there were *two* approaches. He only talked about the one where Caleb and I give each other up and live our separate lives of vastly different lengths.

Lara picks up her menu as though she didn't just drop a bomb, and in a normal tone of voice says, "I just don't like this Romeo and Juliet type of shit."

"Neither do I. It shouldn't be this hard to be with the guy you like." Marissa deflates until, lacking the strength to hold herself up, she leans her chin on her hand. "But I also don't like that the alternative would put her in such danger."

Swallowing hard, I ask, "Do I want to know details?"

They exchange an uncertain glance.

Finally, Lara says, "Information is power. We'll give it to you somewhere we know we won't be heard. And then it's up to you."

That makes my stomach queasy all through lunch, and although we shift topics and mostly talk about how ridiculous it is that Vivienne has asked both Lara and me, for Lara to design a dress for her, I can't keep my mind off of the information I'm missing.

After lunch, the three of us hop on Marissa's car and she locks the doors. Lara's in the backseat, and she scoots to the middle to be able to see both of us.

"Serena," Lara starts, putting her hand on my shoulder. "You could be turned into a vampire by drinking the blood of the vampire king. Of course, he has to willingly give it to you. But that's not the trickiest part."

My head is swimming with just this much information. Shaky, I ask, "What's that, then?"

Marissa's lips tighten into a line. "You could die."

"Unfortunately, the survival rate isn't high." Lara's brow creases. "If the human's body doesn't collapse with the rapid mutation, there's a chance the mind could."

"Oh."

"And I don't want to be an even bigger party pooper," Marissa says, cringing. "But indirectly, the king already decided it's not worth trying to turn you."

"Wait." I press my temples, where a throbbing sensation is building up. "The king? Who is it?"

In unison, both women say, "Cedric Oh."

CHAPTER 74
CALEB

t feels surreal to dress myself for my own funeral.

Or perhaps I've turned into a zombie. That's exactly how I look like through the mirror. My every move is sluggish as I put on the slacks first and then the shirt. It takes me an entire age to button it up, and shouldering the blazer feels like a monumental task that is going to lead to my demise.

My hair is combed to perfection, and after the outfit is complete, I admit I look like I walked out of a catalogue—on the outside. Inside, I'm dead.

Because today is the day of the engagement party to Vivienne Astor.

As part of the preparations, my credit cards were cut, the keys to all my cars confiscated, and the Bad Blood was transported to a different state. There's been security in my building twenty four hours, seven days per week, and Phelan's been camping in my living room. Effectively, there's no way I could even dream of running away.

Doom feels like a handmade Italian suit against my skin.

I take a deep breath that deflates me upon exhaling, and step out of my room. Phelan and three other men in equal black suits wait for me. None of us speak. If any of them were curious if I'm ready, the answer would be no—but I have to follow through with this regardless. Dad says it's for my safety, but it really is for Serena's.

So she can have the life she wants, I'll condemn mine.

I put one foot in front of the other until eventually they lead me to the car, not the Urus I used to ride with Serena before work, but one of those sober Rolls Royces. It would fit my casket perfectly. Alas, I sit in the backseat, alive enough that I can watch the streets pass by, but not enough that it feels like I'm present.

This is going to be reality from now on. An endless succession of events I have no true part of, nor want to experience. And that's going to be the case for some three hundred years.

I look up and think to myself, *I don't pray often but help me.*

That's the last thought before I close my eyes and doze off. I know the venue for the party is removed from the city of Miami, and it'll be a while before we get there.

In my dreams, I see myself going through the exact same motions, except there's a huge smile on my face. I chit chat with Phelan and his team as if I wasn't heading to my funeral, but to an actual wedding. And then the dream transports me to a small church, where everyone looks just as happy to be there —and the woman walking up the aisle toward me has dark hair instead of blonde.

I snap awake with the sound of a car door being slammed closed. When I glance around, it's dark outside and we seem to have stopped.

Phelan turns to me from the driver's seat. "We have arrived."

A small part of me hopes he decided to kidnap me for ransom—thus taking me far away from Vivienne—but in reality he stays as loyal to my dad as I am, or more. Which means that when he says we have arrived, it means to the country club house we rented for this cursed party.

The party is in full swing when I walk into the place. An orchestra plays Frank Sinatra hits, a favorite of my stepmother. The place is done up in red and black, which feels too on the nose to be tasteful.

I heard only trusted people to the kingdom would be invited, which is why there's a fountain in the middle of the ballroom artfully spewing out a red liquid meant to simulate blood. Meanwhile, champagne flutes full of the real deal are being distributed to the vampires in attendance, and more than one holds a glass of blood in one hand and one of bubbly in the other.

"There you are."

Lara is the first one to spot me. She links her arm with mine and keeps me company as the first guests start to give me their congratulations.

After a few minutes of this, I mutter, "Here I am."

She detects the despair in my voice and pats my arm.

I'm trying to be strong, but it's so exhausting to keep myself from falling to the floor and shaking my limbs in a tantrum until I get what I want. I wouldn't even have the energy to do that.

As if reading my mind, my sister-in-law snatches a blood flute and gives it to me. "Drink. You'll need sustenance to last the night."

I down it in one go without even gagging.

Finally, we reach my parents and Daniel. My brother squares up beside me, grasping my shoulder to let me know in every possible way that he's with me. And I appreciate it. Even though I'm aware there's nothing else he can do.

Meanwhile, my parents look me up and down, and by the fact that Diana says nothing, it must mean she approves of whatever she sees. Dad too remains silent. All he does is give me a measly nod in acknowledgement.

The Gonzalez-Blackwell family drop by to congratulate me. After them, the Liu family pays their respects. Then the Okorafors. The MacCains. The Tullys. The Fernandezes. The Villas. One after another, at least one representative from each vampire family parades before me.

It's not just all the faces what makes me dizzy, but the fact that, if the entire vampire kingdom is personally acknowledging this, it means it's real. It's happening. I'm marrying into the Astors and there's nothing that can stop this freight train.

"The day has finally come," Ernst Astor says, shaking Dad's hand.

Money-wise, Vivienne's father is even wealthier than Dad, which has in the past caused friction in matters of our little underground kingdom. But now that the two clans are forming a blood alliance, there should be none of that going forward. It's a win-win for them.

I do imagine Vivienne will want friction between us—in bed. But that's not gonna happen as long as I breathe.

Dad gives one of his carefully modulated laughs. "Indeed, at long last."

"Oh, there she is." Stepmother clasps her hands, as excited as though the woman parting the crowd on her way to us was her real daughter.

Vivienne's wearing a gown as deep red as the blood of our brethren. It matches the decorations. Except, where the bouquets of flowers are delicate and tasteful, her dress is anything but. Every eye in the room is glued to her as she advances, walking so carefully it gives me the feeling even she is worried the measly strips of fabric covering her in strategic places will fall.

Lara yanks me so I lower my ear to her. She whispers, "For the record, I didn't design it."

I don't think anyone did. It looks like a dog went rabid on what once was a dress.

Vivienne is beaming, though, because if anything the gown has served to make everyone's attention fall solely on her. And you know what? I'm kinda grateful. At least for a few moments no one is inspecting me, wondering how the black sheep of the royal family managed to catch the most coveted bachelorette of the kingdom.

Vivienne reaches for my hand the second she joins us. "Honor me with the first dance as a couple."

Over my dead body.

But Dad inclines his head in a way that means *go*, and it becomes an order I can't get out of. I will do it for him, not for Vivienne.

Slowly, I pull Lara's hand away from my arm and offer it to the Astor woman instead. For the first time since I know her, she has a smile that does reach her eyes and it turns her into the most beautiful creature in attendance.

It scares me.

People clear the way for us and the orchestra shifts into the first notes of a waltz. As Vivienne steps into the circle of my arms and places my hands where they should go, a familiar voice makes an announcement through the microphone.

"Ladies and gentlemen, please welcome Caleb Oh and the future Mrs. Oh, Vivienne Astor."

As people start to clap, fierce pain stabs my heart and I can't move.

That it was Serena who made the announcement feels like the biggest wound I could have received tonight, but I forget that Vivienne is someone who likes to pour salt on people's sorest spots.

She gives a twinkling laugh and glues herself to me, against the proper stance for a waltz. In my ear, so low that virtually no one else will be able to hear over the noise, she whispers, "I won."

Hot lava roils in my stomach, wanting to erupt. Holding it back makes me shake from head to toe, but even as the applause begins to wane I can't dance.

I want to run away from here and never stop until my legs give out, or until my heart does. Whichever happens first.

But, gravely ill or not, Dad would find me, and I know exactly what he would say—because he said it to me last night.

"It's time you learn to do things you don't want to, but have to."

And that's it, the rest of my life in a nutshell. Finally I begin to waltz to someone else's tune.

CHAPTER 75
SERENA

'm much tipsier than I should be while on the job. No one cares about the party organizer drowning her sorrows in expensive champagne behind the scenes, though. Especially when things are going smooth.

Now that the happy couple has been introduced to the world, I can sit back and just... exist. The catering team is working like clockwork, the servers have been flawless, a mishap in the women's bathroom was taken care of quickly, and as far as security is concerned, the only real danger tonight is someone tripping. And because this is a family affair —read: an onions and onion-friendly kind of party—there is no press.

If not for one particular detail, the night would be such a resounding success that I'd be tempted to ask for a raise. What use is rewarding my spectacular organizational skills, when my heart is irreparably broken?

That's why I sit in a secluded corner, hiding behind crates of vegetables and fruits. My black suit might get dirty from sitting on the floor, but who cares. I take a big swig of the chilled champagne bottle I smuggled here, and lean my head back against the wall when that much effort leaves me drained of energy.

Moisture in my nose forces me to sniff, and then I do it again and once more, until I'm full-on crying. I bite my lips hard enough to bruise, holding back the sobs. The last thing I want is a bunch of vampires hearing me weeping in the storage area.

My ear piece buzzes and in the next second, someone asks for more champagne. A different voice responds to the request, and I'm glad I get to stay in my sad corner for a while longer. Soon, I'll have to walk out into the light with a straight face, pretending everything is okay.

My phone vibrates in my pocket and when I check it, I find a text from Marissa. *Are you okay? Where are you?*

The valley of tears, more or less.

I'll be alright. Eventually. One day I'll wake up and find it doesn't hurt so much. A different day, I might even stumble upon someone who sends butterflies fluttering in my belly.

But I won't be the same. In the back of my mind, I'll be wondering when things will go wrong. And every day, I'll be wondering if Caleb's okay. If he misses me or has already grown used to his wife. Maybe even fallen for her.

If I could have a superpower, I want it to be traveling back in time, so I can tell my past self never to fall for Caleb Oh. To not stare at him too long, or let him call me by my first name. To not travel anywhere with him. To never feel his arms around me. To spare myself this pain.

I down half of the champagne bottle in one go until the bubbles burn my throat. Then I let my eyes close and for the first time in days, I doze off without a hassle.

"There you are."

The voice snaps me awake with a jolt. My knee knocks the bottle over and champagne spills all over my pant leg and the floor.

Before me, Lara claps her hands. "Perfect. I have an undeniable excuse to get you into different clothes now."

I wipe my face with the back of my hand. A trickle of drool made its way down to my chin. The worst part is that a steady pounding has settled in my head, making me glad for the spilled drink I can't continue drinking.

"How did you find me?"

She shrugs. "I had one of the servers keep tabs on you all night. Anyway, let's go. We have to shower you first."

I take my glasses off and press on the bridge of my nose. "Are you speaking English? Because I can't understand a word you're saying."

"You'll understand on the way."

Lara pulls me to my feet in one swift move with strength an average pregnant woman wouldn't have. I stumble upon the fallen bottle and she catches me. From there on, she keeps an arm around me as she leads me through the service area and to the guest rooms of the massive country estate.

"Where are we going?"

"To my suite." Lara smiles down at me. "We have a makeover to work on."

I frown. "Whose?"

Lara doesn't answer, and only because my mind is blurry do I not realize she's referring to me, until I'm submerged in a scented, bubbly bath. An older lady scrubs my back, and as a second one lathers my hair I finally wake up from my stupor.

"Lara?" My voice echoes in the luxurious bathroom. "What's going on?"

She bounds into the bathroom, her peach colored dress fluttering like a cape. With the pose she strikes, hands on hips and chest puffed up, she could pass up for a very glamorous superhero.

"Dear Serena," she starts, lifting her chin. "Tonight, you must call me fairy godmother."

I mouth the word *what* but can't muster the strength to vocalize it.

Some half hour later or so, I'm bathed, my hair is made up in waves that cascade down to the small of my back, my makeup is something straight out of a beauty pageant—and in lieu of my trusty glasses, I'm forced to wear contacts. They make the world look different, mainly my reflection in the mirror. Because that isn't me.

"Can I please get an explanation now?"

Instead, Lara pushes a deep emerald green gown against me over the bathrobe I wear. She then changes it for a burgundy one. Then a black one. My eyes linger on it. The fabric looks like someone cut a piece of the clear night sky and sewed it together into a dress.

"This one." She tosses the other gowns on the bed. "Put it on."

I sigh. "Lara."

"Look." She grabs one of my hands and forces me to hold the gown, before stepping back. "I'm absolutely heartbroken for the two of you. It may not be any consolation, but Daniel and I tried really hard to convince Cedric that this whole thing is wrong, and obviously that didn't work. So I think, since things are inevitably following their course, that you two should have an opportunity to say your farewells."

My breath catches in my throat.

It takes some effort to keep the tears in my tear ducts, and not ruin the makeup her people so carefully applied.

"Thank you, but—" I start, my voice shaking. "There's no need for goodbyes. We'll keep seeing each other at work every day."

Lara's hands squeeze my shoulders. "You're right, it's not goodbye—it's closure. You both need it and it's the only thing I can give you. And I want you to look spectacular for it."

I hang my head and fix my attention on the dress in my

arms. Is this what Cinderella felt like? Knowing her pretty dress was just a mirage, that reality would soon return her to the rags she belonged to.

Unlike her, though, I can't see this story ever getting a happy ending.

"C'mon, let's show Caleb what he'll be missing."

Lara helps me into the gown, which no doubt was designed by her. It takes both of us and one of her helpers to get me in the dress and secure it in place.

The bodice is stiff and so form-fitting, it almost makes me ask her if she has a mold of my torso laying around in her studio. It cinches tight around my waist, giving the illusion that I have a perfect guitar shape, and it pushes my chest in such a flattering way it looks almost criminal. Since the gown is completely backless, they have to use some fashion tape to prevent any issues, but at least the skirt flows wide all the way to the floor.

Lara completes the look with a minimalist necklace with black stones that catch the light, and earrings to match. "Are you sure you're not an onion yourself? Because your beauty is supernatural."

For the first time tonight—and in weeks—I laugh.

"Wow, that's the worst pickup line I've ever heard."

"No, I'm serious." Lara wiggles her eyebrows. "I'm glad I secured an isolated spot for you guys to meet, because I don't think Caleb will be able to keep his hands to himself."

I rub my arms, where goosebumps are breaking. "Maybe this is a bad idea."

"It's the best idea." Her hand squeezes mine. "Kiss him one last time and then lock that memory in the deepest part of you. There won't be any other chances."

A lump settles in my throat. At the same time, my heart races so fast she can probably feel the throbbing of my veins against her skin.

Every cell of my body wants a last chance too, but a part of me is afraid that I won't be able to let go if he's within my reach.

But that's not worse than the prospect of never feeling his arms around me again. So I follow Lara through the dark corridors of the estate, to the place where Caleb awaits.

CHAPTER 76
CALEB

Vivienne acts like a queen in the arms of her king as the families parade in front of us offering felicitations. Her king is a zombie, though. I feel as though someone ate my brains. I can't nod, smile or say the polite things I'm expected to.

All I can do is stand still, a cardboard copy of Phelan. For the first time, I wonder what terrible thing happened in his life to sap the spark out of him, just as this engagement party and what it represents has drained me of any will to live.

My fiancée leans closer to me, gluing herself against my side. "Smile, sweetheart. People are watching."

Indeed, they are. People aren't even discreet in their stares. Some, mostly the men, have welded their eyes to Vivienne's dress perhaps in the hopes of a wardrobe malfunction. A few people look at her with outright hatred in their eyes, as if she's wronged them somehow. I wouldn't be surprised. If I turn my eyes to her, they will also probably drip venom.

Meanwhile, some of the attention keeps returning to me. There's much the local tabloids have said about me, none of which is true. But in the vampire world, I'm even more of a puzzle. While I've always been in the picture, Dad has never put the spotlight on me until this moment.

Sure, we did get marriage offers from vampire families since I was born. Even the Gonzalez-Blackwell couple proposed I marry Marissa at some point. But it was almost like Dad didn't want the people in his kingdom to pay much attention to me. Until now.

And I hate it. The tacit expectation that I should be brimming with joy right now is killing me.

Vivienne maneuvers my arm around her until my hand touches the bare skin of her back. I pull away, but the next second she forces the contact again.

"I haven't worked so hard for this moment so you can ruin it." Burrowing herself against my side, she rises on her tip toes until her lips are on my ear. Low, she says, "Play along if you don't want your secretary to suffer the consequences."

My body turns to ice.

Slowly, I face her. From the outside, we may look like we're about to kiss. "You already have me, don't you dare threaten her."

Vivienne runs her hand down my chest to my belly, marking her territory for everyone to see. With a frigid smile, Vivienne says, "I may have your body but your heart is still hers, is it not? Until it too, is mine, she won't be safe."

I swallow.

My heart will never be Vivienne's. But I will do whatever it takes for Serena to be safe.

I'm too tired to let rage take over my body, so for now I do as she says and smile. My cheeks start hurting pretty soon, but that's nothing compared to the pressure in my chest.

As more people come to greet us, I churn Vivienne's words over and over. If I was her ultimate objective and my parents were on her side, Serena was the only obstacle.

Is it a coincidence that the recent attacks started since Serena came into my life?

I look at Vivienne's profile, so radiant with the beauty people pay plastic surgeons for. Her heart is ugly enough to concoct attacks like those, or worse. She even admits it openly.

I tear myself away from her. "I need to use the restroom."

The excuse is plausible—I've been standing beside her for at least two hours—and she doesn't hold me back. I weave through the crowd and the only one who dares fall in step with me is Phelan.

"Secure the bathroom," I tell him before disappearing inside.

I stop in front of the row of sinks, hating my reflection. Dad was right all those months ago. I'm powerless. There's nothing I can do to protect those I care about. Or myself.

Worse still, he contributed to turning me into a puppet. How can I possibly even escape this fate if not for jumping into the ocean and never resurfacing again?

And yet, I won't do that. I won't throw away my life, in case there's a sliver of a chance I can right it.

I rip out my bow-tie and pop open enough buttons until I can finally breathe. I wish someone would tell me what I can do to free myself from this sham of an engagement without risking Serena's safety. There has to be a way we can both live —separately or together. It doesn't matter. As long as we're not Vivienne's captives.

If no one will, *I* have to find the way.

A knock on the door makes me freeze. "Phelan?"

"It's me," my brother says, popping his head in through the door. "Your bodyguard gave me a carte blanche."

I sigh. "Maybe I should fire him."

Daniel offers me a small smile. "Are you doing okay?"

"What does it look like?"

He wrinkles his nose. "Like you need to get some fresh air.

Both because you look haggard and because this place sorta stinks already."

"True on all accounts." I run my hand through my hair, and because it falls right in place again, I mess it even more on purpose. "But I don't think my *fiancée* will let me off her sight for longer."

"Lucky for you, you have the best big brother ever." He bends his hand a couple of times. "Follow me."

If Vivienne wants to give me shit for spending time with my family, I'll just ignore her. So I stuff my bow-tie in my pocket and tag along with my brother. Phelan falls in step behind us as Daniel leads us away from the party.

I glance at my big bro from the corner of my eye. "You look like you know where we're going."

"It's because I do," he says with a smile. "But it's a secret until we get there."

There turns out to be a secluded balcony on the second floor. Not a single light is turned on in the hallway leading to the nook or in it, and I'd be stumbling in the dark if I didn't have enhanced sight.

"Wait here." Daniel smacks my back once. "Phelan will be around, but he won't bother you."

My eyebrows rise slightly. "Okay?"

With that, Daniel turns on his heel and disappears into the dark corridor. I have half a mind to follow him, but this time I decide to not rebel against his commands. I have to save that energy for a different time.

Right now, it feels pretty nice to lean against the railing and breathe into the humid air of the night. It smells like damp earth and dewy leaves. This far from the city, the stars pepper the dark sky like diamonds as a gift to my eyes. I take comfort in it. It's the only gift I'll get tonight.

But not a second after I think that, I get another one.

Steps approach from the distance. Two sets, light and click-

ing, of women in heels. There would be more heft to the
strides if one of them was Vivienne. She would be determined
to uncover my whereabouts, and would probably not enjoy the
company of anyone else to do so. So I stay put, facing the
entrance to the balcony to catch an immediate glance of the
visitors.

Then one set of steps stops, and the second one brings me
a vision.

It's as if the night sky melted down around a woman. I
don't need lightbulbs to know who she is. It's in the way her
heart beats fast, in the unique scent of her skin, in the dark
eyes that see through to my soul.

"Serena."

Her name comes out like an exhalation. So out of breath
she's left me.

She swallows so hard that it echoes in my ears. "Caleb."

For a moment, we're frozen. Staring at each other as if we
were an illusion.

Then we meet halfway, pulled together by the same force. I
wrap my arms around her and bury my face in her neck, glad
for the feeling of her skin against my face, against my hands
traveling down her back. Something like a sob tears from her
throat, but she too holds tight. Her arms are around my shoulders, pulling me against her until we mold into one.

This is right. This is where I belong.

"I miss you."

At the same time, she says, "I'm here to say goodbye."

I pull back to really take her in. She's always the most
beautiful woman in the room to me, but right now she's even
more stunning. There's a small tear trapped in the corner of
her eye, and I caress her cheek until the gesture coaxes it to fall.
I catch it with my thumb.

"I'm not really going anywhere." She bites her trembling
bottom lip. "But I still have to say goodbye."

"I know." And it's tearing me apart. "I wish there was a way. I wish we didn't have to…"

Become strangers.

I jolt as she wipes a tear from my face.

"You know what's one of the things I like the most about you?"

The question makes me quake in my shoes. "What?"

Serena's lips bow into a sad smile. "That you're not really an onion, but a sweet little cinnamon roll."

A beam of light pierces through my chest and makes me laugh. It feels foreign, but warms up my entire body.

"And here I thought you would mention my charming smile or my superior abs."

"I like those too." Her eyes crinkle at the corners. "And also these."

With a feather touch, the pad of her thumb brushes across my lips. It sends sensation down to my toes.

"I think you're a cinnamon roll too," I say, smiling against her finger. "You may act all tough and stern, but you're actually warm and sweet. And I like that too. I like all of you."

"Oh, Caleb." She drops her head on my chest. "Why couldn't you be a regular guy?"

I sigh and rub my hands up and down her back, chasing the chill off of her. "My only consolation is that if I was, maybe we wouldn't have met."

"But was it worth it? Meeting and… and developing feelings for each other, only to be forced apart like this?"

I pull away and tilt her chin up. Looking deep into her eyes, I say, "Every moment was worth it."

Her lip starts trembling, and I stop it with mine.

This isn't like the brief but scorching kisses we shared before. This kiss is slow, trying to rob as much time as possible. When it's done, we'll have to embark in a life where we don't belong. I wish I could live in this moment forever.

But too soon, someone clears their throat and Serena and I separate. Tears cascade down her cheeks and she wraps her arms tight around herself. Where her body touched mine, it now feels colder than ever.

"Goodbye, Caleb."

I can't bring myself to return the words, even though it's the right thing to do. Because no matter what tomorrow brings, or what Vivienne tries, Serena steals away into the night with my heart and I have no intention to ever get it back.

CHAPTER 77
SERENA

Oh, no. This is so much worse now.

I run away from the prince like a run-of-the-mill Cinderella. Except I don't leave behind one of my slippers, but my heart.

The makeup must be streaming down my face, now that tears run free. I amble down the dark corridors until eventually, a tall sliver of light draws me to a set of doors that leads out to the grounds. The night air is so chilly that I regret it for a second, but the punishment is what I deserve for thinking I'm the lead of some soap opera.

Watching hours upon hours of romantic dramas didn't prepare me for losing out on real life love.

I find a bench lit up by the moonlight and sit on it. In the dramas, the female lead goes through all sorts of calamities to make her deserving of the inevitable happy ending. It's why I love them, because my life has always followed the opposite pattern, in which only a hardship follows after another.

Even though I tried so hard not to fall for Caleb, in the back of my mind, I hoped this time, with him, it would be different. That finally I would have a happy ending.

"The only person you have is yourself," I say into the night, rubbing my hands up and down my arms. "If you expect things from others, that's your own fault."

I desperately wish this wasn't true. That I had at least one person on my corner at all times. That I wouldn't have to shoulder everything by myself. But that's not the ending in store for me.

"That's a pretty cynical way to view life."

The low voice behind me startles a yelp out of me. In jumping away from the bench, my legs get tangled in the skirt of the gown and I would fall if not for the man zooming out of the shadows faster than my eyes can process. He steadies me by my elbows until it's clear that I'm no longer at risk of acquainting my face with the ground.

"Mr. Oh?" I blink rapidly.

"Sit down, child." He guides me back to the bench. "The last thing I want is anyone to get injured tonight."

"Uh." At the last second I recall the waterworks that exploded in my face, and start wiping it with my hands. "If you don't mind me asking, what are you doing here?"

"Same as you, I think." Mr. Oh sits on the opposite end of the bench, also facing toward the mansion. "I needed some fresh air away from the circus."

He gives me a side glance for a second before shrugging off his blazer and settling it around my shoulders. Immediately, the warmth that seeps into my body is so relieving that I can't think of doing the polite thing of returning the garment to him.

"You didn't have to, but thank you."

Mr. Oh nods. "I've always appreciated your honesty, Miss Lossada. I hope the events that have transpired won't prevent you from speaking candidly in the future."

I think carefully about that one. He might offering an olive branch, a small compensation for putting my heart through the wringer. If I want to stay in his employment instead of walking away, all I can do is accept it.

"When it comes to work, you can count on that, sir," I say, very deliberately.

The older man takes a deep breath and releases it slowly. "It's not comparable, but I'm also affected by the whole situation. No one said it's easy to do the right thing."

I feel that in my bones. Tearing myself away from Caleb tonight, forever, is one of the hardest things I've had to do in my life.

"But I made a promise." Mr. Oh looks up at the starry sky. "And to fulfill it, I have to do everything in my power to keep you safe. Including getting your heart broken in the process."

The words sound so foreign to me, that even after I try to rearrange them in my head I can't identify them as English. Shaking my head, I ask, "What do you mean?"

Even in the dimly lit night, Mr. Oh's eyes are as deep as blackholes when they settle on me. "I heard you now know who I really am, and thus, who Caleb really is."

"Lara?"

He chuckles. "Don't judge her too harshly. She didn't run and tell me what you guys talked about. Instead, she screamed at me that if only I turned you, I could make both my son and you happy. But it's not that simple."

I tighten Mr. Oh's blazer around me to stave off the cold.

"I will confide something." Mr. Oh stretches his legs out before him, crossing an ankle over the other. "The biggest mistake of my life was falling for my secretary."

I draw in a sharp breath.

"I was already married, which is only half of the reason why it was such a mistake." The businessman cringes, as if embarrassed with himself despite the events happening decades ago. "The worst part is that she was a human."

"Oh, no." As my eyes well up, I ask, "What happened?"

"I turned her." Mr. Oh's brow is creased to such degree, I fear he's a moment away from crying. "I thought I could have my cake and eat it, too. I didn't care that my marriage was falling apart, or that my kingdom was judging me as a corrupt king. All I cared about was being with the woman I loved— truly loved. Making a new family with her. Spending the rest of my life with her. So I turned her, and she survived it. When she got pregnant, I was over the moon."

He lets out a harsh breath like he's disgusted with his past self. Mr. Oh gets to his feet and stuffs his hands in the pockets of his slacks, looking into the sky again.

"I was so selfish, I didn't realize I was also hurting the person I loved. While I thought everything had worked out perfectly, she was struggling to adapt to her new life as a vampire."

A sick feeling settles in the pit of my stomach as his voice turns more labored.

"Maybe it was the combination of postpartum depression and the overwhelming rarity of navigating the same world with a different body… but one day she was gone. And only when that happened, did the gravity of my actions hit me."

It takes him a very long while to compose himself enough to face me. But even with my weak eyesight, I can catch the tears rolling down his cheeks and to his chin.

"If I hadn't been so greedy," he continues, his voice faltering. "She would've lived a normal life."

My bottom lip trembles. "But your son would also not have been born."

While nodding, Mr. Oh drops his head. "That's the only good thing to come out of my mistake."

"I'm not asking you to turn me." I sniff, and as moisture trickles down my nose I wipe it with his blazer. "Er, sorry. I don't have tissues."

He offers a tiny smile. "But why? Why aren't you asking me what every human in-the-know asks me?"

"To turn me?" I ask, and he confirms with a nod. Drawing a deep breath, I respond, "Because, what use is living a long life if I can't share it with the person I care about?"

Mr. Oh sighs.

I kick at the grass under my feet. "At the end of the day, me being a human isn't the only reason why Caleb and I can't be together, right?"

"That's right," he murmurs. "I wish the circumstances were different, but I'm just a lowly vampire king. There are other things at play that I can't fix."

That makes me smile. "Thank you, for at least not turning out to be a villain like in soap operas."

"Life isn't as black and white as television makes it out to be." The silent chuckling makes his shoulders shake once more. "Now, let's go back inside. Even I'm getting chilly."

My tears have finally dried, as if they waited for this conversation to finally give up.

Together, Mr. Oh and I head back into the mansion. While he heads back to the party, I follow the clanging noise and smell of food back to the service area. I spend the rest of the night there, with a spectacular dress designed by one of the top fashion designers of our time, and with snooty marks on my boss's expensive blazer—working, among other people in the employ of the Oh family, where I belong.

Cinderella has returned to the life of servitude she's meant for, and this time no fairy godmother will help her reunite with the prince.

CHAPTER 78
CALEB

The very next day, I descend the stairs from one of our private jets and set my eyes on the land of Kentucky.

It's cold as ice.

Well, for a Florida boy like me.

I bundle into my coat and burrow my nose in the thick scarf around my neck. That's as far as comfort as I'll get while spending my birthday in the company of my future in-laws. Happy November eleventh to me.

Behind me, Phelan stomps down the steps like they owe him money. Maybe he's as displeased with being here as I am.

"Don't worry, old boy," I tell him while we walk through the tarmac to the limo waiting for us. "I don't foresee us being forced to stay here for long."

Phelan frowns at me as he opens the door to the limousine. But he volunteers no accompanying words to the gesture, and I don't speak as fluent *Phelan Murray* as he thinks.

When he joins me in the backseat, I say, "I have a plan."

The crease between his eyebrows deepens. While we wait for our luggage to be loaded in the trunk of the vehicle, Phelan activates the partition between the driver and us, and when we're isolated, he finally speaks. "Is it going to put your life in danger?"

"No." I shrug. "Only the family pride. Basically, the plan is to be the most obnoxious possible."

To my shock, Phelan asks me, "How is that any different than usual?"

"Stop, don't make me laugh." I raise my palm at him and continue. "It's so they don't realize we're trying to find information."

"We?"

I nod. "Yes, you're cooperating with this."

From the voices outside, it seems like the vehicle is loaded and we're ready to go. A moment later, the engine roars to life and off we go to the Astor estate. The headquarters of all my nightmares.

"Something Vivienne said last night got me thinking." I fold my arms, recalling her exact words aloud. They don't seem to trigger any eurekas in Phelan, though. "I suspect she's been the one behind all these attacks."

One of his eyebrows goes up.

"Which is why we need to find proof, and if we do, I won't have to marry her."

I still won't be able to be together with Serena, but at least we'll both be safe. That's the best outcome I can hope for.

"Very well." Phelan pauses. "Just don't make me pull out my guns."

"Deal. I'll just use *my* guns," I say, smiling for the first time in weeks. "Prepare for Obnoxious Caleb, level one thousand."

Phelan gives a tiny, almost imperceptible cringe and I have to use all my willpower not to burst into cackles like the villain of a soap opera. I hash out the barest plan of attack with my bodyguard during the ride. It almost makes me look forward to this visit.

I put on my sunglasses and channel my inner diva when

the limo finally stops in front of the sprawling Astor estate. If there's information to be had, I don't expect to stumble into it while I'm busy chafing the Astors's patience raw. The bulk of the work will have to be done by Phelan behind the scenes.

Ernst greets me right at the door, fully decked in golf clothes. "Welcome home, Son."

I ignore his open arms and shiver into my coat. "Do you have a fire going somewhere? I'm freezing my ass off."

Like the southern gentleman I know him to be, the word *ass* makes his smile falter for a second. I mark that as my first victory.

"Of course. Allow my staff to lead you to your room and they'll get the fireplace going shortly."

I walk into the mansion still bypassing my host without brushing the dirt off my shoes.

The inside has been redone since the last time I was here as a kid. It still looks like someone flipped through the pages of a catalogue and selected a random page in a barn chic style. Everything looks spotless and brand new, with not a single sign that someone truly lives here.

It's more or less like looking into Vivienne's eyes.

Speaking of, where is she?

"You're a little early and Vivienne is still with the stylist," Ernst says, as if reading my mind. "But we can go for a round of golf once you've settled in."

I wrinkle my nose. "Oh, I hate golf. It's old men's shit."

In the ensuing silence, I catch the way Phelan's breath hitches and I have to turn away from them not to burst out laughing.

"Anyway, where's my room?"

Through tight lips, Ernst orders one of his staff to bring me upstairs. As we walk up to the second floor, I run my fingers through the furniture, the decorations and worse, across the paintings. On this day, I'm not turning twenty eight years old but eight. My attitude alone will make them rue the day they decided to bring me into their family.

The staff member opens a massive set of doors to a suite. "It's connected to a second room that we prepared for your bodyguard."

"Great." I leap on the bed and bounce on it. "I hate sleeping by myself."

The guide widens his eyes, probably construing more than one meaning from that statement. And to myself I think, great, let the rumors flow. I don't care.

When we're alone, I say to Phelan, "So far so good, right?"

He gives me a strong look of disagreement. "I will go see what I can learn from the staff."

Since I sit by the corner of the bed, I pull the tucked end of comforter free and roll over the bed with it, until I'm an onion burrito. "Go forth, my child. I shall languish here, for I am truly cold as shit."

Sighing, Phelan turns around and heads out of the suite.

Blissful silence and warmth. What luxuries.

I close my eyes and hope no one bothers me for a while. If I managed to sleep for a wink in the nights leading to the engagement it was a miracle. Ironically, it's only been since last night that I've managed to catch up. You'd think getting offi-cially engaged to an evil woman would be the start of a life with insomnia, but ever since I got that little glimmer of hope I don't seem to fear the night as much.

If only Vivienne hadn't been so eager to praise her hard work to trap me, I might not have realized she could be the culprit behind the chaos as of late.

I burrow my face into the pillow, chuckling deeply from my chest. I'll get proof and then I'll be free. But first, a nap.

It feels like too little time has passed before the door opens with a racket. It's impossible to stay asleep with the noise, but I pretend to, anyway. Especially because I recognize the scent of the intruder.

"Welcome home, sugar." The bed sags under Vivienne's weight as she sits on it. "You must be tired after the flight. Why don't you let your fiancée give you a full body massage?"

That's enough to make me roll away from her, which unfortunately unfurls the comforter from around me. "Why is it so stinking cold here, are you all made of ice?"

She laughs. "I can show you just how red-blooded I am."

"Nah, I'm good. I'll just wear more layers."

Vivienne tries to crawl my way and I roll farther until I reach the opposite end of the bed, and spring to my feet. "That door better have a lock."

As she tilts her head, a long cascade of perfectly styled gold hair streams over her shoulder. "Don't tell me you're one of those prudes who don't want to have relations before of marriage."

I jam my hands in the pockets of my coat. "I totally am one such prude when it comes to you. Anyway, I'm hungry. What's for dinner?"

"Me?" She puts her hand on her chest, coincidentally framing the cleavage of her baby blue dress.

"Gross, I'm vegan."

"Still?" Slowly, Vivienne pushes to her feet and treads around the periphery of the bed, stopping just an inch from me. Thanks to wearing like fifteen layers of clothes, I see her hands trek up my chest but feel nothing. "Hmm, I'll have to turn you into a carnivore eventually."

I bat her hands away from me. "Why don't you go vegan instead? Isn't the wife supposed to obey the husband?"

For the first time, her eyes blaze with real fury.

Ah, I've touched a real nerve. And while I'm not retrograde

unlike my words, I'm willing to lean into them as long as they can dampen Vivienne's mood.

"Fine." She turns around so sharply, her hair whips against me. "Let's just go downstairs. Dinner is served."

I follow her, again smudging my fingertips on anything I can reach. She notices it but mustn't find it my most egregious transgression because she doesn't say anything.

Ernst sits at the head of the table, sipping on a glass of bourbon. He's changed out of the golf clothes and there isn't as much gladness in his eyes upon my arrival as the first time.

Vivienne sits to his right and a staff member pulls the chair to Ernst's left for me. I plop on it and put my elbows on the table. Both of their eyes follow the motion with open disapproval.

Wait until I start chewing with my mouth open, I think.

"I hope you find your accommodations comfortable," the head of the Astor clan says to me and I shrug.

"It's okay."

Wow, I really am being a little shit.

Ernst grabs onto his salad fork with extra strength as salads are placed before us. Right away, it gives me another opportunity to be impossible—because the salad has foie gras.

I make a face that comes from the depth of my heart, and push the plate away. "Ew, I can't eat this. I'm vegan."

The Astors grind their teeth so hard that I wouldn't have to be a vampire to hear the crunching noise.

Hours later, after the most awkward dinner in recorded history is finally done, I bar the doors to my suite with half of the furniture. Vivienne's stronger than me and she can no doubt push it out of her way if she wanted to, but at least she won't expect such heavy resistance while trying to first open the door.

Pulling out my cellphone, I select the most strident playlist in my collection and blast it through the room's sound system.

Phelan waits, sitting on the windowsill like a princess in an enchanted forest. I kick his long legs out of the way and sit beside him. Under the music, we share whatever intel we found from day one at the Astors's.

While the findings aren't life-changing, I keep hope that Vivienne will betray herself in the next week. And if I have to use my body as bait, I will.

CHAPTER 79
SERENA

After such a long streak of only bad things happening, finally my luck changes in the week Caleb is gone. Through a friend of a friend of Marissa's, we find a studio apartment that has gone vacant suddenly and the landlady is eager to find a replacement ASAP.

In the course of a couple of days, thanks to her eagerness, my desperation, and the easy logistics of simply not owning any furniture, I end up signing the lease and receiving the keys.

"You didn't really have to leave, you know," Marissa says as she helps me haul the essential stuff I bought at Walmart and Dollar Tree up the stairs.

That's one of the drawbacks of the place—no elevator. Other drawbacks I didn't care about are that the building and grounds are fully non-smoking, and that the landlady doesn't like it when tenants bring significant others to play.

In simple terms, it doesn't refer to someone like Marissa helping me move, but to guys. And since I'm never giving guys the time of the day again, I was more than happy to sign up.

"I couldn't continue imposing," I respond after I catch my breath. Pausing at my door, I'm jealous that four flights of stairs with a heavy load haven't made Marissa even break into a mild sweat. "Oh my word, I hate you."

She laughs at the change of my tone. "Why?"

"You're not even breathing funny!" Grunting, I stick the key in and open the door to my brand new, twenty-five-year-old studio apartment. "You're still welcome into my humble abode, though."

"Thank you for having me."

It takes us a few minutes to bring the boxes and bags in—the ones I'd been carrying. Marissa looped about twenty bags in each of her arms and balanced the two heaviest boxes of kitchen stuff, which helped a ton, but we still have at least two more trips before we empty her car.

"This is exciting, though." She sets out to start unpacking on the kitchen counter, bouncing a little bit with every move. "A brand new start. No gross roommates. A short commute to work."

"Freedom." I spread my arms but the merriment disappears quickly, and I drop them again. "Except for the part where I don't have a car yet."

"I got you, girl." Marissa snaps her fingers. "I'll be your free driver to work and around town for as long as you want."

I push my glasses up the bridge of my nose and look her up and down. "Are you sure you're really an onion, and not an angel in disguise?"

"I can confirm as much." While she balls plastic bags and stuffs them in a single one, she adds, "Angels are pure and holy. Meanwhile, I have very spicy thoughts every time I see a certain someone."

A hidden spark of amusement ignites in me. "I still can't believe it. He's like… a statue."

"You mean a work of art? Oh, yes." Marissa laughs at whatever expression I have on my face. "He's quiet, which sorta makes you wonder what his personality really is like."

I shake my head. "Is that it? Are you attracted to the mystery?"

"Yes, but that's not the reason." She sighs in a way that makes me think she's truly smitten. "You may not know this since you're a human, but among vampires—sorry, among onions—Phelan is a living legend."

After rummaging through the bags of shopping, I find microwavable popcorn and pop it in the device. "Wait until this is done and then you can tell me all the details. We'll just have to sit in the floor and share directly from the bag because I don't have chairs or bowls yet."

A few minutes later, we're doing exactly that and Marissa begins. "You know how, aside from the king, Phelan is the strongest onion, right?"

"I have a vague recollection of hearing something like that," I say while chewing an enormous mouthful.

"Which is amazing in an of itself, but even more when you know he—" Here she pauses and leaning forward, she whispers, "He was born a human."

Half of my popcorn mouthful falls when I'm unable to keep my yap closed.

"Whoa."

"Sorry," I say, picking up the gross mess from my T-shirt and popping it back into my mouth. "You'll understand if my table manners fly out the window because you just dropped a freaking bomb on me."

Fortunately, she's able to move past my nastiness to continue. "Yeah, so like, while everyone admires the heck out of him, some people don't like him because he's not a born-vampire."

I cringe. "Don't tell me you guys have that purebreed versus mutt type of shit too."

"We do." For a minute she chews in silence, her eyes lost in the distance. "And my mom—bless her, she's not a bad person, but she would never let her only daughter marry someone who will, quote unquote, lower our stock."

"Whoa, wait a second." I raise a greasy hand up. "You like him enough to *marry*?"

Marissa's eyebrows go up. "That's what you gathered from all that?"

"I mean it's the first step. We can talk about your mom not approving after."

"He also wouldn't approve." Clearing her throat, she bends her legs until her knees are against her chest. "I've never heard of Phelan dating, period. And strictly speaking, to him I'm just a face in the crowd."

"I'm sure that's not true." I pause in the middle of wincing. "I just don't know he knows how to show much emotion."

"I could teach him." Marissa says this so quick, that the moment she realizes which words came out, her skin glows with a deep blush. As I laugh, she hides behind her hands. "Ugh, I know, I know. I got it bad."

"Entre gustos y colores…"

She groans. "Please, don't tell anyone. I've never admitted this to anybody, not even Lara. She suspects, but I can't bring myself to confirm anything."

"I can't blame you. Knowing her, she'd concoct a plot to lock you up with Phelan in a small room with one bed."

Marissa gasps. "Maybe it wouldn't be so bad after all."

We both dissolve into giggles, and for a while all we can do is gather air into our lungs to fuel the amusement.

This is probably what normal friends do. Except for the part where the subject of the gossip is a lethal vampire, who I have now learned was born a human about a hundred years ago.

By the time we're finally done bringing everything into my studio, and have arranged things in a way that is somewhat functional, I'm thankful that even if things have sucked really bad for the past months, they led me to finding my first actual girl friend.

After she's gone, I sit in an inflatable chair in the living room in the silence. This is the first time I'm truly all by myself. As a child, I lived with my dad. After he was gone, I was one kid among dozens in the orphanage. And from college and on, I've had a succession of roommates, some better than others.

This is the first time I'll have to learn to enjoy my own company, something I've dreamed about for years. I didn't think this momentous occasion would finally arrive after getting my heart so thoroughly broken.

I plug my laptop in and fire it up. Minutes later, I'm watching the sappiest, cutest, Korean drama I can find with a hot male lead and a guaranteed happy ending.

CHAPTER 80
CALEB

'm so happy Vivienne spends hours getting pretty every day. Whether doing her hair, nails, getting massages and who knows what else, she spends hours out of the house every day before coming back looking like a Hollywood star.

I don't give a rat's ass about it, but it allows me plenty of time to roam free across the estate. The staff don't talk to me for anything outside of their duties, so instead I become a ghost. I glue myself to the walls, listening in to clandestine conversations in hushed whispers. So far, all I've gathered is that Ernst is a tyrant and that Vivienne is worse. Nothing I didn't already know.

Every night, I bar the door to my suite and blast annoying music so Phelan and I can confer. He's gathered a bit more information, but so far the only real lead is that a lot of men go in and out of the property. Men who walk in formation and pack heat.

Why does one of the oldest vampire families in North America need a small army?

When Ernst is also out of the house, I put on latex gloves I sneaked in from the staff, and rifle through his office. I don't know what I'm looking for, especially since anything important must be safely tucked behind password in his computer or in a safe. But I look, anyway. Ernst is an organized man, and I have to make sure I leave every drawer, every nook, exactly the same way I found it.

I'm in the middle of glancing through his mail when the door bursts open and I'm caught red-handed. By Vivienne.

"Oh." I look back down at the papers as if nothing was amiss. "It's just you."

"What the hell do you think you're doing, Caleb?"

"Entertaining myself," I answer in a calm tone of voice. Even better, my heart rate is totally normal. If I've learned something in almost a week of behaving like a little shit, is that if Vivienne hasn't retaliated, it's because she can't. "Since my hosts have so rudely left me to fend for myself."

"That's because you've been an insolent piece of—" At my smirk, she stops herself in mid tirade. "I'm going to ask you again, what are you doing here?"

I take my time putting her dad's correspondence back in its drawer, arranging it exactly as I found it. And then, the cherry on top is the way I pull the gloves off my hands. The last one has glued to the skin and makes a horrible snapping sound when I finally succeed in taking it off. I ball them up and put them in my pocket.

"Do you have something to hide, Vivienne?" With deliberate steps, I circle around the desk and approach.

Then a strange thing happens. Vivienne takes a step back.

The subconscious reaction answers my question better than words could.

Humming, I look her up and down. "I think you do, and I think it has something to do with what you've done to secure this blood alliance."

Her nostrils flare. "If only you weren't more important

than you think, I'd be smashing your face against my knee right now."

"Ouch." I put my hands over my heart. "No more seducing, now that you have me in the bag?"

Vivienne advances until there's but an inch between us. I have to clench my muscles not to jump away from her. "Oh, sugar. I can seduce and punish at the same time."

"Maybe with another guy."

Heavy footsteps interrupt this awful conversation, giving me a reasonable excuse to put distance between Vivienne and I. Beyond her, Phelan comes barreling down the hallway.

"There's an emergency," he says from the distance. "We have to fly back right away."

My first thought is Serena. While I've been fooling around here, Vivienne must have found a way to hurt her.

Using all the self-restraint I possess, I bypass her and follow my bodyguard down the hallways, to my suite.

"I've called ahead to get the jet ready," Phelan says. "A limo is already downstairs."

"Crap." I make a quick stop at the suite to pick up my phone and anything else that could be used against me. The clothes I can leave behind. "Let's go."

Outside the door, Vivienne waits like a barrier. "We're family now, how can I help?"

"By getting out of the way," I bark at her. She clenches her jaw but moves away. "Tell your dad I'm sorry to leave without saying goodbye."

"Is that it?" Rage tinges the question.

I take great pleasure in saying, "Yeah, that's it."

With that, I follow Phelan out of the estate. Like he said, the limo waits outside, door open so I can bound in right away.

Only when we're both locked inside, with the partition separating us from the driver up in place, is when I dare ask, "What happened?"

Three words as heavy as blows to the head come out of Phelan's mouth. "It's your father."

The limo starts moving as the world stops spinning.

I stop breathing.

The letter *n* gets stuck in my throat, but I can't fully form the denial. He can't be in danger. Dad's the strongest vampire on earth.

It must be his illness.

"Is he okay?"

Phelan looks more somber than usual. "I'm unsure. All your brother said is that we have to return right away."

I pull out my cellphone and ring Dan. He doesn't pick at the first tone, or the second. My heart is careening now, and I don't know what to do with all the anxious energy coursing through my veins.

Please, don't let me be too late.

"Pick up, Daniel," I growl to the phone, but all it does is ring.

By this point we're driving past the entrance gate of the grounds. A couple of men stand guard, and my eyes glue to one of them.

I hurl myself forward and slam my hands against the partition. "Stop the car!"

The driver hears the racket and has the sense to brake. I crawl on the side seat and observe the guard again.

"Phelan." At the summons, the bodyguard appears beside me, trying to spot what has me entranced. "Look at that guy. Isn't he familiar?"

A second later, Phelan sucks in a sharp breath. He at least has the presence of mind to take out his phone and snap a picture of the guard. "The proof we needed."

It tastes like bile.

"Let's think about this later," I say to Phelan, before ordering the driver to continue on our way.

*

My head is a rollercoaster while we fly back to Miami. I pace up and down the aisle of the jet, and more than once I have to catch myself before I barf all over the place.

The guy standing guard outside the Astor estate was one of those who attacked us in Chicago. I noticed him right away…

Because I drank his blood.

The most important thing right now is Dad, though.

Daniel didn't pick up the phone at all before we took off, but when I land in Miami, I find three missed calls from him. I call him back, and finally the lines connect.

"What is going on now?"

"Dad has pneumonia," he says, freezing me in my tracks. "I have it under control now, but he wants to see you."

Trembling, I ask, "Is he in danger?"

My brother takes a moment before he says, "Not anymore. For now."

The heck is that supposed to mean?

"I'll be there soon," I say instead, shutting off the call. To Phelan, I say, "Gun it."

Wordlessly, he does. Luck is on our side and we don't catch many red lights on the way. The adrenaline rushing through my body doesn't let me relax for a single moment. I stay keyed up from the second I strap on my seatbelt, until the car is safely parked in the private island and I can unfasten my seatbelt.

The hasty travel catches up to me when I try to take a step and I falter like a newborn calf. I brace myself with the car door, draw in a deep breath, and move.

Maria appears at the door, wringing her hand. "They're in the compound."

I nod. It's all I can muster.

At some point, as I make my way through the maze hidden underground below the house, I realize I've been left alone.

Not just because I'm technically safe here, but also because Phelan is an employee, after all, and this is a family matter. I miss him, though. I wish I could suck his unnatural strength by osmosis.

I reach the medical wing and Daniel awaits for me outside the door. "Geez, you look like shit."

"Thanks." I run a hand through my hair. "Is he awake?"

"Yeah, he's with Mom." Daniel gives me a grim smile. "She's taken this setback worse than you."

"Great," I mumble.

Slowly, I push the door open and peer inside. My step-mother sits by the bed, and she's the one I notice first. Even though there's a considerable distance between her and the bed, her eyes remain unfaltering on her husband.

Then there's Dad, hooked to a respirator.

The sight is enough to steal all the energy from my limbs and Daniel has to catch me before I crash to the floor.

"Dad?"

He opens his eyes and when they settle on me, he waves me over.

As if pulled by magnetic force, I rush to his side and grab onto his hand. An IV pumps medicine into his opposite arm. Electrodes peek from under his pajama top, feeding a beeping machine. The respirator swooshes air in and out of his lungs at a steady pace. Before I know it, my vision blurs with tears.

"Leave us, you two," Dad says through the mask. He waits until Daniel steers his mother out of the room and closes the door. "Caleb, it hurts to talk so listen to me well."

I get on my knees, so I'm at eye level with him. "I'm all ears for once."

This entices a weak smile from him. "Son, I feel like my time is shortening, so I have to make arrangements."

Obeying, I say nothing. But I drop my head to the mattress and let the tears soak through the bed covers.

"I want you to get ready." He pauses when a cough racks his chest, and I wait until the crisis subsides, holding his hand. "I'm ordering preparations for your wedding and for the coronation of my successor at the same time."

"Dad." The word comes out of my mouth like an exhalation.

He squeezes my hand with surprising strength. "When that's done, I will tell you the whole truth. Until then, can you trust me?"

A weak sound comes out of my mouth. My mind races trying to comprehend what could possibly be behind the question. What truth? What is Dad hiding from me? Is it related to what I just discovered at the Astor estate?

I should be angry. I should rebel. But I can't bring myself to respond in a manner typical of me.

So, sagging against the bed, I say, "I trust you, Dad. Always."

CHAPTER 81
SERENA

Since we're the only ones who directly assist the Oh family, any news about Mr. Oh are restricted to Jon, Marissa, and I.

Right now, the priority is to keep any possible rumors at bay to keep the company stable in the markets. It's why everyone else thinks Mr. Oh is on a family vacation celebrating his youngest child's engagement.

Even then, I don't know what's really going on. It certainly can't be good if he and his sons are absent. But it's not like I can just text Caleb and ask him.

At first, I saw his holiday to visit his fiancée's family as a good thing, an opportunity to catch my breath and build a wall between us. I shouldn't tear the foundations of that delicate structure this quickly, no matter how curious I am to know what's going on.

Instead, I receive a morning briefing from Jon, telling me to continue assisting the Marketing and Purchasing teams with daily tasks, weed out any rumors before they take root, and be on standby if anyone in the Oh family needs my assistance.

Which is why I'm caught between a rock and a sword when, one morning, Vivienne Astor appears before me.

"I heard you're supposed to help anyone from the Oh family," she says, leaning against my counter.

"Yes," I say, choosing my words carefully. "With the Oh surname."

Her lips stretch into a smile. "Semantics. It's the same to be born an Oh than to soon become one."

Dame paciencia…

"What can I help you with?" I ask, barely concealing the deep breaths I need to take to not erupt. If she's a wolf, I'm the sheep she has clenched in her jaws. Bleating protests is useless.

"Caleb's parents and my dad have agreed to have the wedding as soon as possible." She tosses her hair back with a shrug, and the fake modesty act really doesn't suit her. "I would've preferred to plan the biggest, most spectacular wedding of all time. Something even TMZ wants to take paparazzi shots of. But I guess I don't mind marrying Caleb earlier either."

I remain unflappable on the outside through her rant, a female equivalent to Phelan. But every word that comes out of her red lips feels like a stab to my weak heart.

Meanwhile, Vivienne continues saying, "And seeing what a great job you did organizing the engagement party so quickly, I want your help with the wedding planning."

Getting tortured medieval-style would be preferable.

I glance down at my computer screen, where I have fifty three emails to go through, plus a number of meetings to arrange between the executives, two expense reports to draft, and welcome letters to the grant honorees to send. Technically, I don't need any excuses to get out of this and she's not my employer.

"Thank you for the positive feedback," I say, mirroring her

smile. "However, I'm afraid I'm at capacity with work that I can't set aside, unless my manager requests it."

And since Cedric Oh is undisposed, Caleb isn't going to agree for shit. Knowing him, he's probably looking for a way to not have to marry this woman.

"Is that so?"

Vivienne tilts her head and stares me down for a second. And while, yes, she's intimidating as all get out—I know she could probably pick me up and toss me out the window like a rag—I doubt she wants to commit murder out in the open. Quietly, she removes herself from my vicinity and makes a phone call.

I busy myself drafting the first expense report, keeping watch from the corner of my eye. Her conversation is too hushed for me to make out anything useful, but I have my suspicions.

Sure enough, a moment later she and her awful smile return. "You're going to get a call in a second."

My cellphone buzzes on cue with Jon's name. Slowly, just to annoy her, I take forever picking up. "Hello?"

"Hi, Serena," Jon says, succinct as usual. "I know Vivienne's request is unreasonable but let's go with it, because Mr. Oh really wants the wedding to happen soon."

Well, shit. I forgot that in the absence of anyone named Oh, Jon defaults to my manager. Since he's confirming what Vivienne said, there's no excuse I can come up with that will free me from this.

In front of me, Vivienne settles her chin on her hand.

"What about all the work I have to do?" I ask Jon, trying one last time.

"Do what you can and send me the rest, I'll distribute it among all the assistants."

Damn it.

"Very well," I say, and he disconnects the call right away.

Vivienne claps her hands. "Now, let's go."

I get to my feet and she turns, expecting me to bound after her with the same enthusiasm. And if I'm going to do this, I'll do it well—but it doesn't mean I'm going to be happy about it.

I'm the definition of lackadaisical as I collect my phone, iPad, and a few other essentials, and stuff them in my purse. By the time I join her by the elevators, she shows the first sign of annoyance by how her smile looks more like a sneer. I wonder if she knows that I learned this tactic from her fiancé.

I send a text to Marissa on the way down the elevator. *Legally kidnapped by Vivienne. If you never hear from me again, you know who to blame.*

Excuse me? She responds. After a moment she follows up with another text. *Oh, I just got a note about it from Jon. That sucks.*

I sigh. *You're telling me.*

"Who are you texting?" Vivienne asks me.

Would it be terribly unprofessional if I reply with *yo momma?*

I go for a more middle ground answer by saying, "A friend. Someone needs to know what happened if I disappear in a ditch somewhere."

She hums from her throat and says nothing more. The fact that she doesn't laugh it off *or* get mad, weirds me out.

Three identical black cars erupt with a dozen men who scramble into a neat formation as soon as Vivienne and I walk out of the building. She heads to the middle car and motions at me to get in the backseat with her. I'm beyond weirded out now.

"Are you some mafia heiress?" I ask her, which sounds like a joke if it wasn't because I'm contemplating the possibility.

She scoffs. "Please, that is beneath me. I don't have to kill anyone to get what I want. Otherwise, you'd be dead by now, right?"

I can't hide the shiver that runs across my body. Vivienne

doesn't even bother with an ambiguous smile that might help me take the comment as a joke—because it isn't. Maybe she didn't intend to murder me when she threw me onto the beach, but the possibility also didn't stop her.

The woman sitting next to me is far scarier than an angry vampire chasing me in the night.

"Anyway," she continues, breaking through the heavy silence that falls in between. "There's so much to do, but honestly what I'm most excited about is the dress, so I want to start there."

"I can research for A-list modistes in town." I take out my iPad, if only to busy my trembling hands. "Or beyond Miami, if you're looking for something really unique."

Vivienne waves a hand. "That's well and good, but I first want to have a vision. So we're on our way to a boutique to help me find it. After all, what would any of my men know?"

"Right."

Leaning closer to me like we're friends sharing a secret, she whispers, "Plus, I want the opinion of someone who knows what Caleb likes. I want him to take one look at me and feel like the luckiest guy in the world, you know?"

All at once I realize that this is the real purpose behind all this. Here I thought she just wants to gloat at bagging Caleb, when what she really wants is to hurt us both. Me, obviously, by rubbing the facts in my face. But she also wants to hurt him, by reminding him that she won. That he was powerless against her desire to get him, no matter what. As if he was an object she now possesses.

Bile rises up my throat. I debate just letting it all out and ruining her day—and upholstery. It would certainly be the only revenge I'm capable of. But I choose to behave like an adult again, no matter how much it hurts. Sister Emilia will be proud of me.

I'm so drained of energy already, that when the cars stop at the parking lot of the boutique, my feet stumble upon each other and my axis tilts. One of Vivienne's men catches me by my elbow, and in a swift move he sets me upright. One-handed. No doubt a vampire.

"Thank you," I tell him, looking up at his face in acknowledgement. He nods, and something about him strikes me as familiar.

"Move along," Vivienne says, walking away in thigh-high boots that have heels as high as sky scrapers. It's a shame that she knows how to walk in them and doesn't twist her ankle.

Three employees from the boutique seem to compete over who can give Vivienne the most effusive welcome.

"We have selected ten different gowns for you to try today," one of them says.

"Would you and your companions like a refreshment?" the one in the middle asks.

The third one motions behind her. "Please, follow us. Everything's ready for you."

I gather up my nerve to ask Vivienne as we follow them to the back of the store, "You seem to have everything under control, so why am I here?"

That melodious little laughter of hers comes out. "Like I said, for your expert opinion."

Also known as her version of medieval torture.

I take a seat in the waiting area while she disappears into the dressing room with the three attendants. Two of Vivienne's guys follow, flanking the entrance and exit to the back area like they're guarding the safe at a bank. One of them is the one who caught me before I ate the pavement.

I take out my iPad to pretend I'm working, and take a covert picture of the man so I can inspect his face. I know it's not right to do this, but I promise myself to delete the picture later. Better than creeping on him in real time.

I just can't shake the feeling of having seen him before,

which is weird. You just don't see the same person by accident a second time in a city as big as Miami very often.

Swiping my index and thumb at the same time, I enlarge the picture until it grows too pixelated. And that's when I recognize him.

I almost drop the device in my shock, but I manage to catch it the air with surprising reflexes. My fumbling catches the attention of Vivienne's men, but they soon go back to ignoring me.

I stare at the guy in the flesh for one more moment. He's one of the guys from Chicago who chased Caleb and I into the parking lot of the department store. I'm as certain as I am of my own name.

And if that's the case, why the hell is one of the assailants in Vivienne's employment?

CHAPTER 82
CALEB

catch the tail end of Jon's phone conversation by pure chance. Dad fell asleep in his room and Stepmother wants to be alone with him. My intention to talk with Daniel outside is derailed by something Jon says.

"…Let's go with it, because Mr. Oh really wants the wedding to happen soon."

The only wedding Dad cares about is mine with Vivienne, which means Jon's not talking about the weather here.

From the other end of the line, I hear a familiar voice respond with, "What about all the work I have to do?"

Jon's back is turned to me and I can't see his expression when he tells Serena, "Do what you can and send me the rest, I'll distribute it among all the assistants."

"Very well," she says after a brief moment.

From the end of the corridor I can see my brother approaching, but right now my attention is on the other guy.

"What was that about?" I ask Jon. He must have sensed me a while back, because the sudden question doesn't change his demeanor.

While tapping furiously on his phone's keyboard, he says,

"Your assistant is going to help your fiancee with wedding preparations."

My whole body clenches with the effort it takes to not ram myself into Jon.

Through gritted teeth, I ask, "On whose orders?"

The tone of my voice is enough to finally tear him apart from his emails. Even Daniel freezes in his steps.

Dad's assistant turns to me slowly, eyebrows up. "Essentially, your father's. He wants to hold the ceremony as soon as possible, right?"

Damn him for being in-the-know.

But it's not like I can curse at him for telling the woman I have feelings for to assist the one I'm supposed to marry. He doesn't know about that whole dynamic.

"Phelan," I say under my breath, and the man materializes from the shadows in a matter of minutes. "Send someone to follow them."

"Yes."

Even though Jon clearly looks like he wants to ask what that was all about, I don't owe him answers. Without another word, I walk by him until I reach my brother. I grab Daniel by the shoulder and steer him away from the family rooms. All the way out of the house and into my car. Away from anyone with powerful hearing.

"What the—" my brother says, glancing around him as if he can't believe the change in his surroundings. "What's going on?"

"That's what I'm trying to find out." I turn on the car and even go as far as playing some music.

"Are we going somewhere?"

"No." I turn to face Daniel. "There's just been so much going on with Dad that I put this in the back of my mind. But there's something I need to share with you, and I can't trust anyone else with this."

Daniel blinks several times. "Should I be concerned?"

"Maybe." I tell him what Phelan and I found out about during my brief stint at the Astor manor, as well as what I just heard from Jon's phone conversation. The more I narrate, the more my brother's brow creases.

"So you think Vivienne's behind the attacks?" he asks, scratching his chin. "I wouldn't put it past her, actually."

"Exactly, and I think Serena's in danger," I say.

"That part I don't know about." He lifts his hands in the air in an attempt to pacify my rising temper. "Hear me out. What benefit is she going to get from hurting your assistant at this point?"

I give him a deadpan expression. "My total submission?"

"Ah, yes. There's that." Daniel looks down at the papers he's been carrying all along. "Well, I can tell you at least this much. Dad's exams came out as normal as can be, considering the circumstances. He's out of imminent danger, so you can leave if you want."

I consider the offer for a moment. While it's wrenching to leave Dad's side at this moment, I also can't trust Serena's safety to Vivienne. Especially not after the threats she's made.

"You'll call me if anything happens?"

"Of course." Daniel squeezes my shoulder. "And stay safe, little brother."

I take a deep breath as if about to jump into the ring.

"Oh." Daniel stops with one foot outside the car and one still in it. Twisting, he turns to look at me. "Don't forget your bodyguard."

That word must work the same as his name, because Phelan trawls from out of the house. While they cross paths, my brother says something to the other man that makes him nod. Probably the same as usual, to keep me safe.

After exchanging seats, Phelan drives us out of the private

island and back into the city. I ask him, "Do you know where we're going?"

"Our man sent me coordinates," he says, and that's all the information I get out of him in the half hour it takes from the Oh manor to our destination.

Phelan parks the Urus under the shade of a tree in a nondescript street of upscale homes. The only place that stands out is a bridal boutique, which is where I guess the women must be. I try to open my door, but Phelan has activated the child's safety button.

"Hey!" I protest.

He turns around, his index finger over his lips. "Observe first, act later."

Sound logic—not at all what I want to do. But it's not like I want to tear out the door and destroy the car. Phelan turns back to face ahead and I do the same.

There are three cars parked at the front of the store. Now that the engine of the Urus is off, I close my eyes and concentrate past our breathing, past the dull white noise in the silence of the car. There's a soft breeze outside that ruffles the leaves of the trees, but isn't strong enough to whistle. Traffic is virtually non-existent in this neighborhood, and the biggest noise polluter is the myriad air-conditioning systems.

"Can you hear anything?" I ask Phelan. In response, he lowers the windows just a notch.

It's enough that it allows me to hear past the layer of whirring HVACs. I strain my senses farther still, until I'm able to start catching faraway voices. Someone in a nearby house is fighting on the phone. In another one, there's a crying baby. Then I catch the remnants of a familiar laughter. Vivienne.

"Ugh." The word spills out of my mouth like a reflex.

I focus again, until I hear the voice I most want to hear. It sounds even, not in the high octaves of panic. I relax back in my seat.

I find Phelan's green eyes on me from the rearview mirror. There's a question written on them, and I venture to answer it by saying, "We'll follow them until I'm sure she's fine."

He nods, and that's that.

We sit in silence for over an hour, until the boutique door opens and out comes Vivienne. Serena walks a few paces behind, surrounded by a small army of men in black suits. The entire party boards the three cars and off they go.

I don't have to tell Phelan to make sure we're not noticed. He's an expert. Even though my car must be known to Vivienne, we don't seem to raise any alarms as we follow them through town. They stop at another store for a long time before making a new journey to a restaurant.

It's toward the end of the business day before they drop Serena off back at the Comed headquarters. She stays at the entrance, observing the cars drive away for a moment. I wonder if she fears they'll do a U-turn and take her for a less fun joy ride.

I'm afraid of that too, which is why I tell Phelan, "Let's make sure she gets home safe."

Which means more waiting.

That workaholic woman stays at the office until well into the night. If it hadn't been because Phelan parked the car in the parking lot, I wouldn't have caught her leaving the building along with Marissa and would've thought Serena planned to work until the next day.

"She's safe now," Phelan says as we watch the women get in a car together.

Running my hands through my hair, I say, "I won't feel calm until they're home and no one's breaking into their place."

"Fine." Phelan turns on the car, and we go on another chase, this time after two defenseless women.

I cringe. "We're doing a good thing but why do I feel like a creep?"

To my surprise, Phelan responds, "Because you're doing all of this in secret."

I squirm. It's not like I can tell Serena.

Or can I? Is staying quiet about my suspicions about Vivienne keeping Serena safe? That's really what matters here, not protecting my fragile little heart from getting hurt again.

"Shit," I say after a while. "I hate it when you're right."

So I make a new plan. Which is talking transparently with Serena.

I'm sweating bullets by the time Marissa stops her car at the parking lot of an unfamiliar apartment complex. Serena gets out from the passenger's seat and waves at the other woman as she drives away.

"Oh." The word comes out like a sigh.

I had promised to help Serena look for a new apartment, and it looks like she found it without me. And there will be so many more of her life events that I'll miss the farther apart we grow.

My heart is heavy as I open the door and step out of the car. Knocking on Phelan's window makes him roll it down. "If you see anything weird, engage."

"Yes, sir."

With that, I follow after Serena. The entrance to the building is locked and there's a security camera pointing directly at it. I pretend to stuff a key into the lock like Serena did earlier, and with my back turned to the camera, I break the handle and walk right in. From the distance, I saw her walk up several flights of stairs and soon enough, I stand right outside her door.

This is the closest we've been in weeks. The memory of my hands running across her bare back comes to the forefront of my mind and I have to do a series of breathing exercises to wipe it away.

I knock on the door.

The sound must have startled her, because there's a crashing sound followed by a curse. I'm glad to find she's as clumsy as usual.

She's out of breath when she opens the door. The second she sees me, her lungs stop functioning.

The first thing that tumbles out of my mouth is, "Are you okay?"

Serena squints up at me and I realize she's not wearing her glasses. "Caleb?"

"In the flesh."

She does a double take. "Hold on, I need my glasses for this."

I catch the door open while she goes inside, but remain firmly outside. When she returns, I ask, "Can I come in?"

Serena pops her head out onto the open hallway and sweeps her four eyes up and down. "My landlady doesn't like visitors from the opposite sex and frankly, I don't want to be in closed confines with you."

"Er, are you afraid of me?"

Her nose wrinkles. "No, I'm afraid of myself. What do you want?"

You.

But in lieu of that, I say, "To keep you safe. And I can't do that by saying what I have to where anyone can hear."

Her lips tighten into a line and she spreads the door open further. "Fine, but you have to promise me to stay far away from me."

"Deal."

In doing so, I stay with my back glued to the closed door and watch her make her way to an inflatable chair. "That's a good distance."

I sigh, sagging against the door. "I know Vivienne took you around for the day."

The cringe that comes to her is seismic. "How?"

"This is going to make me sound super creepy, but here goes." I tell her everything from hearing her conversation with Jon, to following her all the way here. By this point, her eyes are as wide as they can be and her jaw drops. I shake my hands in front of me. "I know, even I'm weirded out at myself. But it's because I have a plausible reason to be concerned. I think Vivienne's the one behind all those attacks."

At once, Serena jumps to her feet and startles *me*. "I think the same."

To paraphrase her, I ask, "How?"

"One of her guys from today—I remember him from Chicago." She paces exactly five steps before she reaches the opposite wall and back. "Oh, I'm so glad I can get this out of my chest. It was driving me bananas not being able to tell anyone."

"Shit." I enunciate the word so clearly, it stops her in her tracks. "*Shit.*"

"What?"

I pull at my hair. "Phelan and I also recognized one of her guys at the Astor estate."

Serena draws a sharp breath in.

"But this isn't enough to convince my parents that I shouldn't marry her."

"Then," she says, squaring up. "We need to find hard evidence."

"We?" I shake my head. "No, the reason I'm sharing this is because information is power, not because I want to put you in more danger."

"Too late, the woman hates me." She shrugs. "Even though it's not like I can marry you instead of her."

There's a resounding silence after that. Neither of us can refute that fact.

Lifting her chin, Serena says, "I'm your assistant. Thus, you need to let me assist you."

"Serena—"

"I know you won't let me get hurt." She motions all around her. "Your stalkerish actions of today prove it, along with every other instance where you've saved my butt. Let me return the favor."

I know what the stubborn set of her mouth means by now. It's often made me feel like she's actually the boss in this relationship.

And like her subordinate, I say, "Fine."

By the time I leave her apartment, we have a loose plan. All I can do now is pray it doesn't go awry.

CHAPTER 83
SERENA

"'m so excited about today." Vivienne sits beside me on the backseat of the car. Two beefy dudes sit at the front, neither of them is the one I recognized. "I have flown over one of the best patissiers from Paris and I have no doubt his creations will be masterpieces. I just hope I don't put on any extra pounds tasting them."

Ah, yeah. Today is cake day.

In a deadpan voice, I say, "I'm sure you'll be fine."

"You're right, I'm just going to enjoy it." She chuckles from low in her throat. "It might even be a great excuse to join my fiancé for morning workouts. I hear he really enjoys swimming and I just bought a gorgeous bikini."

The gloating in her face chafes me raw, so I look out the window as we drive down Miami Beach. "Or you could just wear it at the beach."

"Where would be the fun in that?" She lifts one shoulder delicately.

It's winter in Miami, which means it's still ridiculously hot *but* people still want to enjoy a seasonal look. Which is why Vivienne's wearing a turtleneck sweater made of a ribbed fabric that clings to her frame, and also has strategic holes on her shoulders and cleavage. And also why she's talking about bikinis to show off to her fiancé.

I don't understand Caleb. Any other guy in the planet would be absolutely salivating over this woman. Yet, here he is, desperate to find a way to not have to marry Vivienne Astor. And here I am, desperately hoping I factor into the reasons why he can't stomach the prospect of marrying her.

As if I could pull off a sweater like the one she's wearing, or an itty bitty bikini to swim in the pool with…

But anyway, since my ratio of genetics versus effort doesn't approach anywhere near Vivienne's physical level of perfection —and I honestly don't care enough to make the effort—I plan to stuff my face with cake today while I dig for scraps of information that might be useful.

I pretend to fumble with the seatbelt and turn around to straighten it. Behind what essentially is Vivienne's motorcade, and behind a couple of random vehicles, I spot the rental SUV Phelan and Caleb got for today's operation.

Knowing they're on the watch-out puts me slightly more at ease. Just slightly. Vivienne still freaks me the hell out.

The three vehicles stop in front of a residential building right by the beach, not far from where Caleb lives. I follow Vivienne and her men, wondering why a high-end patissier from Paris would be baking goods in an apartment. Only when I walk into the property do I realize that this must be where Vivienne lives when she's in town.

The view of Caleb's apartment prepared me to not be impressed by this one. Yeah, yeah, it's the ocean on one side and the cool part of town on the other. Whatever. Rich people all apparently like the same thing.

Now, the glorious smells wafting in from the massive kitchen do get my attention.

"Pierre!" Vivienne says, spreading her arms wide as a

surprisingly young guy emerges from the kitchen, wearing what I'd describe as a chef's outfit sans the funny hat. The man breaks into rapid French that Vivienne joins in, and I stand aside, watching them hug and kiss each other's cheeks with far more enthusiasm than I would expect for the occasion.

Meanwhile, her men distribute themselves strategically around the apartment, as if not even this place was safe from invisible enemies. What that means for me is that the exit is blocked. While Vivienne and the patissier chat some more, I fire up a quick update to Caleb by text.

At the same time, someone mentions my name. I look up and find Vivienne pointing at me.

"Unfortunately," she says in English to the man. "My fiancé won't be able to attend this session, so he has sent his assistant instead."

I extend my hand out for the man to shake. "Serena Lossada, pleased to meet you."

"Mon chérie, what a pretty little thing you are." The man kisses my cheeks and I do my best not to show the discomfort I feel. Holding me at arm's length, he turns to Vivienne and says, "Are you sure you want this pretty thing around your husband?"

I want to punch him, but I can't see that going well for me so I don't.

Vivienne laughs. "Don't be silly. It's not like Miss Lossada here is any real threat, she isn't one of us."

The man assesses me again. "Oh, I see."

So he's an onion too, huh?

Logically, I don't see why any of these people would look at me like I'm food. I'm sure they're wealthy enough to afford bags upon bags of blood. But it's still strange to be in a setup where I'm so severely disadvantaged in every aspect.

At least there's cakes. Plural.

Three of them sit on the dining table in an arrangement fit

for a grand celebration. They're decorated with intricate flower arrangements, one more exotic than the next, and just the smell of their frosting makes my stomach rumble.

The Pierre guy leads us to our seats and embarks on a lengthy explanation of how he came up with the concept for the first cake. Amid all the fancy French terms he uses that fly over my head, I catch more familiar ones such as pineapple and orange compote and chocolate mousse. I wish he would wrap up his speech quick so I can sink my teeth into the cake.

My phone buzzes and I check it from across Vivienne. The text from Caleb reads, *Remember the mission and stay safe.*

From calories? Or is he reading my mind and realizing that cake is making me lose sight of what matters?

I tell myself to focus. If this is where Vivienne lives, there has to be something useful here.

The first bite of the cake almost sends my brain jumping out the window—it's so damn good—but I take advantage of the tasting to observe my surroundings. I need a good excuse to rummage through Vivienne's room somehow.

Then I look down at the gorgeous, incredibly delicious red velvet cake, and get an idea. Fortunately it's the right time of the month to use it.

I clutch at my stomach and the movement catches Pierre and Vivienne's attention. "I'm so sorry to interrupt but it looks like my stomach is upset. May I use the restroom?"

Vivienne rolls her eyes, which, gee lady, sorry if I have bowel movements during my period. "Vlad, take Miss Lossada to the bathroom."

"Yes, ma'am."

I can't believe one of her guys is called Vlad, but here he is, escorting me to a door in the hallway. Before entering the restroom, I ask him, "Do you think she has feminine hygiene products here?"

Vlad, a massive six foot plus dude, goes pale at the thought.

From the dining area, Vivienne says, "Ugh, take her to my personal bathroom."

"This way." The man escorts me to a different door, farther down the hallway. He doesn't join me as I enter Vivienne's room.

The first thing I see is a bed that fits probably fifteen people. On the wall by the head of the bed, there's a massive portrait of her that is something in the vein of a boudoir pictorial. The decorations are all white with touches of pastel pink —pretty, if it wasn't for the picture.

Inside the bathroom, I remember Caleb's trick for dealing with Vivienne's super hearing and open the faucet as much as it goes. A torrent of water will hopefully muffle my steps after I remove my slippers and walk in bare feet. I'll be out of luck if nothing more incriminating than her wall decor turns up in this room. I can't think of a convincing excuse to go into her office after this.

I rifle through her things quickly, while making awful grunting noises that will hopefully make her think I'm taking the dump of the century.

The things a person does out of love, huh?

But after enough searching, the only incriminating thing I find is that the abundance of mirrors suggests what we already knew—that she really loves looking at herself.

Cursing, I flush the toilet twice and spend a good amount of time washing my hands. My reflection in the mirror shows I have a deep red blush due both to my crimes. It should be convincing in case she doubts I had a hard time in there.

Oddly, there's shouting when I emerge from the bathroom —more accurately, Vivienne's.

"What the—"

I tiptoe to the bedroom door, fearing that a sudden move might send her on an even bigger tirade. Since I'm a lowly human, I can't distinguish the words she's saying until I crack the door open just a notch. Vivienne has Vlad cornered at the end of the hallway, and she pushes him against the wall every few seconds as she shouts at him.

"—You lost them?"

Whoa, speaking of a bridezilla.

The guy murmurs something that makes her face morph from a gorgeous, if angry woman, to an absolute monster. Something in her eyes tells me she *could* kill this guy right here for whatever he said.

I take out my cellphone and hit record. Maybe her horrible temper will be enough to convince Mr. Oh that his son doesn't deserve this marriage?

In a dangerously low tone, Vivienne says, "I hired you and your men to always keep tabs on the Ohs. So again, where is Caleb right now?"

I stop breathing.

This is proof. This has to be freaking proof!

"We're looking all over the place," Vlad says, keeping his eyes down. "We think they were following us until a few minutes ago. I don't know why he's not here already."

I do. Because Caleb told Vivienne he would join the cake tasting without ever meaning to actually join.

Vivienne's body looks like a tight coil about to spring. "You're a waste of space."

The man looks up at her, positively terrified. And so am I, as I watch Vivienne put her index finger on his forehead. He lets out a sound like mewling.

"Look into my eyes," she commands, leaning her face until their noses almost touch. "You'll do as I say."

Stunned, I watch the man's body grow slack until it almost seems like only her finger supports him. "Yes, ma'am."

"Good." Further still, Vivienne closes the gap between them until all he'll be able to see is her eyes. "You will scour the earth and the sea if you must to find Caleb Oh and bring him to me. You have two hours. If you don't succeed, you'll walk into incoming traffic during rush hour until someone runs you over. Is that clear?"

"Yes, ma'am."

Bile rises up my throat. The man's voice sounds as dead as he'll be if he doesn't succeed.

Trembling, I leave the door open but move out of sight. My fingers feel like lead as I send over the video to Caleb, but I have no hope of typing an explanation before the bedroom door opens and Vivienne comes in.

It doesn't matter that I'm not an actress and can't school my face to hide how much she terrifies me. She can hear how my heart pumps three times faster than usual.

Her ice blue eyes fall on the phone in my hand. I don't bother resisting as she takes it from me and crushes the device in her powerful hand.

"Hmm, I was hoping to play with you for longer, but it doesn't look like I can give you any free rein, huh?" Bending forward, Vivienne puts her index finger on my forehead. "Look into my eyes, sugar."

It's as if an invisible force grabs my entire body in a vise. Even when I try to fight it off, I can't move a single muscle. And against my efforts, my voice says, "Yes, Vivienne."

CHAPTER 84
CALEB

'm learning this stakeout business better, which is why for today I prepared snacks.

Phelan and I munch on some homemade wraps made of yucca flour tortillas, stuffed with peanut butter, rolled oat flakes, sliced strawberries, and a sprinkle of cinnamon. Additionally, I poured cold blood in the sippy cups we've grown fond of, because it'd be weird to be caught drinking blood from bags inside a car.

I wash the gross blood down with bites of the wrap, keeping my eyes on the entrance of Vivienne's building. "This is so annoying, I want to see what's happening in the apartment. What if we rappel down the roof of the building and peek in from the windows?"

My question gets absolutely no answer, which is usually enough answer from Phelan.

Sighing, I ask, "Next time, should we install a bug in Serena's phone to listen in?"

"That's illegal." Phelan sips blood from a cup featuring Princess Jasmine. Mine has Mulan, because she's the only Eastern Asian princess and that's why I'm biased toward her.

I shrug. "Not with her permission, right? Oh, speaking of."

A text buzzes in at that moment from Serena. I open it, expecting another quick update, but this time it's a two-minute long video. The still image from the file is too dark for me to guess what's going on, but one thing's for certain.

This isn't about cake.

I hit play on the video.

The image clears up and I make out the backlit figures of Vivienne and a guy. It takes me a moment to process her words, but when I see her pressing her finger on the guy's forehead, my brain seizes onto two thoughts that are equally as loud.

Vivienne looks to be proficient at compelling.

And Serena's in danger.

Faster than I can react, Phelan clicks on the child safety lock. He turns around, saying, "Don't."

"Don't what?" I unbuckle my seatbelt and toss aside the snacks, leaning into one of the backseat doors so I can aim at the other one. "Kick the door open? Too late."

With a powerful kick, I send the opposite door flying off the car. The metal makes an unforgiving crunching noise as it slams against the pavement.

In as long as it takes me to scoot out of the car, Phelan jumps out of the driver's seat and appears in my way.

"Move."

"Use your brain," he says, cornering me against the car. "If you go in there to help Miss Lossada, Miss Astor will retaliate."

"Miss me with the Miss shit." I try to side step him. It doesn't work. "Did you forget why we're in this stakeout? It's to keep Serena safe."

"I thought it was to find proof of Miss Astor being the one behind the attacks."

I try to push him away, but of course that doesn't work

either. "I hate that this is when you decide to use the most amount of words I've ever heard from you."

"It's because no one else is here to reason with you." Then Phelan does something even more shocking—he makes physical contact, grabbing me by my shoulders to root me in place. "We have the proof. A witness is on his way to find you. Once we secure him, we'll ascertain Miss Lossada's safety."

"That'll be too late." A sound like a growling animal comes from my chest. "Serena first—I don't care about anything else."

Phelan clenches his jaw. "No, *your* safety comes first. That is my job and I am not letting you jeopardize it. You will do as I say."

I reel back, but with his grip on my shoulders I don't go far. "Are you trying to compel me?"

The man takes a deep breath, and it wipes his expression back to blank. "Not yet, but I will if I have to."

"I found you!" a third voice says from out of nowhere.

Phelan and I turn to the source—a beefy guy barreling down from Vivienne's building and across the street.

It's the guy from the video. The one who has to find me or die from Vivienne's compelling.

More proof.

If it wasn't for Serena, I'd feel like we're hitting the jackpot. Instead, I question why my chest throbs with a rapid heartbeat even though my heart is hostage in Vivienne's apartment.

"Let's split up," I tell Phelan, grabbing his arms hard enough to break steel pipes—but not him. "Take my phone and send the video to Daniel and Dad, then secure this guy."

On instinct alone, Phelan rolls us out of the way as Vivienne's guy descends upon us. He lands the blow on the rental car, denting the rooftop beyond repair. Not that it already wasn't totaled by me.

As if there wasn't a murderous vampire on us, Phelan calmly asks me, "And you?"

I duck out of a flying kick from Vivienne's guy. "Meanwhile, I'll join my damn cake tasting as excuse to make sure Serena is safe."

Still with his attention on me, Phelan uppercuts the guy's chin so hard, it sends him flying in the air like a rag doll. As the guy lands on the road with a sickening crunch, Phelan says, "And you won't put yourself in unnecessary danger?"

"No, Mom. I'm going now."

My bodyguard frowns, but since he's not blocking my way I guess this is as close as I'll get to him agreeing. I leave him to his task and cross the street.

The guard at the lobby must have seen the whole scene. He's pale as paper, speaking in rapid Spanish to the phone. I catch the word policía, which isn't quite good news.

I wish I could compel him to forget, for his safety and mine, but I'm not strong enough to do that. Only the most powerful vampires out there, who have absorbed the most mutations into their bodies, can develop the skill. Like Dad and his wife, who are the king and queen of vampires after drinking the blood of every vampire family on earth.

And apparently Vivienne.

The guard shakes from head to toe but doesn't stop me, probably because he saw me kick the door out of a car. None of Vivienne's men appear in the way to her apartment, which hopefully means that at this point they suspect nothing is amiss.

My entire body feels hot and cold as I ride the elevator up. I call Serena's phone and a voice message replies, saying the number isn't in service.

For a second, I see white.

I stumble into thin air, and slamming against the walls of the elevator snaps me awake.

Serena's phone not working doesn't mean she's dead. It could just be out of battery. Or got damaged.

If Vivienne hurts Serena *I will kill her*, and I doubt Vivienne would want that outcome. It would ruin the stinking wedding.

"Calm the hell down, Caleb," I tell myself, shaking my head hard.

Stopping just outside the elevator in Vivienne's floor, I force myself to relax my body until my heart rate returns to normal. Showing up to a mundane affair like cake testing while breathing like a horse will not work in my favor.

Finally, I get to Vivienne's apartment. I wait patiently for the door to open and then the sight that greets me is unlike anything I imagined.

Serena and Vivienne sit in the living room, eating cake and chatting like they're best friends.

I'm flooded with relief that Serena is alive and with all her limbs intact. But then I realize something is still wrong. She would never cozy up to Vivienne like this.

"There he is." Vivienne places her plate of cake on the coffee table and jumps to her feet. Her arms are wide like she expects me to run to her. "The groom has finally arrived."

"Monsieur Oh," a guy wearing white says. "It is a pleasure to meet you."

"Mr. Oh." Serena's smile is polite enough, but her eyes are vacant as they settle on me. As though she has no feeling. As if I'm a stranger. "I was just telling your fiancée that you were joining us late."

I take a moment to heed Phelan's order of using my brain.

Vivienne compelled the crap out of Serena. She would never *Mr. Oh* me or buddy up with this sociopath. Which means Vivienne caught Serena recording the video. Which must mean she suspects I've seen it.

Then I recall Serena's phone being off. What if Vivienne

destroyed it? And by compelling Serena senseless, what if Vivienne thinks she's got rid of the proof and the witness?

Also, she must think I'm here because her guy brought me.

Then I focus on Vivienne. Hear heart rate is normal. Her blood doesn't smell heavy with cortisol. There's no perspiration in her skin. In fact, her eyes twinkle like she's pleased with everything. Calm. In control.

Maybe she doesn't think I know. Maybe I should pretend I don't.

"Sorry, I'm late. The traffic was bloody." My joke causes some awkward laughter. I zero in on the guy who looks like a baker. "Are these cakes vegan?"

He gasps. "I did not hear of this requirement."

Bless my food requirements!

I groan as if this was the end of the world. "What a shame, I won't be able to test any of them. Miss Lossada, let's go. We have work waiting at the office."

She jumps to her feet like a robot. "Yes, sir."

I grit my teeth with the effort it takes me to hold back from throttling my supposed fiancee.

Meanwhile, the muscles in Vivienne's jaw pop. "You're arriving and leaving right away?"

I wait until Serena is by my side before I respond. "Yep. Too bad I can't eat the cake."

And figuratively, neither will she. Because I now have enough information to make her sink. If only it hadn't been at Serena's expense.

No one stops us as I guide my assistant down to the lobby. The police haven't arrived yet, and Phelan waits outside with a taxi. Inside, I make out the driver at the front, and Vivienne's guy knocked out in the back. It's a victory, and yet it tastes like bile knowing Serena's mind might be broken.

While riding the taxi, I break down like a freaking baby.

The driver and Serena look at me with the same amount of confusion strangers feel while watching a grown man cry.

CHAPTER 85
SERENA

My boss is crying.

No, scratch that—it's worse. He's weeping.

I'm squeezed between the door and him in the backseat of a taxi. On my boss's other side is Vlad, slumped over. Why is one of Miss Astor's employees here? It almost looks like we're kidnapping him.

"Um." I glance to the front, hoping my boss's bodyguard will have answers. "Mr. Murray, what's happening?"

The man turns around as best as his seatbelt allows. He takes one look at our weeping boss, one at me, and faces the front again without volunteering a response.

I'm starting to sweat. First, there's the fact that my boss continues sniffling and fighting to wipe tears that are then replaced by new ones. And he's not exactly what I'd describe as small, which has me wedged against the door and the handle is jamming onto my hip.

The effort of keeping space between us has me doing a workout here. I just don't think it's right to casually make contact with the person who pays my paycheck.

After a while, Mr. Oh begins to calm down. Or perhaps

he's just grown tired. I sort of want to know what made him so sad. It can't possibly be because he couldn't taste the cake, right?

But I can't ask. That'd be out of line. And we're essentially strangers who see each other at the office every day and then go our separate ways.

I have no idea what, in the life of a billionaire's son, could be so bad as to warrant open weeping. Especially when I do all my little cries in private—and I have tons of reasons to despair. Loneliness? Check. Debt? Double check. An awful roommate? Che—

Wait.

The taxi jolts as it drives through a bad road and I smack my head against the window. As the momentary ache fades, I recall that I now proudly live by myself. But how did that happen? It's like one moment I'm still caught up in the Karyn and Richard grossness, then I'm back at the orphanage, and the next I'm moving into a studio apartment with Marissa's help. Thank goodness for my first friend.

Is she? How did we become friends? We don't actually interact much at work.

My head is starting to hurt. Something feels off and I feel further off for feeling like something is off, when all of these things are facts. But it's almost like getting a math equation where you have the answer, but all the variables are unknown and you don't know how the whole thing can possibly work.

How did I leave Karyn behind? And then how did I leave the orphanage? Things were going okay there.

But wait, why was I living at the orphanage? It's so far from the office.

I clutch at my head. It feels viscerally important to grab onto the thought I'm missing amid the tornado of other thoughts spinning in my head. But I don't know what I'm missing, so how can I search for it?

Backtracking is just as hard. There are holes in my memories of the past couple of days too.

"Mierda." The word spills out of my lips with feeling.

One thing is forgetting to jot something down in the list for grocery shopping, another one is forgetting entire chunks of your day. I'm too young for this shit.

"Don't worry," my boss murmurs beside me, so dispirited I worry he'll start crying again. "We'll find a way to fix you."

"Fix me?"

That gets me no further intel.

One thing is clear—something is wrong with me.

One thing is very unclear—how my boss can possibly do anything about it.

The sky grows dark as the taxi keeps driving past everything I know. The city lights—so numerous that they can blot out the stars from the sky—give way to the more sporadic lamp posts of the highway out of the city.

As we get farther from Miami, I ask, "Where are we going?"

My boss's eyes are half mast, fixed on his lap. "To where we can help you."

Finally, the answer arrives in the form of an enormous mansion straight out of a gothic movie. The taxi driver stops at a gate and we're allowed into the grounds of the mansion after Mr. Murray explains the situation.

The driver parks right at the entrance. "That'll be three hundred and fifty four."

The way I gasp leaves me out of breath.

All that, for a taxi ride? Just how far are we?

My boss reaches into the pocket of his blazer for his wallet and hands over a black card to the driver. While the transaction takes place, Mr. Murray gets out of the car and walks the perimeter to the opposite door from mine. Miss Astor's guy slides to the ground, but at the last second Mr. Murray catches him.

I open my door, thankful for fresh air. How am I going to get back home, though?

First I put one foot on the ground, then the other. But as if this was my first time, my balance tilts and I crash.

The impact is so hard that it leaves me without air. A tiny groan comes out of my mouth while I turn on my back. My shoulder throbs.

What just happened?

Vaguely, I hear someone say, "I will kill her."

"I'm sorry," I say right away, concerned that my boss finds me a total waste of space. Which, right now, I do feel like. It takes more effort than it should to be able to sit up. I can't see jack squat, and it's because my glasses flew off. As I palm the ground around me to find them, I say, "I don't know what happened. It won't happen again."

A blurry figure appears before me. Up next, my glasses are placed on my face and I can see that it's my boss crouched before me. Under the lamp posts in the yard, I note his eyes are bloodshot and swollen.

"Are you okay?" he asks, which makes me jolt.

"Ah, yes. I'm fine. Thank you, sir."

I try to stand, but once more it's like air is tripping me and I'm about to eat the dirt. My boss catches me in mid air, and before I can understand what's happening, he leans down and picks me up in his arms.

I turn into a goldfish, gasping for air and shaking.

"Stop," he commands, and my body responds in kind. My boss looks down at me, and it makes me feel like I'm gonna die. We've never been so close, and as much as I try not to notice it, he *is* gorgeous. "You can't walk right now. Let me help."

It's clear I can't even *think* right now.

I let him carry me into the mansion, keeping my head

down not to see him or anything else. There's no hiding in plain sight like this, even though it's what I most want to do. But my boss smells really good, and with my arms around his neck, flush against his chest while he carries me like I don't weigh a hundred and seventy pounds, I feel like I've crossed a line I never should've crossed.

Immediately, I feel so sorry for Miss Astor. She would be devastated if she saw this scene.

"This isn't right," I say aloud, gathering my nerve. "Isn't there anyone else who could help me?"

My boss swivels around, until I see Mr. Murray carrying Vlad on his shoulder like a rag doll. "Well, he's busy and I could shout for my brother to help, but would that be less uncomfortable?"

"No," I admit. The older son of Mr. Oh isn't my boss, but he's also someone on a different level.

Speaking of, his voice appears from somewhere nearby. "How bad is it?"

"Pretty bad," my boss responds, again in that dead voice. "She can't seem to even walk properly."

They're talking about me.

"Shit."

There's a pause while my boss continues walking. From the corner of my eye I notice that we're in a corridor.

Then, the older Oh son says, "Vivienne must have changed too much."

What are they talking about?

"Do you think we can get it back?" my boss asks.

There's a sigh. "Dad's doing better, but I don't know if he's exactly fit for the task. We'll need Mom's help."

My boss cringes so hard even I feel it. "Shit, I will beg her on my knees if I have to."

A squeaking sound like the rusty hinges of an opening door sounds beside me. I turn my head. We're now entering a massive bedroom with a bed that looks like it'd fit fifteen people.

A bolt of pain stabs my head. For a moment, I lose my bearings.

When I come to again, it's like I'm seeing two scenes overlapping in front of me. One is a huge bed with dark bedsheets and four mahogany posts that go up to the ceiling. Another one is a bed just as big, with white bedding and a huge portrait of a mostly bare woman on top.

My voice comes out drunk. "What is happening."

"Shh." There's something soft beneath me. A hand brushes my forehead softly. "Try to sleep. You'll need the energy later."

All I can do is obey, so I fade into unconsciousness again.

CALEB

The moment I tell Dad what Vivienne did to Serena, he wheezes past me in his wheelchair like an Olympian. It takes me a moment to comprehend his speed, despite being convalescent from a bad bout of pneumonia, but I don't know anyone more remarkable than him anyway.

I lag behind. The entire day's events have drained the life out of me, and if this is how zombies are made then yeah, that's what I am now.

When I reenter my room, Daniel is beside Serena checking her vitals. Dad has migrated from the wheelchair and now sits on the mattress next to her, his index finger on her forehead.

"How did you move so fast?" I ask, and once I've voiced the question I realize that what I want to know is different.

Why does Dad care about Serena so much that he'd rush over in his state?

Back when I first met her, I used to suspect that Dad might have something with her. That was a gross assumption based on his history with my real mother—and some older affairs according to Diana. But that's not it, there have been no signs of an affair.

Rather, Dad does care about Serena. I saw it in the way he put his jacket on her the night of the cursed engagement party, while they sat in the garden talking. It might even be how he developed pneumonia.

And now this.

Dad shushes me, concentrating on what he's doing. Meanwhile, my brother packs his things back in his medical bag and gives me a thumbs up, as if to say she's as okay as one can be when one's mind has been tampered with.

Some vampires go senseless after getting compelled, depending on how strong their minds intrinsically are versus how strong the other vampire's compelling is. And Vivienne is strong. In contrast, Serena is a human. She's naturally weaker.

I want to kill Vivienne. Or I want to *want* to kill her. In truth I'm tired and also scared of her. I want her out of my life altogether.

Finally, Dad pulls back with a deep breath. "About forty percent of her short term memory has been wiped. That's enough to mess with the organism."

I pull at my hair. "Can it be fixed?"

"I don't know." When Dad turns to me, his eyes are glowing as red as my blood. "But I can try. Get me two pints of blood and bring your mother over. This will need both our efforts."

"Leave it to me," Daniel says behind me, clapping my back once before disappearing down the hall.

But they couldn't do it with the assailants we captured after one of those attacks. Can they succeed with Serena?

I stumble and my back is against the wall. There, I sag until I sit on the floor. Gathering my knees in my arms, I say, "Dad, please. You have to fix her. She's innocent."

"I know." Dad's jaw clenches so hard, it's a wonder he's not pulverizing his own teeth. "I will do everything in my power so this child isn't in danger again."

I'm so drained that I can't ask him why. Why all of this is happening. Why I can't do anything about it.

Not long after, several sets of steps echo outside the bedroom. The first one through the door is Daniel, who drags his mother in by her arm. With his free hand, he brings in two containers with the blood Dad requested.

"Drink one," Dad orders his wife.

She scoffs. "Why should I do this?"

"Because I'm begging you," Daniel says, clasping his hands in supplication. "Serena is a good friend of Lara's, and she would be so upset to find out something bad happened to her friend, which would make the baby upset too."

And if my stepmother cares about anything, it's making sure the lineage of her son continues.

Predictably, she says, "Fine."

I stay in my corner, watching as they chug their portions of blood before getting to work. If it was possible, I would add what little compelling skills I have to help them. But I've also never teamed up with Dad or Diana, and I'm only strong enough to sway difficult business negotiations.

Compelling… is an art. The more you do it, the more attuned you get to its intricacies. It's not easy to navigate someone else's mind without losing yours in the process.

Over the years together, Dad and Diana have developed a working relationship where they can build up on each other's compelling strengths. The same can't be said for their marriage, but in this they're unmatched. If anyone can help Serena, it's them.

My brother joins me, sitting beside me and watching in silence. I'm glad to have him on my corner.

A horrible cry pierces the quiet. I jolt to my feet as Serena thrashes on the bed. But before I can reach her side, Dad lifts a hand to halt me. A pair of hands pull me back. Daniel. I look up and catch my stepmother dripping sweat from her chin as though someone poured a bucket of water on her head.

Meanwhile, Serena screams.

"Oh, heavens," I murmur. "Please."

Daniel's grip turns harder. "If you don't kill Vivienne, I will."

This situation lands like an anvil on me. It's as dire as if I was watching Serena go through open heart surgery without anesthetics.

What if she doesn't come out from this? Sometimes it happens with compelling.

Or what if she does, and she's forever changed? Seeing her act like she barely knew me has completely wrecked me. What if I'm forever broken?

Vivienne will pay. I don't know how yet, but I'll make sure of it with my dying breath if I have to.

"It is done," Dad announces, just a second before he tips back and passes out on the bed.

"Oh, shit." Daniel scrambles to pick Dad up. I stumble upon my own feet before I'm able to reach the wheelchair and move it closer to the bed.

Diana staggers on her feet but remains upright. Her arms are extended out like she's trying to grab onto the air for support. She keeps shaking her head every so often.

"I need to check up on Dad." Daniel winces at me. "Can you take care of Mom?"

He knows what that implies. Right now I don't care if my stepmother swipes at my head.

"Yes," I respond.

I wait until he maneuvers the wheelchair around and out of the room. One glance at Serena shows me that she's also out like Dad. Her hair is damp with sweat and her clothes stick to her skin. But her chest rises and falls, and all I can do right now is hope that's a good sign.

Diana grunts and I race to her in time to catch her before she pitches over. It must be so bad that she doesn't reject my touch. Instead, she clutches onto my arms.

"That girl," Diana says through gritted teeth. "She loves you. It's like history's repeating."

An exhalation comes out of me, leaving me empty.

My stepmother staggers, and against both our preferences, I circle my arm around her waist and help her walk out of the room.

All the thanks I get is her saying, "But even if you don't marry Vivienne anymore, you still can't be with a human. Remember that."

"I know." I whisper, focusing on not sending us both careening down the hallway. "Doesn't mean I can stop feeling how I do."

She snorts. "Neither can she."

That's both good and bad. I wish Serena nothing but joy— and no joy can be had when you're pining for someone you can't be with. I should know.

I veer directly to Dad's room after settling my stepmother in hers, expecting him to still be knocked out. Instead, he sits on his bed drinking a fresh pint of blood. Daniel stands by the foot of the bed, glaring at Dad in a way that freaks me out.

"What's happening?"

Daniel's death stare shifts to me. "I will leave you two alone. You need to talk."

I sag. "Am I being scolded for something I didn't do?"

"No." Dad wipes blood off his mouth with a napkin. "I was the one being scolded for something I definitely did."

Daniel shuts the door behind him with such strength, the entire wall rattles. It makes an instantaneous headache settle in my temples.

"I've had enough of today," I say, digging the heels of my

hands against the sides of my head. "But I do have a question you must answer right now."

Dad reaches across the bed to place the empty pint on his bedside table. "You too?"

"I guess I should start by saying thank you for helping Serena." I pause, collecting myself for a second. "But what's your deal with her?"

Slowly, Dad settles against the plush pillows behind him. He rearranges the bedsheets to perfection before speaking. "That's a long story and you're not ready for all of it, but I will share what answers this specific question. Come, take a seat."

CHAPTER 87
SERENA

I haven't seen my dad in eighteen years, but here he is. Looking down at me with a smile so crushingly sweet, I start to cry.

He shushes me and I feel myself shake. "Tranquila, mi cielo. Aquí está tu papá."

How is this possible? Is he real?

When I reach out to him, I see my small, pudgy hands clumsily tap at his chin while he carries me in his arms. That's when I realize this must be a dream. The incessant wailing of my baby version fits the way I really feel.

The dream shifts. I must be older now, because I sit on a chair, watching my dad get ready for work. He struggles with making a decent knot of his tie in the mirror, squinting at it like he does when I'm doing something bad and he's debating how to best discipline me. It's funny.

"¿A qué hora llegas?" I ask him, with the high pitched voice of a child. I check the clock on the wall of our tiny kitchen and it reads five in the afternoon. Why is he going to work this late? "¿Te dejo comida?"

Finally, he's done with his tie. Even though he's wearing a

suit, he kneels before me and kisses my forehead. "Ay, que madura es mi hija que ya cocina."

I remember those words. They once made me feel so proud of being a seven-year-old who could help with chores around the house. But they tasted bitter years later, when I realized all that I lost even before my dad was gone.

This is the night when I lose him. Is this a nightmare or a memory?

I want to scream at him not to go to work tonight, that something will go horribly wrong. That I'll save him dinner but he'll never get to eat it.

Instead, I hear my childish laughter. "Pero no es gratis."

"Sí, sí." Dad stands up to his feet, shaking his head as if he wasn't smiling from ear to ear. "Este finde te llevo al parque de diversiones como te prometí."

We never went. He died that night after an accident at work.

Instead, many years later I finally went to an amusement park with my boss. Caleb. An onion? No, a vampire. The guy who stole my heart before I realized it. Whose father is the same owner of the company my dad died working for.

I snap awake.

Two things happen at the same time. First, I see Caleb's face right above mine. Second, the contents of my stomach rush up my throat. I have to press my hands against my mouth to keep it down.

"Don't worry," he says, much calmer than I'd be in his position. For a moment he disappears from my field of vision, before he reappears with a bucket. "Vertigo tends to happen after getting your mind tampered with. Let it out."

I make a noise and try to shake my head, but the threat is too big.

Caleb settles the bucket between my knees and leans my

head into it. When he starts patting my back, I lose it—and by that, I mean everything that is in my stomach.

Tears stream down my face. The memories rush back to my head faster than I can process them. Dad taking me to school on a first day of a new school year. Caleb sipping juice from a fairytale princess cup during a meeting. Dad's funeral. Caleb and I sitting at the orphanage's cafeteria, talking about how things between us can never happen. Him breaking into my old apartment to see what had made me scream. Me pinning bedsheets to a clothesline. Caleb and I kissing.

And if that wasn't overwhelming enough, now Caleb's patting my back while I hurl into a bucket.

"There, there," he says, his voice lacking the usual buoyancy that made me think he was always amused.

His hand rubs circles on my back until the volcanic eruption finally abates and I slump over the bucket. Slowly, he leans me back and I feel his arm catch me before I collapse. I'm a rag doll as he wipes my face with a damp cloth and puts the bucket away.

With a feeble voice, I ask, "What happened?"

"Vivienne compelled you pretty bad." Caleb still holds me even after he settles me on my back. I'm in a bed, shivering under the blankets, but he's really warm beside me. "She altered so much of your memory that you couldn't even stand up straight."

"Oh."

He tucks me against his side. "It's easier to tuck someone's memories away, or order them to do something, than it is to undo that. It took both Dad and my stepmother to try to restore your mind. But to be honest, I can't promise everything will go back to normal."

No. Never. I will never be the same after my mind was violated like this.

A wail comes out of my throat. Caleb says nothing else as I

cry, but he holds me in the circle of his arms like he's planning to never let me go. I grab a fistful of his T-shirt because I don't want to leave either. The moment I pull away and get up from this bed, I will be confronted by a world that looks a lot bleaker, where I'm completely vulnerable to the predator Vivienne is.

"Serena." I feel Caleb kiss the top of my head, and it's almost enough to chase away the chill in my heart. "There's something more."

I sniffle against his chest. "What now?"

He pauses. "Maybe it should wait."

"No." I pull away enough that I can look at his entire face. "Tell me now, while my stomach's empty."

Caleb bites his lip. "Are you sure? It might—Well, to be honest I'm afraid that it will severely depress you and also make you hate me."

"You're scaring the girl too much," a familiar voice says. "Close the door after you."

I'm confused by the latter part, until Caleb rolls away from me and I see a full quorum. Their features are blurry without my glasses, but I still distinguish Mr. Oh entering the room in a wheelchair, followed by the rest of the Oh clan—a woman I presume to be his wife, plus Daniel and Lara. The room is so large that even this many people don't make it feel crowded.

Caleb helps me to a sitting position as they take a seat in various corners. Then he says to his family, "Give me a second, I need to get rid of this."

I watch, mortified, as he walks out of the room with the bucket of puke. Hiding my face, I say, "I'm so sorry for inconveniencing all of you."

Caleb's stepmother scoffs, clearly inconvenienced.

Mr. Oh shakes his head instead. "I should be the one apologizing."

I stay alone with my confusion until Caleb walks back in, taking his previous spot beside me. He grabs my hand and doesn't let me pull it away, even though his father is clearly watching.

"I had a plan, but never imagined it would go this wrong." Mr. Oh lets out an exhalation that deflates him. "There have been signs of discontent by some families in the kingdom, covert enough that I didn't know *who* was behind it. I needed to uproot the responsible parties before I pass down the kingdom to my son."

Folding her arms, his wife asks, "What does that have to do with the human girl?"

"Mom, let him talk." Daniel shakes his head. Next to him, Lara hugs him like *he* needs protection.

"Miss Lossada's unfortunate involvement is indirect by nature." The king of vampires pauses, as if he too is having trouble navigating his mind like me. "It goes back eighteen years ago."

I frown. How is that even possible? I was a kid and I didn't know any of them.

And then I remember my dad, whose last employer was Comed.

My spine grows stiff and I sit up straight.

Mr. Oh catches me eyes. "Yes, it's as you suspect."

Air fails to reach my lungs.

But he continues. "Arturo Lossada talked about his daughter, Serena, all the time. You don't remember, but I even showed up at your seventh birthday a few months before he died."

A sob tears from my throat. Caleb's hand squeezes mine just a tad tighter.

The next words come out slowly, like Mr. Oh has difficulty getting them out. "That night, I needed a group of men to protect Caleb for a short trip. There had already been a couple of attempts on his life…"

Oh, no.

Slowly, I blink up at Caleb. His eyes are downcast, sparking a recent memory. He looked the same while we rode on the taxi with Phelan and a passed-out Vlad. My chin trembles—the portent of fresh tears.

"That was the biggest operation." Mr. Oh chokes up. "I lost all my men that night, humans and vampires. And they took Caleb.

"He doesn't remember it, or your dad," Mr. Oh continues saying. "Because I wiped what happened that night from his mind. But in the cleanup process, I vowed I would always take care of you, no matter what. So I sponsored your stay at the orphanage. I gave you a college scholarship. And I thought that, under my employment, I would be able to keep you safe and provide the means for the life you wanted. And I've failed."

"You—you—" that's all I manage to say.

I want to punch him. Curse at him. Demand apologies. Hurt him.

But a tiny part of me also wants to thank him. And my body can't contain all these emotions right now.

Caleb's hand starts pulling away and at the last second, I grab onto it with both of mine.

"It's not your fault," I tell him with little energy.

A sniffle that doesn't belong to me tells me he's crying too. I don't care what his family thinks anymore, so I hug him.

That's when, from his corner, Daniel says, "Tell them the rest, Dad. It's time."

And if I thought this was all too much, the rest of the story gets worse.

CHAPTER 88
CALEB

Paraphrasing Serena, while I wipe my face with the back of my arm, I ask, "What now?"

With the way Dad sighs, I'm scared that the worst part of the story is what's coming now. I glance at Daniel and Lara. Something in their expressions makes me think they know what Dad is struggling to say.

"Son," he starts, dark eyes holding mine captive. "You must have noticed that over the years there have been a lot of threats to your safety."

"Yeah, but…" I look at all of them in turns. "Just as many as there have been on everyone."

Movement from the corner of my eye catches my attention. Daniel shakes his head. "No, little brother. None of us have had as many kidnapping or murder attempts, or other attacks."

What the—

"That night, while I looked everywhere for you," Dad continues, rubbing the bridge of his nose. "I decided I would go to any lengths to keep you safe. Even if that meant lying to the whole kingdom and my family."

"Dad, what are you talking about?" Shit, a headache's

forming in my temples, as if someone were hammering my head from both sides. My stepmother doesn't seem to be faring any better.

Beside me, Serena jolts. She lifts her face and through the curtain of messy hair half obscuring her face, she says, "Don't tell me…"

Dad's nodding like he can read her mind without the skin to skin contact required to compel. "Yes."

"Wait." My heart hammers in my chest, physically racing for the answer. "Can someone please spell it out in English? Or any other language I'm somewhat fluent in?"

"I'm also confused," Diana says, squirming as though uncomfortable in her skin. "What am I even doing here?"

Dad takes a couple of deep breaths. When I hone in on him, I can feel his heartbeat almost matching mine. He's nervous.

But Dad's never nervous.

Whatever this is, it's big.

"Caleb." He speaks slowly, the way he did when I was a toddler. "After I retrieved you, I wiped the minds of anyone in contact with you at the time. And yours. I needed to make sure no one had the certainty anymore that you were my heir."

My head hurts so bad that it makes me groan. I'd collapse if it wasn't for Serena holding me up.

Gritting my teeth through the pain, I look at Dad straight in the eye. "Dad, you're not making any sense."

"It wasn't too hard," he continues, as though I didn't speak. "After all, I never publicly admitted to having a son from an affair. Because of that, a lot of people thought my eldest born was naturally the heir."

"Cedric Oh," Diana screeches. "What are you implying?"

Dad faces her. "I also scrubbed your mind. It was the only way. I had to fool my family first to make sure the kingdom focused on Daniel, the son who isn't the rightful heir."

The world tilts.

A fierce stab of pain penetrates through my skull. With a groan, I fall back and for a moment there's nothing—nothing but pain and the lights on the ceiling. I close my eyes, and that's when I see it.

Someone is crying. Me.

My eyes are squeezed shut but there's no hiding the scent of blood… and worse. My cries are drowned by the sound of men shouting all around me, of limbs being torn apart from their bodies, of desperate pleas for mercy.

It feels like forever until the sounds die down, and even then I refuse to open my eyes. Even at eleven years old, I know that if I witness the carnage I won't be able to take it. I make myself as small as possible, and it's a long time until more sounds of fighting surround me.

And then, someone forces me to sit and Dad's voice commands me to open my eyes. I do, because I trust him. He's my dad. And he's finally saving me. I'm crying so hard that I can't even tell him how relieved I am.

"I'm sorry, my child." Dad grabs me by my cheeks, crusty with dirt and blood caked in by my tears. "It's going to be okay now. Just close your eyes and I'll make it all go away."

And again, I obey. Because I know Dad will keep me safe.

The pain in my head makes me writhe on the bed, until a pair of hands pins my shoulders hard to the mattress, and another pair seizes my ankles.

Someone shushes me. "Relax, Caleb. You're safe."

"What?" The question comes out of my throat as if spoken by someone else. I blink through the blur of my tears and find Daniel hovering over me. "Daniel—what's happening?"

His brow is wrinkled. "Your memories seem to be coming back to you by themselves."

Someone is breathing hard from beyond him. It's my step-mother. "You meant to tell me that—"

"Yes." That's Dad's voice. "Caleb is actually your son, Diana."

"No!" she yells. "I cannot—I refuse."

"Lara," Dad commands. "Hold her down."

The pressure around my ankles disappears. When Dan figures I've calmed down, he lets me go and turns away to whatever's happening with his mother. Mine.

"Shit." I curl up. "Shit. *Shit.*"

A gentle hand brushes the hair from my forehead.

Serena.

Blindly, I reach for her until I find her knee. I squeeze my fingers around the fabric of her pants. She doesn't say anything as she strokes my hair, but I feel her body vibrate with silent sobs.

"Stay still, Diana," Dad says. "Let me help you remember."

His wife grunts, maybe putting resistance. But then there's only a silence that prolongs for a while. It ends with a cry.

Through all this, Serena leans down to cover me with a hug.

I love her so much. I can't believe she's trying to console me when *she* must be devastated. And here I am, crumpled up like a useless ball.

My muscles spasm as I struggle to sit back up. The headache isn't as violent anymore, settling instead like a dull but steady throbbing.

Once I gather my bearings again, I find my stepmother— no, my mother—crumpled on a chair in more or less the same state as me. Dad lets go of her hand, probably done trying to restore her memories. His head leans back and he's out for the world.

Right now, I hate him as much as I love him.

He followed through on his promise, all those years ago. He certainly made it all go away. But for years, he piled lies onto more lies. He made me think I didn't have a mother. He made his wife live with resentment. And he also hurt my brother.

"Daniel," I croak out. He pauses in the middle of getting doses of blood ready for the king and queen. "You knew."

That was why he exploded on Dad not long ago.

"Yes." His back is turned to me as he tends to Dad, making the ill man more comfortable on his wheelchair.

"How?"

Sighing, Daniel straightens back up but he doesn't turn. "It was when Dad was assigning Phelan to guard you, after you and Serena were first attacked by those bikers. I accidentally overheard Dad telling Phelan to keep his heir safe with his life if he had to."

I lift one knee and rest my sweaty forehead on it. "So, Phelan knows too."

Daniel snorts softly. "Best guy to keep a secret, huh?"

"Did you know?" I ask Lara, who's been uncharacteristically quiet through this whole mess. But she's so calm, I have my answer even before she confirms it.

"Yeah, Daniel told me."

"I'm sorry," I tell her.

My sister-in-law reels. "What do you have to be sorry about to me?"

I cringe. "You married Daniel thinking one day you would be king and queen."

"No, silly." She shakes her head. "I married your brother because I love him, and funny enough, he seems to love me too."

"I do." Daniel's voice has that grumpy tone he gets sometimes. Right now, it brokers no doubt of his feelings for his wife.

Dad stirs awake, and my brother rushes to feed him a pint of blood. It smells rich in iron, which means it must be vampire blood. With all the efforts Dad has gone through in the past few days, after barely recovering from pneumonia, he'll need more than one pint.

As if on cue, Phelan walks into the room carrying a spare. Dad consumes it too, and only when he's done with it does color return to his face. Phelan picks up the empty containers and marches out of the room, shutting the door.

Shit, no wonder the guy became my shadow.

"So it's true, then?" I hate that my voice breaks but honestly, I feel broken all over. "I'm her son?"

My… mother, is still out cold. Her blonde hair spills over the side of the chair, brushing on the floor.

"Yes, you are the true heir, Caleb." Dad turns the wheelchair to face in my and Serena's direction. "And even though I tried to compel the entire kingdom into believing otherwise, some remained suspicious. So the attacks continued, and curiously enough they increased the moment Ernst Astor started introducing the idea that I should marry you off to his daughter."

The bed shakes almost imperceptibly. It's Serena, whose body betrays her the second the name Astor is mentioned. I pull her against my side and brush her arm to warm her up.

"I still don't understand," I admit.

Dad continues. "My suspicion was that the attacks were a way to seek proof of your real identity. That way, they would have certainty that a blood alliance would ascend the Astors to the top of the kingdom."

"And you still wanted me to marry her?" I wrinkle my nose, my forehead—damn, even my heart wrinkles. "Which, by the way, is *never* going to happen now."

"I never intended to marry you off to the Astors for real." Dad shakes his head. "I just needed to bait them."

"In other words," Daniel says in a deadpan. "Dad used all of us."

Serena stiffens against me. My jaw slackens.

Dad releases a long exhale. "I did, but I didn't expect things to careen out of control like this. I thought putting you right under their nose would blind them and keep you safe. I never imagined they would hurt a defenseless human girl."

For the first time in a while, Serena murmurs, "You underestimated Vivienne's level of evilness."

Dad's eyes twinkle with a smile that doesn't show on his lips. It disappears almost immediately. "You're right, Miss Lossada."

"You're out of your mind," I tell him.

"Maybe I am." Dad pauses, leaning his chin on his hand. "Add reckless too. Proud. But also scared. You don't know what I felt when I thought I lost you eighteen years ago."

A lump lodges in my throat, making it hard to swallow. "So, what now?"

"Now," Dad says slowly. "I have all the proof I need to go after the Astors. But this time I'll have to be more careful."

"And what about us?" I ask, motioning around the room to his wife still passed out, to his eldest son trying to shrink in on himself, to his daughter-in-law who hugs her stomach as if to shield her unborn child from all the drama.

"Us..." Dad's face pinches, holding back his emotions from display. "We'll have a lot of work to do to fix my mess."

CHAPTER 89
SERENA

"Tienes que comer, mija," says Maria, the housekeeper for the Oh family. She puts a plate of soup on the table before me along with some bread. It smells good, like it's all homemade and healthy and the kind of meal I haven't had in forever. But my stomach recoils at the notion of putting something in it.

I shake my head. My Spanish comes out a bit rusty when I say, "Disculpe, no me siento bien."

The woman puts her hands on her hips and gives me A Look. Even though I've never had a Mom, I know it well from every telenovela. It's either one step away from a stern talking to, or from a flying chancla. I don't think Maria would do the latter.

Sure enough, she goes for the former. "Señorita Lossada, usted lleva tres días sin comer bien. ¡Se va a desmayar otra vez! Si me tengo que sentar aquí en frente hasta que se coma todo, lo hago."

I want to whine. Maybe even shake my limbs around a bit too. But that requires much more energy than I have. I pick up the spoon and gather the least amount of soup possible with it. Maria watches with a hawk's eye as I put the food in my mouth.

Flavor explodes in my mouth, like the savory equivalent of having lived in a dark cave all my life and suddenly walking out into sunshine. My stomach groans so loud, I'm sure the entire house hears it.

Maria's face is the picture of proud as she watches me eat. "Muy bien."

Man, I wish I could cook like this. I wonder if she might teach me.

But I shake my head to myself. It's not like I have a right to come to this house again.

Daniel's voice drifts closer. "Maria, a certain someone wants some of your soup."

My heart skips a beat. Is it Caleb?

I've finally showered, brushed my teeth and changed into clean, borrowed clothes from Lara. But I still don't feel ready to face him. What am I going to say?

Except it's not Caleb. Daniel wheels Mr. Oh into the kitchen. As he moves the chairs away to leave more room for his dad's wheelchair, Daniel sniffs the air like a dog. "You know what? I'm open to a bowl of soup, too."

Maria chuckles. "You got it, boy. What about the others?"

"They're passed out." Daniel shakes his head and takes a seat beside his dad. "I think this all was too much for them."

I murmur, "I can't blame them."

Mr. Oh has been watching me all along. I continue eating because I also don't know what to say to him. *I hate you but also thank you* just doesn't seem to cover it.

"Have you noticed any side effects?" he asks me before thanking Maria for the meal she sets on the table.

I tear a few pieces of bread apart and take my time

munching on them. At first, it was a bit tricky to stop having sea legs. The floor seemed to shift with every step I took and I had to grab onto things not to become an acquaintance of the wood boards. But it's got better over the hours.

"I think…" I start, drinking a bit of of water in between. "The lingering thing seems to be a fog that sometimes comes all of a sudden. Is that going to happen all the time now?"

Daniel winces. "I couldn't say. Everyone reacts differently to something like this. The way I see it, you're actually doing great."

Mr. Oh nods. "You have an incredibly strong mind for a human."

That almost feels like a backhanded compliment.

"Thanks."

Daniel narrows his eyes, which while drinking soup makes him look like he has a grudge against it. He turns this stare between his dad and I, back and forth.

"In my opinion," he says very slowly. "Serena is a great candidate to be turned."

"No." The vehemence in Mr. Oh's voice makes his son and I jump in our seats. "I made a promise to her father and I've already botched it up. I'm not putting her in danger again."

"All I'm saying is, if she survived such a traumatic event relatively unscathed, it increases my confidence that she will make it after the turning." Daniel shrugs as if we were talking about the outcome of a sporting event, and not something monumentally life-changing. "In fact, turning her might even make these lingering side effects vanish entirely."

Mr. Oh frowns at him like he can't believe what she's hearing. "But she could die."

"Look, Dad. I never knew my real mother and all I know is the stories." His oldest son pauses, the real heartbreak leaking into his expression for a second. "But Serena and Caleb aren't in the same circumstances as you. And they're different people, too. I think it should be up to them to try if they want to."

"But I don't know that I do," I cut in. When their attention turns to me, it flusters me so much that I can no longer continue eating. I push the plate with the remainder of my food away. "All I've ever known is how to be a human—somewhat. Some days I feel like I wouldn't pass a Captcha. But I also can't picture myself as… as one of you."

Daniel tilts his head. "It's not that different."

"It's very different," Mr. Oh says in contrast. "The heightened sensory inputs alone can be enough to overload your brain, biologically speaking. Some people lose their minds."

In a soft voice, Daniel says, "Like for my mother."

Mr. Oh lowers his head for a moment. "Yes, like Paula."

It's the first time I hear her name, and I get why. The pain attached to his voice is almost palpable. I can't comprehend some of the choices Mr. Oh has made in life, and I definitely wouldn't do the same, but I do know what that pain feels like. I've been carrying it for eighteen years.

There's another reason I can't say aloud to them. Even if I did turn into a vampire, I don't think I'll be able to stand living a long life of watching Caleb from afar. Because now that it's clear he'll become the next king of vampires, it cements what we already knew.

We are two worlds apart.

"Think about it, though." Daniel nudges. "Dad looks like a badass but he's actually a softy. If you really want to be turned and you give him a puppy dog look, he will turn you."

Mr. Oh frowns but doesn't deny the allegations.

His son continues, "And I promise to provide the very best healthcare money can buy, plus my expertise as a vampire doctor. And if that's not enough, I'm certain Caleb will walk with you every step of the way."

Considering how Caleb didn't even bat an eye while I puked my guts out in front of him, I don't doubt it.

But how can I even wish to be with the guy who is going to be at the top of the vampire food chain? I try to reason it but a fog descends in my mind, and for a moment my existence is suspended in nothingness.

When I snap out of it, Daniel is pushing his chair back and as he gets up, he collects the empty plates and brings them to Maria. Before leaving, the human woman pats his cheek affectionately like a mother would.

"My son is unfortunately right," Mr. Oh grumbles. "If you have the conviction of becoming a vampire, I'll turn you."

I don't, though. There's no conviction. Only fear.

"I'm not ready for that." After a pause, I add, "Not right now."

"Understandable, it's been a lot."

"Would you two like dessert?" Maria asks from across the kitchen. "I know you're all talking about some serious stuff, but maybe it can be easier with some pie."

I'm full—of food and worries—but the woman has a point. Some sweetness in my life won't hurt. "Yes, please."

"Hah!" Smiling, she clicks her tongue. "Who's the one who didn't wanna eat before?"

My lips pull into a tiny smile. "I don't know her."

"For me too, please." Mr. Oh raises his hand and for the first time I notice it's shaking. He catches me staring at it and doesn't hide it. "I will, of course, not rush your decision. But the events might accelerate in the coming months... or weeks."

"What do you mean?"

"I'm dying." He delivers this without emotion, and it hits me like a sledgehammer. "And Caleb will have to be crowned king very soon before I'm too infirm for the ceremony."

My jaw slackens and for a good moment, all I can do is blink like a fish.

"And it won't set a good tone for his rule if his first action as king is to turn a human woman he wants to be with. So it would be best for you to be turned by me." Mr. Oh tilts his head in the same way Daniel did earlier. "Like my son said earlier, think about it."

My head swims so much, I fear I may pass out again.

CHAPTER 90
CALEB

Daniel and Dad want to talk the moment I wake up. They hover by my bed, tumbling upon each other to get a word in.

"Son, let's talk."

"I know there's a lot going on right now, little bro, but—"

The problem is, I don't want to listen. My body creaks like the rusty hinges of an old door as I struggle to sit up. The mattress and the bedsheets want to swallow me whole, and I would let them if it wasn't for all the noise.

"Stop." And for the first time in my life, they listen to my request. "I need some fresh air—by myself."

Sighing, Dad says, "Very well."

"Just let me help you." Daniel, ever the generous caretaker, helps me extricate myself from the bed until I'm stable on my feet.

I love my brother. I've always admired him for his intelligence and dedication to his work, but even more for his genuine goodness. I always knew he would make a great king, someone just and kind who could unite the unruly undercurrents behind the veneer of perfection most vampire families portray.

Now, I'm an usurper. Stealing the spot he was raised for.

They stay behind as I walk out of the room. Phelan stands guard outside the door. His expression betrays nothing, even though he's heard everything that's gone down in this house the past few days. But he's the most loyal of Dad's subjects. Even if I'm angry that he didn't tell me the truth, I can't fault him for following orders. It's what he's been trained to do.

I clap his shoulder before I continue walking down the hall of the family rooms. There's a lingering smell of food in the air that makes my stomach churn, but it can wait. First, I need to get rid of this feeling like I'm suffocating.

When I make it out onto the backyard, the earth and the grass are damp with the morning dew and it fills my lungs. If I concentrate past that, beyond the trees, I can catch the scent of the marine breeze. So I don't stop walking and cross the entire golf course we have for a backyard, through my favorite shady path between rows of palm trees. Eventually, I catch sight of the strip of white sand from our private beach, the blue ocean in the horizon.

I kick my shoes off and rip my socks off. When I dig my toes into the sand, I know I'm home.

And shit, it turns out this island might be my home in the future too.

Slowly, I lower myself to sit down on the sand. My eyes get lost in the horizon, which feels apt. I can no longer see what my life might be like. Before, I was on track to take care of the business side of the family affairs and hopefully never have to marry Vivienne. But now…

What do I do?

The entire vampire kingdom thinks Daniel is the heir. And while Dad mostly succeeded in keeping attention from me, what little I got wasn't exactly good. I'm the young son, the irresponsible one, the weak one. None of those things have changed.

I'm still Caleb Oh, the spare. Or that's how I feel like. It's all I know.

Lifting my knees up, I hide my face between them and just breathe in, breathe out. The salty breeze feels like a balm to my soul. If I could stay here forever, rule the kingdom from the shade of palm trees, everything would be perfect. But I can't see this going so smoothly.

Especially with Vivienne in the picture.

A shuffling sound very far behind me makes me turn. I feel her scent before she appears into view.

"There you are." Serena sounds exhausted, but she continues putting one foot in front of the other until she joins me. Like me, she kicks off her shoes and plops up beside me. "I couldn't believe at first that you folks have a private beach, but at second I remembered you're billion-aires. That's more than enough zeroes for a strip of land."

I snort a little. "It was a perfect purchase. No one would suspect the owners of an island in the Caribbean to be vampires."

"Very on the nose." She also brings her knees up to rest her arms on them, then lowering her chin. "Are you okay?"

"I should be asking you that." I dig a little hole in the sand with my index, another beside it, and draw an arch under-neath. A sad face.

Serena takes a deep breath. "No, I'm not okay."

"Me neither." We both linger there for a moment. There's no use in lying to each other. "I'm sorry."

"It's not your fault."

"It is." I brush the sand away, erasing the sad face. "Your dad wouldn't have been killed if it wasn't for me. You must hate me."

She squeezes tighter into a ball. Her voice shakes. "I'm angry, but not at you."

At Dad. And I can't blame her. I wasn't even able to meet his eyes earlier, lest he discover all the shame, anger, and hurt in mine. I can't imagine what Serena must be feeling.

"I understand if you never want to talk to me again," I say, keeping my eyes on the rolling waves crashing on the shore. "If not for the history between us that we didn't know... for the fact I put you in danger with Vivienne. It was reckless to leave you alone with her."

"None of us could possibly anticipate that she would do something like... that." A shiver racks through her body and I want to hug her, but I don't dare find out where we stand after all of this. "She is unhinged."

"To put it mildly. But I will admit I'm a little glad I won't have to marry her after all."

Serena gives me a side eye. "A little?"

Finally, I smile. It feels as if I was being born again. "A lot. Very much. So relieved I could cry. But I already cried for hours because all this other stuff is also too much. So I'm tired. That's mostly what I feel like."

"Same for me." Serena takes a deep breath. "Just know that... I'm still processing everything, but I don't resent you for any of it. Not one bit."

The breeze picks at my hair and I brush out of my face. Leaning back on my elbows, I bask in the sun. It doesn't chase away a certain coldness in my heart. I wonder if it'll always be there.

Her words bring me some relief. But they're not all I need.

"I'm going to break off the engagement." I say, feeling her shift beside me. Looking at her, I say, "Beyond that, I just want to be with you."

Her lips part, and for a long while that's her only reaction.

"I know that all the issues keeping us apart are still there." I remember when she listed them out the first time. Me being rich while she's poor, being her boss, a vampire. "But, I don't want to lose you."

"Caleb…"

"I can turn you into a vampire when I'm the king," I continue, sitting back up. "Then at least we won't be different on that account. As for work, I'm more than happy to quit."

"Caleb." Whereas before she said my name in a wistful way, now it sounds like a warning. Like Serena Lossada, the assistant.

I fight against a grin.

"As for the money." I rub my chin, pondering various angles. "I'd also be happy being a house husband supported by his working wife."

"Caleb!" Serena smacks my leg so hard it leaves a sting. "That's not how things work."

I gasp. "Aren't you a feminist?"

"I am, or I try to be." She shakes her head. "That's not the point. I'm not sure I want to turn into a vampire."

I do a double take. Somehow, I didn't consider this possibility.

"Why not?"

"It's…" She leans forward onto her knees again, making herself small. "It's overwhelming to contemplate. And it's not like I can jump from random-human-barely-getting-by to dating the king of vampires."

"Dating?" I blow a raspberry. "I intend to make you my queen."

With a burst of energy I didn't know she was capable of in her current state, Serena jumps to her feet and away from me. "Are you off your rockers?"

"Yes?" I drag the word as I get up to my feet too. Before she can react, I pull her against me by her waist. Smiling down at her, I say, "I'm off my rockers for you."

Serena smacks me again and tries to free herself, but not with enough power that she'll succeed. "Caleb, you need to think this through. I don't know a lot about your world, but I know enough to imagine that people will say things."

I shrug. "They can talk all the shit they want."

"But it might not just be talk." She worries her lower lip and it makes me want to worry it for her. "Look at what Vivienne and her people have done. Who's to say she and others won't react violently?"

"It's a possibility. But I'm going to be absolutely crushed if I have to let you go from my life. That's a certainty."

Serena shakes her head and when I try to lean down, she brings her hands up against my chest and pushes me away. Not that I go far with her in the circle of my arms. "But Caleb, you can't always get what you want."

"I never do."

This makes her blink rapidly, probably thinking spoiled billionaire plus private yacht plus private beach does not compute. I always got what Dad wanted me to have, but never what *I* wanted for myself. And now that's only one thing: Serena.

"So, trust me," I continue saying. "I'm going to fight tooth and nail for you if I have to. I promise that. Now let me kiss you, woman."

The way she's shaking her head makes me think for a moment that she doesn't want me to, but in the next second she's the one who pulls me down to meet her lips.

CHAPTER 91
SERENA

The plan for now is to pretend like nothing is wrong while Mr. Oh moves his people to identify everyone who is involved with Vivienne Astor.

This means, I go back to the office everyday and pretend like Caleb is essentially a stranger. I try to make note of anyone who might be watching with the intent to report to Vivienne, but days go by and I don't catch any abnormal activity. It might be because I spend half of my time sitting at my desk, with Phelan standing guard by the door to Caleb's office, and the stoic man tends to drive away any curious eyes.

The other half of the time I spend in Caleb's office where, yes, we work, but also where I fight really hard against his charms.

One afternoon, I sit on the couch across from him going over a financial report, and even though I've been speaking for a solid ten minutes on the topic, there hasn't been a single answer. When I glance up, I catch Caleb staring at me in a way that immediately makes my temperature rise.

He has one end of his pen trapped between his lips, which

paired with the lowered eyelids and the disheveled hair typical of his late afternoon, are giving me serious bedroom vibes.

"What?" I ask him.

Without letting go of the pen, his lips stretch into a little smile. "I like that your lips, nails, and shoes match."

They're all red, and with my black dress even I think I look pretty sharp. I wore the outfit for myself, to boost my confidence artificially for just a bit. Anything that can help me feel less scared and confused.

Except for the lipstick, that one I put on specifically because of Caleb.

Clearing my throat, I say, "Yeah, well. I figured if I wore a bold lipstick color you'd be less inclined to kiss me and make a mess that will implicate us."

That's what he gets after kissing me every time we're alone this week—which, on the one hand is delightful, but on the other is terrifying. What if someone walks in on us? And worse, what if I become addicted to the point of no return?

Caleb hums from deep in his throat and finally puts the pen away. "Too bad it's making me want to get messy."

He starts to rise from his seat, but moved by a shot of adrenaline, I jump away from the couch and make it to the door even before he's on his feet.

"Stop." I raise one hand. "We really need to get back to this proposal."

"I have a different proposal for you, though."

Damn it. I can't get my legs to move and take me out of the office, not when Caleb advances in slow mo. He pulls at the knot of his tie, which is honestly one of the moves that hits me the hardest. And sure enough, my knees are growing weak.

He traps me against the door with his body, diving for my lips until he stops a millimeter away. Instead, I feel the pad of his thumb brush my bottom lip. "You don't need to fight the attraction between us so hard, you know?"

"Actually, I do." I push his chest with all the strength I'm capable of right now, which isn't much. "While it's true a few things have changed—some drastically—the ones not in our favor remain the same."

"You're forgetting something." Caleb bypasses my lips altogether and goes for a new attack, placing hot, open mouthed kisses on the column of my throat. By my ear, he whispers, "I'll be king, which means I get to make the rules."

When I shiver, he splays his hands across my back and pushes me flush against him. My body has no choice but to arch against his, as he's so much taller and also the sole reason why I remain standing. I bite my lips so hard that it will leave a mark, trying to stop myself from groaning when his tongue strokes a spot that sends sensation down to my toes.

I need to escape. If I don't, I'm at severe risk of returning the favor.

With monumental effort, I tear myself away from him and open the door.

Outside, Phelan gives me a look like he knows exactly what was going down inside the office.

"Make sure he doesn't follow me," I say to him as I pack up my things in a rush. And maybe Phelan agrees that it's the right approach, because when Caleb tries to open the door and walk out, Phelan holds it shut on brute strength alone.

I mouth the words *thank you* and make a run for the elevators.

My heart is working more overtime than me this week, trying to make up for the time-suck that having part of my memory ended up becoming. And while work is certainly better than sitting at home by myself stewing in my fears, it also comes with a bonus risk. Caleb.

It's not like he's the only one who feels the attraction. Every day I get more and more smitten with him. But letting myself follow the instinctual need for Caleb is impossible, when there's still a major issue at hand.

You know, the one where he's a vampire and I'm a human.

I hail a taxi in front of the office and recite the address of the orphanage to the driver. For days, I've been thinking about visiting Sister Emilia. It will help me to be in the presence of someone who has the best intentions for me, but will also give it to me straight. Lara and Marissa are no help, bless them, because they just keep telling me to latch onto Caleb—their words were: preferably with your legs around his waist—and that's not quite the advice I'm looking for.

Still, when I arrive to the orphanage and the taxi drives away, I can't find the way to broach this conversation with the nun.

Sister Emilia, a lot has happened since the last time I saw you. Mainly, I'm considering being turned into a vampire so I can get it on with my boss's son, who by the way is now going to become the king of vampires.

That doesn't quite work.

"Serena?"

I jump in my skin. Sister Emilia appears behind me with a grocery bag.

"Uh…"

She chuckles. "It's good to see you're sharp as usual, child."

"Now, you're just teasing." I frown, but it's hard to conceal a smile. "Actually, I was hoping we could have a chat."

"That would be lovely, but first I need to deliver this." She lifts the bag up in plain sight.

It turns out to be medicine for one of the nuns, who is nursing a cold. After we make that visit and stop to check in on the kids having dinner in the cafeteria, Sister Emilia and I sit on a bench in the yard, sipping Capri Suns.

"Is everything going all right now?" she asks me, probably

reminiscing about the time I spent here after suddenly being unemployed.

The problem is, so many worse things have happened now.

Sighing, I don't even know where to start the tale.

"I'm employed." I sip on the sweet juice for a moment. "I also moved into a studio apartment by myself."

"That's very good." She faces me for a second. "And yet, you appear distraught."

I wince. "I—yes. I am. Since the last time I was here, I've learned that some things weren't exactly as I thought."

"Like your friends being not quite human?" As my jaw drops, Sister Emilia shrugs just a bit. "There are many things in this world that aren't human."

My head swims a bit at that but I've hit the ceiling for shock already. Rather than absorb more of it, I have to let off some steam. It's what I'm here for.

I tell Sister Emilia how Cedric Oh was linked to my family, all those years ago. It was her who told me that Dad worked for Comed Solutions, and it was I who thought nothing much of it, when it was actually everything.

"And there's more," I say, lifting my glasses to swipe at the first tear that falls. "Dad died while trying to protect Caleb, my current boss."

"The boy who came looking for you that night?"

I nod. "And also the one I might or not have feelings for."

"Oh, dear." She rubs my back in smooth circles. "That is a lot."

"But if I want to be with him," I say, biting my lip. "I have to… change a lot, and I don't know what to think."

Sister Emilia sighs. "That is a difficult conundrum."

"Is it that bad I'm considering it?" I murmur, leaning my head on her shoulder.

"Do you love him?"

"I—Yes, I do." I close my eyes. "Despite everything, I do."

"And does he love you back?"

I think about it and a million little things pop up in my head that point at me saying, "He does."

"And here's the most important question for me," Sister Emilia says, building the suspense. "Does he believe in marriage by the Church?"

"Actually." I sit up straight, grinning. "He's a Christian, so probably."

Of all the responses I could expect, the last one was Sister Emilia laughing. "Then you have my blessing."

Something bubbles inside of me that explodes as laughter. It's not like this solves the challenge of him being the heir to a kingdom, underground or not, and me being just a pauper. But this is a worry I had in the back of my mind, and why I came here to talk about it. Myth says vampires are undead and have no souls.

Caleb, Daniel, Lara, Marissa and even Phelan, they all have souls. They're warm and kind, and some of the best people I've met in my life. Maybe the myth comes from those more like Vivienne instead.

I hug Sister Emilia and later that night, when I'm laying in bed trying to sleep, I think I'm not so conflicted with possibly becoming a vampire bride anymore.

CHAPTER 92
CALEB

On Friday night, I'm working late at the office to pick up Dad's slack. Words I never thought I would string together.

Daniel and I decided to split Dad's workload to allow him more rest. To everyone else at the company, we say he's recovering at home after an accident playing golf.

Naturally, the vampire population goes on high alert. Short of dismemberment, there isn't much we can't pull through from. Jon and Marissa are put in charge of fielding the questions from the heads of the vampire families, as well as squash any rumors about Dad.

Also, because Daniel and I aren't complete fools, we increase security measures around the family. Lara has a whole entourage around her at all times, as well as Daniel. All I need is Phelan. But I did assign a couple of his guys to tail Serena everywhere, and make sure she stays safe through the day *and* night.

Vivienne has tried to contact me for wedding planning bullshit more times than I can count, but I ignore her. The few times when that has been impossible—for example when she's showed up unannounced to Comed—I show her I'm too busy to play with her, and send her packing. Thankfully, she still has that southern instinct of not making a scene, despite very much wanting to.

The last text I got from her reads, *You won't get away from this, Caleb Oh.* I'm sure she means the wedding itself, more than the flower arrangements for it.

What she doesn't know is that I intend to. Soon, I'll break the engagement off. But first, I need to take care of Dad. And the woman who turned out to be my real mother. And that's why I may have to pull an all-nighter today.

Not gonna lie, I miss the days when I was a rich nobody. Just lounging aboard the Bad Blood, which I named after the mistaken belief that I was illegitimate. Yacht therapy is just what I need right now—preferably with Serena next to me. Bonus points if I can get her to wear an itty bitty bikini.

Alas to all those things.

I pull at my hair as I finally finish reviewing a contract with a supplier in its entirety and sign it. Two more to go.

That depressing thought goes out the window as my phone rings. There's a hierarchy of immediate worries that pop up in brain in succession. First, Dad. Second, Serena. Third, Daniel and Lara. My mother would never call me. Dead last, Vivienne.

It turns out to be my favorite option.

"Serena."

"Caleb." She stretches my name to an impossible length. "I'm in trouble."

I jump to my feet like lightning. "Are you home?"

"Yes, but—"

"I'll be there shortly." Running on adrenaline, I shut down the call and burst out of the office. "Phelan, call the guys. Serena's in trouble."

He pulls out his phone and follows me as I barrel down to

the elevators. After a couple of rings, one of his guys picks up. Phelan says, "Status report."

From the other end of the call, I hear, "Coast is clear."

"Check again," Phelan commands before hanging up. He catches me in the middle of rubbing my head. "Calm down."

"When there's a sociopath out in the loose who might harm the woman you love, *you* calm down."

The elevators ding and Phelan joins me in silence. The more I will the journey to be quick, the longer it feels. I probably look unhinged running across the lobby to the parking lot exit, but I don't care. We're not on our way soon enough.

I call Serena again to check in on her and she doesn't pick up, and I feel like I'm going to throw up my heart.

"I swear, if Vivienne's done something again—and don't you dare tell me to calm the hell down again."

Cool as a cucumber, Phelan says, "I didn't use the word hell."

I give him a weird look that he doesn't catch, as he's driving. "Is that really what's most important right now?"

I run out of the car even before it stops when we get to Serena's new apartment complex. I find one of our guys close to the building entrance. He tries to say something but I'm not exactly in listening mode. I break the front door again and make another mental note to ask the guys to fix it tonight, after I've made sure Serena is fine. After all, her safety also needs working locks.

At long last, I get to her door. I slow down for a breath and knock. This is the one lock I don't want to break if I can help it.

Fortunately, she opens the door in a reasonable time. She's not wearing her glasses and her hair is a bird's nest. Also, she sways.

"Caleb?" The smell of alcohol in her breath hits me like a brick to my nose. "What are you doing here?"

I peek around her into the tiny apartment. Apart from her living room looking like a tornado went through, I can't detect any intruders. "What's wrong?"

Serena squints. "I'm in trouble."

"Yes, you said that." Gently, I push her out of the way and walk into her studio apartment. To be safe, I close the door behind me. "What's the trouble?"

She hasn't moved very far and looks up at me from up close. I debate whether to fix her oversized T-shirt—right now it's showing the strap of her bra on one shoulder—but I'm finding I quite like the messy look. In fact, it'd be better if the collar falls just a bit lower at the front.

Then she hiccups and I almost get drunk from the smell alone.

"Whoa." I laugh and push her away. "You've become a distillery."

"I needed something to help me think." She sways and I steady her by her arms. "And Venezuelans are supposed to have rum running through their veins, so I got its help."

I don't think it's too safe for her to walk, so I pick her up in my arms. Serena doesn't complain as I expected. Instead, she laces one arm around my neck.

"What did you need so much help to think about?"

"Us," she says. "And onions."

"Ah." My heart rate slows down now that I know this isn't the kind of emergency I feared. Carefully, I settle her in bed avoiding the laptop sitting in the middle of it. It seems to be showing some sort of soap opera. I shut down the device and put it away. "So, what did you think about?"

Serena laces her fingers over her belly and stares at the ceiling. "Would I have more layers if I become a vampire than now, or does a human have more layers?"

A laugh tears out of me. That's the kind of philosophy alcohol can sometimes induce, all right.

"Hopefully less," I say, sitting down beside her. I make a point of wiggling my eyebrows. "A whole lot less."

"You perv."

I shrug. "It's no secret that I have the hots for you."

Her brow crashes into a deep frown. "Just so you know, we're not gonna have sex unless we marry."

"Then we better marry quick." I smile at the way the frown seems to grow darker. "And for your information, our marriage might last about three hundred years or more, which is plenty of time to make up."

Over and over.

Serena takes a deep breath. "Wow, I actually thought you'd say you can't wait."

"I don't *want* to wait." I try not to laugh at the way her mouth opens. "In truth, I wish you were slightly less drunk and a lot more undressed, and that I could have my wicked way with you in this bed right here, right now. But respecting you is much more important than what I want."

The only warning I get is a sniffle. In the next second, Serena is full-on wailing.

"Er…" I lean forward to wipe away her tears. "Are you okay? I'm sorry if—"

Still crying, Serena pulls me by my tie until my lips crash against hers. I freeze, torn between wanting to kiss her bad enough it hurts, and also not sure it's the right thing to do when she's this drunk.

"Just kiss me, you silly vampire."

Woe on me if I don't please the lady.

I brace my arms around her not to crush her. But when her arms come around my neck to push me against her, it's hard to stay courteous or to think straight. My lips stroke hers in a caress that makes me wonder how much better it will be after we're married and I can peel all the layers off this future onion.

Then I pull away. "Wait, does this mean you want to be turned?"

"I was considering it until you stopped kissing me."

"Oh, in that case," I say, chucking my shoes off.

I crawl over her and caress up her legs. I like that she's wearing leggings—I can feel the contours of her muscles and pretend like I'm touching her skin.

When I reach her thighs, I spread them open and settle in between. Serena gasps and I enjoy the way her eyes widen as I sneak one hand under her T-shirt to feel the bare skin of her side.

"Please, allow me to convince you." With that, I dip my head down to begin a long, dangerous make out session.

CHAPTER 93
SERENA

One second I'm making out with Caleb, and the next I'm dead asleep. The blackout lasts long enough that when I open my eyes next, the place is dark except for the streetlights leaking in between the blinds.

I don't feel awful yet, which must mean I'm still under the influence of Cacique, my favorite brand of Venezuelan rum. However, my mouth feels like it's stuffed with cotton. I need some water.

But something prevents me from turning.

I make out a figure in the dark. It takes me a second to go from panic, to figuring out it's Caleb asleep in my bed. He's been working really hard this week and staying at the office much longer than I do.

Slowly, in increments, I toss until I'm on my side. I prop my head up with an arm. With the free hand, I brush his hair away from his forehead. The fact that he doesn't stir tells me he's out cold.

I whisper under my breath. "You must be so tired."

I can't see how things will improve from here on out. There's so much going on, between overseeing his dad's treatment, to taking care of his fiancée, to dealing with the fallout from his dad's lies. I know he doesn't get along with Diana Oh-Mancini and suddenly finding out she's his biological mother won't change that, but it will definitely force him to reexamine that relationship.

And then there's me. No decision I make is actually going to make Caleb's life easier.

If I decide to stay a human and away from him, it will crush both of us. But if I decide to be turned into a vampire, it won't exactly be a bed of roses. Mr. Oh said as much, and even though he's a proven liar, I believe him in this.

I brush Caleb's jaw softly. His stubble prickles at my skin and I marvel at the texture. He's always so clean shaven I didn't even know he could grow a beard. But it's not like I know everything about him.

I want to find out, though. I want to know what his beard looks like. And to feel it against my skin. As a matter of fact, I want to feel his skin. Just brushing his jaw is not enough.

"I wish things were easier for us." My thumb lingers on his lower lip, soft like velvet. "Why couldn't we have had a normal office romance? You could've been an employee at a different department, who I kept running into at the cafeteria or something."

I sigh. My arm is starting to grow numb, so I lay back down, still staring at him. His chest rises and falls with deep, steady breaths. I'm glad I don't have a couch he could've considered using to sleep, but it's still a struggle not to burrow against his side.

"And in this dream scenario," I continue saying, so low my voice barely comes out. "You would've been human."

I guess this is why people say reality is stranger than fiction. Never in my life did I imagine vampires are real, or that one would be my boss. And that I would fall for him.

"Then it would've been much easier to love you," I say,

closing my eyes and just breathing in his scent, masculine and warm.

"It doesn't have to be hard," Caleb says all of a sudden, making me jump in my skin.

"You were awake?"

"More like I couldn't sleep." He rolls onto his side. The second I try to cover my face, he pulls my hands away. "So you love me?"

My mouth opens into the shape of an o. "How did you come to that conclusion?"

"Easy." He shrugs. "You said if I was human it'd be easier to love me. Meaning, you already do, but the fact I'm a vampire makes it hard."

A yelp is all that comes out of my throat.

Caleb puts an arm over me and pulls me closer. The other arm he sneaks under my head. Our noses brush as he says, "But that's why I say it doesn't have to be hard. Just love me and let me love you for a long time."

"Can I?" I swallow down a lump in my throat. "Do I even have that right?"

Thanks to the dim light, I can see a frown fall on his features. "What prompts that question?"

"I mean." I clear my throat. "If vampire royalty is the same as human royalty, I don't think your subjects will take well to you being with a plebeian. Of color. Human."

He wrinkles his nose. "There'll be people who oppose. Especially those who wanted me to marry their daughters."

"You mean there were more candidates than Vivienne?"

"Nothing as serious." He waves a hand. "But it's not like they'll like everything I do, and I don't want to live catering to their expectations."

I mull it over, biting my lip. "That's surprisingly mature of you, yet still rebellious."

"My brand, ladies and gentlemen." Caleb smiles and he leans closer to place a peck on my nose. "So, stop thinking about others and think about yourself. Or about me and my poor heart beating for you."

"You're so cheesy." I smack him, and an invisible force makes it impossible for me to pull my hand away. Instead, it parks itself comfortable on the hardness of his chest. Trying to turn the tables, I ask, "So you love me?"

"Oh, I do." That renders me speechless, which makes his eyes positively sparkle. "I think it started the moment I saved you from drowning and saw your clothes were fully transparent."

A sound between a groan and a shout comes out of me. "I hate you."

Shaking with chuckles, Caleb gets back on top of me. It's dangerously comfortable to wrap my legs around him. He curls a finger and hooks the collar of my T-shirt lower, allowing him plenty of opening to kiss my throat. There, he says, "I'm kidding, it was when I was wrapped around you in bed in Spain."

I hit his side, and we both jolt when my hand makes contact with his bare skin. Somehow, his shirt got untucked from his slacks and rode up. But when I try to pull my hand away, he grabs it and puts it on his bare skin again.

I'm not complaining. This was one of the things I wanted to do. As he continues speaking against my throat, I brush my hands up the hard muscles of his back.

"You know I'm kidding, right?" Caleb asks before gently biting my earlobe. "I fell in love with you the moment our eyes first met."

"Really? While you were half naked?"

"I mean, I knew I wanted you to get me fully naked right then."

I laugh. "You're terrible."

Caleb's grinning when he pulls away to look down at me. His hand brushes my hair off my face and slowly, his expression grows more serious. "I honestly don't know when it started, but I feel like I loved you since before I met you."

This time there's no trace of joking in his eyes, and I gasp. My chest wells up with something warm, something that activates my factory of endless tears.

"That's funny," I say, not laughing at all. Caleb kisses my temple, where the first tear falls. "Because I feel the same way."

I can't think of one moment when I thought, *this is it, I love this man.* Instead, I gradually fell for him with everything he did. Every smile, every joke, every time he went to incredible lengths to keep me safe, every glance that made me feel like I was truly being seen.

How can I deny this sweet, all-consuming feeling inside of me? How can I turn away from him for an entire lifetime, when I know he exists?

Even worse, what if I actually don't get time with him?

"Caleb." A sob tears out of my throat. "I'm scared."

"Of what, Serena?" With languid strokes of his thumbs, he brushes my tears as they fall. "Of me? Of my family? Of what people will say?"

I shake my head. "Of not surviving it… the turning."

His lips part to release a shaky breath. "That terrifies me too."

I grab onto his face, just wanting to make sure he's real. That this isn't a figment of my imagination. Maybe he feels the same, because he grabs one of my hands and places it on his chest again. His heartbeat is strong and steady against my skin, and I'm thankful for it.

"You're my precious person," Caleb says, his hand over mine. "What am I going to do if I lose you?"

"I don't want that." I pull him down into a fierce hug. "I really don't. I want to be with you for a long, long time."

Caleb brings his arms under and around me. "Then we have to try. I promise, you won't be alone. And when it's all said and done you'll be the queen of vampires, because you're already the queen of my heart."

CHAPTER 94
CALEB

Today is the big day. When I'll break the engagement off with Vivienne.

After working day and night with our people to suss out her collaborators, we found she has a network of gangs in every major city of the US like the motorbike club here. And while we can't imprison them for being employed by Vivienne or the Astors, we do keep tabs on them.

Now we need to make her castle of cards topple over. The first step is to take away what she wants so desperately: the chance of being queen.

I called her up to meet at the same restaurant as before. This time, only Phelan will tag along. Serena is safely sequestered in my parents' mansion, where she'll be working remotely for the foreseeable future.

That is, until the crowning.

I check my watch. Time is passing slower than usual, or that's my anxiety talking. I even ran this plan by Dad, who agreed with it. Yet, there's a sick feeling in my stomach. But Phelan is behind me and all across the building, at least two dozen of our support guys keep watch on all exits.

Pulling out my phone from the pocket of my blazer, I fire up a text message to Serena. *Are you okay?*

As can be, she responds right away. *Everything going okay there?*

She hasn't arrived yet.

After making sure the recorder of my phone is working, I put the device back in my pocket. I'll give Vivienne her pride. She has to be absolutely fuming after ghosting her for all the wedding preparations. If I was her, the lesser revenge I'd take is making me wait.

The other end of the scale would be killing me, but that's what Phelan's here to prevent.

Besides, this time I gave her such short notice she couldn't book the restaurant for ourselves. I chose the appointment smack at noon, which means the place is packed. Business people and older wealthy couples seem to be the main customer demographics at this time of the day. We keep attracting glances, because it's not common to see a guy sitting by himself with another standing guard.

With all these witnesses, Vivienne won't be able to jump at me with her fangs out.

There's a slight shift in the conversations around me, as if something in particular has caught the collective's attention. I know what it is before I turn to confirm, and sure enough Vivienne's strutting in wearing a black dress with more cutouts than anyone else would feel comfortable with.

"Aren't you cold?" I ask her as she sits across the table from me.

Her red lips purse. "Is that all you have to say?"

How pissed would she be if I say yes?

I mean, the purpose of today's meeting is to thoroughly make her lose her shit, but not this quick.

So I grab the menu and peruse it slowly. "Lunch today is on me."

Vivienne laughs low, in a way that makes me fight to

suppress as shiver. I still can't help feeling like she's the one who has all the cards.

"You owe me more than lunch," she says, humoring me by checking out the menu. "I'll forgive you for not doing your part for the wedding planning so far, but that has to stop."

"Or else?" I ask while checking out the salad menu. "Hmm, all the salads have some animal product in them, huh? Do you think they'll mind it if I ask for a vegan option?"

Vivienne snaps her menu shut so hard, the sound makes several heads turn our way. She leans over the edge of the table. "Or else I'm going to show you how dangerous it can be to mess with me."

Time to turn up the asshole-o-meter to the max.

Setting my menu down, I signal one of the servers over. "I would like this salad here, but please replace the original dressing by balsamic vinaigrette. Also, take out any dairy or meat. Replace them by the candied pecans from this other salad, the marinated artichokes from this one and—oh, deep fried tofu would work great."

"Er, absolutely, sir. Anything else?" The poor server looks confused and will probably get the order wrong.

"Yes," I add, handing him the menu. "And a Fanta for the guy behind me."

Typically, the woman should order first. By the time the server turns to Vivienne, there's murder in her face. "A steak for me. Rare."

I make a point of wrinkling my nose at her dietary choice. "You should eat more vegetables."

"Caleb." My name comes out like a curse between her gritted teeth. Vivienne takes a deep breath and leans back. "Fine, be as obnoxious as you want for now. That all will change when we're married."

"How so?" I tilt my head.

"Either you'll finally give into me. Or, you learn not to go against my wishes the hard way."

I take a sip from my water and sigh loudly when I'm done. "Like you've been showing me all these months?"

Subtly, she closes her lips and that's the only reaction I get.

"You couldn't possibly think I'd never notice." I muse, lacing my fingers over my stomach and leaning back into the plush chair. "I have to admit your compelling skills are top notch and it was hard to find proof until I got that text from my assistant. You know, seconds before you tried to wipe every memory of me from her mind."

Vivienne's eyes, as blue as the sky but as soulless as a rock, grow impossibly wide. "So what? That doesn't change anything. We're still going to get married. And it's not like a measly human matters in the grand scheme of events."

"Let me ask you something." I make sure to keep my limbs close to myself, especially now that I know what she could do if she touches my skin. "What were you trying to accomplish by attacking me so many times?"

Snorting, she crosses her arms delicately. "Just because you're the last son of Cedric Oh, doesn't mean I'm thrilled with marrying a weakling."

I pinch my nose. "So, it was like a test?"

"And also a way to show you that my assets are all you need." Her lips stretch into a smile. "Not just my physical assets, I mean. But my security detail. It's what makes this such a great alliance."

"And what were you expecting to get in return?" I shrug, and here's the golden moment. "It's not like I'm the one who's going to be king."

Vivienne's eyes narrow just a bit. If she knew this for a fact she'd barrel through the comment, because everyone in the kingdom is still sure that Daniel is the heir.

But not Vivienne. She lingers in silence for a while longer.

"That may be so," she says slowly. "But like I said, there's power in the Oh name. That's what you'll give me in exchange for my family assets."

It's exactly as Dad said, months ago. It tastes foul to confirm that the reason Vivienne wanted to sink her claws into me is because, essentially, she could.

In theory, being the spare, I wouldn't have access to the larger security detail of the Oh family, leaving me vulnerable. Plus, on the other hand I'm considered to be weak by the vampire community. I've spent more time studying or traveling than defeating vampires to acquire their mutations.

But on the other hand, those were just bargaining chips for the real prize. The zealousness behind her desire to marry me can't just be for those petty reasons.

Her real prize is the truth—that I'm the real heir, and she can only know that if her compelling skills are as good as Dad's. It's the only way she wouldn't be subject to Dad's misinformation.

"And if I don't behave, you'll compel me to?"

"I was hoping you would cooperate instead, but it's an option." Vivienne shrugs. "One that is becoming more and more attractive by the day."

The server arrives with our meals and I wait until the table is loaded to speak again. "What if my own compelling skills increase enough to match yours?"

Vivienne smiles against her glass of wine, leaving a red lipstick stain across the rim. "As if. You would have to seduce the blood out of thousands of vampires to compete against me."

"So that's how you did it, huh?" I stab onto the salad. "Why didn't you compel me already? I'm sure you would rather not wait until we're married to get me to behave."

"Because you won't let me touch you long enough."

I laugh. "Wow, kudos to my survival instinct, huh?"

"But like I said," she continues, not letting me savor the moment. "That will all change at the marriage ceremony itself."

Ah, yes. The way a blood alliance—also known as a marriage—is conducted between vampires is through an exchange of blood. Typically, the couples will bite each other's throats in front of their families as witnesses. In doing this, there's plenty of skin to skin contact. Hands on bare chests and backs, lips on throats. It would be the perfect opportunity for Vivienne to compel me to do her bidding forever.

It's a perfect plan.

Too bad for her, I now have Dad's firm backing to not marry her.

"Unfortunately," I say while cutting an artichoke. "I don't want to marry someone as evil as you."

The food tastes extra delicious watching Vivienne freeze like a statue.

After swallowing, I add, "I sent the video as proof to my dad, and he also agrees that it wouldn't be good to make a blood alliance with someone as dangerously ambitious as you."

Vivienne slams her hands on the table hard enough to topple everything out of place. The wood beneath makes a cracking sound. "You can't do this!"

Calmly, I say, "I can."

"Then I will kill your little call girl of a secretary."

"Try," I say, dabbing at the corner of my lips with a napkin. I fix my eyes on her. "And I will kill *you*."

CHAPTER 95
SERENA

The room I was given in the mansion is four times larger than my studio apartment. Maybe more.

Pacing the length of it up and down is a good workout, and that's all I manage to do as I wait for news. I'm supposed to be working at the desk, where my entire office paraphernalia has been brought over. But there's no way I can focus when I think about Caleb sitting with Vivienne Astor.

I've gone over the scene in my mind enough times. It should be fine. They're in a public place, with lots of witnesses. It would be too hard to wipe the minds of many witnesses if attacking Caleb shows her true nature. It's not like compelling works like the neuralyzers from Men in Black.

Compelling requires the cooperation of the victim, which is why I should've ran the heck away from her that time, and what any freaked out witnesses at the restaurant would do.

I check my phone, but still no further smoke signals from Caleb. At this point I assume she arrived and they're talking. I can't see her possibly taking well to the news. Which means soon, it'll be real dangerous for me to set one foot outside of this place.

"And I just got a new apartment, ugh."

My phone pings and in scrambling to check if it's from Caleb, I almost drop the device on the floor. I pull an impressive feat of athleticism to catch it in the air. My hands shake as I turn it around and unlock it. It's not a text alert but an email, though. And the sender is the last person I expected to have to interact with again.

From: Karyn Johnson

To: Serena Lossada

You can't just pack your shit and leave without paying. You owe me a month's worth of rent now and if you don't pay in fifteen days I'll see you in court.

The email ends there.

I blink at the letters until they lose all meaning. It takes me three more re-reads before I understand that yes, my former roommate is threatening me with litigation.

Rushing back to my desk, I pull open my private email and dig into the past records to find the contract I signed with her. It's a separate agreement from the one she has with the leasing office. My name isn't anywhere in that one. In this second document, we outline the split in pay and it does say I have to give her thirty days notice if I want to move out.

With everything that's happened, I completely forgot. And I can't even blame Vivienne for it.

Cursing, I reply to Karyn's email, saying, *Then consider this my official thirty days notice. All the money you'll get is until then.*

That should fix it. Except for the part where my bank balance is in the reds. I'm absolutely out of funds after putting in the deposit at my new place—which I can't even use anymore, and that *is* thanks to Vivienne. Where am I going to get enough cash to pay for two months of my old rent?

I lower my head to the desk. My glasses dig uncomfortably into my head in this position, but I don't care.

I wonder how much I can get paid for donating blood. Or

could I sublease my studio apartment? But even if I can, will I be able to find someone who can pay up quickly?

The door opens and I sit up straight, fixing my glasses and my hair. Caleb's mother walks in, looking down her nose at me in a way that makes me feel very small. She's dolled up like a movie star from the 1940s, contrasting heavily with my T-shirt and Mom jeans.

"Hi, Mrs. Oh." I clear my throat. "What can I do for you?"

"Let's go for a walk. There's something I want to talk with you about before the coronation."

That said, she turns around and leaves, giving me no chance to even find an excuse. Sighing, I tuck my cellphone into my back pocket and follow the woman. I can't possibly imagine what the queen of vampires wants to talk with me about before her son is crowned the new king, but something tells me nothing good will come out of this day.

"Where are we going?" I ask after we've walked all across the mansion, past the kitchen, and are now trawling outside in the golf field.

She stays absolutely tight-lipped, walking on her kitten heels across the lawn with the ease only someone like her could have. If it was me, I'd have already twisted my ankles. As it is, my feet stumble upon the ground a couple of times and I'm wearing sneakers.

Finally, we break out of the jungle of palm trees and onto the beach where Caleb and I sat together the other time. Someone has prepared an area with fancy tanning chairs, massive umbrellas and tables full of goods. On one, there's a cocktail bar with various concoctions already prepared. On the other one, an assortment of chilled fruit, pastries, and cheeses.

"Sit." Mrs. Oh removes her robe and lays down on a chair. With her sunglasses, the elegant black swimsuit and heels, she's ready for a pictorial.

I sit on the other chair, not knowing what to do with myself.

"Pass me a cocktail."

"Uh." There are like five different ones. "Which one?"

"Whichever."

I grab the biggest and prettiest one, and carefully hand it over to her.

"This role looks good on you," she says, sipping on the cup. "A server."

My entire body freezes, despite the heat of the sun beating down on me.

Mrs. Oh sets the drink on the table beside her. "With the way history has been repeating itself, I thought Caleb took too much after his father. It was just so on the nose for him to fall for his secretary too."

Executive assistant. I can't get my tongue to untangle itself, though.

She chuckles. "But I wouldn't have imagined that it's the same damn thing. How did you do it? Did you wear tiny skirts and bend over to show your cleavage?"

"No," I say through gritted teeth. "I've never done such a thing."

"It doesn't matter." She chucks her heels off into the sand. "The boy's smitten, which—good for you. But you can't possibly expect something formal to come out of this, right?"

Mrs. Oh lowers her sunglasses and gives me an up and down scan.

"See, there are standards to uphold. My husband may have never loved me, but I still brought something to the table." Pausing, she takes another drink from her cocktail. "My family is one of the oldest, most powerful in Europe. The money and pedigree only strengthened the Oh line, even if what ended up coming out of it was Caleb. What do you possibly bring to the table?"

Nothing.

Absolutely nothing.

My only assets are debt. Being turned into a human will only cause controversy among vampires.

And yet… yet, I'm irrevocably in love with Caleb Oh. Not for his family money, or for the power he will hold.

For him. For his smile. For the spark in his eyes. For the warmth in his embrace and the softness of his lips. For the certainty that gleams in his eyes that he will do everything he can to keep me safe. And in any way I can, I want to do the same for him.

Except the only thing I have to offer him is my heart. I'm willing to give it to him, if it will keep *his* safe.

None of that will matter to this woman, so I stay silent.

"It's a shame he won't marry Vivienne," the woman continues with a sigh. "*She* would've brought the same assets I did with my marriage. But it's not like she's the only one who can possibly marry Caleb and continue the legacy. It just definitely can't be you."

I ball my fists at my sides.

"It's fine if you're just his side piece. That's all you're really good for. But you shouldn't set your expectations on becoming the vampire queen."

I get up to my feet. "I hope you enjoy your evening, ma'am."

But she grabs my arm before I turn to leave. I pull it free right away, knowing what I now know of what vampires can do with a little physical contact. My attempts to protect myself only make her smile.

"Just know this, even if you do survive the turning, it doesn't matter how much you two may think you love each other." Her laughter trills in a way that reminds me of Vivienne. "Even if Caleb doesn't grow bored and starts cheating on you like his father did to me, you will still never be accepted by the kingdom."

That's it. I turn and this time she doesn't try to stop me.

While I wish I'd never joined her on this so-called walk, I can't deny that accusation. I'm a complete outsider in this world. If vampires are as old school and stubborn as Caleb's mother, I stand no chance of ever having a smooth life.

Mrs. Oh's mistake is in thinking that her speech will make me choose comfort over the difficulties of trying a life with Caleb. What she doesn't know is that my life until now hasn't been anything but rocky, and I've never given up on it. I'm not going to start now.

CHAPTER 96
CALEB

Ernst Astor tries to hold talks with Dad twice to fix what he describes as the children's mistake. Instead, he and every head of the vampire families receives a formal invitation for the crowning of the next king.

Immediately, the Miami tabloids and beyond put out articles speculating about the health of Cedric Oh. Comed Solutions shares nosedive as most of the articles point at the two sons and heirs of the business. The more respectable one is a scientist without much business knowledge. Whereas the one who went to business school is a total airhead who prefers to spend his time aboard his yacht.

At least they posted a picture of me in a Speedo that favors me. I look like a model in a magazine spread.

In the back of my mind, I can't help wondering if that popular take is financed by the Astors. I'm sure if both Vivienne and her father won't stand by idly if they know I'm the one who will be crowned king.

It's why we send the invitations with barely a couple of days notice. The goal is to not let the Astors have time to prepare a big strike against us.

Meanwhile, we've been preparing for this for days. We called up every single security employee, plus the extended family, and set up camp in one of our country club mansions in the middle of Florida. We will hold the coronation here, where we'll be surrounded by land. It will allow easier escape in case things go awry.

And I'm sure it will go to shit.

The moment it does, we'll have to do everything we can to protect Dad. He will grow weaker after I drink enough of his blood to be able to absorb all his mutations—the vampire ones, not the cancer—especially considering how fast his health has declined in the past weeks. It'll be the prime moment for someone to attack him, and if anyone else manages to drink his blood they will have grounds to challenge me for the crown.

It wouldn't be the first thing something like that happens in history. In fact, it's how my great, great, great, great grandfather took the crown for the family. And if Vivienne can't seize power by marrying me, I'm sure this will be her backup plan.

"Calm down," Serena says as she paces back and forth in front of me.

I'm sitting on my bed, all dressed up in the ceremonial clothes. White button shirt and pants, no socks or shoes. At the end of the night, they will be stained with blood, even if things go well.

"I'm calm," I say, even though my heart is throttling in my chest. "As can be."

"Not you—me. I'm the one who needs to calm down." Serena continues pacing. "I'm not sure I'm doing the right thing here."

She wears a simple white dress that Lara gave her, because the first order of events after I'm the new king is going to be turning her into a vampire.

Dad was against it, and it took me days of non-stop nagging to convince him. I understand his reasoning. He wants me to have a smooth start as the new king. If it turns out he's the one responsible for turning the woman I intend to make my queen, it would be Dad who looks like a villain in front of the vampire families who will feel cheated at a stab to the highest power in the kingdom. Whereas if I turn her, I will look like a despot.

But either way, I will piss them off by marrying her instead of one of their daughters. Meanwhile, if Dad crowns me *and* turns Serena, two things that would require us drinking a considerable amount of his blood, he could grow so weak it may lead to an early grave.

I know he will pass away eventually, but I'd rather not be the one responsible for accelerating that moment.

"Forget what my step—sorry, my mother, forget what she said." I grab Serena's wrist and pull her to me. Holding onto her waist, I bring her to sit on my lap. Her pulse feels too rapid against my hand as I touch her neck. "If you've made up your mind, then that's the right thing to do."

"You make it sound way easier than it is." As she brushes my hair, she worries her lower lip and my attention latches there. "What if something goes wrong?"

"You know," I say under my breath. "I've been wondering the same but maybe it'd be a good idea to stop."

She cringes. "Unfortunately, I don't have the superpower of erasing worries off my mind."

"Neither do I." I force her back to arch down so I can kiss her neck. "But I know something we can do to distract ourselves."

Serena pushes me away and stands up. Her dark eyes travel down my body. "No, the ceremony will very start soon."

I sigh against her skin, too disappointed by that fact to even try seducing her. Unfortunately, this proves to be the right decision when the door opens, and a different voice sounds.

"We're starting."

"Oh, shit," Serena says.

What tumbles out of my mouth is more colorful.

Phelan gives us the most expressive look I've ever seen on his face. Raised eyebrows.

"We're nervous, okay?" I tell him, running a hand through my hair. "Give us one moment."

The man nods and walks right back out, leaving the door open in case I get any funny ideas.

Before I get to the same conclusion, Serena rushes over and hugs me. I wrap my arms around her and feel tremors rack up her spine. I whisper in her ear, "Phelan will take you to the balcony where Lara and my mother will be. I asked Marissa to guard you at all times. Stick with her, no matter what."

"Okay." Her voice is muffled with her face buried in my chest. "Good luck."

I press a kiss to her forehead and try to smile. With the way her eyes tear up, I'm not sure I succeed. "I'll see you after."

I wait until Marissa comes to take Serena away before I'm able to unfreeze my body. It still takes both Phelan and Daniel to prod me to move.

On my right, Daniel is dressed in the same outfit as mine. The plan is that he'll stand by Dad for the start of the cere-mony, and then I'll walk out from the shadows when Dad makes the announcement. Daniel will stay with us, keeping guard when we'll be the most vulnerable.

The problem is that it will also put him at risk.

"Are you sure you want to do this?" I ask him.

My brother clasps my shoulder. "It's my duty, little bro."

"You're expecting a child now." I shake my head. "Your duty is to them."

Daniel gives me a look. "And you think I'd make a good dad if I let anything happen to my family tonight? Or be able to live with myself?"

I groan. "We're a bunch of clowns."

Surprisingly, it's Phelan who retorts. "Yes, you are."

It makes Daniel and I dissolve into chuckles. The sound is jarring, compared to the way I feel inside.

I'm close to showing the heads of every vampire family in the world what shitting in white pants looks like.

Finally, my brother exchanges one last glance with me before parting ways. He walks out onto the courtyard where a stage has been set. Dad sits in the middle on a chair that looks like a throne. It has no special meaning, other than helping him rest for a bit.

I watch Daniel stand beside Dad as Phelan and I stand in the shadows inside the house. Ahead of them, all across the lawn and up to the edges of the forest, are about five hundred vampires representing each of the major families of the kingdom. They've come from every corner of the world and last I checked, booked every hotel in the vicinity. Glad to boost the local economy.

From my vantage, I can see that each of them carries a cooler. If any human is watching this gathering by accident, they'll think it's the weirdest bring-your-own rave, especially because there's no music. But actually, each of the coolers contains a vial with at least one drop of blood from every family member. Safe for a few hundred rogue vampires, it is more or less the blood of a hundred thousand people.

And I'll have to drink all that tonight. It's why I think a Tide pen won't be enough to fix my clothes after the evening is done.

"My kingdom," Dad begins his speech. His voice booms across the eerie silence that extends across the crowd. "As most of you have understood from my continuous absence from the public light, my time is approaching its end."

Murmurs ripple across the vampires like a wave. Directly above me, I wonder what the women in the balcony feel like right this moment. I wish I could hold Serena's hand, to receive her strength and give her mine.

I wonder if Phelan would get pissed if I grab his hand, but the thought vanishes as Dad continues talking.

"My rapid decline has prompted me to call for this hasty crowning, and I want to thank you for your attendance."

Many of the people before him bow, recognizing his gratitude.

"In the same way you have accepted me as your king for centuries," Dad says, making a pause where his voice falters. "I now ask that you accept my son as your legitimate ruler."

Someone starts chanting Daniel's name, and so many voices join at once that I can't determine where it started. All I can do is give Phelan a *yikes* look.

Daniel raises his hands, quieting the crowd. In seconds, the silence falls back. I don't think I would've succeeded so quickly if I was in his spot. Because it's true, they've seen him as the rightful heir for decades and they respect him just as much as Dad.

"Caleb," Dad's voice calls out. "Come, Son."

I'm sure every vampire in a one mile radius can hear the way my heart hammers as I walk out into the lights that illuminate the stage.

Dad finally stands up from the chair, and with difficulty he joins my side. To the crowd, he announces, "Here he is. Caleb Oh, my legitimate heir and your next king."

On my other side, Daniel grabs my shoulder to show his allegiance in front of the crowd.

That's when hell breaks loose—and it's not because of the palpable shock some of the attendants manifest with gasps or shouts of outrage.

No. It's because at that moment, shadows jump out of the forest and attack.

CHAPTER 97
SERENA

Everything goes wrong in the blink of an eye.

The vampires across the property are shrouded in the dark to my human eyes, but even I can see throngs of newcomers appearing out of nowhere. The first one to react is Marissa, who pulls me by my arm so hard I'm afraid she'll dislocate my shoulder.

"Quick," she says. "We have to get you all to safety."

"What's happening?" I ask, as if she wasn't just as shocked as me.

All she can do is shake her head, but I've never seen her paler.

"This way," Mrs. Oh says. Picking up her skirts, she leads the pack out of the balcony and into a hallway. "We have a basement we can hide in. It's not as secure as the compound, but it'll do."

On my other side, Lara glances back and says, "Oh, shit."

That doesn't sound good. I look back and confirm it isn't.

A mass of people wearing all black come barreling down the hallway. And also up the hallway.

Marissa touches an earpiece she wears. "We need reinforcements upstairs!"

"But will they come?" Lara asks, checking out both ends of the hallway. "Because if these guys are here, doesn't it mean they've already got rid of our security team?"

"We'll have to fight," Mrs. Oh surprises me by saying. "There's less men on the right, let's break a path that way."

Her daughter-in-law says, "Sounds good."

"Hop on my back," Marissa tells me.

My brain can't process. "What?"

She glares at me. "Just do it."

I do—almost expecting her to fall over under my considerable weight—but she picks me up like I'm as light as a teddy bear.

"No matter what happens," Marissa says to me. "Do not let go."

"Okay," I say with a weak voice.

My stomach somersaults as the three women break into a sprint. They roar, and their voices don't sound the way I'm used to. Marissa hangs out back and I can't see what the others look like right now, but Lara raises one hand and I see her nails have turned into downright talons.

She swipes at the nearest man with such power, it sends him crashing against a wall. Plaster breaks as the man falls limp.

The world swivels around. Marissa slams the heel of her hand into the forehead of a guy who was coming up behind us. Another one appears from out of nowhere. I warn my friend too late. She's already punching the guy's nose in by the time I scream.

They're so fast. I can't keep up. I squeeze my arms and legs around Marissa even harder. I'll be a goner in no time if I'm left behind. There's no way I can defend myself.

Three men fly across the air. They crash against a window, raining shards of glass down as they fall out of the building.

I hear Mrs. Oh say, "That's what they get for thinking they can hurt their queen."

"Let's go," Lara says.

The three women rush down the stairs. But the ground floor is pure anarchy. An unconscious vampire flies in an arc across the air, crashing onto the spot where we stood a moment before.

One man, dressed in all black, snaps someone's neck before catching sight of us. His face is horribly disfigured by a claw, and also by hatred. "There they are!"

Two of his buddies spot us too. While the odds are good—three against three—no one else is coming to help us. Civilians try to protect themselves from the invaders. Some of the Oh's security team try to fend the attackers off. There's blood on the walls and the floor, where battles have been won or lost.

This chaos is all around us. We're backed up against a wall and the attackers, and the pandemonium beyond. The stairs where we came from are overrun with our persecutors and the odds are no longer in our favor. There isn't a single clear path for us to escape.

And in all of this, as adrenaline makes my heart race at an impossible speed, as sweat drenches my skin and my vision wavers, all I can think of is…

Is Caleb okay?

I pray with all my might that he's not hurt. I know he's strong. Phelan is beside him. His dad and brother too. It doesn't matter what happens to me as long as he makes it out of this safe.

"Let me down," I tell Marissa. "You can't fight properly if I keep slowing you down."

She grabs tighter onto my legs. "But Caleb will kill me if something happens to you."

"Something will definitely happen to me if I get us all killed."

"Can you shoot a gun?" Lara asks at the same time she lifts her dress and pulls out a small gun strapped to her thighs. "That might give you an edge."

Mrs. Oh gasps. "You brought a gun to the ceremony?"

"I know it's forbidden." Lara shrugs. "But you can't expect me to believe none of these invaders are packing heat."

Sure enough, I hear the first pops of a gun going off.

I stutter as I respond, "I've n-never touched one."

Lara pulls the safety off and hands it to me. "All you need to do is pull the trigger. Just don't aim it at us."

My hands shake as I stand there, my back glued against a wall with a loaded gun in my hand. In front of me, the three women become a blur of movement. Marissa and Lara look like professional martial artists. One puts a guy in a chokehold. The other one breaks another man's arms. There are so many screams all around that my ears ring. It's why I don't hear someone approach.

Movement from the corner of my eye is what alerts me. The man with a disfigured face jumps at me. I make myself small. In doing so, I pull the trigger accidentally. The small gun is powerful enough to make me fall on my ass. At the same time, the guy crashes to the floor clutching his knee.

Someone kicks him out of the way. When I look up, Caleb's mother raises her eyebrows at me. "You might not be entirely useless."

Wiping her forehead after dispatching a guy, Lara says, "We have two choices here. Trying to get to the basement right away, or trying to find our men first."

"They'll want the former." Marissa puts her hands on her hips, and while she doesn't seem anywhere as winded as I am, she is bathed in sweat and blood already. "But it's true the yard is closer."

"There's no point in hiding," Mrs. Oh says, taking a deep breath. "We won't survive this either if our men are defeated. Let's go find them."

"What does defeated mean?" I ask with a small voice.

The woman doesn't sugarcoat it for me. "Killed. If they die, we die."

"Sounds reasonable," I say with a nod, and the queen of vampires snorts.

Mrs. Oh flips her blonde hair back, now matted with sweat and blood. "Cover me, we're going to find my husband."

And where Cedric Oh is, Caleb is bound to be found.

My legs shake as I stand up. I have enough presence of mind to aim the gun at the floor as I stick close to the queen's back. She clears a path by brute force alone, and it's clear to me she's as powerful as she is mean. Closely behind me, Lara and Marissa make sure no one is able to stick with our little group for long.

The melee is just as bad when we make it to the yard. This is where the gunshots are coming from. People run this way and that, probably away from the gunmen.

Marissa jumps ahead of our group and motions for us to stick to the outer walls of the mansion, keeping our bodies low. We hide behind a hedge and I shake more than its leaves. The stage where just minutes ago Cedric Oh presented Caleb as his true heir, is now deserted. Where have they gone?

"Murray," Marissa whispers to her earpiece. "Location? Murray?"

"That's not good," Lara says. "If Phelan's not responding, that must be bad."

"Don't panic yet," Diana Oh says, poking her head out over the hedges. "It's not good for the baby."

I give Lara a look and she shares it. If right now isn't the moment to panic, then when is it? When one of these intruders is about to claw our hearts out?

"The plan remains the same," the older woman says with surprising calm. "We find our men and then retreat however we can. Is that clear?"

Lara and Marissa respond in the affirmative, but I can't help asking, "Why are you so calm?"

The woman spares me a glance. "It was worse at Cedric's crowning. Back then, about half of the families were against him being king and they figured if they could kill him before he was crowned, one of them would stand a chance at the title. If you think about what we're seeing now, all the heads of families are fighting for their lives against the intruders, which means they're on our side."

"You're right." There's a frown on Lara's face as she considers this. "It must mean the guys in black are loyal to whoever is paying them."

"Vivienne Astor," I whisper.

"Probably." Lara squeezes my hand.

No further words are needed. It's clear if they catch us, *I'm dead.*

"Let's not be sitting ducks any longer," Mrs. Oh says and off we go to find our men.

CHAPTER 98
CALEB

"Protect my dad!" I tell Phelan.

Dad has the opposite idea. "No, protect Caleb."

With a roar, I grab an attacker by his head and toss him away. "I'm replaceable, Dad isn't."

Behind me, my brother shouts. "None of you are replaceable, you fools. I am!"

Between the triangle made of Phelan, Daniel and I, we keep Dad as safe in the middle as we can. There are so many attackers that for every one we fell, there are three more to replace him. And it doesn't end no matter how hard we work.

They allow us no time to provision ourselves with the blood of the defeated ones. At some point we'll run on empty. Even then, we have to keep going. We can't allow Dad to be killed here.

Shit, and here I thought we'd left the Astors with little time to prepare. I was the fool for underestimating them. By the size of their army, they have been planning for this moment for years.

And still, the hateful woman is nowhere to be seen. As glad as I am for my eyes, I'm worried about what that may mean.

What if she's gone straight to the women? It feels like forever ago since I last saw them at the balcony. I can only hope they're faring okay—that Serena is safe.

Our formation continues its slow journey into the house. Upon the first wave of the attack, our collective instinct was to first, protect Dad, and second, find the women. But the nearest entrance to the house was blocked pretty quick by attackers. Instead, we veered to the side of the building to find one of the side doors.

I run to a wall of men in black. Using that momentum, I kick the chests of one guy with one foot and another one with the other. As I land on my side, I sweep my legs around and make three guys crash onto the ground. One of them pulls out a gun and in the knick of time, I push out of the way before he fires. Someone lands a kick on my side but I roll against his other leg and make him crash. He falls in a great position for me. Hooking my legs around his arm, I break it. The gun in his hand falls against my chest and I pick it up.

The moment I look up, I catch a man jumping at Dad. I aim the gun and fire. The impact is enough to knock the attacker's trajectory off course. With my back on the ground, I shoot at a second one and a third. They all writhe on the floor. I didn't hit any lethal spots, but it's gotta hurt anyway.

Serves them right, for trying to kill my dad.

"Are you okay?" I ask when I return to his side.

He inspects me. "And you?"

Instead of answering, I say, "Let's keep moving."

Phelan tosses two men out of the way as if they were rag dolls.

Finally, the path into the house is clear. We move indoors and my heart leaps onto my throat.

The whole place is thrashed, as if a bomb dropped inside. There are people laying in various states of injury, some in pools of their own blood that tell me they won't recover. While some of them are dressed in white, as the ceremony dictates, others wear the black the intruders chose to identify themselves with.

I spot many familiar faces. The head of the Tullys sits on the floor immobile, his back against the wall and a steady trickle of blood falling from his mouth. His eyes are vacant.

Beyond him, the head of the Okorafors is putting up a brave fight along with one of his relatives. Their opponents are three men, who look worse for wear.

Someone comes crashing down from the second floor and lands so bad, he'll never get up again. I wince, but someone prods my back and I keep moving. A couple of our security guys see us and after putting one attacker to sleep, they rush to join us.

"Sir, are you alright?" one of them asks Dad.

"Have you seen the queen and the others?" Dad asks them, and they shake their heads.

The second guy responds, "We were looking for them too, but they're nowhere to be found."

A third voice sounds from behind us. "I saw them a few minutes ago."

"Jon," my brother says, rushing to steady the man.

Blood gushes down the side of Jon's head where his ear was blown off. He's unsteady on his feet and leans onto my brother for support.

Dad's assistant swallows with difficulty. His finger shakes as he points somewhere ahead. "I saw them go that way, probably to the basement."

Oh, thank goodness. I hope they're safe.

"Let's go find them," Daniel says. "Can you walk alright?"

Jon nods. "Yes—"

"No," Phelan says, cutting him off. "He'll slow us down."

Jon takes out a gun from the pocket of his white blazer. "I can still help."

"You two, bring him along," Dad commands to the two security guys. When they relieve Daniel of the burden, Dad says, "Let's go find the women. Stick close together."

As if he was a general, Phelan and the two security guys respond, "Yes, sir."

Things might be dwindling down because there's less resistance in our path this time. A couple of gunshots sound off and I crouch low. When I turn, I find Jon has felled two attackers. But they don't writhe on the floor in agony. They're dead.

How many people have died tonight, or will die?

Urgency pumps into my blood. I need to find Serena. I can't let her be one of the victims.

We advance down the path toward the basement. I try to help one of the family heads who is being overpowered by two attackers, but Phelan grabs me by the collar of my shirt and hauls me away like a puppy.

"But—"

"No," is all he says.

I follow. He's right. My priorities are my family and Serena. If I can get Dad to the basement where the women are, I can grab Phelan and go back to help anyone else who needs it. And more importantly, to find the mastermind of this debacle.

We finish crossing the lobby, about to enter the corridor that leads to the basement entrance, when a whole contingent of attackers descend on us.

It was a trap and we walked right into it.

I have no time to even curse. I'll be killed if I slow down to breathe. I shut my brain off and let my body move.

Everything Phelan taught me comes out unprompted. A knife tries to stab my face, but I evade out of the way. In the same motion, I knock the arm wielding it away. The knife flies away, followed by a scream. I can't even check to see who it hurt before another guy is onto me. I let myself drop back and watch as one guy in black stabs another, instead of me.

Rolling out of the way, I pick up a fallen knife and throw it at another attacker. It sinks into his chest as if he was made of butter.

Why can no one teleport me out of here?

"Watch out, Caleb!" My brother's voice warns me in time. One guy takes aim at me with a freaking rifle. I run *to* him, which throws him off. Batting the gun away with one arm, I slam my elbow in his face and knock him out. In the same move, I grab the gun and turn around.

Dad is a tornado of destruction, dropping attackers left and right. He has to be fueled by adrenaline. This morning alone, he could barely walk.

Daniel picked some sort of stick along the way. He wields it as a sword, landing crushing blows that break limbs and heads.

I don't even worry about Phelan. The moshpit of men in black keeps spitting out one unconscious guy after another, and I have no doubt Phelan is the one in the middle taking care of them methodically.

I could stand here and pick at anyone who tries to do them dirty, or I could go straight to the basement and check in on the women.

No sooner the thought leaves my mind before a pop goes off. I don't even feel the pain, but my leg jerks and I lose balance. I crash on the floor hard, my side crushed over the gun I'd been holding.

No.

I can't die here.

On instinct, I roll around just as a bullet pierces the floor. My head had been there a second ago.

"Stay still," a familiar voice says.

I don't. Gritting through the explosion of pain in my thigh, I get up to my feet. Jon sways before me, the smoking gun in his hand shaking in the air.

"What the hell?" I ask, shaking my head. "Why are you shooting *me*?"

"To kill you, you bastard." He clutches his side, where a gaping wound pours blood onto his clothes.

"You betrayed us," I say, bracing myself against the wall. "Why?"

"Anything for my true love," he says, advancing slowly.

Foggy as my brain is, it finally clicks. "Vivienne."

He aims the gun at me.

It's as if I'm a stranger. Not his boss's kid, who he saw grow up. As if he hadn't been to my birthdays and graduations.

As if maybe, someone wiped his mind of any memory that gave him any attachment to me.

No wonder tonight's been a mess. No wonder Vivienne's men always seemed to know where I was. How long has Jon been feeding her information?

In exchange for what? A delusion? Because I can't imagine Vivienne cares about him or any of the people she seduces for power.

Jon starts to pull the trigger.

My vision turns into a tunnel. All I see is the bullet exploding out of the barrel. I breathe. My body shifts. Blood pumps through my veins like lava. My muscles coil away from the bullet. It doesn't graze me. In the same motion, I slam into Jon. We crash on the floor. Another bang sounds close to my ear. Instead, I wrestle the gun from him and slam the handle on his temple.

"Caleb," Dad groans. When I look behind me, he's falling on his knees. There's a bullet hole in his stomach.

CHAPTER 99
SERENA

'm going to kill Caleb if he's dead. But first, I need to find him.

The nerves I felt for days leading to today didn't prepare me for how wrong things could go. As we trek across the perimeter of the house, trying to avoid the worst of the conflict in search for the Oh men, I decide that if I survive this night, I will ask any of these people to compel it away from my memories.

I can't stand the sight of all the gore around us. That's why my preferred form of entertainment is dramas and soaps—not horror movies. And yet, that's exactly what we're living. Some sort of horror Hollywood blockbuster.

Bile rushes up my throat when I see a particularly horrible scene. I clamp my mouth firmly shut and swallow back down. If I slow us down to empty my stomach, we'll become sitting ducks.

"I think they're not outside," Marissa whispers from behind me.

"Let's go back inside," Mrs. Oh says.

"What if they're not inside either?" I ask, and the glares I get from the Oh women and Marissa tell me I'm the party pooper.

It's Lara who responds. "That might mean the worst."

Not something I even want to contemplate.

Trembling from head to toe, still clutching her gun, I say, "Okay, let's go inside."

It's easier than when we made the opposite trip. Soon, the reason becomes apparent. There are too many people who are out of commission, lying on the floor or against the walls, a few over broken furniture. Many in states they will never recover from.

A sob tears from my throat.

"Don't look," Marissa says, steering me by the shoulders. "Focus on Mrs. Oh's head."

I do, but her golden hair drips with rust in areas. Her white dress is torn and so dirty it also makes my stomach queazy.

One of the vampires in white catches sight of us, and with a herculean effort gets up from his sitting position against a wall. He leaves a red stain behind, but joins us anyway. "My queen, let me assist you."

Mrs. Oh stops and regards me. "It would be best if you get medical attention."

The man winces. "It's too late for me. Let me just be your shield."

"Very well," she says.

Even more shocking, two more vampires join our little group. Then another. And as we continue advancing across the house, our group gets bigger.

The problem is that for every person who fights on our side, two more attackers crop up out of the woodworks. I stick close to Marissa, whose job seems to be keeping me out of harm. Except maybe the best way to have done that would have been for me to stay the heck away from here.

But who could've guaranteed Vivienne wouldn't have sent her people after me, wherever I went?

That doesn't matter. I need to find Caleb.

Someone makes an awful noise and I turn to it. A vampire in black all but flies through the air, straight at us.

At me.

Before I can react, Marissa takes out a gun and shoots him like a disc at a shooting range. The impact changes his momentum and he lands away. The man falls with a sickening crash.

I can't breathe.

"Keep moving," Marissa says, pulling me by the arm. "We're not safe out in the open."

"I almost forgot that you're a sharpshooter." Lara's voice is shockingly light, as if we were admiring dresses instead.

"I think I'm gonna be sick," I whisper.

"Hold it." Lara's eyes are wide. "If you puke I'll puke too."

I hold it. Instead, I start crying.

"Is that Phelan up ahead?" Marissa asks, narrowing her eyes.

We turn to where she points, and sure enough, there's the bodyguard. He's still relatively far, across the expanse of the ground floor in a hallway. He has a knife in one hand and a gun in the other, and he uses both at the same time against opponents close and far. Phelan moves so fast, if it wasn't for Marissa pointing at him I wouldn't have recognized him. Blood arches across the air where he slashes. Blasts go off as he fires the gun. And yet no one is able to make him move a single step.

"Caleb!" I cry out, he must be around.

Blinded by that thought, I break formation. Someone protests, but there's a rushing sound in my ears blocking every-thing. I slip on a puddle of blood and flail about, but I grab no purchase. I land on somebody, but they don't move or cry out. They must be dead.

In my head, I pray for them—and also that I can find Caleb. Shaking, I get back up to my feet. Marissa intercepts me, bracketing her arms around me in a vise.

"Let me go." I pour all the energy I have into trying to break her hold, but it's impossible.

"Calm down," she screams in my ear. "We'll find him together."

"Watch out!"

The warning comes as two men in black descend upon us. Marissa is forced to let me go to deal with them.

I run. Without looking back, I dodge inert bodies and moving ones. I keep my eyes focused ahead where I last saw Phelan. Pops sound nearby—guns. And yet I don't duck. One foot in front of the other, I keep going. Hoping they'll lead me to Caleb.

Warmth trickles down my arm but I don't stop to look if it's my blood or someone else's. I only stop when someone comes flying from the hallway, just a second before the body would've slammed against me. The projectile is a woman, she crashes on someone else and neither moves.

Oh no.

More gunshots come from the hallway across the wall. I notice my hands are empty now. At some point I lost Lara's gun, but it's not like I have the reflexes to use it against vampires. Especially if they're as quick as Phelan. All I can rely on is luck, and I hope it hasn't left me yet.

Ducking, I walk across the wall and to the opening. The first one I see is Phelan, singlehandedly taking care of almost every attacker. Nearby, Daniel kicks a man in the face so spectacularly, it sends him hurtling into a window. Lara will be proud.

Where's Caleb?

I find Mr. Oh. He's slower compared to his son or Phelan, but just as lethal. If I hadn't seen him coughing up a storm this morning, I wouldn't have imagined he'd be capable of fighting like this.

But then my heart stops. There's a gunshot sound and Mr. Oh's body jerks.

"No!" I shout, not that it does any good. I run out from hiding toward the king. Not that my brain is working anymore, because what can I possibly do in the middle of the fray?

"Caleb," Mr. Oh groans his son's name out as he falls onto his knees.

I slide on wetness on the floor, but this time I don't fall. "Mr. Oh!"

He turns his head, blinking as if my appearance was more shocking than the fact that he just got shot. "Stay away, kid."

I crash on the floor before him. Blood leaks out of his stomach. Shit, what do I do? I grab onto my skirts and ball them up, pressing them against the wound.

"Serena."

I want to weep.

There he is, my Caleb.

He winces as he limps over. His clothes are torn and bloody, especially on his right thigh. But the blood doesn't gush out and I hope that's a good sign.

"Why are you here, kid?" Mr. Oh asks me. "We thought you'd be in the basement."

"We went looking for all of you first." I look up at Caleb, wounded and beaten, but alive. Just because of that, he's never looked more beautiful to me.

Caleb takes off his shirt and kneels down in front of us. Carefully, he removes my hands from his dad's stomach and applies pressure with his shirt instead. He glances between us and I'm not sure if it's sweat or tears what trickles down his face.

"Dad, what do we do?" he asks.

The older man breathes out in a wheeze. "Drink my blood right now."

"But—"

Mr. Oh grabs his son by the nape. "Quick, before I bleed out more."

My chin trembles. I pull Caleb's hands away from his dad's stomach and replace him in the efforts. "Do it, I'll apply pressure instead."

"Shit," Caleb says, sniffling. But for once he obeys.

His dad lowers Caleb's head until it's on his shoulder. An ugly sob racks Caleb's body, until he finally bites his dad.

Out of all the screwed up things I've seen tonight, this is the least of it. Instead, I focus all my energy on my arms, using all my weight to try to prevent more blood from leaking out of Mr. Oh's wound.

I don't want him to die here. The conversation we had the night of Caleb's engagement comes to mind. There's so much I haven't discussed with him. About my dad. About his promise to him. He took care of me even that night, as Cedric Oh put his blazer around my shoulders.

"Please hold on," I say amid sobs. "Don't die."

Caleb's hand finds my knee and he squeezes, even as he doesn't let go of his father yet.

That's when I see her. The culprit of all these crimes. Even through my dirty, broken glasses, even through the distance, I can recognize her figure.

While Caleb and Mr. Oh sit on the floor, vulnerable, Vivienne Astor appears at the end of the hallway running at full speed. Her hand is raised high, fingernails as sharp as claws.

And Caleb's back is bare, turned to her.

"No!"

Before I can string a coherent thought, I get in the way.

The last thing I see is Vivienne's blood red eyes as she spears through my body with her claw.

CHAPTER 100
CALEB

Someone screams, but I'm so sluggish that I can't react.

Dad keeps the pressure on my nape, forcing me to not break contact even as I try to move. His chest vibrates as he screams, "Diana! Hold her back."

What is happening?

I try to pull away, but Dad keeps his arm around my neck in a vise. Exhaustion catches up to me. Or perhaps it's just my energy leaking out of my wound. Maybe that's why I can't hear anything, and why all I can feel is the blood rolling down my throat.

For once, my gag reflex doesn't kick in. My body knows that if I want to survive, I have to absorb the king's mutations into my own body. I won't be a true king until I also drink the blood of the families, but I don't think there's much of it that can be salvaged tonight.

"That's enough," Dad finally says, loosening the hold on me.

I pull away and stagger back, gasping as if I'd been under water. My head spins and spasms travel down my muscles. I don't know if the tears are what won't let me focus on my dad's face, but my vision is blurry and everything seems far too bright.

My heart pounds hard, like a hammer against my ribcage, against my temples, and down my limbs. I crash on the floor but I can't even feel it. What does it matter, when there's lava running through my veins? I writhe and scratch my chest, my stomach, where the heat is stronger. I wish I could take it out.

There are voices around me but I can't make them out. A tinny squeal goes off in my ears and it hurts. Everything hurts.

Then there's nothing but darkness. I feel nothing. I do nothing.

"—leb!"

A groan. It takes my brain a moment to register the sound coming from my throat. Someone calls my name again. And again.

"Shut up."

I don't know who says that, but I agree. I need quiet. Darkness. And an ice cold bath. That would be nice.

"Wake up!"

I snap my eyes open and find my brother above me. His knees are on my shoulders, pinning me down to the floor. "What the…"

"Snap out it," he says, much too loud. "Serena's hurt."

Suddenly, it's as if there's no air. No reason for my heart to beat.

The ceiling shifts above me, beyond my brother's face, and I feel myself pulling to it as if gravity was above me. But it's only because I'm sitting up. At my feet, my sister-in-law lets go of my ankles.

"Go," she says.

I shake my head, trying to clear it from the overload. The ringing is still going in my ears as I roll onto all fours and push up. Everything swims as I look around. Dad is on the floor, staring at me. Phelan is putting pressure on his stomach as Dad motions at me with his hand. He also seems to be telling me to go.

Go where?

I turn around and that's when I see her.

Serena's limp in my mother's arms.

I take one step.

"What the hell?" I ask aloud, taking another step.

The floor feels like it's water slowing down my movements.

And Serena looks as if she's drowned. She's not moving at all. How could she, with such a gnarly wound in her stomach.

"Caleb, Caleb."

I freeze. In the recesses of my fractured mind, I recognize the voice.

"I told you I was gonna kill her."

Laughter. That's not right. No one should be laughing. Not when my heart is breaking in pieces.

Slowly, I turn to the voice. Everything else in the periphery appears as if in slow motion. The fighting, the screaming, none of it makes any sense as Vivienne Astor walks over. Red drips from her right hand. She licks the blood off the back of her hand.

"Hmm, surprisingly tasty for human blood," she says, smiling with red lips and teeth. "Is this why you fell in love with her? And here I thought it was just because she was kinda cute and right under your nose."

I swallow with difficulty. My vision blurs again, and this time I know it's tears.

"Aww, don't cry." Vivienne pouts. "You'll join her soon."

Maybe that would be best. There's no point in living if Serena isn't with me.

Caleb Oh, don't you dare, Serena's voice sounds in my mind, ripe with a warning.

That's right. She would kill me if I let Vivienne win. If I let anyone else get hurt.

Anger boils in my stomach and I release it with a roar. The corner of Vivienne's lips lifts. But she's not smiling when I appear before her in a blink. She's not smiling as I drive my fist into her stomach and she flies back. When she crashes into a wall, it's so satisfying I could stop.

But I don't.

My thighs flex, bare feet pumping the floor so hard I'm propelled in the air like a rocket. Vivienne's extricating herself from the plaster when I'm right there. She gasps—tries to get out of the way. I'm too fast. Or she's too slow. My hand claws at her throat, pinning her against the wall.

I squeeze. Vivienne scratches at my arm, trying to hurt me enough to let her go. But I won't. This ends tonight.

While she makes a choking sound, I sink my fangs on her shoulder through her clothes. I feel one of her hands stab at my bare side, but I don't care. I'm drinking her blood and if she keeps moving, she won't be able to breathe.

Her body grows limp. Even then, I don't let go of her throat or her shoulder. The way her heart beats tells me she's well alive. It's only when my stomach starts tingling that I stop biting her.

Her face is as red as her eyes when I look at her. Then I smile, even though I feel like screaming and crying and cursing at her.

"I won," I say.

Vivienne tries to take a swipe at me. Instead, I hit her over the head and knock her out cold. She crumples to the floor like a puppet whose strings have been cut.

I gasp for air for a while, watching her, half afraid she'll spring to her feet and attack. The other half can't believe anything that's happening. I have enough presence of mind to wipe my blood off her hand so she stays truly defeated.

"Serena," I whisper.

When I turn, I find myself clear across the house from

where my family is. I break into a run, feeling the cuts on the soles of my feet for the first time. Pain shoots up my spine from everywhere. My thigh burns, I might have a few broken ribs and Vivienne's claw was like a knife on my side.

But all I can see is Serena.

I finally reach her side. Daniel is now with her, and he's wrapped her torso up with some fabric.

"Caleb," my brother says the moment he sees me. "We have to turn her right away."

"She's still alive?" I crash on my knees, feeling for her neck until I find her pulse.

It's weak but I can feel it.

How?

Beside her, my mother sits breathing hard. She has Serena's hand in hers. "I erased the memory of Vivienne hurting her. I think that might have lessened the shock."

"Caleb, you have to turn her," Daniel says, keeping his hands firmly on Serena's wound. "Dad's too weak to do it."

My throat is choked up as I look around.

What a mess. Not a single person is unscathed. Out of the five hundred family heads, how many are still alive?

And forget the coolers with the blood from their relatives. Those must be smashed to pieces, the mixed blood scattered on grass and ground.

"I can't turn her," I cry out, digging the heels of my hands against my prickling eyes. "There's not enough blood to finish the crowning."

"That's just a formality." Dad's voice comes from behind me, weak. When I turn to him, Phelan is helping him sit up. "Well, it's important you also get their mutations, but what matters most is *my* blood. Now that you've drank it, what I can do, you can do too."

"That's why you were able to defeat Vivienne," my brother

says, his voice shaking. "You're strong now, Caleb. You can do it."

"If you're going to try," my mother says, her eyes squeezed shut so tight it makes her face red. "Do it now. Her consciousness is starting to fade."

"Shit." Then for good measure, I add, "Shit,"

A hand appears before me, brandishing a knife. I trace the arm up to Phelan's face. "Do it."

I grab the knife and cut my wrist. Daniel opens Serena's mouth and I pour my blood into it. I pray it's not too late as I watch the liquid fill her mouth. That I'm not too weak.

For a while, there isn't any sign that she's drinking it. Blood pools out of her mouth and dribbles down her cheeks.

I gasp for air, feeling like someone is choking me from the inside.

And then Serena's throat spasms. She swallows the blood and, as if knowing this is the only way she can survive, she opens her mouth again.

There's hope.

CHAPTER 101
SERENA

"Levántate."

I recognize Dad's voice with the clarity of eighteen years ago. Trying to open my eyes gets them stabbed by white light and I squeeze them shut again. There was a vague shape before me, but it's not worth putting up with the pain to observe it properly.

"No," I say with a groan.

A female voice I don't recognize says, "Abre los ojos, chiquita. Tu nueva vida te espera."

I want to ask what they're talking about because the words aren't registering. A new life? Man, this is one bizarre dream.

"Vamos," Dad says, in the same way he used to try to make me hurry when we were running late for school. It used to infuse me with adrenaline. Nothing I could be doing was more important than not disappointing my dad.

So, I open my eyes.

The light assaulting my eyes isn't as white as the dream. Instead, it's the sunlight streaming in through the massive floor to ceiling windows. Brightness and heat cook me and it's a wonder I didn't wake up earlier. Everything aches, making turning against the windows a major task.

That's when I come face to face with a sight.

Caleb sleeps in the bed beside me. We're both under the bedsheets, which are bunched up to his waist. He's not wearing a T-shirt and I think he's the reason why the bedsheets feel like an oven. I hope he's wearing bottoms, though.

Wait a second, what am *I* wearing?

I look down and sag in relief. I'm in some sort of T-shirt that fits me like a night gown, and when I check underneath I find underwear. Phews.

The relief is short-lived as everything starts rushing to my mind—the unfortunate side effect of waking up to reality.

The ceremony.

Screaming. Blood.

My heart goes from normal to one hundred in a second. I bolt up right, slamming my hands against my mouth but they can't fully muffle a scream.

"What?" Caleb snaps awake and jolts. He sits on the bed, looking around. "What's wrong?"

A sob convulses in my chest. The large room blurs as the first tears begin to fall. If I close my eyes, I can still see the death and destruction, so I do my best to keep them open and fixed on the abstract painting ahead. It has swaths of royal blue, orange and yellow, and I like it for not having any red.

"Come here," he murmurs, linking an arm around me and gently pulling me to lie down again. I let him squeeze me against his chest. "It's okay. You're okay now."

Caleb's hand rubs up and down my back, chasing the terror away from my body. He smells of soap and the unique scent that clings to his skin. It helps to gradually make my muscles relax, one by one, until I'm the human equivalent of a melted candle against him.

After a while, Caleb pulls away just enough to look down at

me. He brushes my mass of hair away from my face and I touch his face, making sure this isn't a dream. He feels warm and firm against my hand. My heart does something funny when he twists it to kiss the palm of my hand.

There are dark circles under this eyes, and a spark is missing from them. But still Caleb smiles. "You have no idea how happy I am now that you're finally awake."

I sniffle and throw an arm around him. "I'm just glad you're safe. We looked everywhere for you and—"

My horrible memories end at some point, as if my consciousness fell down a dark abyss all of a sudden.

"What happened?" I ask Caleb. The first traces of a headache start to form.

As if sensing this, he caresses my head. "You got hurt."

I grow as stiff as a plank. With some difficulty, I pull myself away from him and palm my body. No limbs are broken, and aside from little aches everywhere, there doesn't seem to be something terribly wrong.

"What do you mean hurt? I'm fine, at least on the outside."

Sighing, Caleb turns to prop his head up with his arm. I *will not* focus on how extraordinarily beautiful he looks right now, with his disheveled hair, a five o'clock shadow and all that bare skin in display. I absolutely should not focus on that.

"Did you notice something?" he asks, and for a second I worry he's referring to the way I'm checking him out. But he runs an index finger down the bridge of my nose and I finally catch his meaning.

"Oh no, my glasses." I feel around the large bed, trying to spot them. The bedside table is also clear of them. "I must have lost them somewhere in the fray. There's another pair at home but—"

And then I catch the real meaning of his question.

I'm not wearing my glasses and yet I can see everything perfectly. The lines of the bedside table. The palm trees beyond the window. The individual strokes of paint on the abstract art piece. I could even count the threads of the bedsheets.

I turn back to Caleb. There must be a question written on my face, because he continues, "You got hurt really bad, Serena. I had to turn you while you were unconscious."

We remain suspended in each other's eyes for a long moment. That's all the mental capacity I have left.

I rub my arms. "I don't remember anything."

Sighing, Caleb sits back up and rubs his tired eyes. "That probably saved you. My mother removed the memory of Vivienne hurting you, and with that she lessened the shock in your mind. I think if you'd have been conscious of the gravity of your injuries, you might have been more willing to surrender to death."

"Whoa, whoa. Hold on. Death?" My voice comes out several octaves higher than usual. "I was going to die?"

"I—yes."

I breathe in and out, in and out. Caleb reaches for my hand and the contact does make me feel slightly better.

"So I'm a vampire now."

He confirms with a nod.

"As in," I continue, swallowing thick. "I need to drink blood to survive now."

Caleb cringes. "I know, it's gross."

Slowly, I release a breath. "I don't know why this is hitting me so hard. I had already agreed to be turned anyway."

"But not under duress." He runs his thumb across my skin. "It was supposed to be a controlled ceremony, and you would've been conscious for the whole thing."

"Alas," I mutter. Shaking my head, I say, "I guess this is what the dream meant, then."

Had those been both of my parents? Did they watch over me from the heavens?

My chin starts to tremble. I'm no longer human. The differences will make themselves known over time, but right now I at least know the world looks completely different—and not just because I no longer need glasses.

"What happened to the others?" I ask, remembering the expedition of women warriors breaking through the battlefield on the quest to find their men. "Are they okay? And Lara especially—are she and the baby okay?"

Caleb nods. "They're all right, all things considered. Lara and the baby are fine, here with Daniel. My mother's fine. Dad…"

I turn to sit while facing him. "Is Mr. Oh okay? He was hurt pretty bad, I was trying—"

"He's recovering," Caleb says, running a hand through his hair. It falls back in a perfect wave atop his head. "The night definitely took its toll on him. I'm not sure how much longer he'll be able to stay with us."

I make a mental note to visit him.

"What about Phelan?" I recall seeing him fighting up a storm, but then I gasp, remembering someone else. "And Marissa? Oh my word, she must have been so pissed when I ran away."

Caleb winces. "Phelan's fine. Marissa isn't quite as well."

I stop breathing.

Blinking rapidly at Caleb, I ask, "Don't tell me she got hurt because of me?"

He has trouble swallowing. "She's alive and healthy. It's just, her father didn't survive the night."

"No…" It comes out as a screamed whisper.

Caleb shushes me and before I'm able to jump out of the bed, he grabs me in his arms. I wrestle him for as long as I have energy, wanting to leave the safety of this room to find my friend. But Caleb won't let me. Instead, he settles me with my back against his chest, and circles his arms around my waist.

"Calm down, she's not here right now." His voice is low and warm on my ear. "If I'm not mistaken, she must be on her way back home right now."

Pulling up the hem of my clothes, I weep right into them. So many lives lost and yet here I am, alive and kicking—and in the arms of the man I love. It feels unfair, like I've received a gift I don't deserve.

"Whatever it is you're thinking," Caleb says, his breath fanning against my neck. "Stop it. None of what's happened is your fault."

"But—"

"No." The firmness of his voice penetrates through the fog in my brain like a balm. "This was all Vivienne's fault and she's going to pay the consequences."

Softly, I ask, "Is there a punishment strong enough on this earth for her?"

"Maybe not." Caleb lowers his head until his face is buried in the crook of my neck. "But as the new king of vampires, I sure will try to find it."

CHAPTER 102
CALEB

Only when Serena falls into a peaceful sleep do I slip out of the room.

While I've never been more powerful in my life, I feel as though I've aged a hundred years in the course of a week. The days leading to the crowning were so charged with anxiety, they chipped away at least a year of my life. Then, the nightmare of the night itself hit me with the impact of forty years of suffering.

But the worst was after that. Days went by with Serena being in so much pain as her body rapidly morphed and evolved, and not even sedatives seemed to put her at ease. My heart broke with every scream, every moan that came out of her throat.

Because I caused that.

And not just because it was my blood what did it. No, every event since we met led us to this moment.

For a while, I agonized that my fixation with Serena caused all the pain she was feeling, and also the deaths of so many. But Daniel took me aside one night and pinned me against the wall.

"Listen to me well, little brother. You are not responsible for what an evil sociopath does. It's Vivienne who caused the deaths of all those people, not you."

"But if I hadn't broken up with her to be with Serena," I said, my voice drowsy, as if drunk on alcohol. But I was just drunk on heartache. "Vivienne wouldn't have done all that."

Ironically, it was Vivienne who spared me from that thought.

In the aftermath of the massacre, I summoned a Council of Elders to help me pass judgement on her. It works more or less as a human law trial, except the Elders of the kingdom are the jury and I, the new king, am the judge. And we're all biased as shit, because a lot of the Elders lost family members that night.

During one of the interrogations of the trial, Vivienne said, "Oh, please. One way or another, I was going to show the kingdom my power. Don't you all find it so unfair that this fool gets to be the king only because he's the son of the former king? Wouldn't it be so much better to be ruled by a powerful, self-made vampire like me?"

Her eyes were completely lucid as she said that, despite being tied by reinforced chains all the way from her neck to her ankles.

That was how I realized, like the fool she claimed me to be, that it was never about possessing me. It was always about gaining power. About Vivienne wanting to be queen of the vampires. If only I'd been a real fool and played along, I would've become her perfect puppet king.

And if that happened, who knows what worse things Vivienne could've done sitting on the figurative throne?

I'll never come to terms with how many people had to die for her last grab to power that night, but as Serena struggled for days and nights since the turning without showing signs of improvement, I did come to terms with the fact things were so out of my control, I had to put them in the hands of someone much more powerful than me.

So I prayed. For a miracle for Serena. For guidance about the future. For forgiveness.

Phelan joined me a couple of times at the family chapel, a mostly unused spot of the mansion.

"I forgot you're a Catholic Irish," I said one time.

He nodded. "Sometimes I forget too."

*

Now that she's finally doing well, I leave Serena to sleep in my room and head back to the chapel. For once, my purpose is to go say thanks.

When I get there, I find Dad sitting in a pew. There's a small cart beside him, a bag of fluids hanging from the top and feeding into my dad's veins by IV.

"Come sit with me, Caleb," he says, without even turning to see who came in. But I now that I have his senses I can understand how he distinguishes the nuance of every person's footsteps.

I sit beside him and we remain silent for a moment, but it's Dad who breaks the quiet with the last thing I expected to hear.

"Forgive me, Caleb."

I open and close my mouth like a fish. "What? What for?"

Dad sighs. "For so many things. I'm old and dying, and it's only now that I'm able to shed my pride and recognize I've done so many things wrong."

I start shaking my head, about to deny what he's saying, but Dad puts a hand on my arm and stops me.

"The saying goes, the road to hell is paved in good intentions, and I had the best of them." He scratches at the skin around his IV. "But wanting to protect my family at all costs doesn't erase the fact that I cheated on my wife or lied to all of you for years."

"Dad, that doesn't matter anymore."

"It does." He looks up at the crucifix that hangs from the wall. "Those were the reasons why I used you all as pawns. It was to protect you all, but also my secrets. And it was why I brought Vivienne into the picture, to suss out how many of my secrets were known before I was able to reveal them."

Dad turns his dark eyes to mine. "And look at what that caused."

I'm at a loss. There's a harsh truth behind his words. His actions had consequences. In the family, they're mostly limited to the tumultuous relationship between my mother and I. Beyond that, they led to so much death. But even if Dad hadn't wanted to protect his empire the way he did, there would've always been a vampire or two coveting his spot, even if he was the most upright and magnanimous of kings.

That's when I realize that in our own ways, we're all just grappling with our guilt. If only we had done something differently. If only we had reacted sooner. If only we hadn't said this or that. And the only one who feels no guilt is Vivienne, the one directly responsible for all the deaths.

Taking a deep breath, I say, "What's done is done. What matters most is how we use the time we have left from now on, and I don't think guilt will help us fix everything that's broken. It's not the same as repentance."

Dad chuckles, and the sound is so startling I jump. "Looks like a king and sounds like a king, he must be one now."

"Oh, stop it." I frown, but the corners of my lips fight against it. "It's just that I've had plenty of time to wallow in my own guilt these days."

"Use that introspective brain of yours to become a much better king than your old man," he says, patting my shoulder.

"I'll try."

"May I suggest how to start?" Dad asks, in that polite way that actually brokers no answer but the one he wants. Resigned, I nod. "Talk with your mother."

I grimace. "About what?"

"Just talk to her." He shrugs. "About anything. Start building a relationship with her. She'll be around for a while longer after I'm gone, and I would like it if you two—well, I can't ask you to get along, but I can ask you to tolerate each other."

I want to ask if I have to, but I know the answer already.

"Fine," I say, bracing myself with the pew in front of us to get to my feet. "I will. I promise."

I debate whether to put it off for later as I leave the chapel, but if I've learned something as of late, is that later might never come.

I do drag my feet across the house, following the faint trail of Diana Oh-Mancini's perfume. It takes me outside where it mingles with the scent of humid grass, damp earth, and beyond to the salty beach.

I appreciate the extra time it takes me to find her while I cross the golf course, but it also fills me with trepidation about how this could go. In the past, the woman went as far as bodily harm as long as it could get me out of her sight.

I pause under the shade of the palm trees, watching her lone figure stand by the shore of the beach.

She turns, spotting me right away. "Are you coming or not?"

I try to remind myself that even though I still have yet to drink the blood of the families, I'm technically the king now. Yet, I feel like a child about to be scolded as I approach her.

"Your father must have given you the speech already," she says, cutting to the chase as usual. "He also pleaded with me."

It figures.

I stuff my hands in the pockets of my jeans. Dad wants me

to talk with my mother about anything, but all I come up with is the desire to ask her for apologies. Not just for slapping me in the face or throwing wine at me, or for making sure to tell me I'd never be good enough no matter what I tried. But for making me feel like I was alone even when I wasn't. Like I didn't belong, even when I did.

Even if I had truly been an illegitimate son, I didn't deserve to be treated like my father's sin was my fault. I bet she will never treat Daniel that way, even after the truth has come out, because now she must see the point clearly.

"I can read your mind." The woman huffs and folds her arms. "But don't forget I was a victim too."

"That doesn't completely excuse you."

"Maybe not, but if it's any consolation you should know this." For the first time, she faces me without the ire that typically colors her expression. "When that human girl jumped between Vivienne and you, risking her life to save yours, I was thankful."

I stagger back, her words landing like a blow.

"It's weird, isn't it? Realizing at that moment that I don't want my other son to die." Her blue eyes set on the ocean, as if it's not the crashing waves what she's seeing but the scene that night. "I was too far to protect you myself. But that girl did. And then my other son tended to her and it didn't matter if he's not really mine, or if the girl was human. I just wanted all my kids to be safe."

I blink rapidly. "All your kids?"

Diana lifts her nose in the air. "That's all the apology you're ever going to get from me."

"I—don't know what to say."

"Unlike what your father thinks, you don't have to say anything." She tosses her hair over her shoulder and turns. "Neither do I. Things aren't going to change just because."

"Of course not."

But even as I say that, I know everything has changed already.

"Now, let's go. We can't be late for the rest of Vivienne's trial."

I watch her back as she heads back to the house. My feet follow after her and it feels like a first.

CHAPTER 103
SERENA

Marissa sits all by herself on a bench under the shade of a tree. Funerals are rough. I'm torn between allowing her time to process through her emotions, and not leaving her alone. But then, there's also the doubt in the back of my mind that maybe I don't have any right to console her.

"Stop thinking," someone says behind me. I turn to Lara. She wears an enormous black hat that covers her from the sun, not that it can burn her skin anyway. She grabs my hand and pulls me along.

Marissa gives us a tiny smile as we take a seat on the bench, Lara to her left and I to her right.

"Thank you for coming, guys."

Lara grabs her hand. "We're your friends, of course we'll be here for you."

I have trouble swallowing. Instead, I focus on my hands, wringing each other on my lap. "Of course, if you want to be alone we'll understand too. And if you don't ever want to see me again, I'll get it too."

Marissa smacks my back so hard and suddenly, I lurch forward and almost fall off the bench.

"Serena Lossada." Marissa uses something that sounds very similar to a Mom voice. "What the hell are you even on about?"

My back smarts, but it's the least I deserve. Sitting back up right, I say, "It's just—you were so busy protecting me that night. He might've survived if you'd been with your dad instead."

"And I might have died instead, or you might have died too." She shakes her head. The netting of her hat sways back and forth, and it must bother her so much that she pulls it away from her face. "Trust me, I've thought about all the scenarios too. None of them change the facts."

Her father is dead, and so are close to two hundred people between innocent vampires, security employees, and attackers.

I've been grappling with my guilt ever since I woke up from the coma. And I know Caleb has, too. Wanting to get rid of it, aside from impossible, only makes me feel renewed guilt. I'm sure it's something I'll have to live with for the rest of my life.

Understanding that helped me forgive Mr. Oh for what happened to my dad. I'm sure he felt the same after so many of his employees were murdered trying to save his son. And if my dad had survived that attack, what if Caleb hadn't?

Only one thing is certain. Sighing, I say, "You're right, there's no point in following those trains of thought. It's an easy way to get lost."

"Well said." Lara gives a couple of quiet claps. "Besides, knowing Mr. Gonzalez he wouldn't want his precious daughter to suffer long."

Marissa winces. "If this was someone else's funeral, Papá would be complaining that it's too dull."

I look ahead of us, where Marissa's closest relatives and friends mingle in the backyard of her family's upstate New

York home. Everyone wears black, just like we do, and there isn't a single smile to be seen. Which I think is fair.

"I tried to convince Mom to play his favorite ranchera during the service, but she vetoed it." Marissa sighs.

From the other side, Lara rubs circles on Marissa's back. "It's okay, she needs to mourn him her way too. We can listen to the ranchera now if you want."

"Deal." Sniffling, Marissa takes out her phone from the pocket of her dress. When the song starts playing, it catches the attention of a few of those in the yard, but no one would demand silence when the household daughter starts singing along.

I don't recognize the song, but the singer imbues so much power and conviction in the lyrics that I immediately like it. From what little I've heard about Roberto Gonzalez, it fits him well.

Across the yard, I spot Caleb standing with Phelan. This is the only funeral I plan to attend, seeing that Marissa is my friend, but it isn't the first or last for them. Caleb has determined to personally mourn as many of the lost as he physically can, and in the process the families have also been feeding him the blood he should've drank from them that night.

So far, he has visited about twenty families. Some fifty more have sent representatives with blood vials for him, as fealty pledges. He still has about four hundred more to go.

"Let's talk about something else," Marissa says when the song is done and she puts her phone away. "How are you adapting to life as a vampire?"

I make a humming sound as I consider it. "I mean, when you exclude all the emotional trauma from that horrible night, it's not so bad."

Lara chuckles. "That's the spirit."

Marissa shows that tiny smile again. "Considering the

horror stories I've heard about how it goes for some turned vampires, you look good."

"To be honest," I say with a wince. "I think the worst of it was while I was unconscious."

Caleb and Daniel won't tell me details, but the way they fretted about me after I woke up hints that it didn't look so good for a while.

"I do feel hungry all the time, though," I add and on cue, my stomach grumbles.

"So do I," Lara says.

Marissa chuckles. It sounds so heavenly that Lara and I exchange a look behind her.

"Okay, but that's different. You're super pregnant," Marissa says to Lara, who emphasizes the point by caressing her barely showing stomach. To me, Marissa says, "And you are probably hungry for blood."

"That sounds like the title of a horror movie." I sigh and it deflates my posture. "But you're right. Sometimes it's so bad, I can practically hear blood pumping in people's bodies and it'll make my stomach roar like a lion."

"I imagine many things are different compared to a human's body, but I wouldn't know how to guide you there." Lara shows all her teeth as she cringes. "I'm afraid I don't have the experience being human."

"But we do know about vampires." Marissa narrows her eyes. "Specifically, female vampires."

"Should I take notes?"

"According to female vampire biology one-oh-one," Marissa says, giving a look that commands my attention. "The most important thing you should know is that our reproductive cycle is a lot longer than a human's."

Lara snaps her fingers. "Oh, that's true. You guys have like a monthly cycle, right? For us it's yearly."

"Whoa." I put both my hands in the air to stop them. "You're telling me I'll only get my period once per year?"

"Yes." Marissa nods. "Unless there's an issue, in which case it might take more or less."

With the way I suck in air, it's a shock they can still breathe.

Lara lifts her index finger. "I know, it's fantastic on that front. But that also means you're fertile once per year. And if you're trying to conceive, it can be tough."

"How long did it take you guys?" Marissa asks her.

"Hmm." Lara taps her chin, eyes lost in thought. "About twenty years? Daniel and I married pretty young, which is why we were able to get pregnant so early."

"Early?" I shriek. "You mean twenty years trying to conceive is a short amount of time?"

"Just like in humans, it depends on a case by case basis." Lara leans forward so she can whisper. "Look at Mr. Oh, it took him and his wife about two hundred years to conceive Caleb, but Daniel was conceived just a few months after Mr. Oh turned his assistant into a vampire."

"Whoa." I reel back with the information. The time difference in those examples is so drastic, I can't even wrap my head around it.

"It's why there are so few of us," Marissa says. "In the past, when the vampire population was in severe decline from humans hunting us, the only way we had to prevent us from dying out was the king turning humans. But some purists don't like that."

"Bah, screw the purists." Lara waves her hand.

"Oh, I guess purists will have a field trip if Caleb and I ever get pregnant."

At once, the eyes of both women zero in on me. It's Lara who asks, "And are you guys trying already?"

"No!" I shout too loud for a vampire funeral, which means everyone as far as the eye can see glares at me. I lower my face, glad my hair falls forward to hide it. "I mean, no—not until we're married."

Lara chuckles. "Caleb's a saint."

"Or he really loves her," Marissa says, smiling.

"So, uh." I clear my throat and for lack of anything better to do, straighten up the skirts of my black dress. "Is vampire royalty the same as human royalty? As in, I'll be expected to produce an heir ASAP?"

"Yes," they say at once.

"And the worst one will be Diana," Lara says, rubbing her belly. "Trust me, I know by experience."

I groan. "I'm so sorry."

"It wasn't terrible. Daniel and I were already decided to be parents."

"No, I mean." I squirm, and it's hard to get the words out but here they go. "You thought your child would one day be queen or king and now…"

"And now they can be whatever else they want to be." Lara grins and reaches over Marissa to squeeze my hand. "I'm partial to astronaut—why are you crying?"

I blink and blink, but the tears win in the end. With a shaky voice, I say, "I'm just so happy to have you both in my life."

Since her fuse is currently even shorter than mine, Marissa breaks into sobs and hugs us both against her. "Me too."

The three of us dissolve into ugly crying and it strikes me that, for the first time in weeks, I might be a bit happy even in the midst of so much tragedy.

EPILOGUE

CALEB

t takes six months to clear the dust. The trial ends and effectively condemns Vivienne. She's now locked up for life in a tiny cell in a prison so secure, she would have to crawl from underground and swim across the Pacific to reach us.

Much harder was dismantling the Astors' assets, but we've had plenty of help from the vampire families with a vendetta. Ernst ends up joining his daughter in the Pacific. While he wasn't the mastermind of the operation, he certainly helped her.

I pay my respects to most of the families who lost someone on the night of my crowning. Dad sends their regards through me, because he no longer feels well enough to travel.

Only when those i's are dotted and the t's are crossed, do we begin planning The Wedding. You know, the one I really care about. And we prepare at lightning speed, before Dad's health keeps declining.

I confess that I've never been more nervous than this moment. Which is weird, because among my family, closest friends, a priest, and a nun—all gathered at the private beach of my parent's home—there won't be anyone to jump out of nowhere and try to murder me.

But my heart races so fast that it threatens with breaking out of my chest as I wait for Serena. My brother squeezes my shoulder, probably because he can hear how fast blood is rushing through my veins. Behind him, Phelan doesn't offer any consolation. He's as still as a statue as usual, which is a comfort in itself. And behind him is Joe, the captain of my yacht. He gives me a thumbs up.

Across from where I stand, Serena's maids of honor smile at me. Sister Emilia, Marissa and Lara are a strange combination, but honestly I've seen more shocking things.

My mother's sole job is to play the music. Like a maestro, she plays the wedding march on a grand piano the moment she hears sounds beyond the palm trees. A minute later, a set of steps and the whirring of an electric wheelchair ring closer.

Serena appears through the trees, her hand holding onto my dad's as he escorts her from his wheelchair. But all I can see is her in her white dress stark against her light brown skin. A veil obscures her face and I can't wait until I can pull out of the way. Until I can kiss her and be called her husband.

Oh shit, this is happening. At last.

My whole body shakes when I finally take her hand from Dad's. It isn't with nerves anymore, but with the effort it takes me to contain the impulse of picking her up and running off. But she wants this, so I have to be patient.

Which is why the ceremony takes ten years.

Or that's how long I feel has passed before the priest prompts me to say my vows.

I clear my throat once. Twice. Serena gives me that look she often wears as my assistant at the office, where she knows I haven't been paying attention and she's annoyed that she'll have to repeat herself. It makes me smile.

That's one of the things I love so much about her, that where I'm messy and scatterbrained, she's sharp and responsible. She'll keep me on task for centuries, and in turn I'll make her laugh.

Win-win.

"Serena Lossada, my love," I say and she blinks fast at the new endearment rolling off my tongue. "I can't promise things won't be hard at times, or that you won't have to work hard at keeping me in line. But I can promise you that my life would be meaningless without you in it. Should you accept the hardships that will come from marrying me, I promise I will devote my entire life to making it up to you."

Maybe I'm breaking protocol, but when a tear escapes from her eye I reach forward to wipe it from her cheek.

"I love you, Serena. Thank you for coming into my life."

Someone coos and that infects someone else with the sniffles.

"Caleb, I—I-" Serena swallows with difficulty and grimaces. "Oh my word, I think I forgot my vows."

I can't help chuckling. "I bet it's my fault, huh?"

Behind me, my brother whispers, "Get used to it, everything will be your fault from now on."

Lara pokes her head out from behind Serena. "That's right."

Meanwhile, Serena has a deep frown as her brain works in overtime. Finally, she takes a deep breath. "Caleb, my future husband in a few minutes, and then husband for a very, very long time."

The cleric members don't know about our true nature so we don't say the v-word, but the rest of us know Serena's talking about the very long shelf life of onions.

"I don't know what the future will bring," Serena says, sober with the certainty that, yeah, it's uncertain.

After today she'll be the queen of vampires, despite

knowing very little about them, and there's so much discontent among the families after what she-who-shall-not-be-named did that they're likely to react negatively to Serena.

Serena continues, "But as someone who lost everything long before meeting you, uncertainty has always been my companion. Now it's going to be you. You will be my certainty, my rock, the fixed point in my horizon. And even though I bring nothing but myself to this union, I hope to become the source of your strength too. And yes, that also means I'll pull your ear when you don't want to work."

I'm not the only one who laughs at that.

Serena's smile is so sweet, it makes her cheeks turn rosy and I want to kiss her. Now.

"So, um." She squeezes my hands tighter. "I love you, Caleb Oh."

Later, when the priest finally announces us as husband and wife, I pick Serena up by her waist and kiss her until it's no longer polite. She's the one who pulls away, bracing with her arms around my neck.

"I love you," I tell her.

"I know." She smiles at the way I gasp. "Don't worry, I've grown to love you too."

"Ugh." I grimace. "It's very clear who has the power in this relationship, huh?"

Serena snorts.

I set her down and together, we greet the attendants as a married couple for the first time.

After the applause dies down, everyone—except Phelan, let's be clear—tumbles over each other to have their turn congratulating us. I practically vibrate with energy as we get hugged, kissed, or shake hands with everyone.

This is when Phelan comes in handy, because the moment he realizes this event is well and truly done, he escorts the nun and priest toward the drivers I have waiting for them. Serena takes an extra moment hugging the woman who raised her before they let go, and I have to dig my toes into the sand to not run at her and pick her up.

"Geez, calm down, tiger," my brother tells me.

I give him the widest eyes. "You have no idea what I'm going through right now."

"I really don't." He laughs at me like only an older brother can, pointing fingers and all.

*

"We should proceed with the next ceremony now that our guests are gone," Dad says, whirling around in the electrical wheelchair and heading back to the house. Closely behind him, Maria and my mother watch out for him.

"Yes." I pump my fist discreetly. This is the part that will bind us in front of the whole kingdom.

I offer my elbow to Serena, who takes it with a calm I don't share. She must have heard my brief conversation with Daniel because she whispers, "You're such a guy."

I lift my eyebrows. "I thought you knew that's what you were marrying."

Serena smacks my arm but doesn't say anything else. I can feel the way her heart races, and that's when it occurs to me that she might be nervous.

Not that I can blame her. So am I.

The massive ballroom is fitted with plush chairs in a circle. Serena and I will stand in the middle for our vampire wedding. Monitors have been set up in the perimeter, where the surviving heads of families will witness the crowning of the new queen.

This is the part I'm nervous about—not the wedding night. The latter I'm anticipating.

When everyone's taken their seat, Phelan gives us a thumb

up as he flips the monitors on. One by one, the families join the live broadcast. Serena and I stand behind Dad, hand in hand as he gives the kingdom one last address.

"In these especially challenging times," he says, his voice deep and calm the way he's always been. "I want to thank you all for tuning to this modest celebration, to crown the next queen of vampires."

The clapping of the family heads sounds tinny through the speakers, but it keeps my blood pressure in check. I'm glad that the ceremony is small, in the comfort and safety of our home, away from anyone who may wish us harm.

Dad whirs around to face us. "Caleb Oh, new king of vampires. Do you accept Serena Lossada as your wife and queen?"

My voice booms out. "I do."

Dad smiles a bit. "And you, Serena Lossada, do you accept Caleb Oh as your husband and king?"

"I do," she says, and although her voice falters a bit, she squeezes my hand.

"You may now bite each other."

And this is it, the big moment an entire underground nation is waiting for—either to laud or feud about.

Serena removes the white shrug she's wearing, which bares her throat and shoulders. I pull my shirt from my pants and tear it off in one move.

It's a bit weird, to partially undress in front of everybody so my wife can get her hands on me, but that's how it is. The families must witness the moment when the spouses willingly give each other their blood to accept a marriage. It's why we often call it a blood alliance instead. And it's even more important when it comes to accepting a new queen or king.

As protocol goes, the heir to the throne must bite their spouse first. Serena is stiff as a plank as I bring her closer to me. I brush her hair away from her skin.

"Relax," I murmur, running my hands up and down her bare arms to warm her up. There are goosebumps on her skin and I can feel the hammering of her heart against my chest.

I don't care if it isn't protocol, but I place a kiss on the base of her throat. The moment I feel her deflate against me, I bite her.

She hisses at the momentary pain as my fangs sink into her skin, and it hurts me more than if she was the one biting me.

Which she isn't doing, I realize.

I guide her head to my neck and she breathes against my skin for a while, until the smell of my blood awakens her new instincts. Her fangs sink into my neck and—

It doesn't hurt. Instead, it makes me fight really hard to remember there's a big audience, and that I can't just tear her dress off of her body and have my way with her.

I remember once telling Serena that there was nothing special about drinking another vampire's blood, but clearly that's because I hadn't yet experienced this moment—the bold declaration that comes from this ceremony. Now the world knows I am hers, and she is mine. That we are one blood. That nothing will tear us apart.

That we are home.

As Dad announces that it is done, I wipe her bottom lip with my thumb, cleaning my blood off them. Her eyes look dazed as she returns the favor. I grab her hand and kiss the palm.

Dad's speaking to the kingdom, but I can't make out the words for the life of me. Everything I am is lost in Serena's eyes, where I plan to live for the rest of my life.

When everyone begins to stand on their feet is when I realize the ceremony is done. I bend down and pick my bride up in my arms.

"Caleb!" Serena yelps.

"Out of the way," I command to family and friends. "I have a marital duty to attend to."

Amid laughter and Serena's protests in both of her languages, I cross the length of the house and drop her off in the backseat of the car that will take us to the Bad Blood. For the first time, Phelan is slower than me and I poke my head out from the backseat as he races out of the house.

"Hurry up, man!" I heckle him. "The bride is in a hurry."

"No, I'm not." Serena's laughing voice comes out muffled from hiding her face behind her hands.

I join in her joy, even though I'm annoyed that I have to wait all the way until Phelan drives us to the Bad Blood.

But in retrospective, that was a short time compared to the long, languid, scalding-hot two weeks we spend in our honeymoon at sea. And anything that happens after that, we'll figure out together.

THE END OF SERENA AND CALEB'S STORY

Thank you for reading this book!

Stay tuned for Marissa and Phelan's story in
MY BODYGUARD BOSS IS A VAMPIRE
coming out this fall!

GLOSSARY OF SPANISH VOCABS

Chapter 1

- Mierda: crap/shit (see also Chapter 27, 85).

Chapter 3

- Dale y ya: do it and that's it.

Chapter 9

- Aleluya: hallelujah.
- Arepas: arepa is one of the national dishes of Venezuela and has no English translation. It's a corn flour "bread" that can be filled with basically anything.
- Carne mechada con pico de gallo y queso de mano: pulled beef with chopped tomato, onion, and cilantro, and a Venezuelan type of cheese similar to mozzarella.
- Qué delicia: what a delight.

- Arepera: this is the place where arepas are sold.

Chapter 11

- Vamos, sí se puede: c'mon, you can do this.

Chapter 13

- Ay, caramba: not a literal translation but something like 'aw, man.'

Chapter 15

- ¿Qué carajo está pasando?: what the heck is happening?

Chapter 19

- Carajo: not a literal translation but something like 'heck.'

Chapter 20

- Señor Oh: Mister Oh
- Güey: Mexican colloquialism similar to 'dude.'

Chapter 21

- ¿Está seguro de que va a estar abierto?: are you sure it's going to be open?
- Sí, señorita. Es el mercado al que voy siempre. Abre hasta las ocho: yes, miss. It's the market I always go to. It opens until eight.

- ¿Y cree que llegamos a tiempo?: and do you think we'll get there in time?
- Sí, está cerquitica: yes, it's very close.
- Gringo: colloquial way of referring to anyone who isn't Latin American, most often used to refer to Americans.
- Necesito sangre. Es para una sopa. Así la hace mi mamá: I need blood. It's for a soup. That's how my mom makes it.
- Ahhh. Por un momento pensé que era para un vampiro: Ahhh. For a moment I thought it was for a vampire.
- Claro que no, ni que existieran. ¿Sí tiene?: Of course not, it's not like they exist. Do you have any?
- Sí, ¿cuánta quiere?: Yes, how much would you like?

Chapter 23

- Posada: inn.
- ¿Qué quieres a esta hora?: what do you want at this time?
- Buenas noches. Disculpe la molestia pero necesitamos que nos aloje: Good evening. Sorry for the bother but we need you to room us.
- El sitio está lleno: the place is full.
- Por favor. Nuestro vehículo se accidentó en la carretera y no tenemos a donde ir: Please. Our vehicle broke down on the road and we have nowhere to go.
- Solo tengo una habitación pequeña con una sola cama: I only have one small room with a single bed.
- La tomamos: we'll take it.
- Buena suerte: good luck.

Chapter 27

- Bueno, ver para creer: well, seeing is believeing.

Chapter 43

- ¿Qué hago?: what should I do?

Chapter 45

- Pues no, nada: Well no, nothing.

Chapter 51

- Nadita de nada: nothing at all.

Chapter 53

- Mira vale: Venezuelan slang, specifically from Caracas, to say 'look.'
- Te amo: I love you.
- Pero yo no te amo: but I don't love you back.
- Mira vale, quietecito te ves más bonito: look, you look prettier when staying still.

Chapter 63

- ¿Qué voy a hacer?: what am I going to do?

Chapter 71

- Jódete: screw you (but the stronger cousin).

Chapter 79

- Entre gustos y colores…: the entire saying is "entre gustos y colores no han podido los autores," which means something like 'authors have not been able to parse among tastes and colors,' a.k.a. to each their own.

Chapter 81

- Dame paciencia: give me patience.

Chapter 84

- Policía: police.

Chapter 87

- Tranquila, mi cielo. Aquí está tu papá: relax, my darling. Here's your dad.
- ¿A qué hora llegas?: at what time do you arrive?
- ¿Te dejo comida?: should I leave food for you?
- Ay, que madura es mi hija que ya cocina: aw, how mature is my daughter who already cooks.
- Pero no es gratis: but it's not for free.
- Sí, sí: yes, yes.
- Este finde te llevo al parque de diversiones como te prometí: I'll take you to the amusement park this weekend like I promised.

Chapter 89

- Tienes que comer, mija: you have to eat, child.
- Disculpe, no me siento bien: I'm sorry, I don't feel well.

- Chancla: the flipflop every Latino kid gets hit with at least once.
- Señorita Lossada, usted lleva tres días sin comer bien. ¡Se va a desmayar otra vez! Si me tengo que sentar aquí en frente hasta que se coma todo, lo hago: Miss Lossada, you haven't eaten well in three days. You'll faint again! If I have to sit here in front until you eat everything, I will.
- Muy bien: very good.

Chapter 101

- Levántate: get up.
- Abre los ojos, chiquita. Tu nueva vida te espera: open your eyes, little one. Your new life awaits.
- Vamos: let's go.

Chapter 103

- Papá: Dad.

ACKNOWLEDGMENTS

I always have to thank the Lord first. Contigo todo, sin ti nada.

To Tara Lush and Avery Keelan for believing in me and supporting my vision of a vegan vampire in Miami. That's what true friendship is about.

To all my readers whether from Radish (who gave MBBIAV 4M reads!), Wattpad, or who have now found me as a self published author. You're the reason I can do this—you're the ones who make my words have real meaning.

To BTS, whose lajimolala fueled the writing sessions that resulted in this literary masterpiece and kept me company while I wrote the first draft of this story while locked up in my apartment in early 2021. Are they the reason I made Caleb half Korean? We will never know. (Spoiler alert: Yes).

Last but not least, I want to thank my mom and my sister, and also my dad up in heaven. Thank you for encouraging me to never give up. Los amo con todo.

ABOUT THE AUTHOR

MC Loyal was inspired by Lord of the Rings to start writing —or more accurately, its shortage of romance did. Now she writes romance with paranormal, fantasy, or sci-fi flares with heroes who would burn the world for their heroines, while also making them laugh. She's unapologetically Latin American and adds a touch of it to spice her stories. Speaking of spice, she writes closed door romance with explosive chemistry and with actual explosions in the background.

Find her:
   Newsletter signup
   Instagram mcloyalauthor